# Venom and Velvet

*Book Two in the Venom Series*

Dani Antoinette

Copyright © 2023 Dani Antoinette

All rights reserved

The characters and events portrayed in this book are fictitious. Any similarity to real persons, living or dead, is coincidental and not intended by the author.

No part of this book may be reproduced, or stored in a retrieval system, or transmitted in any form or by any means, electronic, mechanical, photocopying, recording, or otherwise, without express written permission of the publisher.

Printed in the United States of America

*For all those rooting for the 'villain'...this is for you.*

*He could destroy me...but nothing prepared me for how much I wanted him to.*
DANI ANTOINETTE

# Contents

Title Page
Copyright
Dedication
Epigraph
Introduction
Chapter One ............ 4
Chapter Two ............ 17
Chapter Three ............ 33
Chapter Four ............ 50
Chapter Five ............ 64
Chapter Six ............ 79
Chapter Seven ............ 95
Chapter Eight ............ 111
Chapter Nine ............ 126
Chapter Ten ............ 143
Chapter Eleven ............ 158
Chapter Twelve ............ 176
Chapter Thirteen ............ 196

| | |
|---|---|
| Chapter Fourteen | 211 |
| Chapter Fifteen | 225 |
| Chapter Sixteen | 245 |
| Chapter Seventeen | 261 |
| Chapter Eighteen | 280 |
| Chapter Nineteen | 297 |
| Chapter Twenty | 313 |
| Chapter Twenty-One | 327 |
| Chapter Twenty-Two | 331 |
| Chapter Twenty-Three | 337 |
| Chapter Twenty-Four | 347 |
| Thank You | 351 |
| About the Author | 353 |
| Wild Talk Sneak Peek | 354 |

# Introduction

**Venom and Velvet is a full-length enemies-to-lovers romance. This is book two in the Venom series. It is a continuation of book one and should not be read as a standalone.**

# Prologue
## Day 73

Agent Dobbs sat across from me, dried blood splattered across his wrinkled blazer. Whose blood, I couldn't be sure of. Was it mine? I looked down at my hands, grime and something else I couldn't identify embedded under my nails. I could barely move my right arm, the cast almost completely broken off. A ringing noise flooded my ears, and I hunched my shoulders forward, crossing my arms against my chest.

"Nova." Cian's voice was hoarse. "Nova, look at me."

I couldn't. Not now. Not after everything. The handcuffs around his wrists clashed against the metal desk as he strained to move closer to me.

"Cut it out, Blackwood. Or I'll put a gag in your mouth." Dobbs huffed and wiped the sheen of sweat from his forehead.

"I'd like to see you fucking try," Cian growled and jerked his arms in an attempt to loosen the cuffs.

"Both of you shut up already." Agent Delove scowled and placed a tape recorder on the table in between us.

Dobbs snickered and pulled out a flask. He poured a dark liquid into the two cups of coffee and slid one across to me. "Drink. It'll help calm your nerves, honey."

My hand trembled as I held the cup and took a swig. The liquid burned down my throat, and I welcomed the sensation. It didn't matter. Nothing did. Numbness swept through my whole body. The room was painted a terrible brown color that reminded me of Dobbs' blazer. My stomach turned and I took another sip of my drink. The dim light above our heads flickered for the hundredth time, and the urge to stand on the desk and rip it out of the ceiling was overpowering.

"Nova, are you listening?" Dobbs cleared his throat, and I snapped my attention back to him. "Why don't you start at the beginning."

I threw back the rest of my drink and slid the cup back to him, nodding when he held the flask up. The beginning. How stupid I had been. How naïve and foolish I was. I scoffed, my nostrils flaring as I recalled those first few weeks after being snatched away from my wedding.

"I… guess it started…" My voice trailed off as a commotion in the hallway drew all our attention to the door. People were shouting, one voice louder than all the others—a voice burned into my memory forever.

The door flew open and my chair screeched against the linoleum as I stood up and faced the man who had haunted my nightmares.

Everything was a blur as the men around me scrambled, their chairs spilling backwards, coffee flying across the table.

"Gun, he has a gun!" someone shouted, but I couldn't tell you who. The only thing I knew for sure was he indeed did have a gun.

And it was pointed right at me.

## Chapter One
### Day 3

I woke covered in sweat, a scream of terror frozen in my throat as strong hands gripped my shoulders and shook me.

"Wake up, Nova." Cian struggled to hold onto me as I flailed around, the bedsheets wrapped around me like a vice. "Calm down, you're safe." He dragged me into his lap and held me tight against him. "You're safe, Nova," he whispered as I bunched his shirt in my hands and held on for dear life.

My heart slammed against my chest. Boom, boom, boom.

I was safe. Not being dragged away by masked men who wanted to hurt me. Not being thrown into a dark van to be taken to God knew where.

I was here with Cian.

Safe.

But was I really?

*****

My eyes fluttered open as the sun peeked through blinds and blasted me in the face. My head was on fire and I instinctively reached up to feel the gash on my forehead. The smell of food drifted up my nose, a tray of breakfast on the nightstand next to me. My stomach made an obnoxious growling sound, my mouth filling with saliva. When was the last time I'd eaten something? I peeked under the covers, relieved that I at least had a robe on this time.

My body tensed as I became aware of another person lying in bed next to me. I held my breath and turned my head slightly. Cian lay on his back, fully clothed, his arm draped over his face, covering his eyes.

I squeezed my eyes shut, wishing the pain would go away. Everything was foggy. It was hard to know what had been real and what had been a dream. More like a nightmare. I knew Cian had been in bed last night. He had held me tight against his chest as I'd fought to get away from the man trying to put a hood over my head. I had fought with all my might, yet nothing had stopped him in my nightmare. Except Cian's voice. Calm. Soothing me. I knew that it had been real. But that didn't change the fact that he had taken me from my wedding. He said he'd saved me. Had he? Or was I being held here against my will?

I glanced over as his chest rose with each breath he took, his lips quirked up at the side. He looked peaceful, like he didn't have a care in the world, while I lay here in fear, anger bubbling in my chest.

Time to change that.

I reached over to the tray of food, keeping my eyes on him as my fingers searched around the tray. When I found what I was looking for, I gripped the metal handle tight and slowly sat up. He still hadn't moved, the same steady rise and fall of his chest letting me know he was most likely asleep. I slid the blanket off me and scooted to the edge of the bed.

My whole body was shaking in a way that I couldn't control, and the knife slipped from my hands onto the hardwood floor. I snatched it back up quickly and lay back down, holding it to my chest. So much for sneaking out quietly. I held my breath and prayed he hadn't woken up. I counted to five in my head and risked a glance in his direction.

His arm was no longer flung across his face, and he was definitely not sleeping any more. Dark eyes burned into mine, then down to the knife I was holding onto for dear life.

"What are you doing, little mouse?" His voice was soft, confused.

I launched at him until I was straddling his stomach, the tip of the knife pointed at his neck. My breath came out in spurts, my heart ready to burst out of my chest. "You kidnapped me? You... you... I want answers, Cian." I put a little bit more pressure on the knife. "Or I'll hurt you." I hated the way my voice trembled. Just a reminder that I was utterly unhinged. It had to be shock.

*Of course you're in shock, you dingbat.*

He raised his hands slowly, as if in defeat, then grabbed the top of his button-up shirt, just below where I had the knife pointed. He yanked his shirt open, buttons flying.

I gasped as he grabbed my hand and dragged the knife lower so that it was pointed at his heart, his scorpion tattoo on full display mocking me.

"Always aim for the heart, Nova." He pressed my hand down so the knife was digging into his chest. The blade cut into him, not more than a millimeter, a drop of blood forming.

"Stop," I breathed and tried to jerk out of his grasp. "Let go, Cian."

He grabbed me by the wrists and I shrieked as he flipped us over so that I was lying on my back. He pressed firmly into me, and I bit my bottom lip. He didn't say anything for a moment, his breath just as ragged as mine. Memories flooded my mind of us together at his house, in his car, the phone sex, and I swallowed the lump in my throat.

"Next time you pull a knife on me, you better be prepared to use it." There was an edge in his voice that sent chills up my spine.

In an instant he was off the bed, reaching for his shoes.

"What am I doing here, Cian? Where's Juliet? I want to see her now." I stood in front of the door, hands on my hips. I'd be damned if he thought he could just leave me in this room with no answers.

"Nova," he commanded as he towered over me. "Eat. Shower. I'll send her up. Go."

Oh, really? Was that how he thought it was going to be? He was going to snatch me away and boss me around and I was, what, just supposed to comply? I poked my finger against his chest. "No. Tell me what the hell is going on." Poke, poke.

He sighed, and before I knew what was happening, he picked me up and walked me back over to the bed, plopping me back down. "Eat. Shower." He slammed the door behind him, the lock clicking in place.

I lay on the bed for some time without moving. My chest heaved as I tried to control my breathing. I wasn't thinking rationally. But who could blame me?

I hadn't asked for any of this. Maybe this was karma barreling into me for going along with Ryzen's scheme to pose as his fiancée so that he could close the hotel deal with Covington.

Now look at me.

The smell of food was overpowering my need to find a weapon and break the door down. I nibbled on a piece of toast, but when I tried to eat some eggs, my stomach objected. I choked down what I could, knowing that I needed the energy for whatever lay ahead of me.

The bathroom was old and tattered, and I had a hard time imagining Cian lived here. I peeked through the small window and out into a vast field covered with dried-up trees. No other houses were in sight, just three vans parked in a makeshift driveway. I risked a glance in the mirror and cringed at my reflection. The cut on my forehead was almost two inches long and jagged. Someone had cleaned it up, but it would leave a scar, a constant reminder of something I would rather forget. My fingers skated across my face to my puffy eyes, then down to the dark marks across my neck. The robe fell to the floor, and I gasped at the scrapes and bruises covering my stomach and legs. My shoulders sagged as tears welled up in my eyes.

*Don't cry. You have to be strong. Stronger than ever before.*

What a fucking mess this all was. Nothing made sense. I never imagined being in a situation like this. But having a pity party wasn't going to help anything. I needed to find out what was going on. I leaned my forehead against the shower wall, letting the water pour over me until my skin turned red.

There was a change of clothes on the bed, and I looked around the room to see if Cian was hiding in the shadows. Satisfied I was alone, I got undressed and held the clothes against my body. They were three sizes too big, but I had no other choice.

The sound of keys jingling had my head snapping to the door as my best friend Juliet rushed in. She threw her bag on the ground and was in front of me in an instant. "Oh, my God, Nova!" She wrapped her arms around me in a bear hug. "I was so worried. You hit your head so hard when that man grabbed you..." She pulled back, her face ashen as she looked me over. "Are you OK?"

My throat closed up and I nodded, trying to contain my own tears as relief washed over me. "Are you?" I gripped her hands and dragged her over to the bed.

She sighed, her hands trembling in mine. "Yeah, I've had a few days to get myself together after all"—she waved her hand around the room—"all this craziness."

"Cian won't tell me anything. Have you talked to Grams? Are we prisoners?" My voice rose with each question, and she scrunched up her nose.

"Calm down, Nova." She picked up her bag from the floor and pulled out a bottle of painkillers. She handed me two pills and a bottle of water. "Thora said Grams left before those men showed up at the wedding."

I gulped down the pills and nodded, my leg bouncing up and down.

"We're not prisoners, we're hiding... apparently. I don't know from who. That's all Cian would say while we were waiting for you to wake up. He's been crazy about security around here." She glanced over at the keys still hanging in the door.

"Wait, how long was I out for?" A jolt of pain slashed through my head, and I grunted.

"Two days. Cian was so frantic... I... oh, God, I thought the worst." She squeezed my hands in a vice grip. I didn't have the heart to tell her she was hurting me.

Two days.

What the hell had I missed in those days?

"Nova, this thing with Ryzen isn't good. I don't think him or his brother Riddick are who they said they were." She paced in front of the bed, nibbling on her fingernails. "Thora said those masked men came to the wedding to hurt Ryzen. To hurt you." Her voice quivered. "This is my fault. I should have never encouraged you to sign that fake fiancé contract."

I stood and gripped her shoulders. "Stop it, Jules. This isn't your fault. This is... well, I don't know who's to blame, but it's not you. OK?" I could see the wheels spinning in her eyes, and I shook her gently. "We're going to figure it out. Like we always do." I held up my fingers in our secret code, her lips trembling as she did the same. "What else did you hear?"

"Something about the Mafia. Ryzen owes them money." She walked over to the table where the box of pictures was. "Can you believe that? The *actual* Mafia." Her voice trailed off as she peeked inside the box. One by one she pulled the pictures out, her mouth hanging open when she got to the last one. The one with Ryzen and Iva having sex. She held it up to me, and I nodded.

My jaw tensed at the sight of the picture. Not because of jealousy. Because of what that picture stood for. Deception. Control. Had he made Iva lie to me so that I would agree to marry him? It was so far-fetched I almost couldn't believe he would stoop to that level to get what he wanted. But I guessed I didn't really know him, or Cian for that matter. Hell, for all I knew Iva *had* been sleeping with them both.

"Holy cow. That bitch." Juliet's hand was shaking as she looked back and forth from the picture to me. "What does all this mean?"

I rolled up the sleeves of my shirt and grabbed the picture from her. "I don't know, but I'm about to find out."

I stormed downstairs in the direction of the voices and threw the door open, Juliet on my heels. Cian stood with his back to me, his hands stuffed in his pockets, as he looked out the window. Cian's foster siblings Thora and Eros were huddling together around a table with a third man I had never seen before. He had dark hair like Cian, and was just as tall, but leaner, and covered in tattoos.

My nostrils flared as I held the picture of Ryzen and Iva up. "Tell me what the hell is going on right this instant."

Cian ran his fingers through his hair. "Everyone out." His voice was lethal, and although I was the one who was demanding the answers, I could sense my bravery slowly slipping away.

"Cian." The man I didn't recognize approached him. "We should—"

"Orin, no. Out. Please." Cian turned to face me, still wearing the shirt he had ripped open less than an hour ago.

Orin. Cian's other foster brother. Orin narrowed

his eyes at me, and I stepped to the side as he passed. Eros gave me a salute as he walked by, while Thora grabbed Juliet's hand and tugged her out the door. There was a thickness in the air that was almost suffocating, and I was beginning to regret barging into the room.

Cian turned to face me, his eyes dark as he scanned me up and down. His hair was disheveled, and he had dark circles under his eyes. My eyes instinctively went to the scars running down his face and neck. Not too long ago I had been trailing my lips down them while he moaned with pleasure. He looked like he had been in the fight of his life, and I took a step backwards.

"No," he ordered, taking a step closer to me. "You don't get to run this time, little mouse." He stood in front of me, my eyes chest-level, looking directly at the small cut I had given him earlier.

I swallowed, my throat drier than it had been moments ago. His fingers were soft against my face as he tilted my chin up. It was difficult to decipher the look in his dark eyes. Anger. Frustration. Fear. A combination of the three. What I didn't understand was why.

"I warned you." His thumb traced my bottom lip, and suddenly I forgot how to breathe. "That you were nothing but a little mouse in a den of snakes. Yet you refused to believe me." He pressed against me so there wasn't an inch of space between us. "You shut me out, Nova." There was a hint of bitterness in his voice, and I squeezed my eyes shut.

"Look at me," he commanded. "Tell me why."

"Iva..." I inhaled deeply through my nose, desperate for oxygen. "She said you were lovers."

He scoffed, wrapping his hand around the back

of my neck and weaving his fingers into my wet hair. "And you believed her?" He had me locked in place. I couldn't move even if I wanted to.

"How was I supposed to know, Cian?" I lowered my eyes. "I never thought she would lie. That Ryzen would lie. How could I possibly know that it wasn't true?" My voice quivered, but he didn't let go of his grasp on me.

"Why was it so fucking easy for you to trust him, but not me?" Cian tugged my head back gently. "You made me the monster because you wanted me to be one." Tension rolled off his body in waves, and if he hadn't been holding me up, I might have fallen to the floor.

"That's not—"

His lips crashed into mine before I could finish. Rough. Angry. I could taste the desperation on his tongue as I kissed him back with the same anger. I gripped his arms, his muscles hard underneath my palms.

He grunted and pulled away, turning his back to me. "Fuck," he muttered and shook his head. My fingers trembled as I touched my lips, still tingling from his kiss.

"What do you plan to do with us? Why are we here?"

His shoulders sagged and he was quiet for a moment. "Three days ago, Orin came to me with a tip from a bounty he was chasing." He stood with his back to me. "Regarding the leader of the Voledetti Mafia planning to eliminate the fiancée of the wealthiest billionaire in Chicago."

A chill ran up my spine as I realized what Cian

was saying. "But why?" I gasped.

He shook his head and sighed. "I don't know for certain. Money, we think. Anything is possible with Goodacre." He walked around the desk and pulled out a thick envelope, and dumped a stack of pictures onto the desk. "You want to know why you're here? This is why."

I glanced down at the pictures on the desk, hundreds of them—pictures of Ryzen, Riddick, and a slew of men who had trouble written all over them.

"After he tried to ruin me all those years ago, I vowed to never let him hurt another innocent person." Cian slammed his hand on the desk, and I jumped. "We've been collecting evidence, everything we could find so that we could finally lock him away. And then you came along, and everything changed. I *knew* your engagement was a sham. I just didn't know why you were going along with it."

I swallowed the lump in my throat and looked anywhere but at his face. How the hell was I supposed to explain this to him? That I'd had no choice but to go along with Ryzen and pose as his fiancée or he would have ruined my business? He had held my livelihood in his hands, and I'd had little to no choice in the matter? Would Cian even understand? The more I thought about it, the more ridiculous it sounded. The pain in my head worsened and I cringed as I wobbled over to the couch. Cian rushed over and gripped my hand as I sat.

"You were just another toy to him." His voice was laced with bitterness. "When I found out what Voledetti had planned, I came for you."

I was silent as I took in everything he was saying. There was no questioning what the truth was. It was right in front of my face, in a stack of photographs that showed exactly what kind of person Ryzen Goodacre was.

Heat rushed through my body, and I bit my bottom lip. All my life I had trusted the wrong kind of men, ones who hurt and deceived me. And now it was no different. Ryzen had manipulated me. Lied to me. And I had taken it all in like a naïve, stupid fool.

And now I was here with Cian. Who had come to save me, not to hurt me. My gut told me he was telling the truth, that there was no ulterior motive. But something was nagging at me. "Why didn't you just go to the police?"

"You don't get it, Nova. The Mafia controls the police in this city. Never met a cop who wasn't dirty." Cian scoffed. "We came across four unmarked police cruisers at the edge of the property well before those vans showed up. Whatever they were doing there, it wasn't good."

I swayed to the side and squeezed my eyes shut. This was too much. I lived a normal boring life where my biggest worry was if I ordered enough vibrators. Oh, fuck. "The Shiver Box… Our warehouse? It was on fire…"

"It's gone, Nova. Everything is gone now."

A wave of nausea crashed over me, and I thought I would be sick right there. It was over. Fucking done. That was all Juliet and I had had. And now I was left with nothing. And for what? So I could be a pawn in some sick game that I hadn't even known I was playing?

Cian stood in front of me, lifting my chin. "I would have come no matter what, Nova. Come hell or high water, I would have never let you marry him."

I squeezed my eyes shut and let out the breath

I had been holding. My whole world had been turned upside down more than once over the past few months, and this was all that was left of it. Me, in this room with Cian, a man I had desperately fought to ignore, who had ended up stealing my heart and destroying it. Or so I'd been made to believe. All the angry energy I had had moments ago drained away, and I lowered my head.

"I need to lie down. My head hurts." I stood up. He tried to grab my hand, but I shook my head. "Please, Cian. No more. Not right now." I didn't want to look him in the eyes, to see what was there. Pity, probably.

He dropped my hand and let me walk out without following. Eros and Orin stood in the hallway, their arms crossed against their chests as I hurried by. I didn't know what to say. If Cian was telling the truth, then they had all put their necks on the line to save Juliet and me. And I didn't understand why.

When I got back to the room, I flopped down on my back, staring up at the ceiling. What a fucking mess this was. Juliet's bag was on the bed, and I reached over, dragging it closer to me. On top was a magazine, one of those cosmopolitan magazines that gave you eight hundred ways to wear your eyeliner. On the cover was the actress from that popular vampire movie teenagers went crazy for.

*'How I learned to trust and find love again!' Actress Phoebe Crane details her quest to find her soulmate.*

I rolled my eyes and threw the magazine across the room.

*Oh, shut the hell up, Phoebe Crane.*
*You don't know anything about love.*

## Chapter Two
### Day Four

I lay in bed covered in sweat, the sun having long gone down. How long were the nightmares going to last? Days? Months? Years? I shivered at the thought. In my senior year at college, my economics partner had been held up at gunpoint one night leaving a bar. He hadn't been able to leave his dorm afterwards for weeks. Hadn't been able to go to class. Eventually he'd had to drop out. Life was messed up that way. You worked your whole life towards a goal, and in a matter of minutes, your future could be ripped out right from under your feet.

I didn't want to end up like that. Scared. Hiding. Too afraid to face the world. I had to get a hold of myself. I paced around the room, trying to shake off the image of the monster trying to abduct me. The room felt empty without Cian in it. I replayed our conversation over and over again in my head.

"I would have come for you no matter what."

Butterflies fluttered in my stomach. Had I been wrong to turn my back on him all those weeks ago? It was a lot easier to run and hide than face the person you thought had crushed your heart and soul. I hadn't mentioned the mysterious roses, the giant elephant in the room. I had been receiving a rose in a box tied with lace from an unknown person over the past several months. And now I knew that Cian was responsible for sending them. I didn't think I was mentally prepared for that conversation. Or to face reality.

Everything was gone. Everything I had worked so hard for, just taken from me. I dug my nails into my palms and took a deep breath. Maybe being alone wasn't the best idea.

I tiptoed downstairs and stopped in my tracks when I found Eros sitting in a chair facing the front door, a gun on his lap. A chill ran through me. We were in some type of danger. That was obvious. I took a step back and his head snapped in my direction when the floorboard creaked.

His face softened and he nodded his head toward the room I had confronted Cian in earlier. I mouthed *thank you* and hurried down the hall. The room was mostly dark except for the soft glow of a lamp on the desk. The pictures Cian had pulled out earlier were still scattered there. Cian was lying on the leather sofa, an arm thrown over his face. Even while sleeping he looked ready to fight.

My palms were sweating as I glanced over the pictures of Ryzen and Riddick. Some were innocent enough—dinner, drinks, and lots and lots of women around them. So much for Ryzen's supposed "good boy" persona he had staged to impress hotel chain owner Covington. If Covington had done his own surveillance, he would have found out pretty quickly how much of a playboy Ryzen really was. Then maybe none of this would have happened.

One picture in particular caught my attention,

and I picked it up by the corner. It was a man wearing sunglasses, towering over Ryzen, who was lying on the ground, his hand held up. He looked terrified. I rocked slightly on my heels, shaking my head. I would not want to be caught in a dark alley with that man. I flipped the picture over and laid it back down on the desk.

I didn't want to think about that right now. The last thing I wanted was to trigger another nightmare.

Cian was taking up almost the entire couch, he was so big and wide. A protector. I managed to squeeze myself into the corner opposite of him and pulled my knees up to my chest, using my shirt as a blanket. It was big enough and smelt like him, a hint of the ocean and the forest, wrapped in sexiness. I wondered if that had been a coincidence or some Jedi mind trick to make me feel safe. If it was the latter, it was working. I sank down deeper into the couch and let my eyes close.

I felt myself being lifted and carried up the stairs at some point but was too tired to open my eyes. My head was pressed against something warm and strong, and I nestled my nose into it, inhaling.

Cian.

"You smell nice," I murmured.

His chest rumbled against my head as he chuckled softly. "Go back to sleep, little mouse."

*****

I was eating breakfast alone in bed when I heard Juliet screaming later that morning. My heart skipped a beat as footsteps pounded outside my bedroom door.

*Not again.*

I grabbed my fork, ready to poke someone's eyes out if I had to. I pressed my ear to the door just as Juliet let out another screech, followed by a giggle.

Wait. Was she laughing?

I flung the door open and found her standing outside my door, a water gun in her hand. "What the hell's going on, Jules?"

She pushed inside and slammed the door shut, pressing herself flat against it. She was completely drenched in water. "That big idiot Eros decided it would be funny to soak me with a water gun, so I dumped a bucket of water on him and stole it from him." She chuckled, pure delight across her face.

Eros pounded on the door a second later. "You're on my list, Juliet," he grunted as he tried to open the door. "Mark my words, Miss James." There was a hint of laughter in his voice, and I rolled my eyes.

"You scared the shit out of me, Jules. I thought… I heard you screaming and…" Damn, I needed to get a grip. I sighed. "You freaked me out."

Her smile disappeared instantly. "I'm sorry." She tossed the water gun onto the bed. "I wasn't thinking. I think everyone is going a little stir-crazy. Thora told me everything last night. I just wanted to forget for a minute, pretend we weren't hiding away from the monsters. It was stupid really."

"I understand, really I do." I drew my eyebrows together and rubbed my hands over my arms. "But don't you think we should be more careful? With them, I mean. I don't know if we can really trust them one hundred percent, can we?"

She hopped on the bed, tucking her legs underneath herself. "Nova, you need to wake up and see what's right in front of your face. That man down there"—she pointed to the door—"saved you. They saved us. Who knows where the hell we would be if they hadn't come. So yes, I say we can trust them." She sat up and held her hands out to me.

I sat next to her and squeezed her hands back. "Yeah, but…"

She shook her head. "No buts. I lost everything too, you know. All that hard work building up the Shiver Box, and just poof"—she snapped her fingers—"just gone now." Her shoulders sagged. "I don't know how we're going to recover from this. But I do know that they are good people. We need to trust that they are here to help us."

The weight of the world felt like it was on my shoulders. I flopped down on my back and sighed. "OK."

Everything was far from OK, but I wanted to believe that she was right. That they had our best interests at heart. There were just too many unanswered questions. Today we would find out though. I couldn't hide in this room forever.

"Let's go downstairs and see what the plan is then." She tugged me up from the bed and down the hall.

I wasn't looking forward to whatever was next. It couldn't be good, that was for sure.

We found the four of them standing around the kitchen table when we got downstairs. Eros winked at Juliet, and she flipped him off. She better be careful or she might fall for that Blackwood charm. Speaking of—Cian looked me up and down, his eyes taking everything in, and my body instantly warmed.

"Nova." Thora pulled out a chair next to her. "Come."

We hadn't spoken at all since that day in my

office when she had tried to warn me about Ryzen. She had been so bitter and angry; I had never seen her like that. I rubbed the back of my neck, hesitating. Juliet's words rang in my ears.

*They saved us. We need to trust them.*

Here went nothing. I returned her smile and sat down next to her.

"What's that?" I pointed at her hand. She was rolling a black stone back and forth between her fingers, and she stopped, handing it to me.

"Obsidian. It's for protection against negative energy. Keep it." She closed my hand around the stone.

"Oh, no, I couldn't." I chuckled and tried to hand it back to her.

She shook her head and reached into her pocket, pulling out four more stones. "I've got plenty, don't worry."

Cian was watching us, a smile tugging at the side of his mouth. Eros was stealing pancakes from Juliet's plate, and she smacked his hand. The whole table broke out in laughter, and I couldn't help but wonder if this was what it was like to have a normal family. Well, a form of normal.

"How are you feeling?" Thora's eyebrows drew together. "I've been wanting to talk to you, but Cian…" She lowered her voice and leaned closer. "He's a big brute sometimes."

"I heard that, Thora." Cian tossed his napkin onto his plate and narrowed his eyes at her.

Orin was pacing back and forth around the table, his phone glued to his ear. After a moment, he came over and whispered something to Cian, whose demeanor changed immediately. Cian stood from the table. "They're here."

The hair on the back of my neck stood up. "Who's here?" I looked around the room, waiting for an answer.

Thora patted my shoulder and stood. "It's OK." She followed Orin out into the hallway and Cian came around the table and held his hand out to me.

*Trust.*

I grabbed it and walked with him down to the office he'd been in last night. "Who's here?" I repeated the question.

He rubbed his hands over his face and clasped his hands together. "The FBI."

My eyes widened. "Why?"

He gripped my shoulders as footsteps came closer down the hall. "They are here to help."

The door opened and Orin walked in with two men wearing suits. They were the total opposite of each other. One was older with a potbelly and had his hair combed over to disguise the fact that he was going bald. The other man looked twenty years his junior; his suit was pristine and clung to his body, showing off an impressive physique. If you were into accounting porn, this would be the guy you would want to watch. Orin nodded at Cian, then shut the door on his way out.

Cian stuck his hand out and the younger man shook it and nodded. "Good to see you again, Cian." He held his hand out to his partner, "This is Agent Dobbs. He's very familiar with the situation."

Agent Dobbs sniffled and looked around the room. "Is there a cat in here? I'm allergic."

Cian raised his eyebrows. "No, Agent, not that I'm aware of." They shook hands and Cian touched my elbow. "This is Nova La Roux."

"Agent Delove." The younger man held his hand out, and I shook it, hoping he didn't notice how badly my palms were sweating. "It's good to see you safe, Nova." He sounded sincere, like he actually meant it, and I returned his smile.

"Dobbs, Nova."

Dobbs didn't smile as he gave me a lackluster handshake, completely different from Delove's. I didn't have much experience with law enforcement, especially with the FBI, but something told me I was about to experience Good Cop, Bad Cop. Er, Agent.

Cian guided me to the couch and sat down next to me while the agents sat across from us. The air was thick with tension, and I clasped my knees together, rubbing my palms over my pants. I wasn't in trouble. Was I? I mean, being a fake fiancée to a billionaire wasn't illegal. Was it? Not that they would even know that.

Delove pulled out a briefcase and laid it on the table between us. "Nova, I've worked with Orin Blackwood on several cases, and we've built quite the understanding between us."

Dobbs snorted and wrote something on his notepad. I glanced at Cian out of the corner of my eye, and he shifted closer to me. I nodded and Delove continued.

"As Cian might have mentioned, we've been working on a case against one Ryzen Goodacre, your fiancé."

*My fiancé.*

They didn't know it was a lie.

"We've been briefed regarding the situation at your wedding and understand there was an attempted kidnapping."

I nodded again, although a million questions started running through my head. What kind of case? Was Cian some type of informant? He should have prepared me for this.

Dobbs laid down his pad of paper and wiped his forehead with a handkerchief. "Let's cut the shit, honey. Why'd you blow up your own warehouse? You and your lover boy had a fight and you wanted to pay him back, was that it? Crime of passion?"

*Ladies and gentlemen, let me introduce you to the bad cop.*

My mouth fell open. "Blow up?" I squeaked as heat rushed to the tips of my ears. "I was just almost kidnapped, and now you're saying my warehouse was blown up? How could you even ask me if I could do something like that?" I could barely get the words out, nausea rolling through me in waves.

"Well, considering the kind of work you do, Miss La Roux, it's not out of the question. Quite the harlotry." Dobbs sniffed.

My stomach fell to the floor, along with my jaw. Cian stood and leaned across the table. "Watch your fucking mouth," he snarled.

Delove held up his hand and rolled his eyes. "Dobbs, enough. Cian, sit down."

Cian pressed against me so there wasn't an inch of space between us. Was that why they were here? Because they thought I'd burned my warehouse down? I'd thought they were here to help me, not make me feel like a criminal. The knot in my stomach doubled in size. Cian laid his hand on my knee.

Delove cleared his throat. "Nova, let me break

down what we know so far. On Saturday, at approximately twenty-three hundred hours, five vans were stolen from the Maringo dealership off Highway 88. Those same vans were spotted Sunday on the outskirts of Goodacre Apple Farm, where you were to be married to one Ryzen Goodacre. 911 received a call at fifteen hundred hours from a wedding hostess stating there were masked intruders holding people hostage."

My mouth went completely dry. Oh, God, was it the server from the kitchen? It had to be her.

"Approximately twenty-three minutes later, the sheriff arrived and was greeted by a team of men claiming to be a mixture of local police and FBI, who promptly sent him on his way. No police reports were filed, no investigation inquiries were sent to our local office, and the person who made the 911 call has not been found."

I gasped, my hands trembling as I clasped them together.

"As a matter of fact, if Orin had not contacted me regarding your situation, there would be absolutely no record of what happened to you at Goodacre Farm. Ryzen Goodacre has not made any type of statement regarding his missing fiancée. There have been no posts on social media from any of the wedding guests, who have all been accounted for as safe, excluding the hostess. Life for everyone at your wedding has gone on completely normally the last few days, including your fiancé's. We don't know exactly what happened after you were brought here." Dobbs watched me closely, looking for my reaction.

I didn't acknowledge what they said, just looked at Cian, my eyes wide. That didn't make any sense. How could nobody have said anything or filed a report? You didn't just show up with guns at a wedding and go unnoticed. Cian's jaw was clenched, heat radiating off his body. "How?" I whispered to him. "How can that be possible, Cian?"

Delove opened the briefcase and pulled out a thick manila envelope. "Miss La Roux, can you tell me if any of these three men look familiar?"

He laid out a series of photos of three different men, all of whom looked strikingly similar, with dark hair and tattoos covering their exposed skin. One had a tattoo of a skull and hourglass on his hand, the words "memento mori" over it. Another had the word "omerta" written across his neck. A third was older, maybe in his seventies, leaning on a cane with skulls carved all over it. They looked more than dangerous. They looked downright evil.

I shook my head and pushed the pictures back over to Delove. "I've never seen them before."

"You sure about that, honey?" Dobbs puckered his lips, not trying to hide that he didn't believe me.

Cian put his elbows on the table. "The next time you call her 'honey,' Delove is going to be taking you out of here in pieces." His voice was low, menacing, and the way Dobbs' face reddened, he knew Cian was serious.

"I'll lock your ass up right now, Blackwood," Dobbs huffed, his face twisting in anger.

Cian snickered and rolled up his sleeves. I placed my hand on his arm as Delove ran his fingers through his hair and sighed. "It's OK," I said. "Yes, Agent Dobbs, I'm sure. I think I would remember seeing men like that. What do they have to do with this?"

"They're your lover boy's bosses, Miss La Roux.

You're sure you haven't seen them?" Dobbs was sweating profusely, his eyes drilling into me. "Kind of suspicious you don't recognize them."

"That's it. Dobbs, take a walk and calm yourself before your damn heart gives out again." Delove handed him a set of car keys. "Go check your blood pressure before you keel over."

"Wiseass. Wet behind the ears, giving me orders," Dobbs muttered and stomped out of the room.

I had a feeling that whatever was going on with Dobbs had nothing to do with me. Or so I hoped. Maybe this was how the FBI operated. They put pressure on you and forced you to admit to something you hadn't done. You heard about dirty cops all the time. Hell, Cian had even said it himself earlier.

"My apologies." Delove cleared his throat and scanned the photos on the table. "Agent Dobbs has been building a case on the Voledetti family for over a decade." He pointed to the older man with the cane. "Victorino Voledetti. Retired boss. Handed the reins down to his first son, Kaviathin, age thirty-six." Delove held up the picture of the man with the skull and hourglass tattoo. "He is the leader of their organization, and his brother"—he nodded his head at the other photo—"Althazair, age thirty-three, is his right-hand man."

I crossed my arms over my chest, biting the inside of my cheek. "OK, that's all really fantastic, Agent, but I don't know them and have never seen them before."

Delove leaned forward and clasped his hands together. "This crime syndicate is the biggest threat to the safety of this city. They control everything from street-corner drugs to the police and even government officials. The list of quote-unquote 'accusations' against them is miles long. Money laundering. Public corruption. Weapons smuggling. Tax fraud. Labor racketeering. You name it, they're involved in some way."

I crossed my legs, fighting the urge to bite my fingernails. "What does any of that have to do with me?" Why was he telling me all of this like it was helpful information? The only thing he was doing was freaking me out, and he still hadn't gotten to the point. "Can't you just arrest them?"

Delove chuckled. "I wish it was that easy, Nova. They are smart. Too smart. Every time we come close to getting solid evidence against them, someone either winds up dead or disappears." His eyes drilled into me, and I didn't like where this conversation was headed. "Ryzen Goodacre has been an associate of theirs for many years"—Delove nodded at Cian—"since Mr. Blackwood and him were partners." He studied me for a moment, the room silent. "You don't seem surprised by this news that your fiancé is involved with the Mafia."

I sighed, my shoulders sagging slightly. "Agent, there's a lot you don't know about me and Ryzen Goodacre. But no, based on what Cian has told me, the shock has come and gone."

Delove nodded and pushed a picture of Ryzen in front of me. "He is the key. He is how we take the Voledetti down." He tapped his finger on Ryzen's face and leaned back in his chair.

Dobbs came back into the room, slamming the door behind him. Great, the old coot hadn't keeled over in the back of his sedan.

My mind was reeling with everything Delove had told me. "I already told you I don't know these people. I know nothing about Ryzen and the Mafia. I was attacked, and it sounds like these men might be responsible. So arrest them." I threw my hands up. "I'll give a statement. So will Juliet and Cian." I looked at him for help.

Cian squeezed my knee and nodded. "Tell us what you need."

"The DA is on the warpath. She wants to take these sons of bitches down." Dobbs huffed as he plopped back down into his chair. "And we can finally do that once we have Goodacre right where we want him. Which is where you come in." He looked at me as if he had solved the riddle to the world's hardest puzzle.

"I just told you I don't know anything. Shouldn't we be trying to find the people who tried to kidnap me? The ones who destroyed my warehouse?" I sputtered, my head pounding. "What do you want from *me*?"

Delove and Dobbs looked at each other, the room filling with tension as Delove tapped his pen against the desk. "Your fiancé isn't as smart as he thinks he is. We need you to collect evidence of his illegal business activities. Once we have the evidence, we can use that as a bargaining chip against the Voledetti family. Him or them. Knowing Ryzen Goodacre, he'll choose himself."

The room was completely still as we all looked at each other. A tickle in my throat exploded into full-blown laughter. Delove raised his eyebrows, and Dobbs puckered his lips. He looked like one of those pathetic fish you saw swimming in a dirty aquarium at one of those seafood restaurants, which only made me laugh even more. A tear streamed down my face, and I wiped it away.

"How about hell fucking no?" I slammed my hand on the table, heat rushing to the tips of my ears. "Are you out of your damn minds? You just sat here and told me these men are dangerous, *murderers,* and now you think, what, that I'm just going to put myself right in the middle of it? How would I even get this so-called evidence?"

Delove had the decency to look embarrassed. "You're engaged to the man. He'll have to explain himself and the situation with Voledetti, since he thinks they kidnapped you. Once he believes he can trust you, he'll slip up. You'll find what we need, and we can move forward."

I shook my head, rubbing my temples. "No way, that is not even remotely possible."

Dobbs threw his handkerchief on the table and leaned forward, the buttons on his shirt threatening to pop open at any moment. "Oh, it's possible, honey. You either get the intel we need or you'll be headed straight to prison for insurance fraud and conspiracy. Not to mention domestic terrorism if the DA chooses. There were three employees working the late-night shift in the building next door to your warehouse. You're lucky they weren't severely injured."

My mouth fell open and Cian stood up, bringing me with him. "Get the fuck out. Now," he boomed. "There's no way in hell she's going back to him."

Delove stood and cracked his neck from side to side. "This is the only way out for you, Nova. The DA is ready to press charges with one phone call from us. Help us help you."

My whole body was shaking as I glanced between

the two agents. They were serious. Actually serious about this. My heart was beating so fast, I thought I was going to pass out. They couldn't get away with this. There had to be another way. Conspiracy? Insurance fraud? This couldn't be happening.

"Your plan is flawed, gentlemen." I threw my head back, looking up at the ceiling. There was no way to hide it now. I blew my hair out of my face. "It was all a sham. The engagement to Ryzen? Not real. Not one bit of it. I can't help you."

The two of them looked at me like I had grown two heads. But not Cian. His eyes darkened, his whole body tensing up.

I guessed it was time to tell the truth.

# Chapter Three

The room was silent when I finished telling them my story. Delove leaned back in his chair and breathed deep. I had told them almost everything, from meeting Ryzen in the elevator, to the contract, all the way up to the wedding. I'd left out the parts involving Cian and what had happened with Iva. They didn't need to know about how I had fallen for Iva's lies, which was what Ryzen had been counting on, and the way my world had crumbled around me.

I risked a glance at Cian, his lips set in a hard line. He wouldn't even look at me, and hell, I didn't blame him.

"Makes sense, actually." Delove shook his head. "An empire like Covington Hotels? A money launderer's dream." He whistled.

"Look, I only told you so that you would understand why this plan of yours won't work. Ryzen and I aren't in love. It was all for show." I bounced my leg up and down, the table shaking slightly as I did so. "And you can't honestly believe that I would blow up my warehouse." I scoffed. "I did everything in my power to get that building, and now it was all for nothing." My shoulders sagged, reality sinking in that I had in fact lost everything.

"Excuse us for a moment." Delove stood and motioned for Dobbs to follow him.

When the door shut behind them, I braced myself for Cian's wrath. For him to yell and tell me how stupid I had been. But it didn't come. He sat in silence, his fists clenched. I chewed on my bottom lip, and when I couldn't take the silence anymore, I turned towards him. "Say something."

He looked at me then, his eyes dark with a hint of something I couldn't decipher. "We'll discuss this after they leave."

"But…"

He held up his hand and shook his head. "I don't want them to hear you screaming after I bend you over my lap and punish you for all your little lies." It wasn't a threat. It was a promise.

I gasped, and if I had been wearing pearls, I would have clutched them at that moment. Before I could respond, not that I even knew *how* to respond to that, Delove and Dobbs walked back in.

"Sorry about that." Delove offered a small smile and I relaxed for a moment. Maybe they had talked to the DA and explained, and this could all be over with. I could go back home, and Juliet and I could figure out how we were going to rebuild. "We spoke with the DA and we're all in agreement that this new development works out in your favor. Ryzen still needs to close the deal with Covington, so he needs you. Voledetti won't let something like that go easily. And what better way for you to rekindle your love with Ryzen than reuniting after being kidnapped? You're traumatized. You'll seek comfort in the arms of the man you were going to marry. It will stroke his ego and, believe me, he'll slip up." Delove looked so pleased with himself, I contemplated grabbing the pen on the desk and stabbing it in his hand.

Cian slammed his fist on the table, and I jumped. "There is no way in hell this is happening, Delove. This isn't why we called you." His voice was lethal, and Delove craned his neck, loosening his tie.

"Cian," Delove warned. "This is her only way out of this."

Great, not only were they all experts in my messy fake love life, but I was also apparently invisible. The three of them argued back and forth for a moment, and I rolled my eyes at their pissing contest.

"Hey!" I clapped my hands together, getting their attention. "Can I talk now?" I looked between the three of them. "It's a stupid plan, OK? I won't do it." I scoffed.

Delove placed a series of photos in front of me. One picture was of Ryzen and a man handing him a duffel bag. Delove nodded at the picture. "That's a union official paying Ryzen off." He slid across another photo. "That's you entering the bank and depositing a portion of the money."

My eyes widened as I stared at the photo. I remembered that day. Ryzen had asked me to deposit money at the bank for the wedding fund. There had been no reason at the time to question him. He had said he was busy and that I would be helping him out, which was what I told Delove and Dobbs.

Delove shook his head, his lips in a flat line. "That's conspiracy, Nova. We traced the bills back to the union official. This is dirty money, and you are as clear as day depositing it into a bank account with Ryzen's name on it."

The room suddenly felt fifty degrees hotter, and I rubbed my temples.

"And that's not all." Dobbs pulled out his phone and held it up so that Cian and I could see his screen. A video started to play. It was security footage from the warehouse. Juliet pulled up to the back of the building in our employee Owen's car and I jumped out of the passenger seat with a large box. I knew what this was —it was the night before the wedding, and we'd been running late for the rehearsal dinner. I had forgotten my phone at the warehouse, so we'd stopped so I could grab it and also drop off the box of inventory binders for Owen to go through while I was on my honeymoon. I was gone for no more than forty-five seconds on the screen before you saw me running back to the car. The video cut off after we drove away.

"Care to explain why you're seen running into your warehouse with a box, then running out empty-handed, and less than twenty-four hours later it's been blown to pieces?" Dobbs snickered.

I explained exactly what happened, and Dobbs shook his head and grunted.

"Nova." Delove's voice was stern. "You and Miss James are the only two people seen at that warehouse before it exploded. We searched through the footage. No other people can be seen on camera."

"Well, where's the rest of the video?" I sputtered. "Obviously some of it is missing. Look at the time stamp. It skips." My voice was rising to a high pitch as my heart started to beat dangerously fast.

"That's all that we were able to find." Delove glanced down at his hands on the table. "Look, Nova"— he leaned forward—"the DA is not messing around.

She wants heads to roll, and if you won't help us get Voledetti, she'll take yours."

I opened my mouth and then closed it. No words would come out.

"Fuck!" Cian stood and clenched his fists. "That son of a bitch." His knuckles were turning white, and nausea washed over me.

I knew right then and there that I was screwed. Just when I thought things couldn't get any worse, then bam, world turned upside down. Again. I tugged on the collar of my shirt; it was like it was suffocating me to death. This could only mean one thing. Ryzen had set me up to take the fall for this. Not only me, but Juliet, which was what I told Delove and Dobbs.

"Based on what we know, I would be inclined to agree with you. But with this video, and no other evidence, you and your business partner will be the DA's number one targets." Delove reached across the table and grabbed my hand. "That video is all she needs to indict you and Miss James. She will bury you, do you understand? She is tired of getting dicked around by Voledetti and she's out for blood, at whatever cost. She doesn't want *you*, but she'll take you if you don't help us."

I was fucking screwed. They had me, and we all knew it.

"Help us, and this all goes away. Don't, and we can't guarantee what will happen to you or your business partner."

I yanked my hand out of his grasp and glared at them. So that was it then? I could tell by the look on Delove's face that he knew I hadn't done anything wrong. He frickin' knew, yet wasn't going to do anything to help me because they were desperate. Here I was again, another pawn in a bullshit game I'd never signed up to play.

"It's too fucking dangerous," Cian muttered, his back to us.

That was exactly what I was thinking. What, I was just supposed to show up at Ryzen's wearing a wire and magically get him to confess to every illegal thing he had done? Oh, sure, that'd work. I was sure he'd willingly tell me, "Yeah, I blew up your warehouse, and?"—charming dimples and all.

"We have an informant embedded within Ryzen's organization. They have been providing us with intel for some time, but not enough. They can't get what you could get. They will ensure your safety. You get Ryzen comfortable enough to slip up, get your hands on any evidence you can find and bring it to us, and we guarantee this whole situation goes away and you can go back to living your life." Delove and Dobbs both leaned forward, watching my face closely.

They were talking to me as if I had a choice, and we all knew I didn't. If it was just me, I might take my chances and fight the DA. Grams would help—she would never let me sit in prison. The thought alone was enough to make me shudder. But Juliet? There would be no way she could handle that. She was too sweet and innocent-looking. They would take one look at her and eat her alive. I couldn't be the one responsible for that.

"I need time to think." I sighed and put my head in my hands.

"We don't have much time, honey. Ryzen has his own band of dirty cops looking for you. As far as we can tell, he believes Voledetti has you. You need to get back to him before he realizes Boy Wonder over here was the one who nabbed you." Dobbs scowled at Cian, then gave me a pointed look. "Twenty-four hours. Then we need to set the wheels in motion."

"What happens when Goodacre figures out Voledetti didn't take her? You think of that, genius?" Cian stood with his legs spread, arms crossed over his chest. The look he was giving Dobbs was enough to even make me nervous.

Delove held up his hand to stop whatever Dobbs was about to bellow. "Like we said, we have someone on the inside. We'll make sure Goodacre stays oblivious to your little rescue mission."

We watched them drive off in their sedan a short time later. They left me their files and a warning not to flee. Twenty-four hours, that was all the time I had to make a decision. Of course, it wasn't really a choice, only an illusion of one. Unless some magical arson fairy showed up with a video of Ryzen setting my warehouse on fire, I was one hundred percent royally fucked.

Cian ran his fingers through his hair, his eyes piercing mine. "We can run. We could leave tonight. They wouldn't find us, Nova. I will make sure of it."

*We.*

I shook my head. And, what, be looking over my shoulder for the rest of my life waiting for the FBI to find me—or, worse, for Ryzen to find me? No, I couldn't live like that. "I can't leave Juliet, and you can't leave your family. They need you." I sighed and sank into the couch. "I don't want to drag you into any more trouble either, Cian. I appreciate you saving me, but I'll have to deal with this on my own." I couldn't do that to him. Not after everything Ryzen had put him through. The last thing he needed was to be constantly worrying about me.

Cian dragged me up from the couch and I gasped as he held me tight against him. "Do you think I'm ever letting you out of my sight again, little mouse?" He weaved his hands through my hair, tugging my head back. "I will not let anything happen to you." His soft lips kissed down my jaw and I tried to fight the moan from escaping. "You're mine, Nova."

His lips crashed into mine and I lost myself instantly. I gripped his shirt in my fists, keeping him in place. This was wrong, and I knew it, but you couldn't have paid me to stop at that moment. All the frustration, all the sadness, all the anger I had felt over the past few weeks seeped out of me and into that kiss. His tongue was like velvet, and I moaned when his teeth dragged down my neck, the sensation sending a direct signal between my legs. "Fucking mine," he growled. He lifted me up and I wrapped my legs around him, the length of him pressing into me. I had forgotten what this felt like, this carnal urge to devour someone. He pressed my back against the wall and ground his hips into me, making me moan out. Yes, this was what I needed. My whole body was on fire, burning for him. I reached down to unbutton his pants when a knock at the door had us both freezing in place.

*Crap!*

"Fucking hell," he muttered and lowered me down.

"You guys all right in there?" Eros called through the door, jiggling the doorknob.

I pulled my shirt down and ran my fingers through my hair just as he walked in.

"Oh." He chuckled as he looked between the both of us. "Orin wants to talk." He nodded his head down the hall and Cian let out a deep breath. He grabbed a folder from inside his desk and followed Eros down the hall, but not before promising me that we weren't finished with our talk. Or his punishment. And I knew I shouldn't want it, but the thought of him bending me over his lap and spanking me was almost enough to make me forget for just a moment that my life was in utter shambles.

Thora was out back with Juliet, showing her how to use her camera—probably the same one Thora had used to take all those pictures of Ryzen. Juliet asked me a hundred questions, but I didn't have the heart to tell her. Not yet. Not before I knew for sure what I had to do. She didn't need to carry that burden around when she had been through hell and back already.

I spent the next few hours looking over the files Delove had left me with, my fingers constantly wandering to my lips, touching them, thinking of Cian. I knew I needed to be careful with him—it was too risky and too stupid to put my heart on the line again, especially in the middle of this disaster—but my body and mind were not on the same page. One was in shell shock trying to adjust to the fact that prison was a definite possibility; the other was a horny teenager looking to escape through a mind-blowing orgasm. I couldn't blame either of them, to be honest.

After spending some time looking through the reports, a definite pattern emerged regarding Kaviathin and Althazair Voledetti. Informant A provided intel to the FBI regarding illegal gambling; Informant A went missing. Informant B told the FBI Voledetti was rigging bids for a million-dollar construction project in downtown Chicago; Informant B went missing. Informant C said the brothers were expecting a shipment of drugs to be brought in on a cargo ship at Lake Michigan; the FBI seized the boat and found no drugs, just the dead body of informant C.

There was no doubt in my mind that these people were dangerous. Killers. Drug dealers. Kidnappers. Had they taken me and Juliet, who knew where our bodies would have been found. It was enough to make me sick to my stomach. I rubbed my hands over my face, my eyes squeezing shut as dizziness rocked through me. How the FBI thought I alone was going to take down this crime family was beyond me. But I guessed that wasn't what I needed to do. All I needed was to get Ryzen to slip up. Find the evidence. He had to keep paperwork somewhere. I thought back to when we'd first met, how I'd found it odd that he had so much security around him. It was all starting to make sense.

I picked up a folder labeled 'Goodacre' and thumbed through the documents. Ryzen was clever, but not as clever as Voledetti. The FBI was right. He was their best option at taking them down. The documents went back over ten years: pictures of Ryzen at dinner with the family; shaking hands over drinks; passing of envelopes one could only assume had cash in them. What wasn't in the file, though, was how it had all started. How the hell had Ryzen gone from promising real estate mogul to a pawn in the Mafia's hands? It didn't make sense. But I guessed you never knew what was going on in someone else's mind. Picture-perfect on the outside, dirty and greedy on the inside.

My heart fluttered when I came across a

picture of Cian and Ryzen together at a ribbon-cutting ceremony at their first official office. It wouldn't be too long after that picture was taken that everything would fall apart for Cian. I ached for him, the anger and frustration he must have felt after being betrayed. The documents didn't say who in Ryzen's circle was feeding the FBI information, but whoever it was was giving them a lot of intel—wiretaps on his cell phone before Ryzen got paranoid and threw his phone into a river, copies of new construction projects where the union leaders' names were highlighted. The same leaders were controlled by Voledetti. And so much more.

It wasn't enough evidence though. Even I could see that. It was pure speculation. A hint at illegal activities, a rocky foundation. One that I could only imagine the DA didn't want to risk prosecuting without a guaranteed win.

Cian came back some time later and found me on the floor rubbing my neck, surrounded by pictures of Ryzen. His eyes darkened as he took me in, a crease between his brows as I flipped through the rest of the pictures.

"It's hard to imagine this is real." I held up the pictures and scrunched up my nose. "That Ryzen is this… terrible person capable of the things they are saying."

Cian walked over and stepped on the pictures, stuffing his hands into his pockets. I gulped at the look on his face, knowing I had hit some type of nerve. "He's good at hiding the monster inside of him. After all, he was able to fool you. Even after you were warned, you still didn't believe." There was a hint of bitterness in his voice, and I sighed. "You have no idea who he really is,

Nova."

"And who are you?" I snapped and stood up from the ground. "Huh? Are you some secret FBI agent, or an informant?" My hands trembled and I balled them into fists to get it to stop. He didn't have to keep reminding me that I was the biggest idiot on earth. I was already well aware of that.

He lowered his eyes, his jaw clenched. "I have an arrangement with Delove, that's all you need to know. I have never lied to you, Nova." He took a step closer, not caring that he was getting dirt all over the photos. I knew what he meant by that. *He* had never lied to me, but *I*, on the other hand, was a big fat fibber.

I threw my hands in the air. "I had no choice! I already told you that. Just stop. Please. Let's not do this right now." My shoulders sagged, the weight of the decision I had to make crushing me. "Do you have a computer I can use?"

He walked over to his desk and pulled out a laptop from a locked drawer, then sat down on the sofa without another word. Good. I knew he hadn't given up on the argument, but I was relieved he was respecting my wishes to not continue fighting.

I searched through my emails, looking for my lease with Goodacre Corporation. Something had been nagging at the back of my mind all day, something to do with the lease, but I couldn't figure out what.

And then I found it. The insurance clause. Riddick had been adamant that we had to carry a full coverage policy. It was more expensive, but the landlord, as in Ryzen Goodacre, would cover a portion of the policy for the first year. It was more insurance than was necessary. Way more. Meaning if the DA was trying to implicate us in some type of insurance fraud, this policy was a big fat red flag. I showed it to Cian, and his face said it all.

"That son of a bitch is going to pay for this, Nova. Mark my words." He stood behind me and rubbed my shoulders, my eyes drifting closed. His thumbs pressed into the middle of my shoulder blades, and I let myself get lost in his touch for a moment. The realization was slowly sinking in. There was no way out. Jail or becoming an informant. A life on the run or taking down the monsters.

"Can you go get Juliet? I need to talk to her." I couldn't keep this from her any longer. She had to know. Not because I was hoping she would talk me out of it, but so that she could prepare for what was to come. If I had known how all of this was going to end up, I would have left with Cian. I would have run and never looked back.

Juliet and I sat on the bed in my temporary bedroom, and I explained everything that the FBI agents had told me, from Ryzen being in deep with the Mafia, to the incriminating video of us, and that if I didn't cooperate and try to get information out of Ryzen, they would put us both in jail. By the time I finished her eyes were bugging out of her head.

"Can they do that?" Her voice trembled, and I could sense the floodgate of tears was about to rip open.

I squeezed her hands in mine, both of our palms sweating. "Cian thinks they can. But Jules, I'm not going to let that happen, OK? I'm going to do what they say. It's the only way."

She shook her head. "No way, Nova. It's too dangerous. We'll take our chances. We'll get a lawyer.

They can't just do this to you. To us." Her voice was panicked, as I'd known she would be.

"Jules, I don't think we have a choice. Neither of us would fare well in jail." I chuckled, but she wasn't laughing, and I sighed. "I can do this, Jules."

She jumped off the bed, nibbling on her fingernails. "Maybe I can find something at Riddick's." Her face scrunched up. "I mean, we ended things on peaceful terms. It wouldn't be odd if I showed up at his apartment. He's the lawyer after all—there must be something somewhere in his office." She looked at me, waiting for me to say yes, her eyes big.

I shook my head and scrunched up my nose. "No, Jules. Delove and Dobbs didn't say anything about Riddick or you. Maybe they haven't found out about the two of you, and we should keep it that way."

"But..."

"No, this is my fault. You understand that, right? I got us into this mess, and I'm not going to let you get mixed up in this anymore than you already have. I could not live with myself if something happened to you because of the stupid choices I made, got it?" I squeezed her tight.

"You're squishing me," she mumbled into my shirt. I let her go and we both chuckled. "I'm not going to let you do this alone, Nova." She held up her hand when I opened my mouth and pressed her finger to my lips. "No, gremlin. I know you want to be able to control the outcome of this, but I won't let you do this alone. OK?"

I nodded, knowing full well I would do everything in my power to keep her from getting involved. But she didn't need to know that.

We spent the rest of the night sitting on the bed, talking about anything and everything but the impending doom we were getting ready to face. Thora came up a while later with a tray of snacks and we ate in mostly silence. I didn't want to be the one to say what everyone was thinking. That this was a stupid idea. That I could get myself killed. But the more I sat and thought, the more things became clearer to me.

Ryzen Goodacre needed to be stopped. He had lied, manipulated, and deceived me for his own personal gain. He had burned down my warehouse and made it look like I had done it. I had lost everything because of this one man, this one stupid man I had thought I could trust. And he was going to pay for what he had done to me. To us.

I understood now this need for revenge that burned inside Cian, the frustration he must have felt all these years knowing Ryzen was out hurting innocent people and he couldn't do much about it. It could eat you up though, this feeling of vengeance. And I hoped that by the end of this I wasn't going to be left a shell of the woman I used to be.

Thora and Juliet headed downstairs a little after midnight, and I lay on my back staring up at the ceiling for what seemed like an eternity. The door creaked open sometime later and Cian stepped inside, shutting the door behind him. His eyes looked tired, and I hated that I was the reason for it. I never wanted to be a burden on anyone, and that was exactly what I was feeling with each passing minute.

"Do you want me to stay?" he murmured, his back pressed against the door.

Damn, he looked sexy. I nodded and patted a spot

on the bed next to me. I wanted to get lost in him, the need to forget the last few days overriding common sense that this was a bad idea. That I should stay away from him and focus on how to take down Ryzen. The connection between my mind and heart, right and wrong, was completely lost when I looked at him.

He sat down in the chair across from the bed and leaned back, crossing his ankle over his knee. I propped myself up on my elbow and raised my eyebrows. "What are you doing?"

He let out a deep breath, rubbing his bottom lip as his eyes devoured me. "Sleep, little mouse. I'll watch over you."

My whole body warmed, and I nodded, lying back down. It was the right choice. Of course it was. One of us had to be reasonable, and right now, my body was anything but.

*****

At breakfast the next morning, the entire table was silent. The tension in the room was unbearable. Even Eros, who was always smiling and joking around, sat sullen, his mouth set in a firm line.

After moving my food around the plate for over twenty minutes, not eating a bite, I put my fork down and sighed. Cian glanced at me and threw his napkin on the table.

"It's time. Call them." I nodded at Cian, and he pulled out his phone.

Juliet reached across the table and squeezed my hand. I sat up straight and smiled at her. I could do this. *Had* to do this.

It was time to give Ryzen Goodacre a taste of his own medicine.

## Chapter Four

**Day 5**

Twenty-four hours. That was all the time I had left before I was to go back to Ryzen.

Delove and Dobbs packed up the rest of their equipment and Cian walked them out to their car. He pulled out a cigarette and handed one to Delove. They leaned against the sedan talking for a bit before Cian headed back inside.

I hurried away from the window and busied myself with the items laid out on the table. Cian strolled in, a grin spread across his face. "Spying, Nova?" His tone was playful, and I returned his smile.

"Just getting into character." I chuckled and immediately stopped at the look on his face. I was just trying to lighten the mood. We both knew how serious this was, the danger involved. One little slip-up on my part and it was over. Over, as in dead. That was what Dobbs had said earlier that morning, and it had been scarred into my memory.

"Sorry." I wrung my hands together and exhaled slowly.

Cian came around and gripped me by the shoulders. "You don't have to do this, Nova. One word from you and we're out of here. I promise you, they will never find us, little mouse." His eyes searched mine, looking for something. But I wouldn't give it to him, and he knew it. I wouldn't do that to him—ask him to give up his whole life for a woman he barely knew—especially after everything that had happened between us. And I could never leave Juliet to deal with my mess. No, I was going to do this, and I was going to do it right.

"No, I can do this." I offered a small smile. "I just…"

"What is it? I'll do anything you need." He murmured and stroked my bottom lip with his thumb.

"It's going to sound stupid, but…I'm not that naïve 'little mouse' anymore, Cian. And I never will be again." My voice shook as I got the words out, and I straightened my back. Every time he called me little mouse, it served only as a reminder of all the things I had messed up. The mistakes I had made.

"I understand." He tilted my chin up with his finger, a playful smile on his face. "You're a fierce, strong woman. Brilliant. Brave. And my beautiful star." His lips caressed mine for a moment, and then he released me. His eyes scanned the table and then back to me. "Tell me again."

I knew what he was asking. He had had me repeat it to him several times already. "Tomorrow at eleven p.m. Juliet and I are to show up at the emergency room at Saint Alexus Hospital and look for the nurse on duty with blonde hair and a butterfly tattoo on her right hand." According to the wiretap Delove had obtained from his informant in Ryzen's circle, the blonde was on Ryzen's payroll and had already been alerted to be on the lookout for either me or Juliet. "We're going to tell her that we escaped some men who were holding us against our will, and that we need help."

The nurse would contact Ryzen, who would in turn send his own cops to take our statements, which would never get filed. Ryzen would come to the hospital, and then it was showtime. There was no guarantee this was how it would unfold, just an empty promise from Delove that it *should* work this way. We wouldn't know if the officers we would speak to would be on Ryzen's payroll or not, so we had to keep our story the same no matter what. If there was an issue, Delove and Dobbs would intercept.

Cian crossed his arms across his chest, his jaw clenched. "And what do you tell Ryzen?"

I swallowed; my throat was dry as sandpaper. "I tell him that some men grabbed us from the wedding and that they kept us blindfolded in a dark room. I never saw any faces, and I only heard the name Kaviathin one time." Dobbs stressed that I needed to keep it simple, say we didn't hear or see anything. That way I wouldn't get my lies mixed up and risk exposing myself.

Cian pointed to one of many different recording devices on the table. "Show me how you use this."

"You're quite bossy, you know that?" I scrunched up my nose, and he tried to hide his smile.

"Show me, Nova," he purred and heat moved up my neck to the tips of my ears. His eyes followed me as I walked around the table and matched up the parts that went together.

One was an actual wire with a microphone that I would tape to my body underneath my clothes. It connected to a recording device that would record up to two hours before I would need to replace the tape. I was to wear this one as much as possible when I was around

Ryzen or Riddick. I showed Cian how to hook up the device and where I would place it on my body. I grabbed the watch next and showed him where I would press to activate the camera. Press the button on the right once to take a picture, press the button on the left twice to send an SOS. I hoped I never had to press it twice. The watch was also a tracking device that would broadcast my location to the FBI.

I picked up the necklace with the large onyx stone in the center, a series of smaller black stones surrounding it. A button disguised as a red stone was at the very top of it. There was a camera inside the onyx that would stream a live video whenever the button was pressed. Dobbs had repeated over and over again that I had to press the button in order to activate the live stream, otherwise they wouldn't get any feedback. I had to hand it to them, they were prepared. In all honesty, it almost made you feel paranoid that they were able to put a camera in almost any object and you would have no idea you were being watched or recorded.

"Good." Cian nodded. "What's the name of the office project?" He laid his hands flat on the table and leaned towards me.

"Arlington Office Park. I'll speak with Helen, who will have a six-month lease ready for me to sign on Thursday." Another thing Delove had set up. I would pretend to get back to work as soon as possible to try to salvage the Shiver Box. The new office was in a terrible neighborhood, which was exactly what Delove had said we needed because Ryzen wouldn't be caught dead there. It had a small office space downstairs and an empty apartment upstairs. This was where we would meet when needed and I would hand over tapes, pictures, and anything else I could find.

It all sounded so simple. Easy. But the butterflies in my stomach told me that it wasn't going to be that way. Nothing ever was.

The worst part about this was not knowing how long it was going to be. Would it be days, weeks, months? Nobody could be sure. It all depended on me and what I could get out of Ryzen. I was going to have to lay it on thick, pretend the kidnapping had made me realize that I actually loved him.

Gag.

If by some miracle I could get him to confess to burning down my warehouse, or find the right incriminating evidence, then this could be over within days. I could only hope that I would find some magical box in his office labeled "Mafia" and be done with this.

*"What if it takes a long time, like months?" I asked Dobbs and shivered at the thought of playing loving fiancée for that long.*

"Don't let it take that long, then." He shrugged as if I had asked a ridiculous question.

"What if Ryzen finds out Kaviathin wasn't the one who took us?"

"He won't." Dobbs scoffed and rolled his eyes.

"What if I get a frying pan and hit you over the head? Do you think that would hurt?" was what I had wanted to ask him next, but I hadn't felt like watching him get worked up again. You know, for being an FBI agent, he sure was high-strung. I had a feeling it had to do with the Voledetti. Cian had mentioned that Dobbs had sacrificed years of his time trying to bring them down and had always failed. It showed on Dobbs' face whenever he spoke about them. The fact that I'd caught him constantly pouring liquor from a flask into his coffee was also not a promising sign.

"And what are you looking for again?" Cian walked around and sat on the edge of the table, his arms crossed against his chest. He was so close I could feel the heat rolling off his body. I'd noticed that about him. Always close, never giving me any space. Typically, that would drive me crazy—I was one of those people who hated feeling crowded—but with Cian, it was different. We were like magnets to each other, something that was hard to get used to in my mind, but that my body was loving.

"Nova?" His lips curled at the sides as he followed the path from my eyes to his chest, where his tattoo was peeking out.

"Yes, right, um, muscles… no." I shook my head and rubbed my hands over my face. "Not looking for muscles." I wheezed out a laugh, the butterflies in my stomach starting to rage.

He lifted his hand, and I froze as he pushed my hair behind my ear. "Focus, Nova."

Why did he have to look at me like that? Like he was hungry and had just found his favorite dessert?

"Yes. OK. Documents. Emails." I counted with my fingers. "Anything from Voledetti, Argins Construction, Flocked Builders or anything from a union president or representative." There were so many names to remember, I'd contemplated writing them down, but Delove had insisted that I memorize them. "Bank statements, bid documents, cell phone records, any government documents. Basically, I need to take pictures of anything and everything, especially if it's locked or stashed away."

"Good girl." Cian nodded.

My skin tingled at his comment, and I nibbled on my thumb. "I might have to stay the night at Ryzen's penthouse. That's probably one of the easiest ways to snoop and go unnoticed."

Cian was silent for a moment, the air in the room growing thick with tension. We both were thinking the same thing. Knowing Ryzen and his flirtatious ways, he would try something as he had numerous other times we had shared a bedroom at Covington's.

Cian's eyes darkened, and I could tell he was holding back. His posture said it all.

"And if he tries to put the moves on me, then I'll tell him I'm not ready. That being kidnapped has made me a born-again virgin." I grinned and sat on the table next to him.

Cian gripped the edge of the table, his knuckles turning white. After a moment, he cleared his throat and chuckled. "Born-again virgin, huh?" He quirked his eyebrow and stood, facing me. "Tell me, Nova, what will you do if he grabs you?" He stood between my legs, his hand coming up around the back of my neck, holding me in place.

I gasped as he pressed into me. A never-ending battle of wills was unfolding inside of me. My mind was yelling *no, red alert, this is trouble*, while my body was screaming *yes, you idiot, finally, get your fix, you junkie!*

"Tell me," he purred.

I grinned and bit my bottom lip, trailing my fingers up his shirt to his exposed skin. He narrowed his eyes at me, clearly not liking my answer to his question. I dragged my nails gently against his skin and over his tattoos, his body tensing underneath me. He let out a deep breath as my fingers roamed up his neck until they were weaved into his hair. God, I loved his hair, a dark chestnut color with a splash of gold. It was the perfect length for pulling, which he seemed to enjoy. I tugged his head back and licked my lips as I leaned in closer to him. I kissed the side of his face, just over his scars, then down to his mouth. He froze, his chest rising and falling with each ragged breath he took.

"This." I dropped my arm and slammed my elbow into the crook of his arm, making him release the back of my neck. His eyes widened with surprise, and I took that moment to wrap my leg around his thigh and push as hard as I could on his chest until he fell backwards and landed on his back with an umph.

I stood over him, my hands on his hips. "Nobody touches me unless I want them to." I snickered at the surprised look on his face and stepped over him, walking to the living room.

Not more than five seconds later, he was behind me, his arm coming around my waist, and I shrieked. "Let go of me, you big lug." I beat my fists against his arms, his chest rumbling with laughter against my back.

"Now what, Nova? What would you do?" His breath was warm against my ear, and I had to fight the urge to turn my head and press my lips against his. I struggled in his arms for a moment, but when I realized that there was no way of getting out of his grip, I relaxed my body and let myself hang against him.

"What are you doing?" He chuckled.

"Dead weight. That's the best way to get loose. Don't you know anything?" I turned slightly and grinned.

"This is serious, Nova. Jokes aren't going to help you if he grabs you and won't let go."

"Did I not just put your ass on the ground, Cian? I can defend myself." I huffed, a newfound energy building inside of me at his mocking tone. I jerked again, but he had me pressed firmly against him. We both knew I couldn't get out of his grip. Granted, he was bigger than Ryzen, with wider shoulders and larger muscles, but Ryzen was still a whole lot bigger than me. Annoyance built in my chest, and I grunted.

"If he grabs you from behind, throw your head back until you make contact with his nose. Then smash your heel into his toe. Understand?" Cian's tone was serious now, and I knew the funny moment had passed.

"OK," I breathed, his arms crushing me to his chest. I tapped his hand, and he released me.

Eros and Orin came into the room, both of them raising their eyebrows at us as we faced each other, our breaths ragged.

"Self-defense class, fellas. Wanna watch me kick your brother's ass?" I winked at Cian.

He pointed his thumb at me and turned to his brothers. "This is what I've been dealing with," he grumbled. I took the distraction as an opportunity to yank his arm towards me, then bend it as I circled around him, pinning his arm to his back. Of course he could have stopped me at any time, but he didn't.

Eros hooted with laughter, and Orin smiled for the first time since I had met him. "You see that, Cian? You're not so tough." I pushed him away from me and wiped the sweat from my forehead.

He turned to face me. "You're lucky they're here." He smirked, a promise in his eyes.

"Remember, palm strikes and tiger claws." Eros held his hand up and bent his fingers, pushing his palm out. "Aim for the nose with the bottom of your palm and smash it upwards." He faced Cian and showed me how it should look, and I mimicked his movements. "If you try to punch someone, you will break your hand, and trust me, that's no fun."

I nodded, taking all the information in. They spent the next hour showing me different moves, which I thought was just an excuse for them to roughhouse with each other. Cian took them down time and time again, which surprised me considering how big they all were. I mean Cian was huge, well over six feet of walking muscle, but Eros was just as tall with wider shoulders. Orin was a bit slimmer than the both of them, but definitely not lacking in the muscles department.

I sat down on the edge of the couch to catch my breath, watching them as they tumbled around. It didn't feel real. None of this did. In a matter of months, my whole life had been flipped upside down. Three months ago, Juliet and I had been celebrating signing a new lease and so happy that the Shiver Box was finally growing after all our hard work. And now I was in a room with three men who were practically strangers to me, trying to figure out the best way to stop an assailant from attacking me. Strange how things could change so fast.

My shoulders sagged and I propped my head up with my hands. I needed to stay focused, or I might lose it. Not only was I putting myself in a dangerous situation that had absolutely no guarantees it would turn out OK, but I had lost everything I had worked so hard for. It was still so hard to accept that it was gone. Not only gone, but that Ryzen had made it look like I was the one responsible for destroying the warehouse, and ultimately the Shiver Box. I just couldn't wrap my head around it. Was I really that stupid, or was he just that charming? I guessed we'd never know. The only thing I was able to do now was take him down. And I planned on making it hurt, like he had hurt me.

He was going to pay; I would make sure of it.

Eros and Orin headed upstairs, and Cian stood near the edge of the couch. His lips were set in a flat line, and I tilted my head to the side and tried to smile.

"You don't have to put an act on for me, Nova." His voice was soft, and I let out a deep breath. Was it that obvious? I'd thought I was pretty good at hiding that I was freaking out. Apparently not. "I'll always be close, understand? Minutes away." His eyes burned into mine, and I nodded.

I wanted to be strong, to say I didn't need him to watch over me. But if I was being honest, I didn't know if that was true. If Ryzen was as dangerous as they painted him to be, then I was about to walk back into the life of a monster, one I might not be able to fight on my own.

I leaned back on the couch, something poking my back. One of Eros's water guns was tucked under the cushion, and I shook my head. I was pretty sure it was no coincidence. Something told me he had them planted all over the house just waiting for his chance to get Juliet again.

"I know we were all joking around just now, but we're not taking this lightly. None of us. We will be there, watching, waiting and ready." Cian ran his hand through his hair and let out a deep breath.

Guilt ran through my veins at the look on his face. He looked tied up in knots. I knew a part of him was doing this because he wanted nothing more than to get revenge on Ryzen. But what was the other part of him wanting? Was I even ready to face that answer?

He lifted his shirt up and wiped his forehead, showing off his chiseled stomach. His scars ran across his front to his back, although his tattoos covered them up slightly. But I knew they were there. I had felt them, kissed them. Visions of us tangled up together, my fingers tracing his abdomen, my lips kissing over his body, ran through my mind. An involuntary moan escaped my lips as I watched the muscles in his forearms flex with each movement. He stopped abruptly, his body tensing.

I tugged on the collar of my shirt. "Are you hot?" I reached behind my back and wrapped my fingers around the water gun. "It's hot in here, huh?"

He narrowed his eyes at me. "What are you up to?" He took a step forward and I pulled the gun out, soaking the front of his shirt.

I giggled as his mouth fell open, water dripping down his chest. "You're going to pay for that," he chided and took another step forward.

I squealed and hopped over the couch, pointing the water gun at him. "Stay back, or I'll do it again," I threatened.

"I'm not going anywhere, Nova. You better run, or you're going to pay." He prowled closer and my body hummed as he got nearer.

I walked backwards until my back was pressed against the front door, gun still pointed at him. He looked lethal. Like a predator stalking his prey. And I had never wanted to be eaten alive more than in that moment.

"Catch me if you can," I said breathlessly.

He pounced towards me, and I threw the front door open and ran into the thickness of the trees. Something about being chased felt absolutely primal, and excitement coursed through my veins.

I pumped my legs as fast as I could, not daring to look behind me to see how close he was. I maneuvered my way through the dried-up bushes, the little branches slapping against my shins cutting into them. My chest burned, but I kept moving, faster and faster. He was close, his footsteps pounding through the terrain right behind me. Thump, thump, thump, thump.

I knew that he would catch up to me at any moment. I veered right, stumbling slightly. But who was I kidding? He was letting me win. There was no way that I could outrun him. We both knew it. After a moment, I realized I couldn't hear his footsteps behind me any longer. I pressed my back against a tree, the dead bark digging into me. I could hear my heart beating in my ears as I struggled to catch my breath.

It was eerily quiet, just a low hum coming from the power lines over my head. I peeked around the tree but didn't see him. I bent over, placing my hands on my knees as I tried to catch my breath. A tree branch snapped to my left, just a few yards from where I was hiding, and I took off in the opposite direction. The ground turned muddy, and I lost my footing when I tried to dodge a bush that had menacing-looking thorns sticking out from it.

I yelped and held my hands out in front of me,

but before I could fall face first into a puddle of mud, strong hands wrapped around my waist and tugged me back up.

My chest heaved as I pressed into Cian, his breath just as ragged as mine. "You're mine now, Nova." His breath was warm against my neck as he held me tight against him.

I shuddered at the implication and pushed my ass into him. This was not supposed to be happening. But tell that to my body, which was absolutely not listening to my brain. Hell, who was I kidding?

My mind was screaming for me to let go. Take a chance. Trust. I just wanted a moment to forget—forget about the men with guns, the FBI, Ryzen, the pain, the manipulation, the deceit—and just feel.

"Help me forget, Cian." I turned to face him and gripped his shirt in my hands.

"No, my beautiful little star." He tugged my head back and I gasped. "I'm going to help you remember." His teeth dragged across my neck, biting down gently. "Remember that you're mine."

# Chapter Five

"Oh, God," I murmured as he licked up the curve of my neck. His need for me matched my need for him, and I clung to him like my life depended on it. His lips found mine, and I let myself get lost in that moment. There was nothing gentle about it. It was fierce. Uncontrolled. Greedy. I kissed him back, our tongues intertwined as he crushed me to him.

"I will never let you fucking go again, Nova." He pushed me against a tree. The jagged edge of a decomposing branch scratched along my back, but I didn't care. The whole forest could be on fire right now, and I wouldn't take my eyes off Cian. He lifted me up, my legs wrapping around him instinctively, his lips back on mine. I bit down on his bottom lip, my fingers weaving through his hair, and he groaned.

I wanted more. Needed more. His mouth moved down, and I threw my head back as his lips brushed against my skin. Although we were outside, it felt like there was no air to breathe. My mind was a jumbled mess of wanting to forget about the scary monsters, and the need to be consumed by this man.

He yanked his shirt off and tossed it to the side, my nails digging into his back. His skin was warm underneath my hands, burning for me. I ground my hips against him, his cock pressing into me. It wasn't enough, I needed to feel him. My back pressed into the tree, and I reached down to his belt and tugged, impatience running through my veins. He grabbed my wrists and pinned them over my head, holding me in place with one of his hands.

"Such a greedy little thing, aren't you, Nova," he purred against my mouth. I gasped, nodding. "Did you think I had forgotten about your punishment?" His voice was low as he tugged on his belt with his free hand, it flying out of the loops of his jeans.

Oh, fuck. Was he going to spank me with his belt? The thought made my legs tremble in the most pleasurable way. "Oh, no. I was looking forward to it, actually."

He tossed it to the side, disappointment flooding through me. *Damn.*

"There's my dirty girl." His mouth crashed into mine, his tongue velvety soft as he teased it in and out of my mouth.

"Please, Cian," I begged, not caring how desperate my voice sounded.

"Please what?" His eyes were dark as he kept my wrists pinned over my head. His other hand trailed down between my breasts, under my shirt, until he found my nipple. "You want me to fuck you, Nova? Should I fill you up until you're coming all over my cock?"

I gasped as he rolled my nipple between his thumb and forefinger. My body was on fire, pure need pulsing through me.

"You think you deserve it after your little lies?" he rasped, pushing his cock against me.

"I'm sorry," I choked out as he tugged on my nipple. His hand moved to my other breast as he continued his torturous teasing. Did he want me to beg? Because I would. I would willingly sell my soul right at that moment.

"Don't move your hands, understand?" He gave me a pointed look, and I nodded quickly. Never had I ever let a man boss me around so much. But you know what? I didn't mind. Not one bit. Him taking charge, wanting to control me, was a kink I hadn't known I had.

My legs slid down from around his waist and he unbuttoned my shorts, yanking them and my panties down. He lifted my left calf, then my right, so he could take my panties off, throwing my clothing into the pile with his belt and shirt.

His hands gripped my thighs, digging into my flesh. "Such a pretty pussy, Nova." His breath was warm against my skin, and I threw my head back. "And it's all mine." There was an edge to his voice, and his possessiveness was beginning to make me unravel.

My breath came out in tiny pants as he licked between my folds, his tongue soft as he teased me. Up and down, coating his tongue with my wetness. He had that effect on me. One little kiss, one little hint at pleasure from him, and I was absolutely soaked.

His tongue circled my clit as he pumped a finger in and out of me. I should have been embarrassed at the noises I was making, but I wasn't. I was completely unashamed as I moaned out, begging for more.

He lifted my leg and placed it over his shoulder, his mouth warm as he latched on to my clit.

"Please," I begged, bucking my hips against his face.

He slid another finger inside of me, pumping in and out. "I want your scent all over me, Nova. Let me taste what's all mine."

I started to unravel, my legs quivering as I spasmed around his fingers. "Yes, yes," I gasped as a tingling sensation built all the way from the top of my head, down to my toes. "Oh, God, Cian," I cried out, moving my hips faster. His mouth was relentless, and only when I begged him to stop did he let me go.

I tried to catch my breath, my chest heaving from the powerful orgasm that had raced through my entire body. It was so unlike anything I had ever experienced except with him. It was as if our bodies were made for each other. He stood and unzipped his pants, letting them ride low on his hips. I instinctively reached down and he shook his head, stopping me.

"No. Your punishment is not being able to touch me. Understood?" His eyes burned into mine. You would have thought that would be a laughable punishment, but it wasn't. It was torture. The only thing I wanted more than to have him fuck me was to be able to touch him. All over. But I didn't want to risk what would happen if I did. He was right. I was greedy, and I fucking needed him.

I nodded and his lips devoured mine. I could taste myself on him, and it just made me want him more.

He flipped me around so that I was facing the tree and pushed his leg between mine. My thighs trembled as he rubbed his cock between my pussy lips. Slow, teasing, taking his time as he coated his cock with my juices. His breath was warm against my shoulder as he trailed kisses up the curve of my neck to my ear.

"You're so fucking beautiful, Nova," he rasped out as he slid just the tip of his cock inside of me, then out. He continued this rhythmic torture until I thought I would explode.

"Please. I need you," I whimpered. It was the only encouragement he needed as he slid all the way in, filling me up until I gasped. He drove his hips into me, slow and steady, over and over. I realized he was going slow on purpose, trying to be gentle, and my heart fluttered.

Now was not the time for slow and gentle though. I turned my head and looked over my shoulder. "Fuck me, Cian. Show me I'm yours," I panted.

His eyes turned fierce as he dug his fingers into my hips, a slight flush on his cheeks. "All fucking mine," he breathed and slammed into me.

I cried out, pleasure shooting through my whole body as he pounded into me. He grabbed my hands and pinned them over my head, his other hand coming around to strum my clit. I met him thrust for thrust, a need more powerful than anything I had ever experienced coursing through my body.

"Cian, more," I panted, our skin slapping against each other, making an obnoxious sound. "Please," I breathed.

He groaned, his lips finding mine as he crushed me to the tree, thrusting deeper, harder, faster, until I began to unravel. My orgasm built, flowing through my whole body, and I cried out against his lips, feeling as if I had been struck by lightning.

He slammed into me one last time, groaning out his own release, his lips never leaving mine.

We stayed like that for a moment, our bodies

clinging to each other, covered in sweat, as we tried to catch our breath.

"Fuck, did I hurt you?" He flipped me around and cradled my face with his hands. "Was I too rough?" His eyes searched mine.

"Um, no." I chuckled. "I'm OK—actually, more than OK."

His shoulders relaxed and he tilted his head down until his lips were pressed against mine. Soft, gentle, the complete opposite of what had just taken place between us. My body felt lighter as I melted into his kiss. I hadn't realized how much I'd needed that—not just sex or a quick fuck, but how much I had needed *him*. My heart squeezed in my chest and I sighed, resting my head against his chest.

The air seemed to hum all around us. Quiet. Satisfied. As if it knew something we didn't. He helped me get dressed, inspecting my cuts and scrapes as he did. His jaw clenched as he traced the cut on my forehead. There was something in his eyes that I couldn't make out. I shrieked as he picked me up and tossed me over his shoulder.

"Cian!" I laughed as I tried to grip his sides. "I can walk, you know."

"Mm-hmm," he murmured as he strolled through the trees. His hand came up and slapped my ass, grabbing onto it. "Don't want you to get any more cuts on your legs."

He hiked back, letting me jump on his back after I complained his shoulder was digging into my stomach. We were silent most of the way, just stopping every so often to look up at a bird or a squirrel jumping from tree to tree. It was peaceful, and satisfaction coursed throughout my body at the simplicity of it all. Of course, that feeling didn't last long as we approached the house.

I had to prepare for what was to come. Could I do it? Could I really face Ryzen and pretend he hadn't done such awful things? Not only that, but pretend that I was in love with him? My lip curled at the thought. I would not let him win. No, he was going to pay for everything he'd taken away from me.

Cian found me after I had cleaned up and showered, wearing one of his oversized shirts. His lips curled at the corners as he leaned against the doorframe, watching me as I fiddled with one of the listening devices Delove had given me.

"I have something for you." He walked over and held out his hand. Inside was what looked like a knife handle, and I raised my eyebrows.

"Thanks?" I chuckled and grabbed it.

He shook his head and grinned. "Careful." There was a small button on the side, which he pressed and a three-inch blade popped out. A retractable knife.

"Clever."

"You should know how to use it, since you pulled one on me the other day."

Heat rushed up my neck, and I lowered my eyes. "Yeah, sorry about that." Had that been only a few days ago? It seemed like a lifetime.

He tapped my chin, and I looked up at him. There was a gleam in his eyes as he studied me. "Don't be sorry. It's one of the things I lo… admire about you, Nova." He gripped my shoulders. "You're fearless, and you don't even realize it."

I warmed at the compliment and fought the urge to rip my clothes off and tackle him. I didn't miss his little slip-up. Had he been going to say 'love?' No, he wouldn't have. Would he?

He pulled away and nodded at the knife. "This is small enough to fit down your boot or inside your sock. Always carry it. Understand?"

I nodded and closed my fingers around it, my hand trembling slightly. His face said exactly what I was thinking. Could I actually use it if I needed to? Would I ever be in a situation where I would need to stab someone? I shuddered at the thought. There was no going back after today. The choice had already been made. And I would have to do whatever it took to make sure Ryzen Goodacre paid.

"I promise you that I will do everything in my power to protect you." Cian stroked my cheek, and I closed my eyes. "But you have to promise to trust me. That we're both going to trust each other more. OK?"

He was right. After all of this, it was clear that he was the one I needed to trust the most. I nodded in agreement and pressed my forehead against his.

The rest of the day went by in a blur, a frenzy of mentally preparing and going over everything again and again with Cian until he knew that I had it all memorized. Juliet and I knew what the plan was. Go to the hospital. Talk with the police. And then the rest was unknown. Would Ryzen realize right away I was lying? What would happen if he talked to Voledetti and found out he hadn't taken me? There were a lot of unknowns, but I couldn't focus on them. Stick with the plan and it would be OK.

Cian stressed repeatedly that he would always be nearby if I needed him. Just a call away. He'd promised me that, and I was going to hold him to it. Thora was setting up a new phone for me, a secret phone that only our small group, excluding the FBI, would know that I had. I could use it to call Cian day or night, and Ryzen would be none the wiser.

I wasn't going to lie, it was all overwhelming—not only going after Ryzen, but dealing with my feelings for Cian that had come rushing back. Hell, it wasn't like they had really gone in the first place. Who was I trying to kid? All those weeks of anguish, heartache, all because I'd believed the wrong people. I couldn't beat myself up over it though. How was I supposed to have known that Ryzen and Iva were in cahoots the whole time? The only thing I didn't understand was what their endgame had been. If Ryzen and I had gotten married, where would Iva have fit into all of it? She was obviously after the hotels. It would have made more sense for them to get married, not us. That was what I didn't get. But I knew at some point I would get the answers I needed. They would be exposed. And that bitch was going to pay for whatever part she'd had in it all.

We lay in bed later that night, the house quiet and settled. Cian was fast asleep as I tossed and turned for the hundredth time. It was no use. Adrenaline pumped through my veins, making me restless.

I snuck downstairs in my nightshirt and slippers, passing Eros in the foyer in the same spot he had been in the other night, gun on his lap. I grabbed a bottle of water, leaning against the counter as I chugged it. Maybe I should go for the hard stuff. That might help me pass out. But getting drunk wasn't the solution, so I walked around the bottom half of the house, peeking through the blinds.

Thora was sitting on the carpet in the living

room with her eyes closed, a bunch of crystals surrounding her in a circle. The floor creaked underneath my feet and her eyelids flew open. She smiled and patted the floor in front of her.

I chuckled and sat down facing her, a crystal poking me in the ass.

"Can't sleep?" she whispered, and I shook my head.

"It's been hard to fall asleep lately, and when I do, I've been having terrible nightmares." I rubbed my hands over my arms.

She scrunched up her nose and nodded. "I can understand why. You've been through a lot, Nova. You know you're very brave, right? Going through what you did, and what you're about to do. That takes a lot of courage."

My eyes watered as she spoke and I bit the inside of my cheek to keep the tears from falling. I didn't feel brave or courageous. If I was being honest with myself, I was fucking terrified. The unknown was a scary thing. Especially when you were willingly surrounding yourself with people who were out to hurt you, one way or another. "I'm really sorry about that day in the office, Thora. I was such a bitch, accusing you and not listening to reason and…"

She held her hand up and I stopped talking. "It's in the past. It doesn't matter. And I should have handled that differently too, so I'm sorry for that. But we're good. There is no animosity here, girl." She grinned and squeezed my hand. "But if you hurt my brother, I will make sure you regret it."

I chuckled and shook my head. Sweet, innocent-looking Thora. She didn't look like she would harm a fly, but I was starting to catch on to her. Deep down inside her was a warrior, ready to take on anyone. I could only hope that I could be as fearless.

"Oh!" She snapped her fingers and stood. "I have your phone, hold on." She slid across the floor in her slippers and came back with an iPhone. "It's old, but more importantly, it can't be hacked into. Eros made sure of it."

I grabbed it from her and pressed the button to unlock it. "What's the code?"

She rolled her eyes. "Six nine six nine. Stupid Eros," she muttered.

Of course it was, because a grown man who hid water guns around a house while hiding from the bad guys would obviously find a way to make this funny.

"My friend just came out with a wellness app. It's got some bugs, but I'm loving it. It has everything from meditations, to mantras, to even tracking the hours you're sleeping. It catches you if you're snoring or prone to talking in your sleep." She laughed and pulled out her phone, pressing a few buttons. A moment later, a voice recording popped up of a very sleepy Thora yelling that she wanted chocolate doughnuts with no frosting, followed by a slew of cuss words.

We fell back on the floor, laughing as she replayed it again.

"I guess I turn into a lunatic when I fall asleep." She giggled. "Wanna try one? A quick meditation to help you sleep?"

I shrugged my shoulders and nodded. Why the hell not. I would try anything at this point. We sat up and crossed our legs, hands on our knees, while a woman's voice guided us through some deep breathing.

She then said to imagine a white light surrounding yourself, a circle of positive energy and protection. Anything beyond this circle was not allowed, including nightmares and negative thoughts.

It was actually pretty relaxing, and after ten minutes, I thought I might be able to finally sleep. Thora put the app on my phone in case I wanted to do the meditation again and hugged me goodnight.

When I got back upstairs, Cian was leaning against the table, his head hanging down. I walked up to him and wrapped my arms around him from behind, pressing my cheek against his back. His body was like a furnace, and I welcomed the heat.

"Couldn't sleep?" he murmured and turned to face me.

I reached up and moved his hair from in front of his eyes. He looked tired, like he hadn't had a peaceful night's sleep in a really long time. I was sure I looked exactly the same, if not worse.

"Thora was showing me a meditation." I held my phone up and shook it. "I'm pretty sure I'm not doing it right, otherwise I should be filled with Zen, don't you think?" I scrunched up my nose.

He chuckled and walked me backwards until my legs hit the bed. "Perhaps you would rather be filled with something else, Nova," he drawled, and butterflies roared in my chest. I tossed my phone on the bed behind me, catching a glimpse in the corner of the room of the dried-up rose I had found days before.

"Cian, there's something I've been meaning to ask you." I placed my hands against his chest, my fingers brushing over his scar. His heart was beating so strong, I could feel it underneath my palm. "Those roses I was getting... you sent them?"

He lowered his eyes, focusing on my lips, and nodded. A flush spread across his cheeks, and I thought my heart would explode at how vulnerable he looked in that moment.

"But why?" I tapped my fingers against his chest. "There was no note. I didn't know where they were coming from."

He pushed me back gently until I was lying on the bed, and I chuckled. Sex couldn't always be the answer. Well, maybe it could. He grabbed my leg, placing my foot on his chest. His lips brushed against the sensitive skin there and I laughed as he licked up my ankle and around my rose vine tattoo.

"This tattoo has been burned into my memory since the night you showed up at my club dressed up as Lara Croft" His voice was husky, and I tried to control my ragged breathing as his lips caressed up my calf. "I could not get you out of my mind, no matter how hard I tried." He bit the inside of my thigh, my legs trembling.

That had been on Halloween over a year ago when I had met the masked man, Cian, who had given me the best night of sex I had ever had. But I had never heard from him again. Or so I had thought. "But why didn't you just talk to me, ask me out?" I rasped, then moaned as he gripped me tighter and licked right where he had just marked me with his teeth.

"If I had, maybe none of this would have happened to you." He tensed suddenly, as if just realizing what he had said.

"No." I ran my fingers through his hair. "That's not true. Don't think that, Cian."

His eyes darkened as I caressed his face. I

couldn't decipher the look in his eyes, but I didn't like it. Not one bit.

"I was a coward, Nova. I should have done things differently. My life was a mess and I didn't want to make yours that way, so I held back, even though I could barely handle it. I wanted to know everything about you, from how you took your coffee to all the dreams you had for this world. But I couldn't. The roses were just a piece of me I wanted you to have." He bit down on me again and I cried out. Not from pain or from fear, but because I liked it. Him marking me. Making me his. My thighs quivered as he worked his way up until I was panting. "But never again, Nova. I will not make the same mistake twice." He pushed my panties to the side and buried his face between my legs. "You're mine now."

"Yes," I whimpered and arched my back. His tongue was satin-like as it brushed across my clit. I was ready for him already, and he moaned in appreciation when I bucked my hips against his face.

"Say it, Nova." He pushed my legs back so that my knees were bent and pressed to my chest. I was completely exposed to him, and it made me feel wild. This carnal urge to have him devour me was taking over my whole body and mind.

"I'm yours," I panted and cupped my breasts. "I'm all yours, Cian."

He lapped up my juices, his tongue dipping inside of me, then back up to my clit. "Good girl," he purred. In a flash he sat up, pushed his jeans down, then centered his cock at my entrance. "Don't ever fucking forget it," he growled and thrust into me.

I gasped as he filled me up, arching my back as I gripped his arms. He fucked me slowly, with steady strokes that kept me on edge. I met him thrust for thrust, wanting nothing more than for him to ravish me until I couldn't breathe anymore. He had that power over me, the kind that made you forget anything and everything except for him at that moment.

He reached down, strumming his fingers against my clit as he pounded into me, and I screamed out, his name on my lips, before he crushed his mouth to mine.

We lay tangled together, a sweaty mess, our breaths ragged. Everything would be different tomorrow. My heart ached from thinking that these could be the last few simple moments we had together. He gripped me to him tightly, as if he could read my mind, and I let myself get lost in his kiss one last time.

# Chapter Six
## Day 6

"Operation Black Velvet is a go."

Delove's voice crackled over the walkie-talkie, my body tensing as I sat next to Juliet in the back seat of the sedan.

The whole day had been a whirlwind of emotions, and I was beyond exhausted. I had spent all morning cooped up with Cian in our bedroom. He hadn't wanted to let me go and found small ways to make me stay in bed with him, like bribing me with orgasms and full-body massages. It had been wonderful, and a part of me wished we could have stayed like that forever. Was that what our life would have been like had I not met Ryzen? Filled with laughter, sex, and harmony? I guessed I'd never know.

Delove and Dobbs had come in the afternoon to make sure Juliet and I were prepared. My palms wouldn't stop sweating, and the more I thought about everything I had to do, the clumsier I became. After I spilled a bottle of water, then my coffee, and tripped over my own two feet, Cian had picked me up and laid me on the couch with a warning not to move until I had calmed down.

I couldn't help it. I was terrified of messing it

all up and disappointing everyone or, worse, getting myself into real danger. But I couldn't dwell. I had decided that I was going to do this, and I was going to do it right.

I had finally reached a point in the day where I felt more in control, more relaxed. Until Thora brought out my wedding dress and I almost had a full-blown panic attack. My throat closed up and I dug my nails into my palms at the sight of it. Torn, tattered and bloody, it stood for everything I had lost over these past few months.

My face said it all when I looked at my reflection in the mirror. Absolute disgust. Cian stopped in his tracks when he saw me wearing it, his lips set in a flat line. I smiled slightly and threw my hands up. "Well, this sucks." My voice quivered, and I cleared my throat.

His fists were clenched so tight, his knuckles were turning white. After a moment, he seemed to relax and trailed his thumb over my bottom lip and down my chin. "When this is all over, I'll help you burn it."

I chuckled and closed my eyes as he kissed my forehead. That sounded like a great idea to me.

"You know you're very strong for doing this, Nova." His eyes burned into me. "You are the most fascinating woman I have ever met. One of the strongest. I know that you can handle this, although it's gutting me that I can't be there to help you each step of the way."

My heart melted at his words, and I fell a little harder for him at that moment.

Juliet and I went outside and eyed the pile of leaves and debris in the yard. It wasn't like I could show up at the hospital completely clean with a glowing face from having multiple orgasms. I highly doubted our "kidnappers" were the type to give us hot showers and clean clothes. No, we had to look the part, or it would be too suspicious. We rolled around, getting dirt and muck all over our legs, arms and hair. We looked and smelled terrible, which meant we were doing it right.

Sometime later I stood in the bathroom gripping the sink as I stared at the knife. I knew what I had to do but couldn't bring myself to do it. Cian leaned against the door frame, his eyebrows raised.

"Should I be concerned?" He glanced down at the knife and chuckled softly.

I tilted my head and sighed. "The cut on my forehead. It's been cleaned up and doesn't look fresh. We need to cut it open."

"No." He narrowed his eyes and stalked towards me. "You don't have to do that."

"Cian." I pressed my hands against his chest. "If Voledetti had kidnapped me and thrown me in a dark room, my wound wouldn't look this way. It's not like he would have washed my wedding dress, given me a shower, food, and patched up the cut."

He closed his eyes and grimaced. "Nova."

I grabbed the knife and placed it in his hands. "I can't do it. My hands have a mind of their own today and won't stop shaking. I'll make it worse. Just cut it back open. Please," I pleaded, knowing he didn't want to do it any more than I did. But it had to be done. It was logical. It made sense, whether we liked it or not.

"You're very stubborn, you know that?" He lowered his eyes and gripped me by the back of the neck.

"And you're bossy. Now do it." I grinned and closed my eyes. His breath was warm against my face, a complete contrast to the cold blade of the knife. I held my breath, trying not to move as he did what I asked. It didn't really hurt, just stung, and I said the same to him.

He had a stony expression on his face as he looked at my forehead, and I reassured him that it was completely fine. Now all our bases were covered. He didn't seem to like that though, and he slammed the bathroom door and lifted me up so that I was sitting on the edge of the sink. Before I could realize what he was doing, he crushed me to him, capturing my lips. I could taste the desperation on his tongue. The fear. The worry. I cradled his face in my hands and kissed him softly, trying to show him that it was all OK.

"I can't lose you. I won't let anything happen to you." He fucked me right then and there, not caring there was a house full of people who could hear us. And I loved every second of it.

A part of me was still struggling with what was going on between us. Before Iva had told me that they were sleeping together, I'd been ready to go all in—well, almost. But now, after everything with the FBI and this whole situation, it was just messy. There were feelings there, feelings that I had never experienced in my life, this all-consuming need for him that left me breathless. But I didn't know if it was just the sex. Good sex. Great, mind-blowing, toe-curling sex. You could be completely in lust with someone and not be in love with them. Was that what I was to him? I wanted to believe that wasn't the case. I had tried following my heart before and look where it had gotten me. Only time would tell for us.

Hours later, I sat in the back of the sedan, gripping Juliet's hand. We were half a mile away from the small hospital on the outskirts of a far northern suburb of Chicago. It was dark, quiet, and the cemetery off to the side of the road made it a million times more creepy.

Dobbs turned around from the driver's seat and nodded at us. It was go time.

They'd made Cian stay at the house, not that he had been happy about it. Hell, I wasn't happy about it either, but it was probably for the best. I didn't want to have to depend on him. He was like a safety blanket, but now was not the time for that. Now was the time to be strong, to take my life back and make Ryzen pay. I could do this. I knew I could.

We jumped out of the sedan and started our walk. We were quiet as we got closer, nerves kicking in. I stopped walking when we got close to the hospital and Juliet raised her eyebrows at me.

"We can't just stroll in there all calm. We need to be slightly hysterical."

She nodded and nibbled on her bottom lip. "OK, good point."

"Slap me."

Her eyes bugged out of her head, and she laughed. "What? No." She shook her head and put her hands on her hips. "Slap yourself, you crazy ass."

"Jules," I warned. "You slap me a few times, and I'll slap you. Trust me on this one."

"Nova." She groaned. "This is crazy. I mean this whole thing is crazy, but I absolutely do not want to hit you. Don't make me do this."

"C'mon, Jules. I can't cry on cue. And I know you can't either. It's fine. Just a few slaps to get our heads in the game. I don't want to do it either."

She scrunched up her nose. "Are you sure?

Because it kinda sounds like you wanna slap me."

We laughed, knowing how crazy this all sounded.

"OK, remember that time you bought that big container of specialty marshmallow fluff? And after a few days, you couldn't find it? Remember?"

She nodded, narrowing her eyes at me. "Yes, Mr. Sprinkle Kings Deluxe Limited Edition Cookie Butter Pink Berry. I remember."

"Well, I ate it. All of it. And it was so good. And you tore up the whole damn kitchen looking for that container. And I just let you think that you ate it all."

Her mouth fell open and she scoffed. "You bitch." She laughed.

"And you know that blue cashmere sweater you love so much? The one Peter gave you that you wouldn't stop obsessing over?"

She took a step closer to me, her eyes wide. "What did you do, you little sneak?"

I cringed and scrunched up my nose. "I wore it out one night to the movies and spilt nacho cheese all over it. It was completely ruined. There was no way the stain was coming out. I tossed it in the garbage."

Her hand came up and I closed my eyes as it made contact with my cheek.

My hand flew to my face, my mouth hanging open. "Good one." I chuckled.

"Dammit, La Roux." She threw her head back and groaned.

"Again, one more."

"Fine, but only because you ruined my favorite sweater and *lied*." She slapped me again, and then once more on the other cheek. Tears welled up in my eyes as my face started to burn. "OK, now me." She stood with her hands on her hips, eyes closed. "I know you might not want to do—" She stopped mid-sentence as I slapped her as hard as I could, then once more on the other side. She gasped, her eyes watering. "Wow, why do I get the feeling you have been waiting to do that?"

I chuckled and pulled her tight against me. Of course I didn't want to slap her. She was my ride-or-die, my best friend in the whole world. I would do anything for her, and I knew she would do anything for me. But it had to be done, and better to do it quickly and get it over with. "It's all going to be OK, Jules."

She gripped me back with the same fierceness, her nails digging into my back. "I know, Nova. I'm not going to let anything happen to you either, OK?" She pulled back, tears freely falling now. "I still carry this enormous guilt inside of me for that fight we had and how I let Riddick put thoughts in my head. I can never say sorry enough times."

I sniffled and shook my head. "Jules, forget that. Nobody is perfect, OK? I'm not, you're not, nobody is. We all make mistakes. Life would be boring if we were perfect all the time. Don't feel guilty. It's in the past. Over. I love you."

"I love you too, marshmallow thief." She gripped my hands in hers and squeezed.

"Let's do this."

We ran as fast as we could up the hill and through the bushes. By the time we got to the front door of the emergency room, we were out of breath and sweating. I pushed the door open and ran inside, coming face to face with the blonde-haired woman with the butterfly tattoo.

"Help us!" I breathed deep, my chest rising and falling as I tried to catch my breath. "Please, help us." I gripped Juliet's arm as she slid down to the floor, crying.

Oh, shit. She was better at this than I'd thought. I grabbed onto her shoulders and hoisted her back up. "My friend and I were kidnapped."

The nurse's eyes widened as she took us in, then a spark of recognition flashed across her face. "Lock the doors, Marsha," the blonde yelled to the other nurse on duty, and then came around the desk. "It's OK, you're safe." She held her hands out to us and hurried us down the hall.

It was a small hospital that gave you an ominous feeling. It was mostly dark with very few staff walking around—five I had been able to count, plus a janitor walking around mopping the floors. Marsha herded us into a room, then walked into the hallway, pulling out her phone. The blonde glanced between me and Juliet, then turned her back to us. She must have been talking to Ryzen, just like they had said she would.

The next hour went by in a blink of an eye. Two police officers showed up and started taking our statements. They were young, polished, and definitely not from around this part of town. I told them exactly as I had rehearsed so many times.

"We were at my wedding and I was about to walk down the aisle. But then there was a commotion outside and we saw men wearing masks with guns." My voice quivered. "We tried to run, but they grabbed us before we could get away. They put something over our heads, and we couldn't see anything."

The officer nodded, encouraging me to continue. I reached up and touched the cut on my forehead. "They threw us in a van, and we drove for a long time. They dumped us in a room with no windows. No light." Juliet clenched my hand and squeezed. "They had us face a wall when they brought us food, so we never saw any faces." A tear spilled down my cheek as I remembered how terrified I had been when that man had tried to drag me into the van, how I'd thought I was going to die.

Juliet wrapped her arm over my shoulder. "We couldn't hear or see anything," she continued for me. "They left the door unlocked after bringing us food, so we ran as fast as we could."

"Anything else you can remember? Any names or what the surroundings looked like?" he asked, his pen poised over his notepad.

She shook her head. "No names. Nothing. I don't know how long we were running, but it was daylight when we left. We were in the woods, but it was just… trees. Normal trees."

The police officer listened intently, nodding and taking notes, but I had a feeling that they were going to go straight in the trash. The nurse with the butterfly tattoo, Erin, came by some time later and took our clothes and collected blood and urine samples. The police stood behind her watching as she scraped dirt from underneath my fingernails and put it in an evidence baggy. It all looked and felt legitimate, and if I hadn't known better, I would have said they were doing their job one hundred percent correctly. But I did know better, and based on the looks they kept giving each other, that so-called evidence would never leave this hospital.

I sat on the edge of the gurney, swinging my legs after Marsha patched my cut up and attended to Juliet in the other room. It was definitely going to leave a scar now. I sighed and Erin came over with a bottle of water. "It's OK, hon, your fiancé is on his way now."

I stopped mid-swig, my back tensing. This was it. I was about to face Ryzen. I rubbed my head as everything seemed to go out of focus for a moment.

*Get a grip.*

I jammed my hands into my armpits and counted to twenty. Deep breath in. And out. In and out until my breathing evened out.

I snapped my head towards the door as it swung open, Ryzen standing there, his eyes wild. "Nova!" He rushed towards me, and I froze.

I hadn't thought I was going to feel anything when I saw him. I had convinced myself that my heart was a blank canvas, but now that he was standing in front of me, it was a completely different story. Heat rushed through me, and something else. Not fear. Anger. *Rage*. I opened my mouth, but no words would come out. I was face to face with the man who was trying to ruin my life. The one who was framing me for blowing up my warehouse. The one who had tricked me into believing the man I was falling in love with was deceiving me. And now I was supposed to pretend to be in love with him.

"Oh, my God, Nova. I was so scared." He gripped me to him, and I sat there, unable to move. He leaned back and grimaced at the cut on my forehead. "When I find out who did this, they will pay."

But he already knew who it was. And that was why I was here, in this room. *Time to step the fuck up, La Roux.*

"Ryzen," I breathed and gripped his jacket.

"You're really here?" Tears welled in my eyes. Not tears of sadness or joy like he probably believed. Tears of absolute anger.

"Shh, I'm here, Nova. Don't worry, I'm here." He pressed my head against his chest and rubbed my back.

This son of a bitch was laying it on thick, I had to hand it to him. Which meant I needed to lay it on thicker.

"I was so scared, Ryzen. Those men. They took us!" I sniffled and wiped my nose on his jacket. "I thought I was going to die. I thought they were going to kill us," I whimpered.

"It's OK, you're safe, Nova. I'm going to take care of everything." He squeezed me hard against him.

*I bet you are.* "Ryzen, the men who took me, do you know..."

He shook his head. "Shh, shh, we'll talk later. You're in shock. I'm getting you out of here." He caressed my face with his hands, leaning down to place a kiss on my cheek.

The doctor came into the room and Ryzen grabbed him by the elbow, took him back out into the hallway and shut the door. I stood and walked over, pressing my ear to the door, but could only make out muffled voices.

My whole body was shaking, and I let out a deep breath. I didn't know what I had imagined was going to happen when I saw him, but it wasn't this. Delove had made it sound so easy, but I was beginning to think he had never been double-crossed in his life. Or been in love. Or hate, for that matter.

My mind kept drifting back to Cian. I would give anything to have him here right now, holding my hand, telling me everything was going to be OK. But he wasn't here. And wouldn't be for a long time. No, I couldn't let myself hold onto that thread of hope that he was out there waiting to save me. I was going to have to save myself and Juliet. It had to be done.

Ryzen came back into the room with the doctor, who handed me a prescription for painkillers and said I was free to go. Just like that. No paperwork, no more interviews, they would take care of everything, and I could just... leave with Ryzen.

After changing into some scrubs Erin gave us, Juliet and I walked out of the hospital. A white SUV pulled up and one of Ryzen's security came around and opened the door for us. It was one of his regulars I had seen at his office many times, Valik or Verik something. He gripped my hand and helped me step up, then Juliet. Ryzen climbed in behind us.

Juliet sat facing us, Ryzen glued to my side, gripping me to him. She was doing really well controlling herself, I could tell. Hell, I'd seen that woman experience every emotion in the book, and right now her face was as blank as a stone-cold killer's. Ryzen squeezed my hand and I laid my head against his chest as we drove down the freeway. I wondered if Delove and Dobbs were behind us. Were they watching? Was Cian? Someone had to be, I knew that.

Ryzen was quiet the whole ride. I knew he wouldn't want to talk in front of Juliet, which was fine by me. I stared at her, having a silent conversation with our eyes.

*I hate him, he's a dick.*
*How do you think I feel sitting next to him?*
*You're strong. You got this.*

*We got this.*

*You're going to pay for stealing my marshmallow fluff.*

OK, I didn't know that was exactly what she was thinking, but knowing Juliet, she would find a way to pay me back for that one.

The silence in the car was driving me crazy. There were so many questions I wanted to ask Ryzen, but I knew that it would have to wait. Honestly, I was surprised he hadn't grilled me yet, but that just reaffirmed that he was waiting for the right moment. My leg jiggled as we got closer to downtown, and when we passed Goodacre Estates, my whole body tensed.

"Where are we going?" I stammered and sat up.

"A hotel for tonight." He rubbed my back. "I thought you would be more comfortable."

OK. I guessed. That definitely hadn't been part of the plan. It wasn't like I could have taken the FBI equipment with me to the hospital—it would have been found right away. Delove had said the supplies would be waiting in my apartment for me, and refused to answer when I asked how he planned on getting in there unseen. It was time for plan B, which was to stall any heavy conversations with Ryzen until I got my wire hooked up.

Of course, we pulled up to Covington's Luxury Suites on the Magnificent Mile.

Valik, as I heard Ryzen call him, parked and grabbed a small black bag out of the trunk. He stood in front and guided us to the elevators, bypassing the check-in desk. Maybe Ryzen had a room here all the time for his little dates with Iva. I wouldn't be surprised.

We took the elevator up to the fortieth floor and

walked to the end of the hall. There was a man sitting in one of those metal folding chairs, and he looked like he was about to crush it at any moment. He stood when we got to the door and let us in.

The room was as huge as a three-bedroom apartment. It even had a pool table in the center of the living room area. Ryzen stayed in the hall for a moment and spoke with Valik and his other guard before shutting the door and walking over to the bar. He poured out three shots of bourbon and handed us each a glass, which I more than happily threw back.

"I'm exhausted, and I'm sure you two have a lot to talk about." Juliet placed her shot glass on the bar. "Is there a bed I can stay in?"

"Yes, of course, Juliet. I'll take you." He waved his hand toward the room at the end of the hallway and walked down in front of her. She turned to look at me and mouthed, *Oh, my God,* and I tried to not smile.

I poured myself another shot, then another, slamming them down before he came back.

He cleared his throat and I jumped, turning to face him. "Jesus, you scared me." I gasped.

"Sorry." He stuffed his hands in his pockets. "You're probably tired and want to get some sleep."

"Yeah, you're right. But we do need to talk." I poured two more shots and handed him his glass.

He shook his head, throwing back his shot, and put his hands on my shoulders. "All that matters is that you are OK. That Juliet is OK. We'll talk in the morning."

"I need to tell you something. Something I didn't tell the police."

His jaw clenched, his whole body tensing. "What is it, Nova?"

"When they had us in that room, it was dark. We could barely make each other out. And they didn't speak a lot, but I heard them once through the door. I heard a name." My eyes didn't leave his, his hands digging into my shoulders with more force than a moment ago. "I heard the name Kaviathin. They said it more than once. Do you know who that is?"

His whole face went completely blank. Not one ounce of emotion was there. He shook his head. "No, never heard that name in my life."

*You son of a bitch.* "Are you sure? You're positive you don't know anyone named Kaviathin?" I said his name again, hoping to provoke Ryzen, but it wasn't working. Whatever emotion I'd thought I would elicit from him was tucked away deep inside and it was not going to rear its ugly head tonight.

"I'm sure." He clenched his jaw and let out a deep breath. "Why didn't you tell the police, Nova?" He was the one watching me now, looking for something that I wasn't going to give him.

I sniffled and wrapped my arms around him, hiding my face in his chest. "I was too scared."

He patted my back, not saying anything for a moment. "Get some rest, and we'll talk more in the morning. Do you want me to stay with you in your room?"

My head felt like it might explode, and I squeezed my eyes shut for a moment. "Can you stay on the couch?" I tried to smile, but I knew it came off as flat. "To make sure we're safe," I choked out, wanting to grab the bottle of bourbon and bash it over his head.

"Of course." He rubbed his thumb over my cheek. I shuddered involuntarily, but he probably thought it was from pleasure. "Don't worry. I'm here to protect you, Nova." His lips brushed against my cheek, and I made a mental note to scrub there rigorously before bed.

*Yeah. That's the problem.* You're *here. Not Cian. But not for long.*

## Chapter Seven
### Day 7

I woke to the sound of someone cooking, the smell of bacon in the air. I had slept like absolute shit, tossing and turning all night long. At one point, Ryzen had opened the bedroom door and checked in on me. I actually found it kind of creepy because I had no idea if he was doing it out of concern or to do something harmful to me. I suspected the latter, but it was probably just paranoia.

It was a new day. A day to make wiser choices and not fuck things up and cause chaos. Which was too bad. Footsteps came down the hall, and I flipped over so my back was facing the door.

"Nova, honey, I've got breakfast," Ryzen called out, then swung the door open. "Nova?"

I scrunched my nose up and sighed. *Here we go.*

I flipped over and smiled. "Hi," I said softly. "Be right out."

He stood in the doorway, shirtless with an apron on and a spatula in his hand. "I made pancakes." He grinned. "Juliet left early this morning back home, so it's just us two." He walked back towards the kitchen, not bothering to shut the door behind him.

There was no use delaying the inevitable. I

grabbed the white silk robe from the end of the bed and did a quick check in the bathroom to make sure I looked somewhat presentable, which was quite laughable considering the giant scrape on my forehead and numerous bruises covering my body.

When I got to the kitchen, Ryzen flipped a pancake and stacked them up high on a plate, along with eggs, bacon, and fresh fruit. His smile was spread from ear to ear as he walked over to the high-top table and set them down in front of me. OK, so apparently he was Prince Charming this morning.

"How did you sleep? I hope well?" He cupped my cheek in his hand, and I tried to smile.

"I slept as could be expected after the last few days. Thanks for breakfast, you didn't have to do that." I picked up a pancake and nibbled. "And you?"

He took off his apron and sat down next to me, his arm brushing against mine. Not sure why he thought he didn't need to wear a shirt, but I wasn't all that surprised. I made sure he was looking at me when I glanced at his muscular arms and bare chest, then widened my eyes when he "caught" me looking.

Nova La Roux: Actress of the Year. I was surprised I was able to pull this off so well even though the need to cause him some bodily harm was rushing through me.

I stuffed a pancake in my mouth, doing my best impression of virginal embarrassment, and he chuckled. It was an act. A paid performance. And my payment was a get-out-of-jail-free card if I could pull this off. I just had to think of myself as an actress, that was all. More Stepford Wife and less psycho killer. I could do this. I was a badass and ready to take him down.

"Ryzen, I have a lot of questions. I'm confused why the police didn't know I had been kidnapped. Why didn't you tell anybody?"

He visibly tensed next to me. I didn't think he'd been expecting me to be so blunt. He laid down his fork and turned towards me. "It's complicated." He grabbed my hands in his.

Damn, was he about to confess and I didn't even have my wire hooked up? "OK." I nodded and leaned forward. "I'm listening."

"There's a constant target on my back because of my wealth. I hired extra security for the wedding so that we could enjoy our special day." He gripped my hands tight in his. "Everyone was in the barn when the doors shut. The guests assumed it was part of the processional, except when the doors opened again, Fidora, the wedding planner, came rushing in and straight to my security guards. My team was alerted that there was a breach, and they contained the situation."

My mouth was dry as I listened, waiting for him to drop any clues that he knew it was Kaviathin's men. I nodded, obsessively bouncing my leg on the bar of the stool I was sitting in. "What do you mean contained the situation?"

"They took care of it, but it was too late. You had already been taken and those men were gone." He rubbed his thumb across my cheek. "You'll never know how terrified I was at the thought of something bad happening to you."

I closed my eyes and took a deep breath in. It wasn't adding up. I'd known he was going to lie, but something wasn't right with his story. "But I don't understand why nobody looked for me. My parents, the police."

He sighed, his jaw clenching, as if irritated by my questions. "The guests knew there was a commotion, but they didn't know what. We told them you had gotten ill, and the wedding was postponed. I assume they believed you had gotten cold feet, so I let them think that. And of course I looked for you." His shoulders stiffened and he slammed his hand on the table, making me jump. "I contacted the police that I work with on a regular basis, and they searched right away for you."

*Work with, as in cops you pay to turn their heads the other way and protect you. Got it.* "What about Fidora? She saw the men with guns, just like I did."

"With the right amount of money, people learn to forget things rather quickly, dear." He scoffed and picked his fork back up as if we were done with the conversation.

My hands were shaking as I took another bite of my pancake. It was dry and tasted like cardboard and I glared at him briefly, willing the universe to make him choke on his. "What about the warehouse, Ryzen? It's gone. It's all gone." Tears welled up in my eyes and he stopped chewing, his face expressionless.

"I know. I believe the men who kidnapped you also destroyed your warehouse to get back at me. Insurance will cover everything. I'll handle it. I promise you that." He squeezed my forearm, searching for something in my eyes.

He sure did have a quick answer for everything, didn't he? It was convenient. How many days had he been practicing his lies? The fact that he could say all this with a straight face was making my blood boil. He was good at this, and it was frightening. The answers, his mannerisms, all screamed "I'm here to help you because I care about you," but I knew it was all an act. That was what was so terrifying—how easy it was for him to lie, and so easy for people to believe him.

*I am an actress playing a part. If I can channel the way he lies, the way he acts, maybe I can pull this off without any trouble.*

"Thank you," I whispered and wrapped my arms around his neck. He froze for a moment, then gripped me to him. "And Covington? Is the whole deal over now? Oh, God, I hope all your hard work wasn't ruined." My voice shook, and I hoped he was buying what I was selling.

"Don't worry, I'm taking care of Covington." He hugged me tighter. "I'm going to take care of everything, Nova."

No shit. That was what I was worried about.

I leaned back and looked him in the eyes. "Being taken like that made me realize how short life is. And how I've been too scared to be myself around you." My heart was beating so fast, I was certain he could hear it. "I feel embarrassed saying this, but I've been trying to control these feelings I have for you. Real feelings." *Murderous, crazy feelings.* "And when I saw you last night at the hospital, it made me realize that I don't want to be away from you." I bit my bottom lip, mostly to keep myself from throwing up.

His chest puffed out and a devilish look flashed across his face. "I have feelings for you too, Nova." He stood and stepped between my legs.

Heat rushed through my body, my heart feeling like it was going to stop beating as he lowered his head, pressing his lips to mine. I froze and squeezed my eyes shut.

*Oh, my God, he's kissing me. No, no, no.*

He pulled back. "You're trembling, poor thing. Maybe you need more rest." His body was warm as he lifted me up and cradled me in his arms, repulsion coursing through my veins as he took me back to my room.

I slid out of his arms, tightening my robe around me. "I think I'll shower and head home. There are a lot of things I need to take care of."

"Shall I join you?" He towered over me, grinning. A comment like that coming from him was not surprising. Hell, he had been trying to get into my pants for a long time. The difference was back then I had been stupid enough to fall for a line like that, but now? If he tried anything I would cut off his most prized possession and happily rot in prison for the rest of my life.

I chuckled, and shook my head. "Raincheck."

He seemed satisfied with that answer and let me be. I turned the water to the hottest setting and scrubbed my skin in every place he had touched until it was red. He'd actually kissed me. I would have to keep that little piece of information to myself and not let Cian know. If I had learned anything that past few days, it was that Cian was possessive. My face burned at the memory of us in the woods. That was unlike anything I had ever experienced before. I would have to work quickly to get evidence on Ryzen so that I could go back to my life. Back to Cian.

When I got out of the shower, there was a cream-colored blouse and slacks laid out nicely on the bed, a pair of black heels next to them. Of course nothing comfy and casual, what a stupid idea that would have been. Had he bought these for me? Or were they Iva's? I tried them on and realized they fit like a glove and clung to my curves, so they weren't hers. She and I were complete opposites in almost every way. Her being tall, slender, and blonde with tanned skin. Oh, and a raging bitch. While I was shorter, more curvy with dark hair and pale skin.

I found him in the living room scrolling through his phone. He had showered and changed into a suit.

"You look beautiful." He walked over and handed me his phone. No. Not his phone. *My* phone. He didn't even try to hide the fact that he had been looking through it. How the hell had he gotten it unlocked without the code? I bet he'd put some type of tracking device on there. He also gave me back my purse, which had my wallet and keys.

"I want you to have this." He handed me a black keycard. "It's to my penthouse in our building. You'll feel safer there. I know we said we weren't going to move in together before the wedding, but I think we should revisit that conversation." He grinned that devilish grin that showed off his dimples, and I nodded.

"Of course we'll talk about that. Thanks, Ryzen, I... um, I appreciate it more than you know." I offered a small smile.

*Appreciate that now I don't need to try to figure out a way to break into your apartment and snoop.*

"Valik will take you home, and anywhere else you need to go. Consider him your own personal bodyguard."

I swallowed the lump in my throat. Great, a twenty-four-hour babysitter was not going to help me in any way. But now wasn't the time to bring it up.

He bent down and kissed my cheek. "I'll be in meetings all day, so I'll see you tonight?"

I nodded and he grabbed his briefcase and left me with the muscular guard from last night.

I flipped the keycard over and over again in my hands, thanking the universe for this tiny gift. If Ryzen was going to be gone all day, then I had a golden opportunity to snoop. But first, I had to head home and get my gear.

Valik was waiting at the door for me when I was finally ready to leave. He was all muscle, and covered with tattoos, and I pegged him in his mid-thirties. I didn't like the idea of having him around and reporting to Ryzen, but I had to pick my battles. We made small talk in the car, mostly him asking if I was comfortable with the temperature or if I wanted to listen to music. Nothing on a personal level, which was good. We pulled up to Goodacre Estates and he helped me out of the SUV.

His phone rang, and he held up his hand for me to not move. "Yes, Mr. Goodacre? Uh-huh." He walked to the back of the SUV and opened the trunk. "Yes, I see it. I'll be right over." He pulled out a small duffle bag from the back and shut the door. "Mr. Goodacre needs this right away." He tossed the bag on the passenger seat and turned to me. "My cell phone number is in your phone already. Call me for anything, Miss La Roux. I'll be back shortly." He waited for me to acknowledge him before driving off.

This was perfect. He would be gone for a while

and I would have plenty of time to do some digging. But first, I had to grab a few things.

Back in my apartment, I sank down on the couch and tilted my head back against the cushion. I let my eyes drift closed for a moment, exhaustion overtaking me. It wasn't necessarily physical, but mental fatigue. Everything was going according to the plan, and with any luck, this would be over soon enough.

I searched in the back of my closet until I found the bag Delove had said he would hide. Don't ask me how he, or whomever, got into my apartment undetected by security, because I didn't know. All Delove had said was to not worry about it.

I dragged the bag onto the bed and started pulling out the gear they had given me. First the watch, which I put on and pointed at my face. I smiled and pressed the button, taking a picture so they would know things were going well. Then the small tape recorder, which I stuffed into my pocket just in case. I checked to make sure the wiretap equipment, tapes and necklace were safe in the bag, then zipped it back up and pushed it far back under my bed.

My phone rang and Owen's name flashed across the screen. Fuck. I had been so preoccupied with everything, I hadn't thought to call him. "Heeey, Owen."

"Oh, my God, Nova. Where the hell have you guys been? I've been worried sick to death." He huffed into the phone.

I scrunched up my nose and sat on the edge of the bed. What was I supposed to say? I couldn't tell him about the FBI or Ryzen—not only because I didn't know if Ryzen had tapped my phone, although I was pretty sure he had, but I also didn't want to get Owen involved.

The more he knew, the more of a chance he could be in danger. And I couldn't have that on my conscience.

"Well, funny story." I chuckled and he remained silent. OK. Not so funny to him. "I got cold feet. I panicked and pulled a full-on *Runaway Bride* and, um, made Juliet come with me."

"Where though? You didn't return my calls. The warehouse, Nova! Everything burned down!" He sputtered and I could tell my answer wasn't going to be good enough for him.

"Owen, I know. Everything was a mess, but it's OK now. We're back, and just trust me when I say that it's going to be OK. I'm sorry that we left without saying anything. I left my phone, my purse, everything." I squeezed my eyes shut, hoping he wouldn't ask any more questions. When he started stuttering, I sighed into the phone. "I have a plan, and I'll be in touch in a day or so. OK? I know that's not what you want to hear, but it's the best I got right now. We're going to take care of everything, Owen... take care of you."

"Well, damn. I thought you guys were dead. I couldn't get a hold of anyone. Ryzen wouldn't return my calls. I'm just glad you guys are OK and back home."

We chatted for a few more minutes and I promised to call him tomorrow with more details about next steps. I paced around the living room, gripping my phone. Grams would be worried too. By now, she would have known that the wedding hadn't taken place, but that I hadn't taken her car, money and gun either. My head throbbed and I tried to shake it off.

Later. I would call her later and tell her exactly what I had told Owen—cold feet, that was all. No kidnapping, no dangerous men ambushing us. Just good old-fashioned cold feet. I groaned, thinking about what that same conversation would be like with my parents. There were no missed calls from them though. None. Zero. Zip. It was like I'd disappeared off the face of the earth, and very few people had even bothered to care. That was not reassuring, not one bit. But that just reaffirmed what I already knew—my parents, my sister, they only cared about their image. Not about my actual well-being.

I wondered if Cian was close by. He had promised me that he would always be there if I needed him. There was an internal struggle going on inside of me when it came to him. Yes, we had mind-blowing sex; there was no doubt about it. Did I trust him? Surprisingly, yes. I felt it deep down in my core, this need for him. So unlike anything I'd ever felt. And I thought he felt the same way, although he expressed it a lot differently than flat-out saying "I love you." But once he got his revenge on Ryzen, would I be enough for him? I didn't know if my heart could handle the answer. So I did what I always did: I shoved it down deep inside of me and locked it away until I was ready to deal with it.

I punched the code into the elevator and rode it all the way to the penthouse floor to Ryzen's unit. I held my breath as I stepped out, half expecting one of his guards to be there. But the chair was empty, and I sent another silent thank you to the universe. Once inside, I walked to the floor-to-ceiling windows and peeked down. From this high up, people looked like tiny little ants, scurrying around from one place to the next, oblivious to the madness going on all around them.

Did he have cameras in here? I glanced around casually, looking for anything out of the ordinary that would indicate a camera being pointed directly at my face, waiting for a red light to blast out from the ceiling or an alarm to blare. But nothing happened, and I convinced myself that I was being overly paranoid.

I searched his bedroom first, opening the night table drawers and rummaging through the contents. Condoms, watches, jewelry, aspirin. No documents though, or anything else out of the ordinary. His closet was the same. Slacks, button shirts and blazers, all organized by color, hung neatly with a console holding all of his jewelry in the center of it. I opened every drawer and still found nothing.

Of course it wouldn't be that easy. What kind of criminal hid incriminating paperwork, pictures or video tapes in a shoebox in their closet? That was too cliché, and although I didn't think Ryzen was *that* smart, he also wasn't that stupid.

His office was next. I checked my watch and hurried around to his desk. It had been over forty-five minutes since Valik had left, and I had no doubt that he would pop up soon. I pulled out drawer after drawer until I found a manila envelope labeled "Findlay Construction." It wasn't a name that Dobbs had had me memorize, but I peeked inside just in case. There was a bid request for a new high-rise building on top. It looked completely normal, but I snapped a picture anyways, then snapped a few more of the other documents in the folder. I didn't know exactly what I was looking at, so better to err on the side of caution and go overboard with photos.

I stuffed them all back into the folder and shut the drawer. There was a pink Post-it note crumpled in the wastebasket, and I reached down, unfolding it.

There was a series of numbers written down followed by letters, and a dollar sign with nine billion written after it. I took a picture and put it back in the trash.

The drawer in the center of the desk was locked, and I searched underneath the piles of papers on his desk for the key. It wasn't there. There was a picture frame on his desk with a picture of him and his parents at some type of Christmas event. I flicked the clasps to the side and removed the backing, but no key.

Damn, it had to be here somewhere. I walked over to the bookshelf, tapping my lip with my finger. If I was a secret key, where would I be hidden? All of the books on one shelf were real estate related —construction regulations, city ordinances—but one stood out in particular, a lighter color than the rest. I pulled it out and realized it was some type of journal. There was a gap in the middle, and the key fell out.

*Eureka, bitches!*

I held the key in the palm of my hand and squeezed it tight. The journal had fallen to the floor, and when I picked it up, it fell open to a page that was ripped in half, the bottom part missing. I could only make out the beginning of the first word.

Kav…

*Kaviathin.*

My head snapped in the direction of the office door, a dinging sound letting me know that someone had just come up in the elevator. I put the key back in the journal and stuffed it back on the bookshelf. The hair on my arms lifted, and I bit the inside of my cheek.

*Fuck, crap, fuck, crap.*

Was it Valik? Or, worse, Ryzen? What would he do if he found me snooping in his office? I wiped the sweat from my forehead and pressed my ear to the door, not hearing anything. I counted to three and opened the door just a crack. Still, I didn't hear anything.

What the hell.

Ryzen's bedroom was just across from his office, so I held my breath and ran as fast as I could, pushing the door closed softly. My heart slammed against my chest as heavy footsteps came from down the hall, and I made a beeline for the en suite bathroom and shut the door.

"Miss La Roux?" a loud voice bellowed, and I squeezed my eyes shut. "Are you up here?"

It was Valik.

*Think, Nova, think.*

I ripped my clothes off as the footsteps grew closer, and a moment later, Valik threw the door open and stared at me with his mouth hanging open.

I screamed and reached up, covering my breasts with my arms. "Get out!"

"Oh, fuck, Miss La Roux, I'm sorry." His face flushed and he had the decency to turn his back right away.

"Get out of here!" My voice was on the verge of sounding hysterical, and that wasn't even an act. I had been two seconds away from being caught snooping.

"Yes, sorry, fuck." He shut the door and I leaned against the sink, willing my heart to slow down. That had been close. Too close.

I put my clothes back on and used a damp cloth to cool my face down. There was a cup on the sink and I filled it up with water, pouring it into the standing shower. After a minute, I finally felt composed enough to walk out.

He stood in the living room, his hands stuffed in his pockets. I cleared my throat and he turned, his face still burning red. "Miss La Roux, I apologize. I didn't realize you would be up here. Why are *you* up here, exactly?" He raised his eyebrows at me.

"Shower. Showering. Ryzen has better water pressure. And I wanted to, uh, feel close to him. The shower is a very special place for us." I was pretty sure my face was as red as a tomato, but he didn't acknowledge it.

"Your hair is not wet though." Valik quirked his eyebrow.

"Hm? Oh, you must not have sisters or a wife. Can't wash it every day. Ruins it." I chuckled and dug my nails into my palms. "Maybe if you hadn't washed yours so much, you would still have some." My eyes darted to his bald head, then back to his eyes.

He laughed and shook his head, and my shoulders sagged slightly. "I shave it, actually. The ladies seem to enjoy it." He grinned, and I returned his smile. For being a bodyguard—well, Ryzen's bodyguard—he definitely didn't give off creepy vibes. Maybe he wasn't going to be a problem for me after all.

"Can we keep this between us?" I pointed my finger from me to him. "I don't want Ryzen to freak out about you seeing me naked. He gets territorial."

Valik's eyes got big, and he nodded. "Absolutely. Our secret. And I'm sorry again."

"No, it's OK. I should have let you know. Anyways, I should take a nap—um, but in my apartment, so you're free to go do whatever you need to do." I grabbed my purse from the couch and walked around him.

"I'll come keep guard." He followed me to the elevator and pressed the down button. "Mr. Goodacre told me not to let you out of my sight. And he doesn't like it when people don't follow orders."

I sighed and rubbed the back of my neck. Was there any point in arguing with him? It wouldn't get me anywhere to object. Besides, I was a "kidnapping survivor." Wouldn't I want someone watching over me? "OK, Mr. Bodyguard. Let's go then."

One thing was for sure, Valik took his job very seriously. When we got down to my unit, he opened every door to make sure nobody was hiding ready to snatch me up again. He even checked in the shower and the pantry. After he was convinced I was completely alone in the apartment, I gave him a chair from my dining table set and let him sit outside my front door.

I was going to have to figure out a way to ditch him. Some way, somehow. I couldn't have him around me twenty-four seven. That could compromise everything, and I wasn't going to let anyone get in my way of finding out the truth about Ryzen.

No matter what the cost.

# Chapter Eight
## Day 14

"Not hungry?" Ryzen watched me closely as I moved food around my plate.

"Just a lot on my mind." I scooped up a big piece of fish and shoved it in my mouth, smiling. The waiter refilled my glass of water and hurried off to another table.

I choked the food down and went back to picking at the vegetables on my plate. It had been a long few days. We were spending a lot of time together, and it was taking its toll on me mentally. There was a lot of resentment burning inside of me because of this man, and being in close proximity to him was becoming harder and harder.

"Your grandmother?"

I nodded, not looking at him. She was in the hospital with chest pains, and I worried that me going missing had something to do with it. Of course, when I talked to her on the phone, she swore it had nothing to do with me. She was actually ecstatic that I hadn't gone through with the wedding. But if she had known the real reason why, it would be a completely different story.

I sighed, replaying the conversation over and

over again in my head. All that mattered was that she was getting better. It was more of a false alarm, but they wanted to keep her there for a few days for observation.

The wire I had taped across my chest was making my skin itch, and I had to stop myself from scratching the area. Wearing the wire all the time around Ryzen was putting me in a constant state of panic. What if he could see? What if he tried to grab me and found it hidden underneath my clothes? I hated it, but it had to be worn.

"That's a beautiful necklace." He nodded at the onyx stone hanging around my neck. It was the necklace with the hidden camera, recording everything around us. "Where did you get it?"

I looked down at the necklace, heat flooding my cheeks. "Birthday present from Juliet last year."

"It's lovely. Goes perfect with your pale skin." He eyed my breasts appreciatively and went back to eating his steak.

*My skin, huh?* "Thanks," I mumbled and laid my fork down. "Have you talked to the insurance company? I haven't heard back yet."

He chewed his steak more aggressively, his shoulders tensing. I was beginning to see a pattern here. He did not like being questioned at all. Which was making it more difficult to get him to open up and trust me.

I placed my hand on his knee and squeezed. "Just eager to get the process started so we can get the Shiver Box up and running again," I grinned, and he seemed to relax.

"I'm taking care of it." He eyed my breasts again, his jaw working as he chewed.

*Choke, choke, choke.* "Jules and I are renting a small office space on the South Side in the meantime. We need to get our bearings and figure out how to get through this mess."

"Is that so?" He raised his eyebrows, finally swallowing that wretched piece of meat. He already knew, but was pretending this was new information. Valik had taken Jules and I to meet the realtor yesterday to sign the lease, and I knew he was reporting back to Ryzen. I'd had Valik wait in the car because I wasn't clear if the FBI or even Cian was going to be in there, but it was just the real estate agent. She was cold, unwelcoming, and I didn't know if she was having a bad day or just hated her job. Either way, the conversation was quick and to the point, which was perfectly fine by us. It was definitely a terrible location, one that Ryzen would not want to come visit. Graffiti covered the outside of the building, and a group of men on the corner had looked awfully suspicious.

The office came furnished with scratched-up desks and tattered chairs. The real estate agent had pointed to a door with a stack of boxes in front of it and mentioned it led up to an apartment up top, but it was off limits. OK, so maybe she wasn't working with the FBI.

"I could have given you an office on my floor, Nova." He reached over and squeezed my hand. "So we could be closer."

I had to stop my eyes from rolling to the back of my head. Had he always been like this? So fake and convincingly charming? No wonder I had believed every word out of his mouth before. The way he stroked my hand and smiled would have most women swooning.

"Thanks, Ryzen, but I don't want to be a burden." I tugged my hand from underneath his and went back to eating. The waiter filled up my wine glass, and I sipped it slowly, feeling eyes on me.

Was it Cian? Or the FBI? I turned my head casually and glanced around the room, but didn't see anyone with a familiar face. Dessert came, and Ryzen spoon-fed me tiramisu while I did my best to appear as if he was the sun to my moon. To the outside world, I'm sure we looked like a couple madly in love. But if they only knew the truth...

He wiped chocolate from the side of my lips and then sucked on his finger, not taking his eyes off of me. Oh, boy, he was really laying it on, and had been the last two nights when I had stayed over at his penthouse.

It was the only way to stay close and keep an eye on him. When I had told him I felt frightened to sleep alone, he'd been more than eager to offer me a spot on the bed next to him. And when he wrapped his arm around my stomach and pulled me tight against him, I wanted to scream. To fight. To hurt. But I couldn't do any of those things, and I knew it. I knew I had to play this part—scared, worried, needing the big muscular man to save me from the shadows in the night. I fucking hated it, but it had to be done. He had tried many times already to get me to sleep with him, but I had told him I was still too shaken up, that I wanted to take things slow so that we could do it right this time. Gag.

I scanned the restaurant again, the feeling of being watched intensifying. There was a man sitting at a table near the back, dressed in all black with his head down. We made eye contact, and he narrowed his eyes at me.

"Ryzen, there's someone watching us," I breathed and gripped his hand. He followed my gaze, his face reddening.

"Don't worry about it, Nova. It's nothing." He yanked his hand out of mine and typed something into his phone.

I peeked over his shoulder, the man still sitting there openly staring at us. He didn't look like any of the men in the pictures the FBI had shown me, but now was a good chance to bring it up again. "OK, whatever you say. I just… I googled that name, Kaviathin, and found a lot of scary information online." I took a drink of my wine and leaned closer to Ryzen. "I think he's in the Mafia," I whispered.

Ryzen clenched his jaw and stuffed his phone back into his pocket. His eyes were dark when he looked at me, and a spike of fear raced down my spine at his expression. "Let the police handle it, Nova." He wrapped his hand around the back of my neck and tugged me close. "Stop looking things up before you get yourself into trouble." He kissed my forehead and released me.

A warning. Was it meant to be a threat?

The hair on my arms stood up, and I rubbed my neck where he had grabbed me. I had hit a nerve, that was obvious. Based on his reaction, I didn't think it was going to be easy to get him to spill his guts. No, I would have to find evidence elsewhere.

When I looked back up, the man was gone, and I breathed a sigh of relief. Was he with the Voledetti or just some random pervert? Something told me he was up to no good, that was for sure. A sting of disappointment flooded inside of me as I realized

Cian hadn't been the one watching. Not that I would probably know—it wasn't like he could make himself seen in front of Ryzen—but I hadn't heard anything from him over the last few days. Not the FBI or Cian. It was unnerving to say the least. I didn't want to dwell on it, but a part of me felt like I was being abandoned. Get the evidence so Ryzen would be locked up in prison, that was my goal. Sex with Cian was just a bonus, I guessed. It wasn't like we had professed our love for each other. Him saying "you're mine" when fucking didn't necessarily equal "I love you." I'd seen enough porn to know that. Although I wasn't ready to accept that just yet.

Valik drove us home and I told Ryzen I would be up as soon as I changed into pajamas. I couldn't exactly change in front of him while wearing a wire.

Tonight was the night I was going to grab the journal and take more pictures. I hadn't had a chance the last two days to go snooping, but I would tonight. I squeezed the baggie in my hand, the sleeping pills crushed inside. Ryzen had a routine, and every night he liked to check emails, talk with Riddick, drink a bourbon and then go to bed. It was the same pattern—unlucky for him, but great for me.

I changed into silk pajama pants and matching top and tucked the baggie into my waistband. Valik was sitting outside Ryzen's front door, and I smiled at him as I entered the code and walked in. I could hear Ryzen typing in his office, so I went behind the bar and grabbed two glasses, pouring bourbon in each of them. My hands trembled as I took out the baggie and poured the contents into his glass, mixing it with my finger.

"What are you doing?" I jumped as Ryzen leaned

against the door frame, watching me.

I dropped the baggie on the floor and kicked it into the corner of the bar. There was no way he could have seen me pour the baggie into his drink, the tabletop was too high.

I smiled and held up the glasses. "Making us a nightcap so we can wind down."

He grinned and prowled over to me. "I like the sound of that."

I handed him his glass and held my breath as he glanced at it. He placed it on the table behind me.

*Drink it!*

His hand gripped my waist, and I yelped as he lifted me up and sat me on the edge of the flat-top. He stepped between my legs and dug his hands into my thighs.

"How about we unwind another way?" He leaned in and kissed the side of my neck, his breath warm.

Chills ran through my body as he dragged me closer, his cock pressing into me. I chuckled and pulled back. "How about"—I tapped my finger against his lips—"you get relaxed on the couch and I give you a nice well-deserved massage? How does that sound?"

He grinned and nodded. "Sounds perfect."

*I bet it does, you frickin' pervert.*

"Ah-ah, take your drink." I handed him his glass and clinked my own against his. The liquid burned going down, and I didn't take my eyes off of him as he threw his back and placed it back on the table.

*Good dog.*

"Let me just freshen up and I'll be out in a minute." I hopped off the bar and walked to the bathroom. I let out the breath I had been holding in and pressed my back to the door, sliding down until I was sitting on the carpet.

Ick. The last thing I wanted was for him to be touching me, or, worse, me touching him. But I knew Ryzen, and the way to get him to back off was to offer the possibility of sex, even though I had absolutely no plans ever to fuck him—I would never lower myself to that. Hell, I didn't even want to willingly kiss the man. I had to sacrifice my pride and ego if I was going to do this right, but if he ever touched me like that again, I couldn't guarantee he wouldn't end up bloody.

After a few minutes, I sighed and realized I couldn't hide in the bathroom all night. My only hope was that the sleeping pills were already working their magic. I pinned my hair up and walked down the hall to the living room. I found him on the couch, his head tilted back and mouth open, a soft snore coming from him.

"Ryzen," I whispered and tiptoed over to the couch. "You fall asleep, big guy?" I waved my hand in front of his face and bounced up and down in front of him. He didn't move an inch. Great, now that that was taken care of, I could get what I came here for. My palms were sweating as I raced down the hallway to his office and shut the door quietly behind me.

*Get the journal, open the desk drawer, and get the pictures I need for the FBI.*

I turned his desk lamp on and went over to the bookshelf, biting my fingernails as I searched the same row for the journal.

It wasn't there. Crap. Maybe he'd put it somewhere else. My eyes darted from row to row, searching for it, but it was nowhere to be found. If it was gone, then so was the key to the desk. I yanked on the drawer to the desk, but it wouldn't budge.

*Think, Nova.*

There was a letter opener and I grabbed it, placing it in the slit. I had seen this so many times on television, it couldn't be that hard to get a stupid drawer open. The metal hit something and I jiggled the opener around, trying to knock something loose. There was a clicking noise and I yanked the drawer open.

*Holy shit, it worked.*

There were three red folders and I pulled them out, opening each one. The first folder contained financial statements from different banks. My eyes bugged out of my head as I saw the balance on each one. Twenty million, eighteen million, thirty-five million. I snapped pictures of everything with my watch. The next folder had more financial documents and what looked like balance transfer requests. Same bank, same amount, just different account numbers.

The last folder had a stack of real estate appraisals for different properties. There were different ones paperclipped together, so I spread them out and snapped pictures. I didn't know what I was looking at exactly. There would be one property with five appraisals, four of them all around the same amount, but one of them over a million dollars higher. It didn't look right, even to me, so I crossed my fingers and hoped it was good enough for Delove and Dobbs.

Just when I was about to close the drawer, something caught my eye. A little black jewelry box was tucked towards the back, and I pulled it out, opening the lid. My hand froze as I stared at the contents. Was that… was that hair? I squinted my eyes, realizing it most definitely was hair. A woman's hair, most likely, braided and tied with rubber bands at both ends. There was also a silver necklace with an angel pendant next to it.

Ick. I didn't think I wanted to know why he had this hidden away, and I really hoped I wasn't going to open a closet or cabinet and find his dead grandmother's skeleton in there. Chills ran through me at the thought.

I put everything back exactly how I had found it and shut the desk drawer. My heart slowed down when I heard the click, realizing that the drawer had locked itself again. I took one quick look around the office for the journal. When I didn't see it, I reached over and turned off the light and opened the door, running right into Ryzen.

"Nova?"

*Oh, fuck my life.*

"Did you put the pot roast in the oven?" He rubbed his forehead. "Don't burn it again or Nana will be angry."

"Um, what?"

"Riddick stole my Easter eggs. You're going to punish him, right?"

My shoulders dropped and I sighed. *He's sleepwalking.*

"Yes, Ryzen." I turned him around and pushed him into his bedroom. "I'm gonna spank his ass real good."

"OK, thanks, Nova." Ryzen flopped down on the bed face first and went back to snoring.

*****

I wiped my forehead and chugged the glass of water. Another nightmare had me tossing and turning all night. But what had woken me was that damn app Thora had put on my phone. When she said it had some bugs, I didn't realize she meant it would start blaring weird chants at five a.m., making me have a panic attack.

Ryzen was sitting up in bed rubbing his eyes when I got back to the bedroom.

"Hey, sleepyhead. You passed out on me." I handed him a glass of water and reached for my purse.

"That's never happened to me before," he mumbled and stretched. "Must have been really tired."

"Seems that way." I turned my back to hide my smile. "I gotta get ready. Long day ahead of us."

I left before he could ask any questions, giving Valik a salute on my way to the elevator. No doubt he would be right behind me soon enough.

After a hot shower and a change of clothes, I called Juliet and told her we would pick her up in twenty minutes. Today was our first official day back at the office. We had a lot of catching up to do, and I wasn't looking forward to it. Owen was going to meet us there in the afternoon to help out.

Valik picked up Juliet and we cruised down the freeway to the South Side of Chicago towards our temporary office space. When the Backstreet Boys came on the radio, Valik started humming along, and Juliet and I glanced at each other, trying to hold in our laughter. I guessed he wasn't so bad for a bodyguard. By the time we got to the office, we were having a full-blown concert in the backseat, with Valik holding up a pretend microphone for us to sing into.

"OK, big guy. You don't need to stick around here. I'll call you when we're ready to go home." I held onto his hand as I jumped out of the back seat.

"But Mr. Goodacre…"

I shook my head. "Are you really going to sit out here all day? Just go, take care of errands. It's almost that time of the month, you know. Do you want to go buy me some tampons?"

He flushed and cleared his throat. "If you need them, then yes, ma'am."

I sighed and threw my purse over my shoulder. "You're not going to listen to reason, I can see that." Juliet tugged my hand and we headed inside our office.

Yes, I mostly wanted him gone because I didn't want him snooping around when Delove and Dobbs showed up later. But at the same time, how boring must it be sitting around babysitting a twentysomething who designed dildos for a living? I just hoped that D&D would sneak in upstairs without being seen.

The office smelled like old dirty clothes and I was pretty sure I had seen a rat run into a closet after lunch. I put our cell phones in the small refrigerator in the makeshift kitchen, something I had seen on one of the documentaries about serial killers. Supposedly it would block any signal and if someone was spying on you through your phone, they wouldn't be able to hear. I caught her up on everything that had been going on with Ryzen, her jaw falling to the floor when I told her about the sleeping pills.

"Nova, that was really risky." She bit on her fingernails and I smacked at her hand.

"It's under control, Jules."

We spent hours catching up on emails. There were thousands of them. Not only did we have to respond to everyone, we had to cancel hundreds of orders that had come in over the past few weeks. It was not a good look for us.

When Owen finally showed up, we squeezed him in a bear hug and put him to work right away. Of course, he had a million questions, but we kept our responses short and to the point. No use getting him tangled up in this mess. As far as he was concerned, I had gotten cold feet and taken Juliet on a short honeymoon trip until I decided to come to my senses and go back home to Ryzen.

I spoke with La Madam Orgo directly on the phone, explaining the situation with the warehouse. She was our top customer and had ordered five thousand of our rose stimulator toys before our warehouse was destroyed. It killed me to cancel such a huge order, but there was just no way to fulfill it. It would be months, most likely, before we would be up and running again. That was assuming the insurance paid out and oh, yeah, that I wasn't in prison. She was beyond understanding, and I had to hold in the tears when she offered to help in any way she could. I hung up with a promise to let her know when we were back in business. She'd said she would be ready to place another order when the time came.

Owen sent out a mass social media post explaining how we had hit a hardship, and that we weren't accepting any new orders until further notice. By the time five rolled around, we had almost caught up on everything, minus a few phone calls that would just have to wait.

I peeked out the window and watched as Valik leaned against the SUV, checking his watch every few seconds. He had been out there for most of the day, only disappearing once or twice for a few minutes at a time.

"Jules, have Valik take you home." I closed the blinds and nibbled on my bottom lip.

We looked at each other, having a conversation with our eyes. She knew I was supposed to meet the guys upstairs soon, and no, I didn't need her to stay.

"Awesome, maybe he can give me a ride too? I took the bus here, and, uh, don't feel like getting mugged on my way home." Owen scrunched up his face and we chuckled.

"Go on, you two. Tell him I'm still working and I'll be ready by the time he gets back."

Well, I hoped I'd be ready.

By the time they left, I was ready to go upstairs. I moved the boxes out of the way, almost having a heart attack when a giant rat scurried from behind the boxes. It was the size of a squirrel, and there was no way it wasn't on steroids. Maybe it would run out the door. Wishful thinking. It wasn't like I would ever be able to kill it. Or want to. He *had* been here first.

The stairs leading upstairs were covered in cobwebs and had an unpleasant smell like a flea market. I covered my nose with my shirt, and opened the door to the apartment.

It was a lot nicer in there than I'd thought it was going to be. It was as if someone had been living there for some time and had just recently moved out. I rubbed my finger over the TV stand and raised my eyebrows. Not a speck of dust. If I was being honest, it was a hell of a lot cleaner and fresher-smelling up there than it was down in the office space. Maybe the FBI had had someone come in and clean up the place. I shook my head at the thought. That didn't make any sense either.

I snooped around opening one door after another, not finding anything of interest. It was almost time for them to get here, and I wiped my palms against my pants. It wasn't like I had any reason to be nervous. This was just a check-in. Something wasn't sitting right in my stomach, but I chalked it up to nerves and waited on the living room couch.

Exactly at five thirty, the back door to the apartment squeaked open and Delove walked in, followed by Dobbs. I stood and wrapped my arms around myself, offering a smile. But when Cian walked in and slammed the door behind him, my face fell. I hadn't been sure he was going to come. But he had come.

And he looked pissed.

## Chapter Nine

"You drugged him?" Delove's eyes were practically popping out of his head. The FBI agents sat opposite from me while Cian leaned against the kitchen counter with his arms crossed over his chest.

I tugged on the collar of my shirt and looked everywhere except Cian's face. "Well, you said to get evidence by any means necessary."

Dobbs howled with laughter and slapped his knee. "Good one, kid."

See, at least someone in the room appreciated my antics. It wasn't like it was all that dangerous. What was the worst that could have happened anyways?

"Nova." Delove held his hands up. "You need to be careful. That was…"

"Reckless," Cian muttered, his eyes drilling into me.

"Fine." I sighed. "But did you at least get the pictures, the video? It's good, right? Is it enough?" *Please tell me it's enough.* My leg bounced up and down to the rhythm of the ceiling fan clanking. The look on their faces said it all though, and I squeezed my eyes shut for a moment. Of course it wasn't going to be that easy, I should have known better.

"Oh, we got the pictures, and a sneak peek at

your little show, Miss La Roux." Dobbs tossed a stack of photos on the coffee table between us. It was all the pictures I had taken over the past few days, and video stills of me and Ryzen at dinner and at his apartment.

There was a series of pictures on top of the pile of Ryzen shirtless, walking towards me and standing between my legs. I flipped it over and glanced at Cian. He stared at me, expressionless, which only made my heart beat faster. I clasped my hands together to keep them from shaking and turned back to Dobbs.

"Well, obviously nothing happened. There was no *show*." I shuffled through the pictures, finding the ones with the bank statements. "Look, this is suspicious, right? Has to be something shady."

Delove nodded and flipped through the photos. "It's a good start. He's layering the money, trying to make it seem legitimate before he withdraws it. We need more though. See if you can find more statements."

I rubbed my hands over my face. "OK, what about these appraisals?"

Dobbs grunted and leaned back into the sofa. "He's overvaluing to get a bigger loan. Still not enough." He sipped his coffee. "We need more."

Yeah, yeah, of course they did. I didn't understand anything they were saying. Layering, overvaluing—they might as well have been speaking in a foreign language.

Cian walked over and glanced down at the picture of the black box with the hair in it. I handed it to him, and he raised his eyebrows.

"Should I be worried about this?" I nodded towards the picture. "It's very Norman Bates of him." A chill went down my spine, and I shook my head. Maybe I was just being paranoid. It was still creepy though.

Cian was quiet as he studied the photo, his eyes narrowed to the bottom right-hand corner. "What's this, Nova?" He held the photo in front of my face and pointed to part of the angel pendant.

"Oh, the photo cut off. It was a silver necklace with an angel pendant. Why?"

Cian shook his head. "It's familiar, but I can't place it." He put the photo down and went back to leaning against the counter.

"You need to wear the onyx camera necklace more. We need to see who Ryzen's with, where he's going and what he's talking about. So wear it. Got it?" Delove gave me a pointed look and I nodded. "Now, we need you to place this in his office. There is a wireless camera and microphone embedded in it. Put it facing his desk, but where he won't see it." Delove handed me a little black object the size of a button.

"How am I supposed to put this in his office without him seeing?" I scrunched up my nose. Did they think I was Houdini or something? I stuffed it into my pocket and placed my head in my hands.

"You'll figure it out." Dobbs shrugged and I desperately wanted to wipe that smug smile off his face. "Just put it in there and click the small button to activate it. We'll take care of the rest."

Delove collected the photos and piled them back into his briefcase. "We'll be in touch. In the meantime, wear the necklace, get closer to him, Nova. The sooner you find what we need, the sooner this will all be over." He offered a small smile, and they headed out the back door.

Cian locked the door behind them, and I stood, scrunching up my nose at what was to come. Was he going to yell? Tell me how foolish I was for drugging Ryzen? We stared at each other, not saying anything. The silence was deafening, and I threw my hands in the air. "I'm sorry."

He quirked his eyebrow. "For?"

"Well, you know. The pictures of Ryzen. Nothing happened." I was rambling, and heat raced up my neck. It wasn't like any rules had been broken between us. So why did I feel so guilty?

"Nova." He stalked over to me, pushing my hair behind my ear. "I thought we were going to trust each other more?" He wrapped his hand around the back of my neck and tugged my head back. "I trust you. I fucking hate that I can't be there to protect you from him. That he thinks he can touch you. I want to rip him limb from fucking limb, and the only thing that's stopping me is you." He growled and crushed his lips against mine. I let myself get lost in his kiss. Everything else drifted away. Ryzen, the FBI, the threat of prison if I didn't get what they wanted. It all vanished when he touched me, and I never wanted the moment to end. He kissed me until I had no air left in my lungs. I pulled back, gasping.

"I… you didn't call. I haven't heard from you." I exhaled.

"I was giving you what I thought you needed. Time to adjust. It was foolish of me. It won't happen again." He trailed his thumb over my bottom lip and down my chin. "I've been yards away from you at any given moment. We're all taking shifts to ensure your safety. I don't trust the FBI to take care of you, so you can fucking bet that I'm going to."

The fierceness in his voice sent goosebumps up my arms, and my face warmed. God, he was intense. Heat rolled off his body in waves, taking all the air out of the room. "I didn't realize you were around. I thought maybe… I don't know." I shrugged, feeling like an idiot.

"What part of 'you're mine' don't you understand?" His eyes darkened. "Do you think I'm going to let you go now that I have you?"

I shook my head from side to side. He was serious, that was abundantly clear. And I didn't want him to ever let me go. Our tongues tangled together, and he held me tight against him. There was a neediness inside of me, this craving for him that I couldn't shake no matter how hard I tried. "I need you," I whispered against his lips.

"I'm all yours," he growled against my lips.

*Damn straight you are.*

Our hands were everywhere, ripping off clothes, lips brushing against flesh, nails dragging against skin. I pushed him down on the couch and straddled him, positioning his cock at my entrance.

"Take what's yours, my beautiful star." His jaw clenched as I lowered myself until I was filled up with him. A gasp escaped my lips, and I threw my head back at the sensation of him. My whole body was on fire, and it only wanted one thing. Only craved one thing.

Cian fucking Blackwood.

His hands grazed across my stomach and up to my nipples, rolling them between his thumb and forefinger. "I'm all yours." He thrust his hips up and I screamed, my nails digging into his shoulders as our skin slapped against each other. "And you're mine."

"Yes," I panted and moved my hips faster. "All yours." I didn't know how we had gone from speaking with the FBI to fucking in a matter of minutes, but that was how it always seemed to be between us. Unpredictable. Ravenous. Pure lust-filled passion. This need I had to give every part of myself to him came over me every single time, and I didn't want it to ever go away.

I tugged his head back, licking up his neck as his hands gripped my ass, slamming me down on top of him until we were in a frenzy of sweat and guttural moans. I worked my hips in a circle and then down, a whimper coming from my mouth as I came completely unraveled. My orgasm hit me like a ton of bricks, and without warning I cried out and arched my back, Cian licking up and in between my breasts before grunting out his own release.

My chest heaved and I collapsed on top of him. I would never get tired of this. Of him. He lifted my face and cupped my jaw, placing small kisses around my lips and nose. I chuckled and rested my forehead against his.

"Promise me you'll be more careful," he murmured.

"I'll try." I squealed as he slapped my ass, then gripped the flesh.

"You are strong, Nova. Fearless, and one of the toughest women I have ever met. But you are also dealing with a desperate man. And that makes him dangerous. Do you have the knife I gave you?"

I pointed to the pile of clothes on the floor, the knife lying next to my panties. "I always carry it."

We gathered our clothes and dressed, the mood growing somber as the minutes passed. I didn't want him to leave, but I knew that he had to. Valik would be back any second and God help us if he came searching for me. I would have to find a way to get him to lay off, and I mentioned that to Cian.

"He's trying to keep you safe." Cian's jaw clenched. "So let him. I'll find a way to get to you; I always do. Remember, Nova, I'm always around, even if you can't see me."

We said our goodbyes and he left quietly through the back door. I waited downstairs for Valik to come back, not in any rush to go home to an empty apartment —or, worse, to Ryzen's. Having these moments with Cian, no matter how brief, were like a lifeline, one that I needed to cling to keep my sanity. There was no denying the connection we had. The things he said… oh, God, it was all enough to make me weak in the knees. There was so much happening at once, but one thing I knew for sure: I was falling madly in love with him, and that scared the shit out of me. After everything we had gone through, I hoped I was enough for him. That once Ryzen was locked away in prison we would have a fighting chance. That it wasn't just lust-filled sex, and our need for revenge wasn't the glue holding us together. Only time would tell.

The night dragged on, slow and boring, which was a nice change of pace. I texted Ryzen that I was safe at home, that I missed him today, and even sent a kissy face emoji to lay it on extra thick for him. He loved the attention. My fake adoration for him was fueling his ego, and it was obvious. And grossing me out beyond belief.

I smelled my shirt—it smelled just like Cian, and I decided I was going to sleep in it. Valik knocked on my door right when I was about to sleep, and I popped it open, hand on my hip. "You aren't staying out in the hallway all night, are you?" His face turned a shade of pink, and I shook my head. "Why don't you come inside if you're so intent on staying?"

"Oh, no, Mr. Goodacre would not like that. I'll be fine out here." He plopped down in the metal chair, and I rolled my eyes.

"I don't like you being uncomfortable all night, Valik. I'm going to talk to Ryzen. I don't need a babysitter twenty-four seven." I walked down the hall and grabbed the throw blanket from the back of the couch. "Here, at least take this." He hesitated, and I tossed it in his lap. "Don't be stubborn, you big moose."

I would talk to Ryzen tomorrow and have him pull Valik off my day and night duty. It was too much. Suffocating and unsettling. I knew Cian was supportive of the idea of Valik being around, but if I was going to get the evidence that I needed, I couldn't have Valik being my shadow twenty-four seven.

*****

I went to Jules' apartment for breakfast the next morning. There was no need to go to that shit-hole office every day, and the fewer rats I had to deal with, the better. We put our phones in the freezer, and I caught her up with what the FBI had said.

"Did you show them the hair? That's so creepy." She shivered.

"That's what I told them. Cian had a weird look

on his face, but he didn't tell me anything else about it. I think he might be hiding something."

"Oh, boy. Not the trust issues again."

I shook my head and took a bite of my croissant. "No, not like that. I mean… maybe he didn't want to say something he was unsure of." I shrugged, "I'll ask him next time I see him."

"And how are things going between you guys otherwise?"

My skin heated as I thought back to our last moments together.

"You're blushing!" She chuckled and leaned forward. "Tell me all the details."

And I did, because that was what you did with your best friend. You told them all about the mind-blowing sex you'd had with the sexiest man you had ever been with. By the time I was done, she was fanning herself, and whistled.

"Damn, I don't think I'll be able to look him in the eyes next time I see him." She chuckled. "So this is actual love? Like looove love?"

I nibbled on my bottom lip, and nodded. "I think so. Everything is a mess, but he… he makes it all a little less messy."

"Do yourself a favor. Tell him." She squeezed my hand. "Don't do what you always do and hold your feelings inside. After everything you've told me, you can bet your sweet ass he feels the same way."

"I'm scared, Jules." I squeezed her hand back.

"Nova, it's a good thing. I mean, I know we're in a total shitstorm right now and everything around us is bonkers, but… it'll work out." She held up her fingers in our secret code, and I did the same. "It always does."

On the way home, I had Valik stop at Mr. Sprinkle Kings. Ever since I had confessed to Juliet that I had eaten her marshmallow fluff, there was this feeling of guilt stabbing me in the back of my head. I ordered four cartons of fluff and three boxes of marshmallows. It was overkill, but I knew Jules would love it.

The camera Delove had given me was burning a hole in my pocket. I knew I had to get it into Ryzen's office, but wasn't sure how I was going to be able to do that. Maybe it wasn't going to be that hard—just show up for lunch, leave it in there, and we'd be good to go.

We drove past our old office, and I had Valik stop so I could get out. A "for lease" sign hung in the window, and I traced my fingers over it and sighed. If only things had been different. If I hadn't moved into Goodacre Estates, if I had just found a way to not sign the contract... but wishing wasn't going to make it go away or make it better.

"OK, look." I walked over to where Valik was leaning against the SUV. "I'm going to grab an iced coffee from my favorite place down the street, and then I'm going to that park"—I pointed over his shoulder —"so that I can lie in the sun and get centered. You stay put. I don't want to see your face for the next hour. Got it?" I tilted my head to the side and gave him a pointed look. "I mean that in the nicest way possible. But I need space."

He chuckled and gave me a salute. I punched his shoulder for mocking me, since I was the one who had been saluting him since we had met. "Don't touch those marshmallows or Juliet will kick your ass. She's feisty, don't let her fool you."

With that, I walked over to Stan's, my favorite

diner in the city. Stan, the owner, was so excited to see me, I couldn't help but laugh. He loaded a bag up with all my favorite pastries and I grabbed my ice coffee and headed to the park. I took off my shoes and jacket and lay in the grass with my arms and legs spread wide. It felt good to soak in the sun; it was giving me life. Finally, I felt like I could breathe again. The weight of the world wasn't keeping me down. It was just me, the sun and birds, and my bag of pastries that I planned to devour. I hit play on the meditation app and was about ten minutes in when it shut down and stopped working.

OK, well, there went my Zen.

I wasn't ready to go back to Valik or deal with any other adult responsibilities, like keeping myself out of prison, so I grabbed my bag of pastries and lay on my stomach facing the row of empty benches. Well, not so empty anymore. A woman was sitting by herself, her face in her hands. Her shoulders shook, and I realized she was crying.

She pulled out a tissue and dabbed the side of her eyes, then froze when she saw me watching her. Well, this was ridiculously awkward. I knew if I was upset and crying in a park and looked up to see some random stranger with cherry filling on her chin watching me, I would be really uncomfortable too. So I did what any normal person would. I grabbed my bag of pastries and walked the thirty feet over to the bench.

"Hi." I sat down next to her and pulled out a napkin and pastry, holding it up to her. "This is the best pastry you can get in this city and is known to solve all your problems with just one bite." She sniffled and hesitated. I wiggled it in front of her. "Your parents probably warned you against taking food from strangers, but I promise, it's safe."

A smile spread across her face, and she grabbed the pastry. We ate in silence for a moment, the awkwardness slowly slipping away as she moaned in appreciation.

"Told you." I chuckled and took a sip of my iced coffee. "Bad day?"

She inhaled sharply and I regretted the question almost immediately. There was something about her that was familiar, but I couldn't place it. She was quite beautiful, with long flowing black hair. The way she was dressed, like she had just stepped off the catwalk at a model show, indicated she was probably not from around here. Diamond earrings dangled from her ears, and she had a ring on her finger that was bigger than the engagement ring Ryzen had given me.

"I just get so sick of men trying to control every move I make," she whispered and took a big bite out of her pastry.

"Amen to that," I scoffed and held out my hand. "I'm Nova."

She didn't offer her name, just shook my hand and went back to chewing.

"Sometimes it helps to vent to a stranger," I said. She glanced at me from the corner of her eye, and I shrugged. "I'm all ears."

"Have you ever loved someone so much, it hurts to breathe?" She looked off in the distance. "So much that being without them feels like you're dying inside?"

I froze, an uneasy feeling nestling deep in my stomach.

"Yesterday I was in Rome with the love of my life. And today, I am in America because my father deemed the man I loved not good enough for me." She turned to face me all the way, and I noticed she had one blue eye and one gray eye. "And I'm completely lost now." She looked at me expectantly and I stopped mid-chew.

Crap. I had not been expecting such a deep answer.

"I'm sorry to hear that." And I was. You could hear the pain in her voice, a pain that I was all too familiar with. "There's no way to get back to Rome?"

She shook her head, a tear spilling down her cheek. "No, I'm trapped here."

"Do you want me to call someone for you?" I pulled my cell phone out of my pocket.

"It's too late now. I tried to explain to my father, *al cuore non si comanda,* but he wouldn't accept it." She placed her hand over her heart. "The heart wants what it wants."

"I know what it's like to love someone and then lose them. I'm sorry. I hope that you find your way back to him." I placed my hand on her arm and squeezed.

"You don't understand," she whispered. "He's dead." A dinging noise sounded from her purse and her hands trembled as she pulled out her phone.

Well, obviously I'd picked the wrong bench to sit on.

"Are you in danger?" I looked over my shoulder and around the mostly empty park. "I have a car close by. I can take you wherever you need to go."

She stood and dropped her pastry on the ground. "No, I shouldn't have said anything. I have to go." She took a step in the opposite direction, then turned back to face me. "Thank you, Nova. I won't forget your kindness on this otherwise dark day." She hauled ass down the path, and I lost sight of her once she got around the bend.

Well, that was downright strange. Did crazy tend to attract crazy? Because that was exactly what it felt like. The hair on the back of my neck stood up and I looked around, searching for anyone who might be watching me. I reached down and touched the knife I had stuffed in the side of my sock. It was still there. And I was ready to use it if I had to.

The park suddenly didn't feel so peaceful and calming, and I grabbed my pastries and coffee and went in the opposite direction she had run in. By the time I got back to Valik, I was out of breath, and he jumped out of the car right away.

"What's wrong? Are you OK, Miss La Roux?" He gripped my shoulders.

"I'm fine." I sucked in all the air I could, my lungs begging me to slow down and breathe. "I just wanted to make sure you weren't eating all the marshmallows."

He raised his eyebrow and let go of my shoulders. "You're a little strange sometimes, Miss La Roux."

"Cut the La Roux crap and call me Nova already, Moose."

We both laughed and he helped me get into the back of the SUV. I had him stop at Jules so I could drop off her treats, which she held tight against her chest.

"We're still not even, you thief."

I had barely spoken a word to Ryzen all morning, and that wasn't good. I had to keep up appearances, make him believe I couldn't get him off of my mind. Delove's words echoed in my ears.

*Get closer. Get the evidence so you can go back to living a normal life.*

I would bring up the wedding again. And Covington. Sweeten the pot a little bit. If he thought that I was ready to tie the knot and help him secure his deal, maybe he would open up more. It was stupid, and something I didn't want to do, but it was my best option. But first, I had to plant the camera in his office.

I had Valik drop me off in front of Goodacre Corporation, and when he tried to get out and follow me upstairs, I shook my head and held my hands up. "No, no. You go take care of your business. I'm here with Ryzen. In a completely secure building. Absolutely nothing is going to happen to me here."

He hesitated, and I could tell he would need more convincing. "You said you needed to get your niece a birthday present. So go take care of it. Or I'll tell Ryzen you saw me naked." I put my hands on my hips and tilted my head to the side.

"You don't play fair, Miss La... Nova."

"Go." I pointed down the road and smiled.

After he drove off, I took the elevator to Ryzen's floor. Memories flooded my brain as I thought back to the first time Juliet and I had walked into this office together. We'd had no idea that we were stepping into a lion's den. Well, more like a snake's den, as Cian liked to call it.

Ryzen's secretary's jaw practically hit the floor when I strolled in, but she quickly recovered and greeted me with a smile. "Miss La Roux, I haven't seen you since... the wedding." Her voice trailed off, and I couldn't tell if she was trying to take a jab at me or was being sincere.

"Yeah, those darn cold feet really got to me. Is he in?" I tugged on the glass door and gave her a pointed look when it wouldn't open.

"Oh, um, he's in a meeting, but you can wait in his office. He should be done shortly."

She buzzed the door, and I walked down the hall, my heart slamming against my chest as I got closer to his office. I knocked once, twice, and when nobody answered I went in and shut the door. I had to be quick. He could come back at any moment. My mind still felt scrambled after that weird incident in the park. Something was weird about that situation, but hell, I had my own problems to worry about. Like prison.

I tossed my purse on the chair and glanced around his office, looking for the perfect spot to place the camera. There was an abstract sculpture behind his desk to the side, and excitement coursed through me as I realized it was the perfect spot. You could see anyone who came and went, and also see his computer screen.

There was a deep nook at the top of it; it was one of those pieces that had a lot of mounds and sharp edges, so the camera would blend in perfectly. I pulled the camera out of my pocket and it fell to the ground, rolling under his desk.

"What are you doing here, Nova?" I jumped at Ryzen's voice, my hand flying to my chest as I turned and saw him in the doorway.

"Hey, you." I smiled from ear to ear, willing my heart to slow down. "I missed you last night, so thought we could grab lunch."

Crap. Crap. Crap. I glanced down and saw the camera had fallen next to his wastebasket. He came closer and I rushed over to him before he could pass his desk, throwing my arms around him and squeezing.

He chuckled and pulled back, puckering his lips

and lowering his head. I turned my head slightly so his lips grazed the side of my mouth. "How about it then? You've probably been working hard all day."

He checked his watch and sighed. "I have a meeting with Riddick in two minutes. How about dinner?" His hands roamed down my back and I bit the inside of my cheek.

"Sounds lovely." I grinned and tapped the tip of his nose.

I didn't know how many times I was going to get away with love taps on the nose, or side-mouth kisses, but I hoped he wouldn't try to take it any further. I shuddered at the thought.

He squeezed my hand and brought it up to his lips, kissing my knuckles.

"Walk me out?" I asked.

He nodded, his hand on my back as he led me back down the hallway. Halfway down, I stopped and slapped my forehead. "I forgot my purse in your office. Go to your meeting, I'll grab it and see you tonight."

"Sounds lovely." He kissed my cheek and left me in the hallway.

I pushed my hair behind my ear and speed-walked back to his office, shutting the door behind me. That had been close. Too close. The anxiety of sneaking around like this was going to give me wrinkles.

Maybe he had more incriminating documents in his office, but I decided against trying my luck and grabbed the camera from the floor. I reached up high and placed it in the nook. It blended in perfectly and couldn't be seen from any angles that I could tell.

Freedom was in the air, and I was hungry for it.

# Chapter Ten
## Day 24

I was getting restless. The nightmares kept coming and waking up in the middle of the night drenched in sweat wasn't helping. Especially waking up next to Ryzen. We were spending a lot of time together, and it was making me feel dirty. And guilty. Like my body and mind knew I wasn't supposed to be within ten feet of this man. And his constant need to try to fuck me was keeping me on edge.

Last night when he'd tried to pull me to him, I had laughed and swatted him away. He was enjoying it, this game we had of him trying to get into my pants, and me playing coy and embracing my newfound virginal persona. The only way to get him to stop was to mention Covington. That got his full attention.

"You've really been taking good care of me, Ryzen, ever since I was… taken." I stabbed my palm with my nails, willing the gods of crying to give me one fake tear. "So patient and caring. And I know you've been keeping Covington at bay while I recovered emotionally and, um, mentally."

He leaned in closer, holding his breath as he hung on to every word.

"And I want you to get what you deserve."

*Prison. A kick in the ass.*

"So whatever you need me to do to reassure Covington that I'm back on board, that we're madly in love and ready to get married…" I bit my bottom lip and lowered my head. "I'm ready to do that for you. You mean that much to me. Let's close this hotel deal."

*And the winner for Performance of the Year goes to… Nova La Roux!*

"Sweet Nova." He exhaled and gripped my hand. "You're sure that's what you want?"

I nodded and tugged my hand gently out of his grasp.

"OK, if that's what you want." He caressed the side of my face, my nostrils flaring. "I'll set up a dinner this week."

*****

## Day 28

There was a lot to do regarding the Shiver Box to ensure we didn't go under and have to permanently close our doors. Ryzen wasn't giving me much information regarding his side of the insurance claim, which was maddening. I knew it was going to be a slow process, and I had no idea if the FBI was making the insurance company stall. So we had to just keep going and proceed as if they weren't involved.

Ryzen said he was working with a building inspector and a long list of engineers and architects to determine the extent of the damage. I found that odd, considering the building was just a pile of rubble with a fence going around the property. Juliet and I had hired a public adjuster to help us with our side of the claim and they'd helped us already by getting the insurance company to cover Owen's wages in the meantime. We also hired a forensic accountant. She was amazing and helped us analyze our invoices, calculate our inventory losses, and get everything ready to submit to the insurance company. The only thing we could really do while everything was up in the air was try to maintain a presence on social media and keep people interested in our products.

Valik had finally laid off babysitting me twenty-four seven and I was getting as much evidence as I could, taking photos of anything and everything that looked like it might help the FBI, and wearing the necklace with the camera in it. Ryzen questioned why I always had it on, and I told him that it helped me feel closer to Juliet when I was afraid. He bought it, or at least I hoped he had. He didn't bring it up again. I had met with Delove and Dobbs one more time in the past week, and they had said the same thing as before.

*It isn't enough. We need more.*

A plan had been brewing in the back of my mind, and when Ryzen locked himself in his home office in the morning, I knew that today was the day. I pressed my ear against the door, his voice slightly raised as he spoke on the phone with someone. He sounded angry and panicked. Was he talking to Voledetti? Whatever it was, it was serious. He flung the door open, and I stood there smiling, a cup of coffee in my hand.

"Here you go," I handed him the cup and batted my eyelashes at him. "Everything OK?"

He sighed and ran his fingers through his hair. "Everything is wonderful, Nova." He turned me around and ushered me down the hall. "Why don't you do a spa day. On me. I've got to head out in a little bit to an important meeting." He handed me his credit card and walked me to the elevator bank.

*Paying to get rid of me, huh?*

I ran back to my apartment and changed into leggings and a black hoodie, tucking my knife into my combat boots. There was an empty feeling in the pit of my stomach, but I shook it off as I tossed my cell phone onto my bed and grabbed the secret phone Thora had given me. Couldn't have Ryzen tracking me, not today. I tugged my hoodie over my hair, keeping my head down as I took the elevator to the parking garage, hauling ass out the side exit. A cab pulled up and an elderly couple got out. Before the driver could pull off, I opened the door and slid into the back seat.

"LaSalle and Van Buren, please." I pushed the sunglasses up my nose and kept myself small in the backseat. If Ryzen wasn't going to his office first, then this was going to be a big waste of time. But deep down in my gut, I knew he was going to show up.

*Please let him show up.*

"Park here." I pointed down a side alley that gave a clear view to the front of Goodacre Corporation. The driver looked at me with raised eyebrows when I didn't get out. "I'm waiting for someone. Keep the meter running." He shrugged and put the car in park.

Five minutes passed, then ten, and I was beginning to think that my grand plan wasn't so grand after all. But close to the twenty-minute mark, a familiar black SUV pulled up to Goodacre Corporation, and I leaned forward, peeking through the front window.

"You following your husband, lady?" The driver chuckled.

"Fiancé," I mumbled, not taking my eyes off the SUV. A minute later Riddick came down with a duffel bag and jumped into the backseat.

"I'll give you a hundred bucks on top of the cab fees if you follow that car." I pointed at the SUV as it made a U-turn in front of us and headed in the opposite direction it had just come from.

"No problem. As long as he doesn't have a gun, then I'm good." The driver took off behind them, and I leaned back into the backseat, keeping my head down. It wasn't like Ryzen would be able to tell it was me. I was covered in black from head to toe, including the jeweled necklace with the camera in it.

We followed them around downtown, the cab driver shaking his head and chuckling when I told him not to get too close. "Believe it or not, this isn't the first time I've been paid to follow a cheating spouse. And believe me, they are almost always cheating."

Fifteen minutes later and we were on the outskirts of a manufacturing park. A large sign over twenty feet wide was posted to the fence, with the name "Goodacre Corporation" plastered across the front of it. There were construction crews all over, the sound of trucks beeping, pouring cement, cranes moving large metal beams from one point to another. The SUV turned down a gravel road and parked.

I handed the cab driver a hundred dollars. "Wait here. I'll be back in ten minutes."

He shrugged and took the cash, and I ran behind the building looking for a way in. Either Ryzen was having a typical real estate meeting, or he was doing something shady. And I would bet my life it was the latter.

There was a staircase going up the back of the building at least three floors up, and I climbed to the top, my boots making a thumping noise as I went. My back pressed against the back door, and I peeked through the window, jiggling the doorknob. The door swung open and I held my breath as I poked my head around the corner. All clear. This was kind of easy. Maybe the universe was on my side today. I gripped the necklace and pressed the button on the side, ensuring the video was recording.

It was dark and dingy with barely a shred of light except what was streaming through a few broken windows. Boxes filled with old computer equipment littered the area, and I gasped when I tripped over a pipe, banging my knees on the metal grating.

My leggings were ripped at the knee, and I held back a groan at the blood covering my skin. OK. Maybe I wasn't as smart as I'd thought. The air smelled like old rubber and something else. Something… not right. A chill ran up my spine as mostly darkness surrounded me. When I finally got through the maze of boxes, I realized I was on the top floor of a makeshift storage area that wrapped around the whole building. It opened up in the center and when I got closer, I peeked over the railing and saw several old utility vans parked.

Voices came from below where I was standing and I scooted back a few feet away from the railing and kneeled behind an old desk.

"Let me do the talking. He's already pissed off at you."

*Riddick.*

"He's pissed at us. Not just me. I'll handle it." Ryzen cursed.

He was definitely up to no good. Two large black trucks pulled in, dirt flying in the air and surrounding Ryzen and Riddick. I crawled as close to the edge as I could and pointed the necklace at the men below.

Six men stepped out of the vehicles, all dressed in black suits and sunglasses. They were big, way bigger than Ryzen, and a wave of nausea passed through me when I noticed they all had guns hanging over their shoulders. This was serious, and more than I had bargained for when I had decided to follow him.

But it was too late now. I was about to get exactly what I needed in order to be free from this mess.

A man stepped out of the truck and lit a cigarette, blowing a circle with the smoke up in the air. I was almost right above them. Had it not been dark as hell up here, they might have been able to see me. My hand trembled as I pointed the necklace at the man and followed his path as he walked towards Ryzen and Riddick. The men with guns parted for him, and as he got closer, I realized I was looking at none other than Kaviathin Voledetti.

Excitement raced through me. I was about to capture exactly what I would need to get out of this whole situation with the FBI. It was quickly followed by panic as I realized that Ryzen was about to find out Kaviathin hadn't been the one who had taken Juliet and I.

Kaviathin blew smoke in Ryzen's face, and Ryzen waved his hand, huffing.

"Do you have my money?" Kaviathin purred, this time blowing smoke at Riddick, who seemed to be smarter than Ryzen and let the smoke waft over him without moving.

Ryzen kicked the bag to the man standing to the right of Kaviathin. "It's all there. You can count it if you don't believe me."

Kaviathin chuckled and tossed the cigarette on the ground. "If I thought you were stupid enough to double-cross me, you'd be dead already."

Ryzen tensed, his fists clenching at his sides. Oh, he could not be happy being talked to like this. A man like him who was all ego and thought of himself as the king of all men? No, he was seething, and it was obvious.

Kaviathin stepped closer, the tips of his shoes touching Ryzen's. "The next time you ball your fists up in my presence, you better be prepared for what's next."

Ryzen paled and took a step back and Kaviathin chuckled. Even from up here I could feel his power. His evilness. This was not a man you wanted to run into at night in a dark alley. My hand trembled as I held the necklace out further, making sure I was capturing everything.

Kaviathin turned on his heel and walked toward the truck. Ryzen ran his fingers through his hair, arguing with Riddick for a moment. When Riddick took a step forward, Ryzen grabbed onto his jacket to stop him.

"We're handling the situation with Nova and Covington. You don't need to interfere like that again." Riddick's voice wavered slightly when Kaviathin turned and gave him a lethal look.

"Riddick, shut up." Ryzen tugged his arm.

"Taking her like that almost messed everything

up. We got your point. We'll handle it from here."

Kaviathin raised his eyebrows. "Interesting."

Something warm brushed against my leg and my eyes widened as a rat scurried from behind me. I jumped backward, hitting my head on the edge of the desk.

The men all grew quiet, and I held completely still as they looked up.

"Check that out," Kaviathin barked, and heavy footsteps sounded on the stairs.

Oh, fuck. Oh, fuck.

I backed up slowly, the necklace falling from my hand and landing over one of the grate holes. *Oh, no, please don't fall.* If it fell, it was going to land within feet of them, and then I'd be royally screwed. Just as I was about to grab it, strong hands wrapped around my waist, tugging me back, a hand coming over my mouth. They dragged me backwards into the corner behind a stack of boxes.

My heart slammed against my chest, and I clawed at the hand, trying to free myself.

"Quiet, Nova."

*Cian.*

"Don't say a word. Understand?" His breath was warm against my ear, and I nodded. He let me go, the footsteps almost to the top of the stairs.

He picked up a small pebble and tossed it to the other side of the room. The footsteps stopped suddenly, then came the sound of boxes crashing to the floor. I squeezed my eyes shut, my blood running cold, knowing that whoever was up here with us had a gun, and we didn't stand a chance. Cian held his finger up to his lips and gave me a pointed look. I nodded, my stomach dropping to the floor when he pulled out a gun himself and pointed it in the direction of the man.

"Fucking hell," a man's voice grumbled from about twenty feet away. His footsteps banged down the stairs. "Was just a disgusting rat. Filthy shithole."

I let out the breath I had been holding and stayed completely still.

"Let's go." Kaviathin's voice boomed, and a moment later I heard the trucks start up and drive away. Riddick and Ryzen could be heard arguing, but the adrenaline was pumping through my whole body and I couldn't understand a word they were saying. Cian disappeared around a stack of boxes, and I curled my shoulders forward, hugging my knees to my chest.

A moment later Cian came around the corner and kneeled in front of me. He lifted my head up, cupping my jaw. "Are you OK?" he whispered.

I nodded, my mouth suddenly dry. This might not have been the best idea I had come up with. I'd wanted to catch Ryzen doing something illegal, but I hadn't been mentally prepared to actually be within feet of dangerous men holding guns again. Images of the masked men at my wedding grabbing me ran through my mind, and I shuddered.

Cian reached over and grabbed the necklace, stuffed it into the pocket of his pants. He grabbed my hand and tugged me up from the ground. "We need to wait a few minutes so they don't see us leave."

I nodded, his arms wrapping around me like a blanket. My whole body was shaking. Was it from fear, or just the adrenaline? Either way, it was almost unbearable. The only thing I could think of at that moment was that I had exactly what Delove and Dobbs needed—Ryzen on camera giving Kaviathin Voledetti a bag full of money. This had to be it. I was almost free from all of this.

After what seemed like an eternity, Cian walked us to the back door and left me standing there while he went outside and looked around. He grabbed my hand again and we ran down the back stairs in the opposite direction of where I had asked the cab driver to wait.

"Wait." I tugged on Cian's hand. "Someone is waiting for me over there."

He shook his head and dragged me under his arm, making me run with him. "They left as soon as you went into the building."

Well, shit, so much for trusting strange cab drivers to do the right thing. I guessed I couldn't blame the guy. We ran down the gravel road, behind a bunch of parked cars until we got to a small sedan. Cian opened the back door and told me to get in and lie down in the back. He jumped in the driver's seat and sped off, hopefully in the opposite direction Ryzen and Kaviathin had gone in.

"Cian, what..."

He held his hand up and I stopped talking. "I'm two seconds away from climbing back there and spanking your bare ass for being so stupid, Nova. Keep your head down until we get where we're going."

"But..."

"One more word out of your mouth," he growled and I puckered up my lips.

I was tempted to give him a sassy comeback, but decided against it. Not because I didn't want the spanking, because you know I did. But the tone in his voice told me he was not playing around, and I didn't think I wanted to push that boundary. Not yet.

We drove for some time, and the tall Chicago buildings I saw from where I was lying in the back indicated that we were back downtown. He pulled into a parking garage, and I sat up when he opened the back door and held out his hand to me. We took the elevator up to the top floor, not saying a word the entire time. Heat was rolling off his body, and I knew that I was in for it—I was about to get yelled at. Or have mind-blowing sex.

I followed behind him as he walked over to a bar and poured a shot of alcohol before slamming it down. He poured another and handed it to me, and I did the same.

The apartment was beautiful, with dark-colored walls and large bright paintings covering the entire room. A large white sofa was in the center of the living room, and he walked over and sat down.

"Where are we?" I asked and sat down next to him.

He was leaning forward with his elbows on his knees, hands clasped together. "Our apartment." His voice was low, and I knew that he was still pissed off.

Ours? As in mine and his, or his and his family's? I didn't want to ask because something told me we were about to get into a big fight.

His back was completely tense, and when I reached over to touch him, he turned suddenly and grabbed my wrist. "Do you have any idea how stupid that was, Nova? You could have gotten yourself killed. You know that, right? Answer me."

I flinched back from him and tried to pull my wrist away, but he wouldn't let me.

"This isn't a game. If they'd found you, you would be dead right now. Fucking dead. Don't you get it?" His voice rose with each word. He was more than just angry. He was scared.

"But I got the video. I got the evidence, Cian. That's what matters."

"It doesn't fucking matter. It was stupid. Reckless. Use your head." He dropped my wrist and stood, grabbing the bottle of Jack Daniels from the bar.

"Of course it matters!" I threw my hands in the air. "Now he's going to pay, Cian. Ryzen's getting everything he deserves. So my plan, although risky, was the right thing to do." I stood and placed my hands on my hips.

"It was foolish. Don't ever do something like that again." Cian's chest heaved up and down, his eyes drilling into me.

"I don't understand why you're so upset. This is what we wanted." I was pleading with him to understand. "Revenge. We both want it, and now I have the video that's going to get it for us."

He clenched his jaw and stalked over to me. I took a step back, the back of my knees hitting the couch. I couldn't decipher the look on his face, and the knot in my stomach grew. "Fuck revenge, Nova." He reached up and wrapped his hand in my hair, tugging my head back. "If anything happens to you because of this, I will hunt each and every single one of them down and kill them. I will burn the whole damn world down to keep you safe, do you understand?"

"Yes," I whispered, my lips trembling.

"I am nothing without you. You are my everything, and I can't lose you over this. I won't let that happen. You're mine, my beautiful bright star. Forever."

It was like all the air in the room had been sucked away, the intense look in his eyes making my whole body tremble. His words were sinking in, the pain on his face evident. I darted my tongue out to moisten my lips, my mouth suddenly dry.

He loved me.

I was his, and he was mine.

And I never wanted to see the pained look on his face again.

I lifted my hand up, placing it on his chest. His heart was beating so fast, and I hated that I was the reason for it. "I'm sorry," I whispered. "I didn't think."

He grabbed my hand, brought it up to his mouth and kissed my knuckles. "I love you, Nova." His voice was hoarse, and my heart squeezed in my chest at his words. "I fucking love you so much. Don't ever, ever do that to me again."

"I love you too, Cian," I whispered, lowering my eyes.

"Look at me." He tugged my hair gently. "Say it again."

"I love you."

His mouth crashed into mine, taking my breath away. I let myself get lost in him as I had so many times before. But it was different this time. I had finally said the one thing I was scared of saying, terrified of showing him, because I hadn't wanted to get my heart broken again. But it didn't matter. It would all be worth it. Just for this moment, in this room with him. With the man I loved. The man I would do anything for.

He wrapped me in his arms, his lips never leaving mine, and took the stairs two at a time. He tossed me on the bed, and I leaned up on my elbows, watching him as he ripped his shirt off, his scars slashing across his body.

I would do anything to take his pain away. Pain his parents had caused, Ryzen had caused. I would take it all into myself if I could. Now I understood what he had meant before—that he would hurt anyone who hurt me—because I would do the same for him. If anyone ever hurt this man again, they would have hell to pay.

He leaned down, kissing me gently, and there was no other place I would have rather been at that moment than in his arms.

## Chapter Eleven

We stayed in bed for hours making love. It was different this time, maybe because I had finally taken down the wall around my heart and let myself feel free with him. I explored every inch of his body, from his muscular calves, up to his stomach where my favorite tattoo of his was, up and over his scars across his chest and back, to his neck. I was familiar with every inch of his flesh, as he was with mine.

I lost track of how many orgasms he gave me. At one point, I had to beg him to stop, but he still wouldn't listen. If I had learned anything, it was that Cian was more than a giver—he was a giver until you couldn't take any more. And I loved every second of it.

I didn't want our time together to end, to go back home and deal with Ryzen or getting evidence. It was consuming my whole life, and I just wanted it to be over. The frustration, the fear. All of it.

"Tell me something, how did you come up with the idea for the Shiver Box?" Cian rolled over onto his side and propped his head up with his hand. We had ended up in the middle of the living room, on a plush white carpet, my new favorite thing in his apartment.

"Well…" I lay on my back staring up at the ceiling. "Jules and I met in our freshman year of college and became best friends right away. Completely inseparable. We ended up in the same business class where we had to come up with a business idea and a plan for how we would launch it. We were supposed to be brainstorming ideas, but she went out on a date instead, and it ended in disaster. When she got back to our dorm, we started talking about how a vibrator could never disappoint us like men did." Cian poked me in the side of my stomach, and I giggled.

"And the idea just came to us for a sexual wellness shop. We planned every little detail, and although the professor was not thrilled about our business idea, we frickin' loved it. And that's what started it all. We worked out all the kinks so that by the time we graduated, we were ready to set up shop. And the rest is history."

It had been hard at first, not as easy as we had hoped. But we'd gotten through it, and without taking money from any of our families. Neither of us had wanted that.

"I love that about you." He cradled my cheek in his hand. "Such determination and passion for what you do. When this is all over, I would love to help you rebuild." I shook my head, opening my mouth to say no, but he pressed his finger to my lips. "It's not a handout. I know you, Nova, I know you don't want that. That's not what I'm offering. You guys are great at what you do, empowering others, and that's something I want to get behind. When the time is right." He kissed me deeply, making me forget about any objection I was about to give him.

He lay back down, dragging me on top of him so my head was resting on his chest. "What do you think of the apartment?" he mused as he trailed his fingers up and down my back, giving me chills.

"It's beautiful." And it was. There were red and white roses in the living room, purple lilies in the kitchen and bedroom, and a rainbow of colored tulips scattered in between. All my favorite flowers. The bookshelves were overflowing with books and pictures of Cian and his family, and in the center of the living room hung a massive painting of *The Swing* by Jean-Honoré Fragonard. I had been obsessed with that painting in high school after I'd had to write a paper on it in my art literature class. A grand piano was off to the side, facing the floor-to-ceiling windows. We were high up, maybe fifty floors, and the view of the lake took your breath away.

"What did you mean by *our* apartment? Like your family's?" My face heated. I didn't want to sound like I was insinuating he meant my and his apartment.

He stroked my hair, his chest rumbling as he chuckled. "Ours, as in mine and yours, Nova. For as long as we need."

I turned my head and grinned. "You rented it?"

"I own the building. We're only four blocks away from your apartment." He pushed my hair behind my ear, trailing his fingers down my cheek, and I giggled.

"Oh... how many buildings do you own?"

"In Chicago? My portfolio varies, but as of now about twenty-three commercial buildings downtown, about eighteen properties out in the suburbs. Some residential, some commercial. Plus the Hellfire Club and the Heathens' Lounge. A lodging chain in Montana, plus a few other acquisitions in other states."

"Wow." I reached up and planted a kiss on his

lips. "Very impressive."

"I do all right." He laughed. "The clubs have been my focus lately." His eyes darkened and he stared off to the side. "I'm not like Ryzen, Nova. Constantly chasing money, working twenty-hour days, living in a state of stress, always greedy for more." He shook his head. "You find the right deals. Focus on those, and the money will come. Then you have the freedom to spend time on the important stuff." The way he looked at me then had my heart skipping a beat.

"Can I ask you a question then? Did you even want the hotels? Covington's?"

He snickered and sat up, bringing me with him. "Not in the slightest. I was only there for two reasons, which quickly turned into one."

I squealed as he carried me down the hall into the master bedroom and dropped me onto the bed. Oh, God, please no more orgasms. I didn't think I could take it anymore. Or could I?

He sauntered over to the shower, turning on the water. Over the king-sized bed hung another one of my favorite paintings, *The Three Graces* by Peter Paul Rubens. Actually, now that I was coming down from my sex coma, there were several other pieces of art in the apartment that I had loved growing up. I trailed my finger over the bookshelf, and grinned when I found *The Hitchhiker's Guide to the Galaxy* and the book *Outlander*. How in the heck would he even know I loved this stuff?

He walked up, wrapping his arms around me.

"Why, Mr. Blackwood, have you been stalking me?" I feigned shock. "How did you know these were my favorite books? And the paintings? The flowers?" I turned around in his arms, placing my hands on his chest. "Don't tell me you're psychic?"

"Close." He kissed my forehead and reached down to the bookshelf, pulled out a box, and handed it to me.

My mouth hung open as I stared at the contents. All of my diaries were in there, the ones I had tried to sneak out from my parents' house the night Ryzen had announced our engagement. I had completely forgotten about them. And now here they were in my hands again. All my secrets, all my fears, all the little moments of joy, which were few and far between, tucked between these pages, and Cian had read them all. There were things in there I had never shared with anyone.

"You're upset?" He frowned and blew out a deep breath. "I'm sorry, Nova. I couldn't help but read them. Such an… intense, optimistic, fragile child you were, who turned into this beautiful, powerful woman. I didn't mean to upset you."

"Stop talking." I chuckled and put the box back on the bookshelf. "I'm happy you read them. Honestly, it's like giving a small part of myself to you, if that makes sense. Read them all, if you haven't already."

He nodded, his face growing serious as he gazed at me. "I'll take all the parts you're willing to give, Nova."

God, how was he able to make my heart burst without even trying? He carried me into the master shower, the water pouring over us. I soaped up a loofah and started at the top of his shoulders, working my way down his chest. When I got to his scars, I cleaned them gently, letting the water wash off the soap before trailing little kisses over them, down his side, to his back, and then front again. His chest heaved as I kissed my way down his scorpion tattoo and his abs.

I stroked the length of his cock, already hard for me. "Such a beautiful cock, Cian." I licked the tip, and he lowered his lashes, jaw clenched. "It's so perfect, like it was made for me." My tongue swirled around the tip and then down. I tried to take him all the way in my mouth, but he was too big.

"Nova, let me take care of you first." He reached down and I slapped his hand away.

"Stop ruining my fun," I teased, and stroked him up and down.

He balled his hands into fists as I worked my hand up and down, my lips wrapping around him and sucking. His whole body was tense, and the guttural moans he was making had my hand working faster, my lips following my strokes.

"Fuck," he growled, weaving his hand into my hair and tugging gently. "You're so fucking beautiful like this. On your knees, ready to take my cock."

I moaned around him, letting him fuck my mouth the way he wanted.

"Look at me, my beautiful fucking star."

My eyes were on his as he pumped his hips. He thrust deeper, and I opened my mouth wider, trying to fit as much of him in my mouth as I could. Precum dripped on my tongue, and I reached up, caressing his balls as his thighs trembled.

He had me up in a flash, his mouth crashing into mine, biting my lower lip. "Let me fuck that pretty pussy."

My chest heaved as he flipped me around and pinned my hands over my head. Water poured over us, the tiny drops making my skin tingle in the best of ways. He thrust into me, and I gasped, still sore from the hours of lovemaking that had taken place all morning.

"You feel so good." He licked up the side of my neck, his teeth grazing my ear. "So fucking wet for me all the time, greedy girl."

"Yes," I breathed and pushed back into him. "Fuck me, Cian. Please."

He wrapped his hand gently around my throat and pumped his hips, faster, harder. The noises coming from my mouth didn't sound human, but I didn't care. All that mattered was that he didn't stop. He reached his other hand down and rubbed my clit, his hand on my throat squeezing just a little tighter. "Oh, God, don't stop," I moaned.

"Never," he growled as he hammered into me.

A tingling sensation started at the top of my head and moved down my spine until I shattered around him, screaming out his name as I came. He grabbed onto my hips and fucked me without mercy, our skin slapping against each other as he growled out his release a moment later.

I laid my head on the bathroom wall, gasping for air as my body came back to earth. He turned off the water and wrapped me in a giant towel, carrying me to bed.

A while later, he left a message for Delove. We waited for Delove to call back, but he never did, and the frustration of realizing I had to go back home was enough to make me sick. Tomorrow. Tomorrow this would all be over. It had to be.

*****

"What the hell do you mean there's no video?" I stood in front of Delove and Dobbs in the apartment upstairs from our temporary office, my nostrils flaring. "How can that be possible?" I was on the verge of tears. Not because of sadness, or even desperation, but tears of absolute anger.

"Nova, calm down." Delove held his hands up. "Let me show you." He opened a laptop and pressed play on the screen. The video was grainy, and dark, and you could just make out the boxes of old computer equipment. It cleared slightly, and I could see the railing, but once I got closer to the open area, the video turned to static and stopped completely. "See? There's nothing here."

Cian stomped over to the kitchen, slamming his hand on the counter. "Fuck," he muttered and lowered his head.

"Maybe you turned it off," Dobbs said, his tone accusing.

"Oh, yeah, that's a real smart theory, *Agent*. How about your stupid equipment doesn't work the right way, and you guys are the fuck-ups here, not me?" I snapped. There was a rock the size of a boulder in my stomach, and bile rose in my throat.

"Calm down, Nova." Cian dragged me down to the couch and wrapped his arm around me. I didn't miss the surprised look that flashed across Delove's face. "Can you get the video back?" Cian asked, his voice a lot calmer than mine had been moments ago. My leg bounced up and down, and I stared daggers at Dobbs. He loosened his tie and looked anywhere but my face.

Delove sighed, shaking his head. "No. There's nothing there. I get the feed directly as a live stream, and nothing came through. There's nothing to get back."

I threw my hands up in the air. "Well, what now? I was there. I saw Ryzen meet with Voledetti. I saw him give him money. That's worth something, right? I could testify. Cian saw it too. We could both testify." I looked at Cian, my eyes pleading. "Right?"

He squeezed me closer and nodded.

"What exactly were *you* doing there, Blackwood? Kind of odd you just happened to show up." Dobbs narrowed his eyes at Cian, and it took all my willpower not to jump over the coffee table and strangle him.

"I was doing what you were supposed to be doing—making sure she's safe. Looks like you can't even do that, Agent Dobbs." Cian's voice was low, menacing, and Dobbs stiffened, but didn't say anything else.

"I'm sorry, Nova. I really am. But you have to continue." Delove sighed and closed his laptop. "If Ryzen met with Voledetti once, he'll do it again. And then we've got him."

"We just had him," I snapped and stood up. "I'm taking all the risks here. I'm finding all the evidence. Do your damn jobs, because I am sick of this." I stormed towards the door connecting the units.

"Where are you going?" Delove called after me.

I turned around, my hands on my hips. "To get ready for my fucking dinner with Covington and Ryzen, because you fucks can't do your jobs right, and now I'm fucking stuck in this bullshit still, you fucking fuckheads." I slammed the door behind me and stormed down the stairs.

Juliet raised her eyebrows when I walked in and scrunched up her nose. "Didn't go well?" She rushed over and wrapped her arms around me, my whole body shaking with anger. "Oh, honey, it's OK. Tell me what happened?" She squeezed me tight, and I let her hold me. There was something comforting about being around her when I was stressed. She always knew how to make me feel better.

I repeated the conversation that I'd had upstairs with Dumb and Dumber, and her mouth fell open. "Those idiots. Can't they see that you're doing everything they asked? They're the ones messing up this whole thing. Did they say why testifying wouldn't be good enough?"

"Not exactly, but I think the implication was that it wouldn't be safe for me. Or for Cian. They want a solid foundation to build their case. Not just the word of some silly woman." I rolled my eyes and plopped down into my chair.

"I hate that I can't do anything to help you. I wish I could take some of the burden off your shoulders." She scrunched up her nose, and sat on the edge of the desk. "What if I wore your wire, and met with Riddick? Pretended I wanted to rekindle the flame?" She rolled her eyes and chuckled.

"Jules, I love you, but I would never put you in danger like that." I squeezed her hand. "Riddick is… he's just as fucked up as Ryzen. It's better to stay away."

Her shoulders dropped and she sighed. "OK, but if you change your mind, tell me. You know I'll do anything for you." She patted my hand. "Let's not give up hope yet. It's almost over."

But I had a feeling that wasn't true. For some

reason, it felt like things were about to go from bad to worse.

Valik came and picked us up an hour later. After he dropped off Juliet, he moved the rearview mirror so he could see me better. "Bad day, Nova?"

I sighed and stared out the window, pausing for a moment before I answered so I wouldn't freak out again. It wasn't his fault. He seemed like a good guy—at least I hoped he was.

"Can I ask you something, Valik?" I faced forward, and he nodded. "Why are you working for Ryzen?"

His eyebrows rose and he puckered his lips. "Well, long story short, I was having a hard time, and he took me in and gave me a job. Mr. Goodacre's a good man. You're lucky you two have each other." He smiled, and I died a little bit more in that moment.

He had no idea who he was working for. How many other people worked under Ryzen and thought he was a god, a helper, a provider for the community? Ugh, it was sickening. I offered a small smile and nodded.

"Want to stop at Stan's? We could get some pastries?" Valik said in a sing-song voice.

I fought the smile that was threatening to break across my face. I had taken him to Stan's last week, and he had become obsessed. And rightfully so. He was worse than me now when it came to those little tiny puffs of heaven.

"They have Nutella today. But *only* today, Nova." He drummed his fingers on the steering wheel, and I rolled my eyes, chuckling.

"OK, but quickly because I have to get ready for dinner."

An hour later and we were pulling up to Goodacre Estates, both of us with chocolate smeared around our lips. I handed him a napkin and giggled at the face he made. "Clean up, you big moose."

I texted Ryzen that I was going to shower and be up shortly. He had been planning this dinner for days. Covington, the man Ryzen was trying to purchase the hotels from, and his wife Lorraine were coming into town specifically to see us. Ryzen thought it would look better if we had dinner at his home, instead of a fancy restaurant. A more family feeling, he had said.

Heaviness set over me as I thought back on my conversation with Delove and Dobbs. This was one of the worst days out of all of them. To be so close to being done with this all, and then having it taken away from me—it was defeating, and my shoulders slumped forward. Tears threatened to spill over, but I balled my hands into fists, refusing to succumb to the desperate feeling of defeat. Not yet. No, I would make this work.

Ryzen had sent down a dress, a white bodycon dress that covered all my tattoos and clung to my curves. I put on the necklace and watch, not wanting to miss another opportunity to get some evidence if there was a chance. My hair cascaded around my shoulders, and I sprayed a splash of perfume on my neck before taking the elevator up to the penthouse floor.

My stomach was tied in knots, and I let out a deep breath when the elevator doors dinged open. Valik stood there talking with one of Ryzen's other security guards, and he nodded in appreciation when I walked by.

Something was... different. The apartment smelled amazing, like someone had been cooking all day, but that wasn't it. There were pictures scattered around the apartment. Pictures of me and Ryzen together, some of us kissing, a lot of me laughing and looking adoringly at him. Us out to dinner or holding hands on a bench. It was creepy and made my heart beat in a way I knew wasn't healthy. Most of them were posed, of course. They had been taken months ago, even before the wedding. I wanted to throw up just thinking about it all.

"Hey, you," Ryzen called from behind me.

*It's showtime.*

I turned to face him, plastering a big smile on my face. "Hi, there." I walked over and he pulled me tight against his chest.

"You look good enough to eat." He grinned, showing off his dimples. Had this been months ago, I would have been drooling over how adorable he looked. But now, all I wanted to do was cover his face with a pillow and smother him.

"Thanks to you. The dress is lovely." I chuckled and wiggled out of his arms, doing a spin in the dress.

"I have something for you." He held up his hand and went into the other room. A moment later, he came back with a little blue box and held it out to me.

I did my best to act flustered as I pulled out a huge diamond ring, my mouth hanging open. "Ryzen, you didn't have to do that."

He grabbed the ring and slid it on my finger. "Of course I did." He leaned down and kissed my cheek. "Besides, Covington will be expecting you to be wearing an engagement ring."

"It's beautiful." I held my hand up, the light from the chandelier making the ring glisten.

"I hope that one day, when you're ready, we'll make it official. Not just for Covington and to close the deal. But because you mean that much to me." He stroked my cheek and I leaned into his hand.

*Oh, you rotten little snake.* Two could play this game though.

I bit the inside of my cheek, and lowered my eyelashes. "I would love that, Ryzen." I turned my head, rubbing my cheek against his hand. "So much."

He grinned, his eyes devilish as he pulled me to him. He lowered his head, his lips puckered just as someone cleared their throat from behind him.

"Sir, your guests are in the lobby." His security stood holding an iPad in his hands. "I'll go meet them." He turned on his heel and left.

"Ready?" Ryzen squeezed my hand, and I nodded.

A moment later, Covington walked in with Lorraine on his arm.

"There you are, you slick son of a gun." Covington stepped into the main room and Ryzen beamed as he approached.

"Great to see you, old man." Ryzen chuckled and gripped his hand tightly, then leaned in for a hug. "Lorraine, lovely as always." He kissed her on both cheeks. "Please, come in. Nova, come say hello."

I grinned from ear to ear, and did my best to act like seeing them was the most wonderful moment of the day. "So happy you guys could make it up here." Lorraine gripped me in a hug a little too tightly, and I held my hand out to Covington, who scoffed and pulled me in for a hug as well.

"You look wonderful, darlin'," Covington boomed and lifted his pants up a little higher. "What you got cooking, Ryzen? Better not be no damn city food."

We walked to the dining room where the table was set up beautifully with flowers and several wine bottles laid out. I know one thing Ryzen had planned tonight, and that was to get them drunk and agreeable. Which might work in my favor.

One of Ryzen's staff poured us each a glass of wine and then started serving the food. I should have known Ryzen wasn't actually going to cook them a meal, but rather use a personal chef. We started off easily enough, chatting about the city as we ate our salads, and then into some projects Lorraine was working on back home, then Covington talking about his plans after retirement.

They had both glanced at my ring more than once, and when dessert was being served, I decided to take the plunge and get it over with. I held up my glass of wine and cleared my throat. "I'd like to make a toast."

They all held up their glasses, looking at me expectantly.

"To the two of you wonderful souls for coming up to visit us, and to Ryzen." I tilted my head to the side and smiled. "To the man who has been so understanding, patient and caring. I couldn't have asked for a better man to spend the rest of my life with." Guilt spread through my veins as Cian's face flashed in my head, and I tried to swallow the lump of guilt in my throat. "You've changed my life in more ways than you know. Salut."

We all clinked our glasses together and took a drink. My hand trembled as I laid my glass back on the table and cleared my throat. "I just want to say how much it means to us that you're here." Ryzen gripped my hand and squeezed. I thought back to that woman in the park, to what she had said about the love of her life, and channeled her for strength in that moment. "Have you ever loved someone so much, it hurts to breathe?"

Lorraine let out a little sigh, covering her chest with her hand, while Covington wrapped his arm around her and pulled her closer to him.

"That's how I was feeling. And it scared me so much and I had to leave. The wedding… it was too much. The overpowering feeling of love for this man was just too much to handle. And I regret leaving like that and disappointing so many people. But Ryzen has been nothing but forgiving and understanding. And I just want you to know that I'm going to make this right. All of it."

Make it right by locking up this manipulative bottom feeder in prison for hopefully the rest of his life.

"I can see the love all over your faces. You hang on to each other and never let that go," Lorraine cooed and pulled Covington down for a kiss, while Ryzen leaned over, pressing his lips to mine.

Damn, were they really that gullible, or was I just that good at faking it? Either way, it didn't matter because they bought it hook, line and sinker. We spent the rest of the night drinking wine and listening to Covington tell old stories from his glory days. Some of them were actually pretty funny, and I had to remember that not everyone in this room was a monster.

Lorraine pulled me aside before she left and gave me a little pep talk. "I'm glad you came to your senses, Nova. Ryzen is a good man, and you are a good woman. You make the perfect couple. I can't wait to see the babies you two make." She chuckled and stroked her hand down my arm.

"Oh, you." I leaned into her and patted her arm, laughing as if that was the most wonderful idea in the world.

"You hang on to him, honey, and we'll see you at the wedding." She kissed my cheeks and left with Covington a moment later.

I plopped down on the couch and sighed, throwing my head back and staring at the ceiling. Putting on a show like that made me feel dirty, like a liar, and ashamed. I knew it was for a good reason, but still, it didn't make it any easier.

"You did amazing, Nova." Ryzen leaned against the door frame, his hands in his pockets. "Covington is very pleased that the wedding is back on. In fact, he wants me down in Dallas this weekend to finalize some paperwork and tour a few of the hotels. Things are moving forward again."

"That's great, Ryzen. I'm happy for you. For us." I chuckled and stood. "I've got a little headache, so I think I'll head downstairs."

I stopped in front of him, and he reached down, running his thumb over my bottom lip. "OK, sweet Nova. I have to make some calls anyway." His lips grazed mine, and for the second time tonight, I had to hold back the bile from coming up.

I said goodnight to Valik on the way out and breathed a sigh of relief when the elevator got to my floor.

Things had gone well tonight, and they were about to go even better. With Ryzen out of town all weekend, I was going to rip his apartment apart looking for what I needed. Because Delove and Dobbs had been right before. Ryzen wasn't that smart, and I knew there was something in there that was going to help me end this madness.

There had to be.

## Chapter Twelve
### Day 34

"Valik, for the tenth time, Juliet and I are having a girls' night, and you don't need to hang out in the hallway all night." I poked my head through the crack of Ryzen's front door. Valik stood with his arms crossed, giving me an all-too-familiar look. "We're just going to get drunk and watch chick flicks on Ryzen's eighty-inch TV."

I tapped my foot and opened the door a little more. He glanced over my shoulder at Juliet, who was busy pulling wine bottles out of her grocery bag and lining them up on the kitchen counter.

"Yeah, Valik. I'm sick of men and need to vent." Juliet walked over with a glass of wine and stood with her hand on her hip. "So unless you want to stick around and hear me complain about Jimmy Finnigan"—she took a sip and held up her thumb and pointer finger in the shape of a small "c"—"who really overestimated the size of his…"

"OK," Valik huffed, holding his hands up in front of him. "I don't need to hear any more. Go. Vent. Be magical unicorns for all I care. Just do it safely." He checked his watch. "I'll check on you in a little bit."

I rolled my eyes and grinned. "OK, Dad."

"Yeah, thanks, Daddy." Juliet winked at him, and his cheeks turned a shade of red.

We chuckled as he jammed the down button on the elevator panel and got on without turning to look at us again.

"I think you scared him, Jules." I shut the door and walked over to the kitchen, grabbing a glass of wine.

"Then I did my job." She sat on the barstool and swiveled around in a circle as she sipped.

We were going to tear this apartment apart if we had to. Ryzen had made a mistake somewhere, and I was going to find it. "Ready?" I turned to Juliet and raised my eyebrows as she put on a pair of plastic gloves, snapping the rubber at the bottom against her wrist.

"What?" She shrugged and tossed me a pair. "Just covering our bases."

I scrunched up my nose and nodded. She was probably right.

We started in the kitchen, pulling out every drawer and opening every cupboard. I took pictures of everything that might be of help to the FBI, from phone bills, to handwritten notes on Post-it notes. No nook or cranny was left unchecked.

We went room to room, searching all the obvious spots, then the not-so-obvious ones like under the carpets, behind his paintings and under the cushions of the couch. We even unzipped the pillows and checked the stuffing in case he had anything hidden in there. But we weren't finding anything that looked overly suspicious. I had been counting on finding the journal with the key back in its original spot, but it wasn't. Maybe it had been just dumb luck the first time I had found it. But we searched his office from top to bottom, and it was nowhere to be found.

We were on a mission, and so far, we were failing at it. We took a quick break and ordered some pizza, devouring the slices and chugging wine. Juliet caught me up on her conversation with the claims specialist. It was taking longer than usual to process our claim, and Juliet said the agent had sounded nervous over the phone. It just confirmed what I already knew but hadn't been willing to accept—that the FBI was in fact interfering. A part of me had hoped they had been bluffing, trying to scare me shitless so that I would help them. But oh, I'd been wrong. So, so wrong.

A little while later Juliet called out to me from the floor of Ryzen's closet. She had a box opened in front of her, pictures spread out. "Come look at these."

I sat down next to her, my heart fluttering in my chest when I realized I was looking at pictures of a young Ryzen and Cian together. They were wearing football uniforms in some of them, so this must have been back in high school. Photos of them wearing matching Halloween costumes, drinking with friends at a bar. Just hundreds of pictures. So odd that Ryzen would keep these after all these years, especially after what he had done to Cian.

There was a woman in a lot of the photos, and I picked up one where the three of them were huddled together around a miniature replica of the Chicago skyline.

"That's Gretchen." My hand trembled slightly as I grabbed another photo. "Cian's ex-fiancée." Something in the photo caught my attention and I peered at it closer, unable to tell if I was looking at what I thought I was. "Hand me the other photos of her."

Juliet scanned the floor, handing me a few pictures, and an unsettling feeling ate away at my stomach. "I'll be right back." I went to Ryzen's office and used the letter-opener to jimmy the drawer open. The black box was still inside, and I brought it over to Jules.

"Ugh." She cringed when she saw the hair.

"I know, so damn weird. But look. It's the same necklace, right?"

"Oh, shit, it is." She stared from the photo to the necklace and then back again. "Why would Ryzen have this with, I'm assuming, a piece of *her* hair?"

"I have no idea, but I'll take pictures of it just in case."

We stayed up until three in the morning looking for evidence. A feeling of hopelessness had settled inside of me, even though I tried hard to fight it. I had taken a ton of photographs of the inside of Ryzen's apartment. Something, anything, had to be a lead… the beginning of a trail. I just hoped it was good enough.

*****

Day 35

Valik kept his word and didn't hover around us, although he was texting pretty regularly to check that we were OK. I knew he was just doing his job, so I couldn't hold it against him.

Cian said he was having a family dinner at our apartment and wanted Juliet and I to come. Every time he said "our" apartment, a jolt of happiness spun through me. When this was all over, and I was free from the chains of the FBI, maybe we would actually have a shot. Maybe with Ryzen gone, the FBI not meddling, maybe, just maybe, we could start a life together.

I held onto that thought as we got ready to walk the four blocks over to the building. I told Valik that we were going out to the movies and dinner and not to bother us, and surprisingly, he didn't put up a fight this time.

When we walked inside the apartment, Juliet whistled, nodding her head. "Very nice, you guys."

My cheeks heated as Cian walked over and tugged me to him. "I missed you," he murmured. His lips grazed mine and what started out as a kiss hello quickly turned into me gripping his shirt in my hands while he squeezed my ass.

"Get a room, you two." Eros chuckled and popped the cork from a wine bottle.

I pulled back, breathless, and Cian chuckled. "I think I'm ready for dessert first." His eyes pierced mine, and I sighed. I didn't know how he did that. Just one kiss, a few little words, and I was beyond flustered.

"Nova, Juliet!" Thora squeaked from behind Cian. "Come on, let me show you what we're making." She grabbed our hands and dragged us to the kitchen.

Orin pulled a huge pot from the oven, and we all let out a collective moan as the heavenly smell of pot roast enveloped the kitchen. "I made mashed potatoes and baby carrots too. They are to die for. The trick is to put a little bit of brown sugar on them while they're roasting," Orin said in one breath, and we all stared at him. He was usually the quiet, grumpy one, but apparently not when he was cooking.

"Smells great, can't wait to eat." I chuckled as Cian wrapped his arms around me from behind.

"I can't wait to eat *you* later," he whispered in my ear, and I bit my bottom lip.

"OK, OK." Thora held up her hands. "You guys are adorable and everything, but I do not want to see my brother getting fresh with his girlfriend right before dinner." The whole room laughed, and my cheeks warmed.

Girlfriend. My smile stretched from ear to ear as Cian pulled out my chair and I sat down. Orin and Eros brought the food to the table, and we were all salivating by the time he served each of us.

"Wow, Orin. If you ever decide to give up chasing bounties, then I think you have a future in cooking." I chuckled.

"How did you become a bounty hunter anyways?" Juliet asked and shoved a huge piece of roast in her mouth.

He leaned forward and put his elbows on his table. "Well, it's not as glamorous as you might think. We"—he nodded at Eros—"used to get ourselves into a bit of trouble back in the day. Nothing crazy, but then I met Ralph, my mentor, and he gave me a job, and as it turns out, I'm good at catching the bad guys. We can't all be a real estate genius like Cian over here."

"I'm hardly a genius." Cian laughed, his eyes never leaving mine. "Just made some smart moves after all that shit went down. Connected with the right investors, the right developers, was smart with my choices. And that's it."

I elbowed him in the side. "Oh, yeah, sounds so easy."

Juliet took a bite of a baby carrot and moaned. Eros put some of his carrots on her plate and leaned closer to her. "Here, eat up, girl. I could listen to you all night." He winked.

"Oh, stop, you big flirt." She rolled her eyes, but I could tell she liked the attention. I couldn't blame her.

"Hey, what do you expect? I am named after the god of love." He chuckled.

I didn't know why it had never clicked before. Eros. Thora. Orin. "Wait," I said. "So Thora, is that supposed to be reminiscent of Thor?" I raised my eyebrow.

Thora beamed and nodded. "Our mom was obsessed with mythology and anything mystical. Always talking about gods and goddesses, crystals and harmony. She's the reason I am the way I am, I suppose." Her voice trailed off, a hint of sadness in it, and the room got quiet for a moment.

Cian held up his glass of wine. "To Naomi, for giving me the best sister and brothers I could ask for." We all held up our glasses. "And to that hillbilly hospital down in Texas that typed Orin on the birth certificate instead of Odin."

Orin glared at Cian and lowered his glass, while the rest of us broke out in uncontrollable laughter.

We spent the next few hours like that, sitting at the table telling stories and laughing. It felt good to be around people who were caring and gave their love so easily to each other. Eros was too excited to know how "two hotties," as he liked to call us, had started a "sex store," to which we both rolled our eyes and huffed out, "Sexual wellness store!" They got a kick out of our design disasters, and Juliet loved to tell the story of me demonstrating to the manufacturer how their little adjustment to the anal beads ruined the whole product. Not demonstrating on myself, but on a doll, I explained when everyone's mouths hung open.

Every time I looked up, Cian's eyes were on me, a smile spread across his gorgeous face. His eyes were lit up with happiness, and I thought my heart might burst out of my chest. He was always touching me—a hand rubbing my back, a soft caress to my cheek, a kiss to the forehead, whispering "I love you" into my ear. It was one of the greatest nights that I had had in a while.

Eros lit up three cigars, handing one each to Cian and Orin. I went into a sneezing fit, which seemed to amuse everyone at the table.

"I'm sorry, Nova, I'll put it out." Cian stabbed the cigar out and gave a pointed look to his brothers.

"Oh, no, no, no, it's fine. My father used to smoke them all the time, and for some reason, it just always tickled my nose. Regular cigarettes don't do it. Just some weird thing about me." I chuckled.

"I hate to break it to you, but that's not the only weird thing about you, Nova." Eros cackled at his own joke and moved to put out his cigar, but I stopped him.

"OK, God of Love, real funny. Smoke it, I'll go get some fresh air on the patio." I held my hand out to Cian. "Wanna come?" I grinned at the devilish look on his face.

When it was time to leave, I didn't want to go. It felt like I belonged in this house with Cian and this family. Not out there up in a penthouse belonging to a man I loathed and despised, who was hell-bent on ruining my life.

Things became clearer in that moment as we

walked the four blocks home, Eros trailing behind us in the distance. I would do anything to bring Ryzen down and get back to normal. So long as Cian was a part of that with me.

*****

I got the best news when I got home that night. Not only was Grams out of the hospital, but Ryzen was going to be gone the rest of the week. Things were going so well with Covington, all thanks to my performance at dinner, that Covington had invited him to stay even longer. Ryzen wasn't sure when he would be back, but it wouldn't be sooner than Friday.

Which meant one thing. I had at least five days of freedom, and I was going to take advantage of every single minute of him being gone.

Over the next few days, we fell into a nice and easy pattern. Juliet and I went to the office for a few hours a day where we tried to handle as many emails and phone calls as we could while Owen worked on our social media. We didn't need to actually be in the office to do any of the work, but it was important to build back up a sense of normalcy, especially for Owen. He could have walked away at any time, but he hadn't.

Valik would chauffeur us all home and sit around outside my door for a bit until I changed into gym clothes and told him I was going to work out, and no, he didn't need to follow me. I would go for a run, which I fucking hated to do, and my prize was Cian waiting for me four blocks away where we spent the next few hours together, mostly in a state of blissful orgasms.

But it was more than just sex now. We spent hours talking about everything and learning all we could about each other. We talked about our childhoods, me telling him how my sister Grace would terrorize me, and him explaining a little bit more about how he grew up. It pained me to hear about his abusive father, and how his mother did nothing to help him, to help any of them. How people could be so cold-hearted, I could never understand. I learned more about the young Cian, the sports fanatic who loved playing football, who turned into a real estate junkie after starting college. And even though Ryzen had been a huge part of his life during that time, we both refrained from mentioning him. He was the dark shadow hanging over our heads, and all I wanted to do was forget about him.

The night before Ryzen was to come home I had a special night planned with Cian. I had sent Valik on a wild goose chase around the city running errands for me, and by the time he got back, he was more than willing to take a hike because he was sick of picking up "my girly shit."

I laid out the lingerie set on my bed, tapping my lip as I hummed. Sexy outfit. Check. Trench coat. Check. Sex drive of a virgin freshman in college about to fuck the quarterback. Check. I held the roses up to my nose and sniffed for the hundredth time. Cian had sent over a bouquet earlier in the day, and my heart had sung for the rest of the afternoon.

My phone dinged and I smiled as 'Pizza Delivery' flashed across the screen, my secret name for Cian.

*Pizza Delivery: Change of plans, little mouse. Meet me at 723 Donahue at seven. Can't wait to see you.*

I scrunched up my nose at the nickname slip and shrugged. Maybe he was going to surprise me with something. Excitement raced through me as I changed into my lingerie and trench coat and checked my hair for the millionth time.

I got a cab and we took off, getting to the location just before seven. The driver left me at the end of a long driveway, and I had to double-check the address on my phone and the mailbox. It was the right place, but something seemed off. The house was pitch black, and there were no cars in sight. Uneasiness settled in my stomach and I hesitated to walk up the path. It was just paranoia. It had to be. Cian was probably inside waiting to surprise me, and I was standing out here in slutty lingerie being an idiot.

But there was one thing I had learned since this whole ordeal had started months ago: I needed to trust my gut more. And right now my gut was screaming, *Bitch, get the fuck out of here.*

I moved to the side of the driveway, out of sight from anyone who might be inside peeking out the windows. Thora picked up on the second ring.

"Hi, love, what's up?" The sound of plates clinking in the background and light music made me realize she was probably out.

"Hey, sorry to bother you. Um, this is going to sound crazy, but... I'm supposed to meet Cian for a date."

"Uh-huh. OK, Nova, I'm just gonna stop you right there. I love you and I love him, but I don't think I can give you any kind of advice that you're probably looking for. That sounds like a Juliet job to me." She chuckled.

"No, the thing is he texted me and changed our

meet-up spot. And, well, I just got here, and the house looks empty. Um… I don't know, I'm probably being stupid and he's inside waiting for me." I forced out a laugh.

"What's the address?" Her tone turned serious.

"723 Donahue," I whispered.

"Hold on." Her side of the line went silent, and I paced in the darkness, sweat forming on my forehead. "Cian's not answering and that property is listed for sale. I don't like the sound of this. Orin is out chasing his bounty, but let me see if I can get Eros to run over. Do you have a gun?"

Did I have a gun? She said it so casually, as if I should obviously have one with me. "No." My voice was nothing but a whisper as a sense of dread washed over me.

"OK, it's fine. Better to be safe than sorry. Hold tight, and I'll send Eros. Just wait outside, OK? Don't go in there, because we can't be sure what's going on."

"OK. I'll wait here for Eros." I hung up and wiped my forehead. This was stupid. I was getting worked up over nothing, and now I was probably going to ruin Cian's surprise and Eros's night.

I waited in the bushes. Five minutes passed, then ten. I tried dialing Thora again, but she didn't pick up this time. Great, she'd probably realized that I was being an idiot. After a few more minutes and nobody showing up, I decided that either I was being really stupid, or if something was wrong and Cian was inside, I had just wasted twenty minutes sitting out here for nothing.

My phone dinged with a text. It was from Cian.

*Pizza Delivery: Don't keep me waiting, my love.*

Fuck it. I was going in.

I straightened my back and marched up to the house, mace in hand. The light outside had been turned on in the time I had been hiding, which only confirmed that someone was inside, and it was probably just Cian. I knocked once, twice, and when nobody answered I tried the door handle and it swung open with a creak.

"Cian?" I called out.

It was quiet. Too quiet. I flipped the nozzle on my mace and held it out in front of me. *Where are you, you little sneak?*

"Cian?" Still no answer. I stepped inside and saw a dim light down the hall. I called out his name a third time, but still nothing. My heart was beating so fast, I thought it might explode out of my chest. What the fuck could be going on? I held my mace up, ready to spray anyone who stepped out, and walked as quietly as I could toward the light.

*You can do this.* The hair on the back of my neck stood, and I hesitated when I got to the door. Did I really want to push this door open and see what was on the other side? But what if Cian was hurt? Or what if he was laid out naked on a plush velvet throw waiting for me?

I swung the door open and stepped in, ready to pepper-spray the fuck out of anyone who was there. It took a moment for my eyes to adjust from the darkness to the dim lighting, but once they did, I had to swallow the scream that threatened to come up.

Cian was tied to a chair in the middle of a nearly bare living room. Three men stood around him, one pointing a gun at his head. He struggled in his restraints, and when he saw me, his eyes widened. "Nova, run!"

But there was nowhere to run. I knew they could

catch me, so I held my hands up in front of me to show that I wasn't a threat, and stepped forward.

"Don't hurt him," I whispered, taking another step forward.

A man stepped forward from the shadows. Someone I had hoped I would never have to see face to face.

Kaviathin Voledetti.

"Miss La Roux, nice to finally meet you in person." He came forward and stopped in front of me. His gaze traveled up and down my body, and I wished I hadn't worn something so provocative outside. "Stunning." His voice was low. "I see why Mr. Blackwood is so taken with you. Come." He held out his hand to me.

I had no choice. What was I going to do? Run, fight? That wasn't going to help me, and that definitely wasn't going to help Cian. No, I needed to keep calm so we both got out of this alive. I placed my hand in Kaviathin's and he walked us over to two metal folding chairs on the other side of the room. He waved his hand at the chair and nodded. "Please, sit."

"If you fucking touch her, I will kill you with my bare hands," Cian growled, jerking roughly to the point I thought he might actually be able to get loose. But the man holding the gun cocked it and pressed it to his temple. Cian stopped struggling, his chest heaving.

Kaviathin chuckled and sat down across from me. He pulled out a pack of cigarettes and handed me one, which I took. I wasn't a smoker, but if I was about to die, then now would be the time to become one. He leaned close and lit my cigarette, then his, blowing smoke up in the air. "Miss La Roux, I'm sure you're well aware of who I am and what I do."

It wasn't a question, more of a statement, and so I nodded.

"Good." He took a long drag, smoke billowing around us. "Then why have you inserted yourself into my business?"

Oh, fuck. Oh, fuck. Did he know about the FBI? That had to be it. I took a drag from my cigarette, trying to figure out how to answer that question. "What do you mean?"

"You have accused me of kidnapping you, have you not?" he purred. His nonchalant tone wasn't to be taken lightly, I knew that. Although he was being polite, as far as "*I have a gun on your man and will kill him*" went, there was a hint of anger in his voice that I didn't miss.

"But"—I narrowed my eyes at him—"you *did* try to kidnap me."

"Is that so?" He leaned back and watched me for a moment, his expression unreadable. What the hell was he getting at?

"You're going to pay for this, Kaviathin." Cian jerked in his restraints.

"Shut him up."

The man with the gun hit Cian in the back of his head with the butt of his gun, and Cian's head lowered. I gasped, my whole body shaking.

"Much better." Kaviathin smiled and turned his attention back to me. "Ryzen has assured me that he has Covington under control, as well as you." He glanced at Cian, and then back to me. "But I can see that is not exactly the case. Imagine my surprise when I have you followed, and I find that you are sleeping with Ryzen's enemy."

I bounced my leg up and down, the movement

not going unnoticed by Kaviathin. What was I supposed to say to him? The truth? I didn't know how much he knew about the real situation, so I puffed on my cigarette.

"Quite the web of lies you find yourself in, Miss La Roux. Quite fascinating." He tossed his cigarette on the floor and smashed it with the tip of his shoe. "My father always had a soft spot for Ryzen. I never understood why. The man is a gutter rat. But I'm in charge of this family now, and I am not my father." He leaned forward and took the cigarette out of my hand, my fingers trembling, and dropped it on the floor. He squeezed my hand. "Everyone is disposable, Miss La Roux."

Well, that didn't help me feel any fucking better in that moment. Was he going to kill us both now? He couldn't. It couldn't end like this. Not after everything.

He snapped his head around and looked over my shoulder, and I turned as I heard a mousy voice mouthing off.

Thora.

Fuck.

One of Kaviathin's men, an older-looking guy, was dragging her through the door by her arm. "Look what I found outside snooping."

"Get off me, asshole. You're hurting my arm." She kicked his shin, and he yanked her even harder.

Kaviathin's face darkened and he stood, barking something in a different language—Italian, I thought. The older man froze, letting go of Thora. She rubbed her arm and glared at him. "You're lucky you have a gun, otherwise I would kick your ass, you fuck."

Kaviathin walked over and towered over the

older man. "What have I told you about this?" he growled and the man's face turned ashen. "You do not place your hands on a woman like that. Ever."

"But your father always said—" The man stopped talking when Kaviathin reached up and gripped his chin.

"I am not my father, Gustavo. It'll serve you well to remember that." He held his hand out to his side and one of his men walked over and handed him a gun. He pressed it against Gustavo's forehead. "Apologize."

The man's eyes widened, and he sputtered. Everyone in the room held their breath as Gustavo's eyes darted to Thora and back to Kaviathin.

"I'm sorry, sir," he mumbled.

"Not to me, you imbecile," Kaviathin growled.

"I'm sorry!" Gustavo was visibly sweating, and I didn't want to keep looking at him, but I couldn't tear my eyes away.

Kaviathin turned to Thora. "Do you accept?"

Now it was her turn to widen her eyes. She nodded her head fast, and Kaviathin lowered the gun and handed it back to the other guard. "Get out of my sight, Gustavo."

Gustavo pressed his back against the wall and side-stepped until he reached the door and hurried through it.

Kaviathin snapped his fingers at the other man, who rushed over. He whispered something to him, and the man followed after Gustavo. I didn't think I wanted to know what was going to happen to him, but whatever it was, he probably deserved it. Kaviathin pointed at a chair in the corner and nodded at Thora. "Sit, and don't move. Understand?"

She glared at him, but nodded, doing as he said. He walked back over and sat down in front of me, gripping my hands in his again. I desperately wanted to yank them away, but after what I had just seen, I knew it wasn't going to do me any favors.

*Just keep calm. Don't admit to anything, and maybe we'll all walk out of here alive.*

"I'll get straight to the point, Miss La Roux. I'm growing tired of Ryzen's schemes and incompetence. This deal he's working on with Covington needs to take place. And you are the glue apparently holding everything together. So you need to do your part to ensure that we're all successful." He glanced at Cian, then back to me. "And I see now that you may require a different kind of motivation than I had originally planned."

What the fuck was that supposed to mean? The knot in my stomach grew, and I exhaled slowly.

Kaviathin walked over to Cian and slapped him, and my hand went to my throat. Cian groaned, then opened his eyes, looking between me and Thora. His face twisted with anger, and he started thrashing again. I couldn't help it when my eyes watered, not because I was terrified of dying, but because I didn't know what Kaviathin was getting ready to do to him.

Kaviathin pulled out a gun, and I stood. "No!" I yelled.

"Sit down, Miss La Roux." His voice was laced with irritation.

I sat down on the edge of the chair, not taking my eyes off Cian. *It's OK,* I said with my eyes. *We're OK.* His chest heaved as he watched me, and he nodded slightly.

Kaviathin placed the gun against Cian's shoulder

and looked me dead in my eyes. "You make sure Ryzen does his part. Or your lover here will die. Do you understand?" His voice was low, but clear, and I didn't doubt for one second that he was lying.

"Yes, yes," I whispered and nodded. "I understand."

He smiled in a way that was anything but reassuring and pulled the trigger, shooting Cian in the shoulder.

Cian howled in agony, blood splattering around him, and I screamed. Thora yelled and tried to get up, but the man pushed her back down into the chair.

"Do not underestimate me, Miss La Roux." Kaviathin handed the gun to his associate and whistled, twirling his finger in the air. They marched towards the door, and Kaviathin turned around one last time as I ran towards Cian. "Let's keep this rendezvous between us, shall we?" He glanced at Thora, then walked through the door.

"Cian, Cian!" I tugged on the ropes, desperate to untie them. Thora rushed over and placed her jacket on the wound. "Cian, it's OK. We're going to get help."

He groaned. "Nova, are you OK?"

"You're OK, Cian. I'm not going to let anything happen to you."

"Apply pressure, Nova. We need to get him out of here now." Thora pulled out her phone and punched in a number.

I couldn't understand a word she was saying. It was like I had tunnel vision, and all I saw was blood and the gaping wound in his shoulder.

He couldn't die.

I couldn't let him die.

DANI ANTOINETTE

## Not now.

## Chapter Thirteen

I gripped the cup of tea in my hands, willing them to stop shaking. But they wouldn't. Dried blood stained my coat, the sound of Cian moaning in pain etched in my memory forever. Thora sat next to me and placed her hand on my forearm.

"He's going to be OK, Nova. Don't worry. He's tough."

Yeah, he was tough, but that didn't make me worry any less. The events of the last few hours replayed over and over again in my mind, until the throbbing in my head became unbearable. If only there had been some way to avoid this. But I knew there was nothing I could have done differently. If Kaviathin had wanted to find us, threaten us, then he would have found a way, no matter what.

We were in a small house not far from downtown. It had the same look and feel as the house Cian had kept us in after saving us at the wedding. Had that only been six weeks ago? It seemed like a lifetime had passed since then. We had tried to take him to the hospital, but he was adamant about not going.

*"No hospitals. No cops. Thora, call Henrick." He had groaned as I put pressure on his wound.*

We had raced here, Eros and a man with a

medical bag already waiting for us. They had been in the room for over an hour. Every so often Cian would yell out, and I had to cover my ears and squeeze my eyes shut at the agony in his voice.

Eros walked into the kitchen, Henrick right behind him. Thora and I both stood, gripping each other's hands.

"He's stable. The bullet went through and through without causing any major damage. I've stitched him up." Henrick smiled slightly. "He'll make a full recovery."

My hand flew to my chest, the pressure lessening as the news sank in. Thank fucking God. Thora squeezed my hand, her face lighting up.

"Told you," she whispered.

Henrick reached into his bag and pulled out a bottle of pills. "Give him two pills every four hours for the pain. Keep the wound clean and dry and keep an eye out for an infection." He handed the bottle to Eros and shook his hand. "Call me, day or night. I'll be here."

Eros walked Henrick out and came back a moment later.

"Why did his medical bag have a pawprint on it?" I quirked my eyebrow.

"He's a vet." Eros chuckled at the look on my face. "Well, now he is. But when I knew him, he was a combat medic in the army."

I nodded, nibbling on my bottom lip. "Can I see Cian?"

He nodded and rubbed his hands over his face. "He's resting, so try not to wake him."

I walked down the hall and peeked inside the room. Cian lay on the bed, his eyes closed. He looked so vulnerable in that moment, and my heart broke. Things could have ended up a lot worse than they had. I sat in the chair next to his bed, watching his chest like a hawk as he breathed. There was a huge bandage on his shoulder and dark marks on his face where Kaviathin's men had beaten him. I moved his hair out of his eyes and pressed my forehead against his for a moment.

Something inside of me was awakening. Not fear, not helplessness, and not even sadness. It was full-on fury mixed with a splash of vengeance. Kaviathin was going to pay for this. If I could make him suffer the same way we were, then I would. He was going down, and if that meant getting to him through Ryzen, then even better. I was going to make him regret his choices tonight. Some way, somehow.

Rage fantasies flashed in my head, and I dozed off in the chair next to Cian's bed thinking of all the ways I was going to torture Kaviathin when the day ever came. And Ryzen. Maybe tie them up together and unleash a fury of hornets. Or push them off a bridge. Either would work.

I awoke sometime later to fingers being dragged through my hair. I sat up with a gasp, and Cian chuckled. "Sorry to wake you, little star."

"You're awake!" I leaned over the bed and squeezed him as hard as I could.

"Nova, my shoulder," he wheezed.

"Oh, fuck." I pulled back. "I'm so sorry, Cian." I caressed the side of his face, and he turned into my palm. "I was so scared. I thought you were going to die." Tears welled up in my eyes, and I sniffled, trying to fight them off.

"It's not going to be that easy to get rid of me." He

grinned and tried to sit up. He let out a small groan, his hand flying to his shoulder where the bandage was.

I helped him sit up—not that I could actually do much since he was the size of a house compared to me, but I did my best. When he was fully seated, he wrapped his hand around the back of my neck and tugged me to him. "Get over here," he coaxed, and I climbed into the bed with him. His lips crushed into mine, his tongue velvety soft as it tangled with mine. I pushed away gently, my chest heaving as I searched for oxygen.

"OK, cowboy, turn it down a notch. You *were* just shot." I smiled and laid my hand against his chest.

His face darkened. "I'm going to kill that son of a bitch."

"Why didn't you want to go to the hospital, call the cops?"

His face twisted in anger, and I rubbed my hand over his heart. "We can't trust the police, Nova. The hospital would have called them. It's better this way. You saw all those reports Delove had. Kaviathin won't let anyone get away with trying to take him down the legal way." He flinched in pain, patting his shoulder. "He could have killed us all if he had wanted to. He just wanted to instill fear." He looked at me and lowered his lashes. "If anything had happened to you..." He trailed off.

"Don't think like that." I pressed my lips to his cheek.

"I am nothing without you, Nova."

My heart fluttered in my chest at his words. It was hard to grasp the number of emotions running through my body at that moment—fear that I was going to lose him, love for not. There was also an undertone of anger threatening to rise up to the top and spill over. "I'm going to fix this. All of it. They are going to pay. I won't let anything happen to you. I am nothing without you, Cian." I whispered.

He chuckled and pressed his forehead against mine. "My strong warrior woman. I'm the one who's supposed to protect you." His lips met mine again, a desperation in his kiss that I was all too familiar with. The need to be consumed by him was overpowering, but now was not the time.

"Get some more sleep, OK? We'll talk when you wake up." I tried to get out of bed, but he gripped me to him, and I shook my head, laughing.

"Stay. You belong here, right next to me." He tilted his head back against the headboard and shut his eyes.

After a while his breathing slowed down, his chest rising and falling in an even rhythm. I lifted his arm from around my shoulders gently and scooted down the bed as quietly as I could. He looked peaceful now, probably because the painkillers had finally kicked in. I shut the door gently behind me and checked my watch. It was after midnight, but it felt like days had passed, not just hours.

I found Thora in the living room lying down on the floor, a crystal on her forehead with soft music playing. I chuckled; I should have known.

"How is he?" she whispered, not opening her eyes.

Damn, she was good.

"Good. Better. He's sleeping again." I lay down next to her and she pulled a crystal out of her pocket, handing it to me. I placed it on my forehead and shut my eyes. Before I had met Thora, I would have never imagined I would be the meditating type, but there was really something to it. Most people were afraid to look at themselves, like really look deep inside. And that was what meditation helped you do—check in with your body to see how you were feeling and acknowledge all those thoughts, the good, the bad, and the wickedly ugly.

We lay there for some time, not saying anything as the music played. At some point in between meditating and actually falling asleep, the music stopped, and she groaned.

"This app is driving me crazy." She chuckled. "My friend had the right idea, but not the best execution apparently."

"Can I ask you something?" I turned on my side and faced her. There had been something nagging at me, and I needed to ask someone who could possibly give me answers.

"Go for it."

"I haven't told Cian yet, because I wasn't sure how he was going to respond. But when I was searching in Ryzen's apartment, I found a lot of pictures of him, Cian and Gretchen in a box. Like hundreds of photos."

"Hm, interesting." She sat up and tapped her fingers together.

"Well, that's not even the weird part. The weird part was I found her angel necklace in Ryzen's desk, along with a chunk of braided hair. I'm pretty sure it's hers. It has to be."

"What a fucking creep." Her face twisted in disgust. "I don't know why he would have any of that… the photos, the necklace, and especially the hair."

She scrunched up her nose. "Especially not after what happened."

"Yeah, that's kinda what I wanted to ask you about. I don't want to ask Cian because I don't want to upset him. I mean he told me bits and pieces, but not exact details."

She sighed and stared up at the ceiling. "They were high school sweethearts, he tell you that? She was always around, and I loved her like a sister. I was just as shocked as everyone else when Cian found her and Ryzen in bed together the night before their wedding. We were all staying downtown at the Grand Hotel. Gretchen was screaming down the hallway and when we got there, we found Cian and Ryzen in a full-blown fight. I had never seen him so enraged. I was terrified. It took five of the hotel security guards to pull him off of Ryzen.

"Soon after that, Ryzen accused him of stealing money from their company. He told everyone, even got his dirty cop friends involved. It was a nightmare." She shook her head.

God, the anger and betrayal Cian must have gone through. It was amazing that he hadn't actually killed Ryzen.

"We found out that Ryzen was working with the Voledetti family, but not until much later. After it was all too late. Ryzen told all their investors not to trust Cian, that he was a thief who took after his drunk of a father. Cian was ruined. Nobody would work with him —no investors, no developers, no agents. It took him six years to rebuild his reputation. He found a silent investor who wanted to remain anonymous and gave him just enough for his first property. And he built his empire up from there, one property at a time. Because that's just the way Cian is. He's a survivor. Unstoppable."

I nodded, taking all the information in. Ryzen was a bigger piece of shit than I had realized.

"I don't know what happened to Gretchen." She scrunched up her nose. "We never talked about her again. I tried asking soon after the fight, but Cian refused and said to never mention her name again." She stood and stretched her arms over her head. "But this thing with the necklace, and her hair... I would talk to Cian about it. He needs to know."

I clutched the crystal in my hand, the sharp edges digging into my palm. She was right. I would talk to him about it. Uneasiness swept through me, but I shook it off. I ended up back in bed with Cian, unable to keep my eyes open any longer.

The next time I opened my eyes, Cian wasn't next to me, but standing and staring out the window.

"Hey, how are you feeling?" I mumbled and rubbed my eyes. The clock on the nightstand flashed seven a.m. and I groaned. I would have to go home soon. Valik would be texting me within the next few hours to check up on me, and the last thing I needed was him finding out I wasn't at home where I'd told him I would be.

"I'll survive." Cian ran his fingers through his hair, then clenched his fist. "I should have been more careful." He turned to face me. "I'm sorry I didn't protect you last night, Nova. It won't happen again."

"Cian," I scoffed and walked over to him. "Don't you dare blame yourself for something that was out of your control." He wrapped his arm around me and tugged me close to him. "How did they get you to that house?"

His back stiffened, and I rubbed my hand up and down, gently gliding over his scars. "I was in the parking garage in our building and a van pulled up. Before I had time to react, four men jumped out and tackled me. I tried to fight them off, but there were too many of them. They must have knocked me out, because the next thing I know I was tied up in the chair and you were walking in the door." He slammed his hand against the wall. "I was fucking careless, and I'm so sorry."

"It was four against one, Cian. You couldn't have done anything." I cradled his face in my palms. "I'm just glad that you're alive. That we all are." I planted a kiss on his lips. "What do you think Kaviathin meant when he said I *accused* him of kidnapping? Did you hear the way he said it? It was… strange."

"I haven't stopped thinking about that either. Something is off about that." Cian clenched his fists, letting out a deep breath.

I shrugged, trying to shake off the feeling of dread. "They will get what's coming to them."

"I will never let anything bad happen to you, Nova. You are such a remarkable woman, caring, strong, and I won't let them dim your light. I will always take care of you." He brushed his lips against my forehead, and my whole body warmed.

"Come on, you need to rest." Cian let me drag him to the bed and we lay down. His hands roamed over my body, and I slapped them away. "I said rest, not sex."

He chuckled, his breath warm against my cheek. "Something tells me that I would heal a lot faster if I was buried deep inside of you." His voice was husky, and I bit my lip.

Damn, he was good at changing the subject. But I knew sex was the last thing he needed right now. Besides, I had to get something off of my chest. I sighed and faced him. "I need to tell you something."

His face turned serious. "You can tell me anything, Nova."

"OK, it might not be important, but... when I was searching through Ryzen's things I found a lot of pictures of you, him, and Gretchen in a box in his room."

Cian quirked his eyebrow up and nodded.

"That angel pendant, the one you thought looked familiar? It was hers. I saw it in hundreds of photos. And I'm assuming the hair was also hers."

He narrowed his eyes, rubbing this thumb across his bottom lip. "You're right. I couldn't place it before, but now that you've said it, she did wear that all the time. Her grandmother gave her that necklace when her grandfather died."

"I'm sorry if this upsets you, I just thought that you should know. Plus, it's, um, super fucking creepy of Ryzen to have those things."

"Why would I be upset?" He tilted his head to the side, staring at me.

"Well, I mean, it's Gretchen, and I don't want to open old wounds." It wasn't like I was jealous. Not at all. I just didn't want to unlock a door that he had sealed shut years ago. Well, that I had hoped was sealed.

"Nova." He tugged my head back. "That was almost a decade ago. I don't care about her. I haven't in a really long time." His eyes searched mine, and a wave of relief washed over me.

"But Ryzen and your revenge? I thought that…"

He shook his head, his nostrils flaring. "Goodacre tried to ruin me. The revenge I was after had nothing to do with Gretchen, not after time went by, and everything to do with him being a sadistic fuck. Believe me when I tell you that I haven't thought of Gretchen in a long time. She tried to talk to me, to beg for forgiveness, but it was too late. The last I heard she had moved to France. And that was it. End of story." His mouth was on mine, warm and feverish. I moaned as he bit my lip, his hand moving down my back to grip my ass. "You are the only woman I care about. Now, and forever."

God, why did he have to say things like that, things that would make me melt instantly? His words settled deep into my soul, and I didn't know how I'd ever thought of him as the bad guy. The villain. I had a lot of making up to do. I reached up and clutched him to me.

"Fuck, my shoulder," he hissed and I leaned away from him.

"I'm sorry." I covered my mouth to hide my laugh. "You can't say things like that and not expect me to want to tackle you."

His eyes turned dark, a grin spreading across his face. "Tackle me, then. Just not on the left side."

I shook my head. "No, no. I have to get going soon before Valik realizes I'm not home. Get some rest before I tell Eros on you."

"Tattletale." He winked and sprawled in the bed.

Damn, he looked good, even with a bandage wrapped around his shoulder. His muscles flexed and he rested his hand over his abs. I knew what he was doing though. Trying to entice me, make me weak and make me give in to him. He looked inviting, like I should just crawl into his lap and stay like that the rest of the day. But I knew I couldn't.

*****

I nibbled on a piece of steak, struggling to keep my food down. Ryzen poured more wine into my glass, and I chugged it. I was getting so sick and tired of these stupid dinners with him.

It was like night and day from yesterday to today. I had been running on adrenaline for the past twenty-four hours, and it was all catching up to me now.

He raised his eyebrows as I gulped the wine down and shook his head. "You OK, Nova? You look…" He gave me a once-over, his lips in a flat line. "Well, forgive me, but you look like hell."

I chuckled, trying to mask the bitterness raging throughout my body. "Didn't sleep well. The nightmares got the best of me." That wasn't exactly a lie, although the nightmares I was having now were of Kaviathin, and not of masked, mysterious men. A shiver ran through me, and I reached for the bottle, filling up my glass. And now I was here again with Ryzen, when I should be with Cian taking care of him. Annoyance bubbled in my chest and I swallowed it down with my wine.

"How was it with Covington? The trip went well?" I decided to change the topic to something that didn't involve the way I looked or felt, otherwise I might end up yelling at the top of my lungs.

"Great. Perfect, in fact. He's ready to sign

everything." Ryzen laid his hand on top of mine. "As soon as we are married."

I nodded. I'd known this was going to come up again at some point, and I was ready for it. "I think it's time to move forward too."

*With getting you to confess, that is.*

"But Ryzen, I need you to be honest with me." I was the one gripping his hand now. I needed to push him, get him close to the edge, and the best way to do that was to get him flustered. Because although he tried to portray himself as a strong and powerful man, I knew that when he got flustered, he got sloppy.

He quirked his eyebrow. "About?"

We were silent for a moment as I tried to figure out the best way to approach the topic. My original plan of beating around the bush went right out the window. "Are you working with the Mafia? Did they take me to get back at you?"

His face reddened, and he tried to take his hand from underneath mine, but I gripped him tighter. "Why would you ever ask a question like that, Nova? I'm a reputable businessman. I don't work with scum like the Mafia." He yanked his hand away and threw his napkin on the table. "Who put that thought in your little head, huh?"

"Nobody. I was just looking for more info on that Kaviathin man and found some unsettling news. If you're working with him, then you should tell me before we get married. I have a right to know if I'm going to be in danger because of your work."

He reached over and gripped my chin. My eyes widened. I had expected him to deny it, but not actually get physical with me. I glanced down at the knife on the table, then back to him.

"And I told you to stop snooping before you get yourself into trouble, Nova. You don't want to mess with these people." He let go of my chin and went back to eating.

*Ah-ha.*

"So you *do* know them?" My leg bounced, moving the table slightly.

"No, I don't," he huffed. "But I know enough that you should never dig into the Mafia, or you're bound to find trouble." His nostrils flared. He was visibly upset now. I had struck a nerve. Good. That meant that I was getting closer.

I stood and walked behind him, wrapping my arms around his shoulders. "I'm sorry if I upset you. But you can trust me, Ryzen. I only want what's best for you. For us."

*Like prison time.*

He shrugged his shoulders so that I would let go of him. "Just… don't bring it up again, Nova."

We finished our meal in mostly silence, Ryzen glaring at me when he thought I wasn't looking. I was laughing on the inside. Good, I hoped he was flustered. That meant that he would make a mistake. And I would be there when he did.

After dinner, I changed into pajamas and crawled into his bed. This was one of the worst parts about doing all of this, that I had to stay in the same bed as him. It couldn't be avoided though. If I had all these supposed strong feelings for him, then I wouldn't sleep downstairs in my apartment all the time. No, I would be here. With him. And it made my stomach sick. But as long as I could keep his hands off of me, and he knew that he wasn't getting any sex from me until after we were married, then I had to just suck it up and deal with it. I had a goal, and I had to remember that that goal was bringing him down. No matter what.

I checked my phone and realized that I had dozed off, the bed empty. I threw the covers off and tiptoed down the hall. A soft light came from under his office door, and I stepped closer, pressing my ear to it.

"I need more time. Another week or two max," Ryzen hissed.

He must be talking to someone.

"I know what you said, but the old man won't budge on this marriage shit, baby."

*Baby? That's interesting.*

"I miss you too, Iva. Just give me more time and I'll make this right. We'll be home free soon."

*Iva.*

That bitch. I balled my hands into fists. And where the hell had she been all these weeks? Apparently sneaking off with Ryzen, from the sounds of it. Good. Let her get impatient. It would probably help me more.

"Oh, fuck, baby, I'm so hard for you. I can't wait to cum inside that sweet fine pussy."

I gagged, my hand going to my chest. OK, I didn't need to stick around for this part. I hauled ass back to the bedroom and hid under the covers.

I needed a shower.

A scalding hot one.

And something to forget what I had just heard.

## Chapter Fourteen

**Day 39**

"Here, try this one on." Orin handed me a gold ear cuff shaped like a "C" that fit over the top of my ear and wrapped down and around my earlobe. Little golden leaves dangled from it with tiny diamonds at the end. It fit perfectly, and I admired my reflection in the little handheld mirror.

"They're not real." He chuckled.

"That's OK. Hopefully no one will get close enough to be able to tell." I laughed and puckered my lips in the mirror. "This is actually adorable."

"Nova, focus." Orin pulled the cuff off and held it in front of my face. "The mic is right here in the first leaf, and the earphone is at this end that loops over the top of your ear. If you wear your hair down, just make sure the mic doesn't get covered. Got it?" He pointed to all the pieces, and I nodded. I held out my hand, and he dropped it into my palm. "This runs on an eight-hour battery, so that should be enough time."

Ryzen was having a party with several important investors, and since I was his fiancée, I was required to be there. "Just mingle and smile," was basically what he had told me. It was going to be at his mansion in Highland Park, a posh neighborhood where everyone had manicured lawns and money to burn. Out of his five homes in the city and suburbs, this was the one I hadn't been to yet. And I was itching to get inside. I needed to get my hands on that journal, and if it wasn't at his condo, the penthouse, his office or stashed away in one of his many cars, then it might be there.

"OK, let's make sure it works. Just press the button here." Orin pointed at one of the leaves, then pulled out a set of headphones and put them on. I did as he asked and walked down the hall into the bathroom and shut the door.

"Cian used to sleep with a stuffed bear in his room when we were younger," Orin said in my ear.

I chuckled and shook my head. "Oh, boy, don't let him hear you say that."

There was slight static and the sound of shuffling, and then Cian's voice was in my ear instead of Orin's. "Don't listen to him, little star. He's lying." He chuckled, then Orin muttered something in the background.

I walked back to the office and laughed as Cian had Orin's arm pinned behind his back. "Say mercy, brother."

"Cian, let him go before you hurt your shoulder." I giggled and sat on the edge of the desk.

Those two were always going at it, and you couldn't help but laugh. Maybe because I had grown up with a demonic sister who didn't have a bonding bone in her body. Grace was more likely to murder me than play a game with me. I hadn't even heard from her since the wedding—not one call, text, or email. It wasn't like I had expected anything from her, and I trusted her as far as I could throw her, but her silence just confirmed what I had always known: she didn't give a shit about me. And honestly, I was done caring. I would rather surround myself with people who showed me love, honesty, and compassion than a money-obsessed psychopath.

Ryzen's mansion was gated and covered several acres, so even though Cian wanted to be close by, it wasn't as easy as it sounded. Ryzen's security would be all over the place, and I didn't want to risk them finding Cian, Eros or Orin. No, they would have to stay away. Orin had offered to make us a makeshift walkie-talkie so Cian and I could communicate if I needed him. I was hoping I wouldn't need to, but things were unpredictable, especially when it came to Ryzen.

I had met with Dobbs and Delove earlier in the week. It was the same broken record as always. The good news was that at least some of the things I was finding were actually helpful and definitely incriminating. They were building a case against Ryzen, but not even close to getting what they needed on Voledetti. The case against Ryzen was weak though—possible money laundering, but it just wasn't enough. I almost lost my shit when Delove said that, and I let him know that if he said it wasn't good enough one more time, I was going to take that necklace and shove it where the sun didn't shine. He hadn't been too happy with me after that.

Dobbs had tried to grill Cian on his injury after he spotted fresh blood on Cian's shirt, but Cian wouldn't say a word, and when Dobbs looked at me, I shrugged my shoulders. If Cian believed that Kaviathin was serious about hurting us if we spoke about what had happened, then that was good enough for me.

Now I checked my watch and groaned. "I have to

head back soon. Valik thinks I'm out for a run. And Jules will be stopping by soon too."

Cian glanced at Orin, who packed up his bag and headed for the front door. "Have fun, you two." He winked at me and I grinned, shutting the door behind him. He had done almost a complete one-eighty since I had first met him. I wasn't sure what had changed. Maybe he'd finally realized that I wasn't out to hurt Cian. Pretty much the opposite. Especially right now.

"Sit, let me check your bandage." I walked over to the couch with the basket of gauze, alcohol and other items necessary to clean his wound. He peeled off his shirt and relaxed on the couch. I leaned over him and removed the bandage carefully, his hands rubbing up my thighs as I worked. "It looks good, healing nicely." I kissed his cheek and taped a new bandage over his wound.

"Mm-hmm. Thank you, Nurse." His hands roamed over my ass, and I clucked my tongue at him.

"Why, Mr. Blackwood, is that any way to treat a medical professional, sir?" I swatted his hands away and giggled as he huffed.

"Nurse La Roux, I have another ache I need you to take care of."

"Is that so?" I smirked and straddled him. My hands weaved into his hair, tugging his head back. "Let me guess where it's at." His cock pressed firmly into me, a shudder going through my body. I could never get enough of him. My body was always ready, greedy, begging, and by the looks of it, so was his. My lips worked up his neck as I trailed little kisses over his scars, then bit down on his earlobe. "I can't leave my patient suffering, now can I?"

"No, ma'am." His chest heaved, and I paid close attention to not touch his shoulder area. God, he looked good enough to eat—hair disheveled, cock hard for me, a playful grin on his face. I stood and stripped off my shorts and panties as I watched him stroke himself. His eyes never left mine as he worked his hand up his shaft, and down, a groan leaving his lips when I stood in front of him naked.

"Come take what's yours," he growled.

Yes. All fucking mine. I climbed into his lap, and he rubbed the head of his cock between the lips of my pussy, up and down, over my clit, teasing me in a torturous rhythm that had me panting. I gasped, throwing my head back when he plunged into me, filling me up in such a delicious way that it sent goosebumps up my arms.

"You're so fucking beautiful like that. Filled up with my cock. I love you so fucking much." He raised his hips up as I slammed myself down. A frenzy of hands roaming, lips biting, and skin slapping overcame us until we were both moaning. I gripped his head in my hands, my tongue swirling around his. More. More. I needed more. His hand moved up to my throat, squeezing gently, and I moved my hips faster until I was chanting his name. The need to come was overpowering, and I yelled out his name, little black dots in my vision as I came all over his cock.

"That's right, my beautiful star, scream for me." He pushed us down to the floor, my ankles on his shoulders, and fucked me with a relentless passion I was growing so used to. "This is my pussy, Nova. I own it. Don't forget that."

"Yes, Cian, I love you," I whimpered and dragged

my nails up his back. He let out a guttural moan, filling me up with his release a second later.

We lay on the floor, trying to catch our breaths. "Your bandage got messed up." I looked at the torn gauze and scrunched up my nose.

"Fuck the bandage." He chuckled and gripped my hand in his.

Less than an hour later, I ran home, a smile spread from ear to ear. A dark van pulled up next to me, and I froze. It felt like my soul left my body for a moment, and I shook my head when a young guy stepped out and ran into the restaurant I was passing. I looked over my shoulder, worried Kaviathin and his men would pop out at any moment. It seemed that was all I had been doing all week, looking over my shoulder for monsters, but they never showed. Couldn't say that I was relieved, though. Because I knew they were out there. Waiting.

And I was sick of it.

Juliet was in the lobby when I got home, and I squeezed her in a big bear hug when I saw her.

"You're glowing." She swatted my ass when we got inside my apartment.

"Oh, must be a runner's high." I tapped my chin.

"Bullshit, Nova. We both know you hate running." She chuckled. "I'm glad you're so happy now. I mean, under the circumstances. Cian's a good guy. But if he hurts you, I will kill him." She gave me her serious mother face and I pinched her cheeks.

"I know you will. And I'll be right next to you with my own bat."

She pulled out a stack of forms and a pen and handed them to me. "I've been working with the forensic accountant all week. She's a beast, fucking love her." Juliet spread the documents out. "She also has a fraud examiner on her team, and they went through everything with a fine-tooth comb. These are their final assessments on the fair market value of our property and assets. They are also ready to testify. We just need to sign these so they can send them to the insurance company. This is the last step, Nova, so hopefully good news is coming our way." She held up her fingers in our secret code, and I did the same.

We went through and signed all the documents, making sure we hadn't missed anything. If this was the final step, then we needed to be thorough.

"Oh, are we still meeting Grams this weekend for brunch? She said to bring Owen too for some reason." She chuckled.

I placed my hand over my heart. Grams was doing a lot better now. I was doing my best to not show her any stress when we met here and there. She had lots of questions, and I thought she knew deep down something was going on. But luckily, when I told her everything was going great, she didn't ask any more questions.

"How's Cian? His shoulder is better?" Juliet stacked the documents on the table, evening them out so the tops were all level.

"Yeah." I smiled. "Considering everything, he seems to be in good spirits."

"There's something I want to tell you, but don't want you to freak you out." She bit her bottom lip, and when I glared at her, she held her hands up. "Not about Cian. Well, not really. I'm probably overreacting… but the thing with Gretchen and the hair was really bothering me. And I know you said she moved to France."

I nodded. "Yeah, that's what Cian said."

"Well, that's the thing. I checked. She's not in France. Actually, she's not anywhere. It's like she disappeared off the face of the earth."

My heart skipped a beat, and I cleared my throat. "What do you mean?"

Juliet shrugged. "I don't really know. I tried every search imaginable to find details on her, but nothing showed up. Eros and I were talking, and he called up a buddy in Europol, and his buddy got back to him last night."

"And?" I leaned forward.

"And... nothing. There's no Gretchen Mastillo in Europe, in the US... there's just nothing." She threw her hands up.

"I mean, she could have gone anywhere though." I clasped my hands together, a million thoughts racing through my mind.

"No, I know. That's why I didn't want to make a big deal about it. It's just, well, we've seen enough serial killer documentaries to know what a box with someone's hair and favorite necklace in it means." She scrunched up her face.

Ryzen, a killer? That was a whole new layer of fucked up. I mean, he was crazy, but killing someone like Gretchen? That made no sense. She was probably off living her best life in Jamaica or something. "Eros didn't say anything when I saw him."

"I told him not to freak anyone out." She rolled her eyes. "He's dramatic sometimes."

"Since when are you guys so close?" I smirked

and raised my eyebrow. "You little minx."

"Oh, no, no, no no." She held up her hands. "It's not like that."

We FaceTimed Owen and caught him up with what was going on with the insurance claim. He was beyond excited that we were hopefully getting closer to getting it resolved. Little did he know there were a ton of other problems we were handling right along with this one, but I would never tell him that. He was rebranding our website and excitedly showed us all the new tweaks he had made.

He was so happy, and I hoped his efforts weren't being wasted. If I wasn't able to pull this all off, then Juliet and I would be in jail for arson and insurance fraud, and website updates would be the least of our concerns.

*****

Valik drove Ryzen and I up to his estate in Highland Park a few hours later. Valik was as quiet as a mouse the entire ride, and I suspected he didn't want to let on to Ryzen that we had become close buddies. I could understand that, so I didn't try to mess with him. The last thing I needed was Ryzen yelling at Valik for being a decent human being.

I tucked my small bag by my feet and kept it out of Ryzen's sight. It had my makeup, the ear cuff, my knife and my other supplies, including my second phone, the one Ryzen didn't know about. I had learned my lesson after last time when the necklace hadn't uploaded the feed to Delove, so this time, I would also record with my phone. I wasn't taking any chances.

There were butterflies in my stomach as we got closer to the mansion. It felt more dangerous this time. The stakes were higher, not only because I was running out of time and ideas stalling Ryzen and the wedding, but because Kaviathin was expecting results from me as well. The complete opposite results of what the FBI wanted. And if I didn't produce them, Cian might end up dead. I would never let that happen. Over my dead body would I let Kaviathin hurt a hair on Cian's head. Not again.

Orin had tried to give me a small gun, but I had refused. First of all, I didn't know how to use one that well. Cian had taken me shooting once, but that had just ended up with us having sex in the middle of the woods again. Secondly, I had no place to put it while I was at Ryzen's mansion. It wasn't like I could stuff it down my cleavage. I had snagged the garter belt I had worn with my Lara Croft costume the night I had met Cian, before I'd known it was actually him. It was just strong enough to hold my knife and my phone. Anything else and it would probably fall down my leg.

Besides, I didn't think I would actually need it. It wasn't like I would pull a gun on Ryzen and force him to confess, although the idea had crossed my mind a time or two. I wanted nothing more to see him quiver with fear, confess all his dirty sins, and get handcuffs slapped on his wrists. But no, I had to play this smart. And carrying around a gun was not smart.

I glanced at Ryzen out of the corner of my eye as he read the newspaper. The road up to the house was bumpy, with gravel rocks flying as we drove up. He couldn't be a killer. Could he? As of late, he had more and more reminded me of a soft guy. Not in the cuddly kind of way, but in the way that he didn't like to get his hands dirty. Money laundering, stealing, lying, yes—that was right up his alley. But actual murder? I didn't think he was capable of pulling it off. Although ever since my conversation with Jules that morning, there was a rock the size of a boulder in my stomach.

We pulled up to the gate, and my eyes widened at the size of it. I should have known it was going to be lavish. It almost reminded me of Covington's estate. It even had a grand waterfall statue in the center of the circular driveway. "It's beautiful, Ryzen."

He puffed his chest out and nodded. "Thank you, Nova. Although it pales in comparison to your beauty." His hand stroked my cheek as his gaze went up and down my body. I clenched my jaw and laughed.

Valik saved the day and opened the door, holding his hand out to me. I stepped down and slammed the door.

"You're quiet today," I whispered as we walked to the back of the SUV and opened the trunk. He stuck his tongue out at me as Ryzen came around the back with his briefcase, and I chuckled.

"Ready, dear?" Ryzen held his arm out to me, and I looped my arm through his.

*As ready as I'll ever be.*

I wasn't sure what to expect tonight. Ryzen had said I didn't have to do much, just mingle and make small talk. Try to avoid any talk about the wedding or the kind of work I did… yada, yada, the same rules as always. But that was fine, because the only thing I hoped to accomplish tonight was finding that journal and anything else that might help me get dirt on Ryzen.

He gave me a brief tour of his home, showing me all his toys, including the eight-car garage filled with luxury vehicles. None of that mattered to me; a Ferrari was just another car in my opinion. But he was really excited, even kneeling down and rubbing an invisible speck of dust off his Rolls-Royce. I oohed and ahhed, boosting his ego, and he loved every second of it.

"Very nice, Ryzen. Maybe you'll take me for a ride in one?" I placed my hand on his biceps. "That would be nice."

He gazed down at my lips, an evil grin spreading across his face. "Great idea. This one has a sleeping nook in the back." He nodded at a boat-sized car in the corner, and I laughed, patting his arm.

Ugh. I had to keep him mellow, unsuspicious, and flirting was the easiest way to do that. Even though it made me feel dirty as hell.

We walked up a circular staircase, a beautiful skylight above us. When we reached the hallway, he grabbed my hand and yanked me towards a room with double doors that swung open towards us. "Look at this. I got it at a museum auction several years ago. One hundred percent authentic."

I stopped short when we walked through the doors. To my right was one of those medieval knights' suits of armor. He tapped his finger against it, making a dinging sound. "It's real. Can you believe that? Paid a pretty penny for it too."

"Wow, that's amazing." What the fuck was I supposed to say to him? Cool metal outfit? I chuckled and glanced around the room, noticing that we were in some sort of office. There were bookcases covering each wall, and a large mahogany desk close to the windows.

*Thanks, Ryzen.* Now I knew exactly where I needed to snoop first. He showed me to a room that I could get ready in and pulled a box out of his pocket. "I got this for you."

I tugged on the ribbon and opened the box, an extravagant gold necklace laced with diamonds inside. "It's breathtaking, Ryzen." I trailed my fingers over the diamonds and lifted it out the box. It was beautiful, very heavy, and not something I would typically wear.

"I want you to wear it tonight. It will go great against your skin." His fingers caressed my neck.

"Oh, but I have my other necklace, the one Juliet gave me." Fuck.

He shook his head. "No, this one, Nova. It will really make me happy to see you looking so beautiful."

I nodded. It wasn't like I could argue with him over it, otherwise it might look too suspicious. If a man you supposedly had feelings for gave you jewelry, you wore it. There was no way around it, and I knew it.

"That connects to my room if you need anything." He pointed to the door off to the side. "Anything at all." He lowered his head, his lips on mine. My whole body stiffened, but he didn't seem to notice. His tongue pressed forward, trying to gain entry into my mouth, and my stomach turned. I had been really good at keeping him at bay, telling him I wanted to take things slow. Just a little flirting here and there, and he had seemed fine with it. Probably because he was jerking off on the phone with Iva, or hell, he was probably fucking other women that I had no clue about. Either way, I didn't care, as long as he kept his hands to himself.

"Ryzen," I breathed, "we should get ready." I placed my hands on his chest and pushed slightly, but he wouldn't budge.

"I can't help it, Nova. You're so damn beautiful." He brought his head down, his breath warm against my neck as he kissed me there. Bile rose in my throat, but I swallowed it down.

"Good things come to those who wait." My voice quivered slightly, and he groaned.

"You're right." He sighed and checked his watch. "OK, I'll see you in a little bit, beautiful." He kissed the tip of my nose.

Great, now I was going to have to shower again.

I didn't like these little surprises of his. He knew I didn't want to have sex with him until after we were quote-unquote "married," and for some reason, that seemed to only make him try harder to fuck me.

Maybe I should have listened to Orin and taken the gun.

No, that wouldn't have been smart. It just meant that I needed to try harder tonight. That journal had to be here, and I wasn't leaving this place without it.

# Chapter Fifteen

"How are you doing, little star?" Cian's voice echoed in my ear, a warm feeling spreading through my chest.

"Better now that I can hear you." I sighed and grabbed the necklace Ryzen had given me, putting it on. It felt like it weighed ten pounds, and was more like a leash than an actual present, but I supposed that was what most wealthy men like Ryzen did—provide their girlfriends with lavish expensive gifts so they would turn their heads the other way at any wrongdoing.

"You're doing great, Nova. You can do this," Cian purred. "Tell me what you've seen so far."

"Well, a bunch of cars have already arrived. At least fifty of them. His security is everywhere also. Do you think it's because of Kaviathin?" My voice hitched when I said his name.

"Don't worry about Kaviathin. Eros is tailing him as we speak, and he's miles away from you."

My shoulders drooped and I said a silent thank you to the universe. Kaviathin was the last person I needed to be worried about tonight. "Awesome, that makes me feel better." I brushed my hair, letting it cascade over my shoulders. The earpiece was slightly hidden by my hair, not that it mattered. To anyone else, it looked like a cool piece of jewelry. But to me, it was my lifeline to the only piece of sanity I had left.

"Ryzen's room is right next to mine, so I can gain access to that pretty easily. Once I know he's occupied, I'll check there first." I applied some lipstick and puckered my lips in the mirror. "He has some sort of office filled with trophies and books just down the hall. He might have documents hidden in there."

"Good, very good, Nova. Just stay perfectly calm. You are in complete control, OK?"

"Yes," I whispered. The ache in my chest spread. Cian was out there watching over me, but still so far away. Desperation seeped out of every pore in my body. I was reaching a breaking point. "Tell me again what's going to happen," I breathed.

His voice was soft, calming. "You're going to find what we need tonight, and once you do, I'm hauling ass up there to get you. We're going straight to Delove and Dobbs, and if they choose to remain unreasonable, then we're leaving. Scotland. Ireland. The Bahamas. Anywhere you want to go, Nova."

I chuckled and closed my eyes. That would be a dream come true. Of course, it was a white lie, and we both knew it. There was no way I would ever leave Juliet, and I would never ask Cian to leave his brothers and sister. A life on the run, always looking over my shoulder to see how close the FBI was, or, worse, Kaviathin Voledetti? It just couldn't happen that way. No, every moment counted tonight.

"OK, I'm going downstairs now. Wish me luck."

"You got this, my queen."

I walked down the circular staircase and glanced

down at all the people walking around. There were a lot of them, at least sixty, and that was just in the main room. A waiter passed by with a tray of champagne and offered me a glass, which I quickly grabbed. Just a little something to calm my nerves.

Ryzen was standing near the fireplace, a group of five men and women surrounding him. His eyes brightened and he waved me over. I plastered a huge smile on my face as I approached the group.

"You look stunning, Nova." He kissed my cheek, and Cian grumbled in the background. Ryzen held my hand and introduced me to the group of people, who didn't try to hide their stares at my breasts, or the giant piece of jewelry collared around my neck. I spent the next thirty minutes dangling on Ryzen's arm, offering a smile or laugh when necessary.

"I'm just going to run to the ladies' room," I whispered in his ear and kissed his cheek.

"OK, honey. I'll miss you." The women awwed and the men chuckled at his supposed adoration.

"I'm going to fucking kill him," Cian muttered.

"Calm down," I giggled and walked casually up the stairs. "It's all for show, Cian."

"It doesn't matter. He's a fucking dead man for touching what's mine." Cian sighed. "I hate this."

"I know," I whispered softly to avoid looking like a mad woman talking to herself to anyone who might be looking at me. "I'm going upstairs to check his room first."

I went to my room first and locked the door behind me before opening the connecting door to our room. Ryzen's briefcase lay open on his bed, and I shuffled through the contents. There appeared to be architectural drawings of a high-rise building right on top. Underneath, I found a letter from the insurance company.

"Listen to this." I read through the letter. "It says they have been working with law enforcement to ensure there's no fraud taking place. It lists Delove's contact information at the bottom. Why didn't Delove tell us that?"

"I don't know," Cian murmured, "but I don't like it."

Had Ryzen been in contact with the FBI? That seemed like something Delove or Dobbs or, hell, even Ryzen would have mentioned to me. I snapped pictures of everything with my watch and cellphone and put it back in his briefcase. I went around the room, opening every drawer and looking through, trying to find the journal or anything else that could be useful.

"Seven minutes, Nova." Cian's voice was tense.

"Just one more minute." I walked over to a large armoire and searched through it, not finding anything. "There's nothing here." I sighed.

"Get back downstairs, little star."

"Yes, sir." I chuckled and went back through to my room, then back down the circular staircase. I looked around, not seeing Ryzen, so decided to mingle with the crowd, offering a smile and hello. I was shocked when I saw the SNM triplets in the corner, and walked over to them. I hadn't seen them since we had met at Covington's fundraiser fiasco where Ryzen had won the bid.

"My favorite triplets." I grinned and they reached down, embracing me in a hug.

"Miss La Roux, stunning as always," one of them

said. I glanced down at his cufflinks and saw the letter "S".

"Thank you, Scott. You all look just as handsome as ever. What do I have to do to get a drink around here?" I chuckled when they all raised their hands at the same time, three waiters stepping over and offering me a glass of champagne.

"Watch it with them, Nova," Cian growled. "They like to share."

My cheeks heated, and I bit my bottom lip to stop my laugh. It wasn't surprising; they were pretty sexy. And triplets? C'mon. What grown woman would turn down a night with three sexy men? Well, I would, because Cian was more than enough for me to handle. But maybe I should introduce them to Juliet. She would probably have the time of her life.

We spoke for some time, them telling me about a new complex they were building that would have a high-end shopping experience and the largest fitness facility ever built on commercial land. I nodded with enthusiasm and asked a lot of questions, because I didn't want to come off as rude, especially after they had always been so nice to me.

"Sounds very exciting, gentlemen. Humor me for a minute. Are any of you single? I have a friend, my business partner, who I think might be perfect"—I looked between the three of them—"for you."

They all nodded in unison. I was pretty sure Cian was right about the whole sharing thing.

"Take our number, we'd love to meet her if she's anything like you." Scott winked and I could almost feel Cian's jealousy seeping through the earpiece.

"She's pretty great. I'll pass it on." I excused

myself and worked my way around the room.

Ryzen snagged me again soon after and introduced me to more and more people. It was honestly exhausting walking around with a fake smile for so long. But my prize was waiting for me, and the faster I got this over with, the faster I would get home to him.

My stomach growled, and I walked over and grabbed a piece of toast with goat cheese, grapes and honey. I moaned as I swallowed it down, grabbing three more and stuffing my face before anyone could see me. I pulled out my phone and casually took a video of the people in the room, and stopped in my tracks when I turned around the corner.

Iva Covington.

That little sneaky liar was sitting on a chaise lounge, talking with an older gentleman. Her eyes caught mine, and she waved her hand, signaling me to come over.

My hands trembled as I gripped my champagne flute. I felt like I could snap it in half at that moment. I plastered a smile on my face and walked over.

"Nova, you're a sight for sore eyes. Get over here, girl." She stood and hugged me. Her breath reeked of alcohol and I quirked my eyebrow. She was a giggling mess. Was she drunk already? This ought to be interesting. She grabbed my champagne and chugged it, waving a waiter over. She grabbed two glasses of red wine, handed me one. "Sit, let's catch up."

*Yeah, let's do that, you snake.*

She patted the edge of the chaise, and I sat down next to her, taking a sip of my wine.

"I'm surprised to see you here after"—she looked

around the room—"you ran off at your own wedding. Not a good look, honey, not at all." She clucked her tongue, and I imagined reaching over and strangling her with that stupid silk shawl she had over her shoulders.

"Yeah, well, what can I say?" I laughed, shrugging my shoulders. Ryzen was watching us, and I waved at him. I decided to take a page from her book. "I just couldn't stay away from Ryzen. He's so…"

"Vile. Disgusting. A pig?" Cian offered in my ear.

"He's just been so great. And the sex!" I placed my hand on her knee. "Girl, when I tell you that he has me screaming all night, every night… he's an animal."

Her face reddened and I took a sip of my wine, hiding my smile.

"I'm going to spank your ass red the next time I see you," Cian growled, and I giggled softly.

"You, uh, you guys are intimate?" She tilted her head to the side, and I scrunched up my nose.

"Of course, we're engaged." I snickered and rolled my eyes slightly.

She turned her head towards him, her nostrils flaring. I wondered what Ryzen had been telling her. Probably that he wanted nothing to do with me, that he only had eyes for her. Her reaction was everything I had hoped it would be.

"We just saw your grandparents not too long ago. It was so nice to see them. I'll be happy when this whole hotel business is done with, so I can spend more quality time with Ryzen." I sighed happily and glanced at him. "He sure is something."

"Yeah." Her voice was low, bitter. "He sure is."

"Oh, look at the time, I should get back to my

man." I stood and held my arms out to give her a hug. She looked surprised, but reached up, and just as she did, my wine glass slipped and fell into her lap.

"Oh, no!" I covered my mouth. "Iva, I'm so sorry, how clumsy of me."

Her jaw fell to the floor as the wine dripped down all over her dress. She grunted in anger and stood, the liquid running down her legs and into her heels.

"Oh, honey, let me see if the housekeeper has something you can borrow while we get that out." I reached for the napkin and dabbed at the stain.

She stepped away and narrowed her eyes at me. Something told me I might not have been as good as an actress as I had thought. Because the look she gave me said she knew *exactly* what I had just done. I scrunched up my nose and shrugged my shoulders as she stormed off, the people standing around giving me a peculiar look.

"What happened?" Cian asked.

"Oh, nothing, just spilled my wine all over her. An accident, of course."

"Of course." He let out a throaty laugh.

Ryzen headed over in my direction with a small plate of food. "Everything OK?" he asked, handing me the plate.

"Oh, yeah, I think she's just drunk." I chuckled and averted my eyes. "Thank you for the food."

"Of course." He rubbed my arm and leaned down, kissing my forehead. "Come mingle when you finish, OK?"

He went off and stood with a group of men, who looked at him as if he was king of the world, and I rolled my eyes. Now was my time to move. He would be occupied for a while now. I set the plate aside and walked casually to the back of the room and then up the staircase. "I'm heading for his office," I whispered.

When I got to the two-sided doors, I swung them open and slipped inside, locking the door behind me. "OK, bookcase first. Maybe his journal is here." I scanned each book, looking for the journal or any other book that looked out of place. "It's not here, Cian." I moved some things around the bookshelf, searching for anything. "There's nothing on the shelf."

"Try the desk, Nova," Cian breathed. "Be calm, you have plenty of time."

My chest felt heavy, adrenaline pumping through my veins as I walked around the desk and turned on the lamp. I yanked open each drawer, searching for anything and everything. Invoices, contract documents, the same old shit he had at his other home office. I had *seen* this already.

Where was the journal?

I opened the middle drawer and rifled around, half expecting to find another box with women's hair in it. I breathed a sigh of relief when I didn't find one. "There's nothing in here, Cian." My voice shook, and I tried to compose myself.

"It's OK, Nova. Keep looking."

I slammed the drawer shut, but something was stuck, and it wouldn't close all the way. "Wait, there's something wrong with the drawer. It won't close." I pushed and pulled, but something was blocking it from closing.

"Is there something underneath it getting stuck?"

He was right, maybe something was stuck in the

back or the bottom, like a pen. I kneeled down on the floor and felt around, not finding anything. Just when I was about to give up, my fingers grazed over an object. It was square, and I tugged, tape ripping off the wood.

"I found something." I was breathless as I held the tiny stick in my hand. "It's a flash drive."

"Great, Nova. Take it and get back downstairs."

"Wait, there's a laptop right here. I want to see what's on it." Ryzen's screensaver, a bunch of dollar signs floating in a circle, was on the screen and I pressed enter, the password screen opening. "Damn it, it's locked." My shoulders slumped forward.

"Try 'I am a king six nine eight.'" Cian's voice was low, a hint of worry in it.

Would that actually work? I typed in the password and the main screen popped up. "Holy shit, it worked. How did you know that?" My voice was breathless as excitement raced through me, and I inserted the stick into the laptop.

"It was his password back in the day. Kind of a stupid move not to change it."

"OK, it's loading." I tapped my fingers on the desk as folders started to pop up.

"I don't like this, Nova. Take it and go downstairs. We'll come get you and check it together."

"No, Cian, it's right here, one second."

I opened the first folder and a bunch of electronic bank statements popped up. They looked similar to the ones I had found at Ryzen's home office, but the deposit and transfer amounts were much larger. The next folder I opened had several scanned letters, all on casino letterheads.

"What is it, Nova? What do you see?" Cian's voice

was tense, and my anxiety went up another hundred notches at his concerned tone.

"Bank statements, letters from a casino. Hold on. I just found a bunch of pictures."

Pictures of the entire Voledetti family popped up on the screen—some of Althazair, some of Kaviathin and a lot of Voledetti senior. It looked as if Ryzen had taken them with his cellphone, as there were snippets of his hands and body in some of the corners of the photos. I scrolled through, and gasped. Pictures of Voledetti senior with pallets of drugs and guns. Lots and lots of guns.

"Cian," I breathed, my voice shaky. "There are pictures of Voledetti with drugs and weapons."

He let out a deep breath. "OK, Nova, take it and go. I'm coming for you."

"Hold on, there are audio files here too. And videos." One in particular caught my eye. It was dated the day before my wedding. I held my breath and pressed play. It was security footage from our Waveland and Ash building. A small car pulled up and a man—I was assuming it was a man based on his size—dressed in all black jumped out with a backpack. "It's a video of our warehouse. Two guys just pulled up." I checked the timestamp on the video, my mouth falling to the floor as I realized it was the missing chunk of video Delove had shown me.

The screen changed angles and picked up the man's movement as he ran to the back of the building, staying close to the wall and keeping his head down. He took out what I could only assume was a bomb based on the size and placed it behind the dumpster. He tossed the bag into the dumpster and ran back to the car.

"Oh, my God, it's Riddick." The video went back to the car where the man jumped in and took off his hood, showing his face. It was Riddick clear as day on camera. "Riddick blew up the warehouse." I wiped my forehead and blinked rapidly. "We got them, Cian. We fucking got them." A laugh escaped my throat and I had to stop myself from jumping up and down. "Let me record this with my cell phone so I can send it to you. I'm not taking any chances." My hands trembled as I pulled my cell from my garter and hit record.

"You've been gone too long, Nova. Hurry."

"Just give me a sec—" I stopped talking and lowered my phone as voices came from down the hallway. Oh, fuck. "Hold on, someone's coming." Maybe they weren't coming into this room though. Maybe it was just security. Maybe—I heard Ryzen's voice and my heart dropped. "It's Ryzen."

"Fuck," Cian hissed. "Hide, Nova." His breath was shaky, and I realized that I was about to be totally fucked if Ryzen found me in his office. I yanked out the flash drive, shoving it down my cleavage, and put my phone back in my garter. I pushed the screen of the laptop down and looked around the room.

Panic was running through my body and up my spine. There was a closet. Or under the desk. No, they could find me easily if they came in here. Someone tugged on the doors, then said a slew of cuss words when they realized it was locked. The sound of keys jingling had me sprinting across the room to the only other door. I stepped in and shut it quietly behind me.

"I'm in the bathroom. What should I do?" God, why was I so fucking impulsive sometimes? I should have listened to Cian. Grabbed the flash drive and gone.

But no, I hadn't listened, and now here I was.

*It's OK. Take a deep breath, bitch.*

"You're not doing anything wrong. You just came up to use the bathroom. That's all. Turn on the faucet and start singing."

"What?" I hissed.

"Sing. Be natural. Just do it, now."

I turned on the faucet, running my hands under the cold water. "'Beautiful moon, so bright and white, won't you be my lucky date tonight?'"

"Keep going, you're doing great, Nova. Keep singing and walk out naturally."

My heart slammed against my chest as I heard the doors to the office swing open. "He's coming," I whispered. My whole body was on the verge of shutting down. Never in a million years had I experienced as much fear as I did in that moment.

"'Love me wrong, love me right, you belong to the night.'" I hummed the rest of the song and flung the door open as the footsteps approached.

"Holy shit, Ryzen! You scared me half to death." I reached up to my throat instinctively.

He towered over me, his jaw clenched. "What are you doing in here, Nova?"

I stepped around him and chuckled, my laugh coming out forced. "Using the bathroom, silly. Am I missing all the fun?" My back was to him, and I dug my nails into my palms. He spun me around and I gasped, his eyes dark.

"You shouldn't be in here." His eyes searched my face, and I tried to relax my expression.

"Oh, sorry. You know I couldn't stop thinking about your medieval knight over here." I nodded my head in the direction of the metal uniform. "And I wanted to send a picture to Juliet. She'll get a kick out of it. And, well, nature called."

*Please believe me. Please believe me.*

He was silent, glancing over at the knight, then back to me. The silence in the room stretched, the tension growing, and I knew that I had no other choice.

"You know, that knight is pretty sexy." I trailed my fingers up his chest. "Maybe we should try some roleplaying. I'll be the damsel in distress, and you can be my knight in shining armor."

He quirked his eyebrow, his arms wrapping around me. "Sounds kinky. And I like kinky." He smashed his lips to mine, his tongue pressing forward, and I opened my mouth. Not because I wanted to, but because I had to. This was a life-or-death moment as far as I was concerned, and if that meant kissing the son of a bitch, then I had to do it.

I pulled back, breathless. "Wow, well, let's get this party over with so we can start our own party in your bedroom." My palms were sweating, and I rubbed them down my dress. "C'mon, you sexy knight. Let's go back downstairs." He let me grip his hand in mine and tug him towards the door. We were almost out the doors when he stopped and turned around.

"Let me turn this light off." He walked over to the desk and was about to flick the lamp switch, but froze, staring down at the ground.

No, not at the ground, at the drawer that was half open still. His face twisted in anger as he reached under, searching for, I could only assume, the flash drive that was stuffed between my breasts. His movements were jerky, frantic, and then he noticed the laptop and opened it up all the way, his eyes widening.

"You bitch," he snarled.

"He knows," I whispered, and Cian yelled into my earpiece, but I couldn't understand what he was saying. All I could focus on was Ryzen and the murderous look in his eyes. He flung the lamp across the room.

"Where the fuck is it?" He took another step forward.

Adrenaline pumped through me, and when he took another step closer, I used all my strength to push the knight over. It crashed at his feet. That was all the distraction I needed as I ran out the doors and slammed them shut. I took off the belt from my dress and wrapped it around the handles, taking a step back. The doors shook, Ryzen yelling from the other side. He was enraged like I had never seen before. I turned to go down the hall, but one of his security guards was coming around the corner, so I hauled ass in the other direction.

"Nova, what's happening? Please answer me," Cian pleaded, and I pumped my legs faster.

"I got away; I'm running," I gasped as I found a narrow hallway with stairs leading down. I took them two at a time, almost breaking my neck as I flew to the bottom and ended up in the back kitchen. A group of servers stared at me with their mouths open, and I pushed through them until I found the back door. Cold air blasted me in the face as I ran, then turned the corner. Valik was leaning against his car, and I yelled his name.

"Valik, drive!" I screamed and his eyes widened as I approached. "Get in the fucking car and drive."

I threw open the back door and jumped in, and he

hopped in, starting the engine. "Nova, what the fuck is going on?"

"Just go, go now." I looked over my shoulder and tried to control my breathing when I didn't see anyone behind us.

A walkie-talkie beeped, and a panicked voice came over the line. "Do not let Miss La Roux leave the premises. I repeat, do not let Miss La Roux leave. She is considered armed and possibly dangerous."

We were silent for a moment, both our chests heaving as we stared at each other through the rear-view mirror. Before he could say anything, I reached down and pulled out my knife, and held it against his neck. "Do not fucking move, Valik."

His eyes were as big as saucers, and he held his hands up. "Nova, what are you doing? You don't want to do this."

"You're right, Valik. I didn't want to do any of this. But here we fucking are. Throw the walkie-talkie on the dashboard."

He pulled it from a clip on his belt and tossed it onto the dash.

"Now your gun."

"Nova, you're not going to hurt me. Just tell me what's going on so I can help you." His voice was pleading, but I couldn't trust him. Couldn't trust anyone who worked for Ryzen. I pushed the blade into his throat, a drop of blood forming at the tip.

"Never underestimate a desperate woman. Now give me or your gun, or I'll fucking cut your throat." My voice was low, controlled, and in that moment, I could see the fear in his eyes. He knew I was serious.

He reached his hand down and I put more

pressure on the knife, a hiss coming from him as blood dripped down his neck. He pulled it out and I snatched it from his hand, pointing it at his head. "Get out, now." I turned off the safety, my hand trembling.

"OK, OK. I'm going." He opened the door and stepped out and I climbed over the front seat, slamming the door in his face.

Static came over the walkie-talkie, a frantic voice saying, "She's out back, go get her!"

I pressed my foot on the gas and sped down the dirt road.

*Fuck, fuck, fuck!*

"Nova, speak to me, please. What's going on?"

"I got a car. I can't see shit out here. I'm on a different road. It's not the one we came in on."

"Fuck, OK, hold on. I'm pulling the map up. OK, do you see a creek nearby?"

I reached up and tugged my seatbelt on, the car flying down the road. I didn't know why they always made car chases look so fun on television. There was nothing fun about this. I was going so fast, the car swerving all over the place. A huge boulder appeared out of nowhere and I swerved, shrieking as the back of the car spun out of control for a moment. There was a creek to my right, and I said a silent prayer. "I see it on my right, now what?"

"The main road is three miles south. Just keep going and take a right when you get there and that will take you to the highway a few miles down. I'm coming, little star, I promise, just get to the highway."

Lights flashed behind me, and I gasped as a set of headlights raced towards me. How had they gotten to me so fast? *Just focus, Nova. Two minutes and then you'll be there. Two minutes and you'll be safe.* I slammed my foot on the gas and held my breath. "Someone's coming, Cian. But I think I can make it. I think I can get to the main road... I can see the lig—"

I screamed louder than I had ever before as a huge tree log lay in the middle of the dirt road. It was too late; I was going way too fast to stop or to swerve. I didn't stand a fucking chance and I slammed into the log at full speed. My head was spinning as I realized I was up in the air, the car upside down as I went flying, and then... darkness.

*****

Lips were on mine, blowing air into my mouth. I wanted to scream and beg for death as pain ripped through my entire body, but I couldn't move. I couldn't speak. It was just utter and total darkness with voices yelling around me.

"I want that bitch alive."

Ryzen.

He'd gotten me.

*****

There was light, then darkness again, a never-ending cycle as I struggled to open my eyes but couldn't. The pain—oh, God, the pain. It felt like my whole body was broken in half. A blurry version of Ryzen was all I could see, fear roaring in my ears at how close he was.

"Give her more. No, I don't pay you to fucking

think. Now give her more or you're fucking done."

*****

Oh, my God, my head was killing me. I reached up to rub my temples and gasped at the cast around my arm. My gaze traveled over my body, my eyes widening. I was covered in scrapes and bruises, a bandage wrapped around my thigh and one around my foot. A steady beeping noise came from the right of me, and I squinted in that direction. A man stood there in a white coat and a clipboard. A doctor, but I was definitely not in the hospital. It was a bedroom in a house from the looks of it.

"Where am I?" I croaked out and moistened my lips with my tongue.

He handed me a cup of water. "Here, drink this, Miss La Roux."

I chugged the water and held the cup out for more. Two more cups later, I was finally able to speak without my throat hurting. "Where am I?"

"You're home, Miss La Roux."

Home? This didn't look like my home. I furrowed my brows and looked around the room. Nothing looked familiar.

"I got it, Doc." A man stepped from behind the doctor and peered down at me. He brushed my hair out of my face and stroked my bottom lip.

"What's happening? Who are you?" I whispered as his eyes drilled into me. I could have sworn a smile flashed across his face before his mouth set in a thin line.

"Oh, Nova, it's me." He cupped my cheek in his hand. "Ryzen. Your fiancé."

My mouth fell open at his words.

*My fiancé?*

That didn't make any sense.

I had never seen this man before in my whole life.

## Chapter Sixteen

**Day 50**

Retrograde amnesia. That was what the doctor called it.

I sagged into the bed and squeezed my eyes shut. The more he talked about amnesia, and trauma, and dissociation, the faster my heart beat until my whole body began to shake in a way that I knew wasn't right.

"Nova. You were in an accident and sustained some head injuries." Ryzen leaned in closer to me and I tried to push him away, a shot of pain running through my arm that was wrapped in a cast.

"Get away from me." My eyes darted around the room. "This can't be happening."

"Doctor, help her." Ryzen nodded and the doctor pulled out a needle.

"What is that? I don't want that." I shook my head and tried to back away, but there was nowhere to go. My legs were tangled in the blankets and when he tried to put the needle in my arm, I smacked him away. "Get away from me. I don't know you people!" My voice rose to a high pitch, and I sounded hysterical, even to myself.

"Hold her." The doctor grabbed the needle and Ryzen held my shoulders down.

I flailed my arms and legs, trying to do anything to get them away from me. But it didn't work, I was too weak and every movement I made felt like someone was poking me with a cattle prod. "Stop, let me go!" My arm stung, and I realized the doctor had injected me with whatever was in the needle. Within moments I stopped trying to fight Ryzen off, my head rolling from side to side. And then the sweet embrace of darkness came again.

**Day 52**

I woke up with a gasp, my head throbbing like I had been hit with a bat. Ryzen sat in the chair next to my bed, his head in his hands.

"Nova, you're awake. Thank God." His lips set in a flat line, and I gripped the blanket to my chest. My movements felt slow, like I was moving through water.

I didn't know how long I had been out for. Was it hours? Days? "What's... what's going on?" My speech was slightly slurred, and I realized that they must have been giving me some sort of painkiller or relaxant.

"Please stay calm. I know this is stressful, but just bear with me for a moment." He ran his fingers through his hair and sighed. There were bags under his eyes, his clothing wrinkled. "What's the last thing you remember?" His eyes burned into mine, and I looked away.

"Um..." I stared at my fingers, a giant diamond ring on my left hand. What the hell? My head throbbed, and I closed my eyes. "Uh, I was with Juliet. We were moving into an office. Our business, the Shiver Box. We were just moving in days ago." I shook my head.

Ryzen's face was unreadable as he gazed down at me. "You and Juliet moved into that office three years ago, Nova."

My mouth fell open as his words sank in. Three years? I was missing three years of memories? No, it couldn't be. Ryzen paced around the bed, his hands stuffed into his pants pockets.

"We met last year when you moved into my building. It was love at first sight. We're engaged, Nova. Happy. In love." A dimple appeared on his cheek when he smiled, and I blinked my eyes rapidly. He grabbed a stack of photos from the nightstand and handed them to me. "See for yourself."

My hands shook as I grabbed the photos. I stared at the one on top without blinking for a moment. It was a picture of me, except I was dressed like a rich bitch, and Ryzen's arm was draped over my shoulder. The smile on my face was spread from ear to ear. The next photo was nearly the same. They were all of me smiling or laughing, Ryzen kissing my cheek or holding my hand, or us kissing. To say it was jarring would be an understatement.

It was me, but I didn't recognize myself. Who the hell had I turned into? There were so many photos of us, and in almost all of them, I was looking adoringly at him. Clinging to him, kissing him. He handed me a newspaper clipping, our picture front and center under the wedding announcement section.

Another man walked into the room and shut the door softly, taking a seat in the corner. He was big and bulky with a bandage wrapped around his neck. I went back to looking through the photos, trying to find the right words.

I had just lost three years of my life.

I was engaged to this man.

This man I didn't know, but obviously loved based off of these photos.

What was I supposed to do? Could it be fixed? A desperate feeling washed over me, tears welling up in my eyes. I needed to see Juliet. She would help me understand all of this.

"Is Juliet here?" I looked around the room, peeking behind Ryzen at the man in the chair.

"Nova." Ryzen shook his head and sat on the edge of the bed. "You and Juliet are no longer friends."

The man sitting behind Ryzen narrowed his eyes for a moment, but when he saw me looking tried to hide his expression.

"What?" I breathed, my hand flying to my chest. "What do you mean?"

Ryzen's shoulders slumped forward, and he sighed. "I didn't want to tell you this right now, but… you broke off all contact with her over a year ago. You said she wasn't a good friend."

I reached up and rubbed my temples, shaking my head. "Why? Why would I say that? She was my best friend," I choked out. This was the icing on the cake. Not only had I lost my memory, but also my best friend? My ride-or-die? The one person in this world I would kill for. Was Stepford Wife Nova a total bitch?

"Don't worry about it, Nova. You are much happier without her, believe me." He gripped my hand and smiled.

"What about the Shiver Box, our business?" I

whispered.

He shook his head. "Inoperable at the moment."

My palms were sweating, and I hoped he wouldn't notice. This was all terrible. Everything coming out of this man's mouth was making me nauseous. The need to crawl under the blankets and burrow into a dark hole was overpowering.

I nibbled on my bottom lip. "How did we meet, me and you?"

"You moved into a building I own, and like I said, it was instant love. We've been inseparable since." He scooted closer to me, moving my hair out of my face.

I searched his face, screaming inside my head for me to remember something. Anything. Just one sliver of information. But nothing, not a single memory or feeling, was there. "You own a building?"

"Several."

"You're rich?" I scrunched up my nose. Great, non-amnesiac me was probably a gold digger who didn't need friends because she had a rich fiancé.

He chuckled, rubbing his thumb across my cheek. "Yes, and now so are you."

Was that supposed to make me feel better? Because it didn't. I'd been brought up around money, and I'd seen what it did to people. I had always sworn I would never be that way. I'd work hard, be dedicated, never take a handout. But apparently, I'd also lied to myself.

"I'm scared, Ryzen." My voice trembled and I tried to swallow the lump in my throat.

"Don't be. I'll take care of everything, just like I always do. I love you, Nova." He reached over, brushing his lips against mine. I moved back away from him, shaking my head.

"Sorry, I, um, can't." I pulled the blanket up to my neck and scooted away from him.

"That's OK." He poured water into a cup, handing it to me with two pills. "Drink this, it'll help with the pain."

I hesitated for a moment, and he grinned. "Be a good girl, Nova."

The man sitting in the corner of the room cleared his throat. Ryzen snapped his head towards him and motioned for him to come over. "This is Valik, your bodyguard, although I guess you wouldn't remember that considering your current situation." There was a hint of laughter in his voice.

I stopped mid-sip and looked at him. Had he just made a joke about my condition? No, he couldn't have. This Valik guy peered down at me, his face twisted with concern as I took both pills. "Hello." I offered a smile.

"Hi, Nova." He let out a deep breath.

Ryzen clapped his hands together, his eyes gleaming. "Great, I have to get some work done, but I'll come back to see you soon, my love." He leaned down and pressed his lips to my forehead. "Get some rest." He nodded to Valik, who followed him out into the hallway and shut the door behind them.

This was all too much to process. How could you just forget a part of your life? My smiling face stared back at me, and I flipped the photos over. I would remember. I had to.

The voices in the hallways grew louder and I flung the blankets off and walked over to the door.

"I'll send you right back where I found you. I'm doing what's best for her. How dare you question me." It was Ryzen, and he sounded angry.

"But sir…"

"No! Watch her and report back to me. That's your job. Do it. Or else."

I held my hand against the door and leaned so that I wouldn't tip over. The pills. They were making me drowsy already. What the hell were they, horse tranquilizers? The room spun slightly, and I stumbled back to bed, letting my head hit the pillow as I passed out.

## Day 56

Everything fucking hurt. My head, my arm, everything. It was like being stabbed with little tiny needles all over my body. I was exhausted, not only physically but mentally as I struggled with the loss of my memory and of my best friend. Maybe I could fix it. There had to be a way to make things right. It was like I had just been with her yesterday, and now she was just… gone. No stupid fight could have been worth losing her over. Non-amnesiac me was really starting to piss me off.

Valik sat at the end of my bed, reading to me from a magazine. Every time I had opened my eyes over the last few days, he had been there talking or reading to me, even though I hadn't heard a word he was saying. The pills they were giving me were strong, too strong. I decided I liked him; his eyes were kind and he acted like his job was to make me laugh.

I thought it was odd that I wasn't in a hospital recovering, but Ryzen said that because of his wealth the paparazzi would be all over us at the hospital, so it was better to rest and recover at home in private. *Our* home, apparently—one I couldn't even remember. I was staying in a large bedroom with a giant window that I could see out of from my bed. There were trees as far as you could see, and when Valik opened the window, the sound of water nearby.

He flipped through the pages, reading off the top twenty ways to please your man. "Hmph, I don't think you wanna know what number twenty was, Nova." He clucked his tongue. "Definitely not appropriate." He chuckled and tossed the magazine into my lap.

A face stared up at me, and I blinked slowly, focusing on it.

*How I learned to trust and find love again! Actress Phoebe Crane details her quest to find her soulmate.*

I knew this from somewhere. But where? The realization sent a jolt of happiness through me as I looked at the publication date; it was only three months old.

"I've seen this before." I held up the magazine.

"Really?" He leaned forward and smiled. "That's awesome, Nova. Do you remember anything else, like where you saw it?"

Where had I seen it? *Think. Think!*

My shoulders sagged and I shook my head. "No."

"That's OK, it's still progress. Ryzen will be happy to hear it."

Ryzen. I hadn't seen him once since the other day. But I guessed I couldn't say that for sure, since I had been sleeping for most of the time. Today was different.

Today I wanted to get out of this damn bed and outside.

"Can you take me outside? I'm tired of lying here."

His mouth set in a flat line, and he hesitated. "Well, you're supposed to rest."

"Please, Valik." I gripped his hand. "I'm getting cabin fever."

He looked over his shoulder at the shut door, and sighed. "OK, let's do it. But if you get too tired, then we come back, OK?"

I clapped my hands together and threw the blankets off. "Yes, sir!" I stood up and immediately stumbled to the ground. "No, no, no, I'm fine." I gripped the side of the bed and dragged myself up, Valik's arms coming around my waist.

"Up ya go." He lifted me up back to the bed. "Jeez, Nova, you're like a baby giraffe." He chuckled.

Twenty minutes later, after Valik insisted on helping me stretch out my entire body, we were walking barefoot in the grass outside, being careful to avoid the small granite rocks that were everywhere. We were on an island off the coast of Maine, Valik had mentioned. It was breathtakingly beautiful and so green. Exactly what I had imagined an island paradise would be.

"Do I live here?" I gripped onto his forearm as we walked at a snail's pace.

"You live in downtown Chicago in the same building as Ryzen. This is the first time we've been here."

"Am I happy?" I glanced at him from the corner of my eye, gauging his reaction.

He chuckled. "I would say yes. There are some days you are glowing with happiness. There are others where you look like you want to murder someone."

We reached the edge of a bluff, and I peeked over the edge, little pebbles of granite falling down below. It was a good hundred feet to the bottom. Valik gripped me close, making sure I didn't get too close.

"Tell me about Ryzen. Is he a good man?"

He was quiet for a moment, and I tried to read the expression on his face. His whole demeanor had changed, and the hair on the back of my neck stood up.

"Yes," he said softly, and walked us away from the ledge.

"I heard him yelling at you. Is he always that way?" I stopped walking and he looked down at me.

Valik's lips were set in a flat line, and he shrugged. "It's complicated." He didn't offer anything else.

"OK, I can see you are not in the divulging secrets mood." I punched his arm softly, almost losing my balance. "We're friends, right? Me and you? I can tell. You're pretty great, Valik, and I'm happy that you look after me." I smiled at him.

"You're a pain in my ass, is what you are."

"Oh, hush. Are you going to tell me what happened to your neck? That's a pretty nasty cut." I reached up and traced the mark there, and he froze, his whole body tensing.

"It was a misunderstanding," he said softly.

I blew out a deep breath. "That's a scary misunderstanding. I'd hate to be in the room with the person who did that to you."

His eyes widened, and his body shook with laughter. "You have no idea, Nova."

We walked for some time, the fresh air making

me feel alive for the first time in a while. I had so many questions and wondered where the doctor was. Why weren't we doing something about my memory loss? There should be tests or a psychologist or something, anything. But Ryzen hadn't mentioned any of that. I thought back to what I had heard him tell Valik the other day.

*"I'm doing what's best for her."*

Of course he was. He was my fiancé. I shouldn't doubt him, should I?

We made our way back to the house and found ourselves on a terrace of sorts. Ryzen was sitting at a table with a woman, and waved us over when he saw us.

"You're up, sweetheart." He stood and kissed me on the cheek. "Getting a little exercise, are you?" His smile didn't meet his eyes when he looked at Valik.

"Yes, sir. Just helping her stretch her legs."

"You can go now." Ryzen nodded his head towards the house and Valik left.

I nibbled on my bottom lip as I watched him walk away. That had been rude of Ryzen, and totally unnecessary. Valik was helping me so much. Ryzen should treat him better. Was Ryzen always like that to him? Maybe Ryzen was jealous for some reason. I would talk to him about it.

"Nova, this is Iva, a friend of ours." He helped me sit down next to him and pushed my chair in.

"Hello." I smiled and pushed my hair behind my ear, hissing at the pain in my arm. "Sorry, I'm having some issues right now remembering you."

"Is that so, honey?" She smirked and looked me over, her eyes cold. When Ryzen said "friend of ours," I had a feeling this was no friend of mine. Something about the way she was looking at me wasn't right. There was anger there, and I wasn't sure why.

"Car accident, so I'm told."

"So I've been told as well." She snatched up her glass of wine and took a sip.

Well, this was awkward and not what I had been expecting from the day. I laid my hand on Ryzen's forearm and leaned closer. "Can you pour me some water?"

"Of course, love." He poured water in my glass, and handed it to me, kissing me on the cheek.

Iva's eyes were practically popping out of her head, and she chugged the rest of her wine. "So...we're friends then?" I asked.

She was silent for a moment, looking between me and Ryzen. He nodded at her and her expression changed just like that. All of a sudden, she was beaming at me and reaching over the table to squeeze my hand.

"The best of friends, Nova." She laughed, and it reminded me of the Wicked Witch from *The Wizard of Oz*, high-pitched and full of crazy. Was I supposed to fall for this act? Because this woman was obviously a snake and had something for Ryzen. It wouldn't take a rocket scientist to figure that out, especially since she wasn't trying to hide the adoring looks she was giving him while practically glaring at me.

*Let's test this out.*

I leaned closer to him, and he wrapped his arm around my shoulder. Iva followed my hand as I placed it on his chest. She gripped her glass so hard, her knuckles were turning white.

I'd known it. The question was, did Ryzen know it too?

"Is there something going on between you two?" I sat up and looked at Ryzen and then back to her. Both of their faces registered shock. Was Stepford Wife Nova a chickenshit too afraid to speak her mind? Because the old me sure the hell hadn't been. Especially not after finding my sister Grace in bed with my then-fiancé, Dalton.

"Don't be silly, we're all friends here, Nova." Iva grinned, but her leg was bouncing up and down, making the table shake.

"Nova, that's very out of character for you," Ryzen scolded. "Iva's just come to say hello, that's all. Riddick will be here later today as well."

*His brother. He told me this already.*

Ryzen stood and walked over to a little bar, turning his back to us. He mixed a drink and came back to the table, handing it to me. "Here, your favorite."

I scrunched up my nose and looked at the glass. Lemonade was my favorite drink now?

"Drink." He grinned from ear to ear and lifted his glass up for a cheers. "To my beautiful fiancée. I thank God every day that she's all mine."

Iva blinked rapidly and held her glass up, her nostrils flaring. I clinked my glass against theirs and took a sip. Ryzen put his hand under the glass and tipped it up, encouraging me to drink it all, which I did.

A housekeeper came out with a tray of food and placed a salad in front of each of us. My stomach growled and I nibbled on a piece of lettuce, wishing it was something else like steak. It didn't really matter though, because in a matter of minutes, my head was falling backwards, my eyes closing.

*****

My head was fucking pounding when I woke up, and for once Valik wasn't in the chair next to my bed reading. What the hell had happened? One second I'd been eating lunch, and the next I'd passed the hell out. Was it because of my head injury? Or worse, had Ryzen put something in my lemonade? Uneasiness washed over me at the thought.

It was dark outside, and my stomach growled in an obscene way. Well, this wouldn't fucking do. I was tired of always sleeping and being in bed. It was maddening. After going to the bathroom and freshening up, I decided to go look for Ryzen and, hopefully, dinner. Typically, there was a tray of food and tea left next to my bed every night, but that wasn't the case now.

I headed downstairs and was about to call out for Ryzen or Valik when I heard voices coming from a room down the hall. The door was cracked slightly, but before I could push it open, I stopped in my tracks at the heated conversation.

"Have you lost your fucking mind?" A man in a wrinkled suit was pacing in front of Ryzen's desk. "The FBI came to our office looking for you. I stalled them, but I don't know for how long."

"Were you followed?" Ryzen leaned back in a chair, completely relaxed.

"No, I made sure of it. I switched flights three times. But, Ryzen, shit is hitting the fan. Blackwood is onto us. He chased me down in the parking garage, him and his stupid fucking brothers. I barely got away." Riddick huffed and wiped his forehead. "And don't get me fucking started on Voledetti. He wants to see you. Now."

"Riddick, calm down, I have it under control." Ryzen smirked and placed his elbows on the desk. "And I'll handle Cian. You can count on that."

"What the hell happened?" Riddick waved his hands in the air and plopped down in the chair across from him.

"She found the flash drive." Ryzen's voice was low, angry.

Riddick was quiet for a moment, his fingers rubbing his temples. "You were supposed to get rid of that. Why do you still have it?"

"Insurance against Voledetti. But she saw the security footage. She knows."

"Why the fuck would you even save that? Are you trying to get us both locked up?"

"Don't worry, I got it all back. I have a plan, Riddick."

"Was her almost dying part of your plan? Fuck, Ryzen!"

"That was her fault. She tried to get away." He smirked.

"What are you going to do when she remembers, Ryzen?" Riddick's voice was laced with panic.

My ears perked up, confusion clouding my brain. Remember? Were they talking about me?

Ryzen chuckled and held up a bottle of liquid, shaking it. "She won't. Believe me."

Riddick shook his head. "This is fucking crazy.

Things have gone from bad to worse, to just…fuck!"

Ryzen poured out two drinks, handing one to Riddick. "I'm taking care of it, like I always do."

The knot in my stomach grew to the size of a boulder, and I backed away from the door slowly. What the hell was going on? Something wasn't right, that much was clear. Why would the FBI be talking to them? And who the hell were this Blackwood and Voledetti? There were too many questions, but there was one thing I knew for sure.

My fiancé was hiding something.

And I wanted to know what it was.

## Chapter Seventeen
**Day 63**

It had been over a week since I had overheard that strange conversation between Ryzen and Riddick. He hadn't bothered sticking around and had been gone by breakfast the next morning. Iva too; she was nowhere to be seen. Not that I was complaining. Something was going on between the three of them, and I had a dreadful feeling that I was involved somehow.

Being on the island felt isolating. Ryzen spent most of his time locked in his office and would only stop by my room at night before bed. I wondered if this was what our relationship had always been like. The pictures he had shown me reflected a loving couple who were very much taken with each other, but there was a coldness about him that had me feeling uneasy at times.

The only other people I had contact with were Valik and the doctor, who barely uttered a few words every time I saw him. The good news was that the cast on my arm could come off in as soon as two weeks. I was getting stronger, moving around as much as I could. During the day, Valik would take me on walks around the property where I would try to get as much info out of him as possible. He answered almost all my questions, except the ones about Juliet. I would get random images of her smiling face in my head; they weren't old memories, they were definitely recent, and I was excited about that. But Valik would stutter and try to change the subject when I asked about her. I wanted to trust him. Deep in my gut, I felt that he didn't mean to cause me any harm. But he was hiding something. Just like Ryzen.

I had tried asking him more about my accident on his routine nightly visit where he would bring me tea and pain medication.

"I already told you, Nova. We had an argument over the wedding date, and you got upset and left. You had been drinking too much that night, and you slammed right into a tree." His lips were set in a flat line. "I warned you about your drinking before. This is the wakeup call you needed."

Great. I was apparently a drunk also.

"Now, take your pills." He handed me two pills and a cup of tea.

I had tried telling him that I was feeling much better, that I didn't think I needed them anymore. But he didn't listen. Just said "doctors' orders." End of conversation.

I popped them in my mouth and sipped the tea. At his pointed look, I chugged the whole cup and handed it back to him empty.

"Get some rest. I love you." He leaned down and kissed my forehead.

"Thanks," I mumbled and lay down, shutting my eyes.

He turned off the lights, leaving me in the dark, and as soon as he shut the door behind him, I swiveled my tongue and spit out the two pills I had hidden there. I reached under the mattress and pulled out the baggie of pills I had been collecting over the past few days and added the new ones in there.

Stepford Wife Nova had apparently gotten herself up shit creek somehow. And I was going to have to fix it. First thing, no more damn pills. I was sick and tired of always being groggy and in a state of confusion. Sometimes it was hours before I could even have a rational thought. Second thing, I needed to find a phone.

Ryzen stalled every time I asked him for one, since mine had apparently been ruined in the crash. And he wouldn't let me use his, not even to check the weather. "Nova, you've lost three years of your memory. Looking at news or anything else might be too jarring for you. The doctor said you needed to recover first."

Sounded like a pile of horseshit to me. For whatever reason, he didn't want me talking to anyone else. Was it a control thing? Possessiveness and jealousy? Or was it something much worse? I mean, I couldn't even use a laptop. There were none to be found in the whole house, except for the one in Ryzen's office. When I asked Valik if I could use his phone, he said Ryzen had confiscated them all from the guards. That he was worried about being tracked by the media, who were like bloodhounds. They all communicated with walkie-talkies only.

Another thing I found strange was there wasn't a single knife anywhere. No sharp objects. I knew, because I had looked all over after I realized I wasn't allowed to cut my own food. I searched every drawer and cupboard in the kitchen. No knives. I even went as far as searching the living rooms and bathrooms in case they had them stashed away somewhere. Nothing. Not one damn knife. Now tell me why that was. Was I a danger to myself? Or to someone else? None of this was making sense, and the clearer my head became, the more I realized that Stepford Wife Nova had fucked up somewhere.

It was late in the afternoon when Valik and I were walking around the property. I had been getting little snippets of memories back, random things that didn't make any sense, like Juliet and I hugging a blond-haired man in an office or petting a cow in the rain, and a man with scars on his face. He was... helping me with something. My body hummed with excitement when the flashes happened, as if they were happy memories, and things that had happened recently. But that made no sense.

Some banging noises drew my attention to a small structure behind the tree line. Valik halted, putting his finger against his lips. I nodded and wrapped my arms around myself. After another thirty seconds, we heard the noises again. He pulled out his gun, and my eyes widened. I knew he was a bodyguard, but hadn't realized he was actually carrying a weapon. It seemed almost silly, considering there were only a handful of us actually on the island: Ryzen, three or four security guards, and the housekeeper.

Valik walked over to the shack, his gun pointed at the door. The shuffling noises started again, and he pushed the door open slowly, yelling when a little black cat came running out.

"Holy fucking hell," he bellowed.

I grabbed my stomach, laughter rolling through

me as the small cat ran right over to me and started rubbing on my legs.

"Aww, look at this cutie. He's probably hungry." I picked him up and he snuggled right into my arms. "Oh, my God, he's so adorable. Let's take him back and get him some food."

"Nova, I don't think Ryzen is going to like that."

"Well, Ryzen isn't here, I'm here. And I say we take him." I put one hand on my hip and quirked an eyebrow at him.

"Whatever you say, boss lady." He chuckled and searched inside the shack for any other stragglers. "All clear."

I rolled my eyes and laughed. We started our walk back to the house, and when we got closer, I saw Ryzen speeding off in one of his fancy cars.

"Where's he going?" I looked at Valik. The island was isolated, with only a handful of shops and locals, according to Ryzen.

"Maybe to blow off steam." Valik shrugged. "Sometimes he does that."

"Interesting," I whispered and walked up the steps into the house. If Ryzen was gone, then that meant I had a shot at going through his office. I glanced at Valik out of the corner of my eye, my mind racing.

We went into the kitchen, and I pulled out some leftover meat from the night before, shredding it with my fingers for the cat to eat. "We should call him Dracula. Look at those tiny little fangs." I chuckled as I petted him.

"I guess he is kind of cute." Valik petted him while he was eating, which Dracula seemed to enjoy. When he was done eating, he shot down the hall and then back to the kitchen, looking at us with wide eyes.

"He's happy, see?" We both awed at the little black ball of fur as Dracula ran around wild, practically falling over himself when he rounded the corner and went straight for the open door leading into the basement. "Valik, go get him before he gets lost." I hoped he hadn't heard the eagerness in my voice.

"Great, now I'm babysitting a cat." Valik shook his head and walked down the stairs, and when he got to the bottom, I shut the door quietly and locked it.

This might be my only chance. I raced down the hall, and not more than thirty seconds later, I heard Valik calling my name. I'd have to be quick before he got out. A man his size could break down that door with a snap of his fingers if he really wanted to. I hesitated when I got to Ryzen's office door. What if he came back and found me here? *No, no. Just be quick and see if you can find a cell phone.*

I rushed in and shut the door behind me. My heart was beating so fast, I could hear it in my ears.

*Quick, Nova.*

There were pictures of us all over his office, similar to the ones he had shown me before. But now wasn't the time to look at those. I opened the top drawer first, moving the papers and folders around, but didn't find a phone.

*Come on. He has to have a phone or laptop in here somewhere.*

I yanked open the side drawer to the desk and stared at the bottles there. Pain medication. And lots of it. But none of the bottles had my name on it. *Houston, we have a problem.* Fentanyl. Codeine. Vicodin. Xanax. Holy shit, it was like a damn narcotics lab in the drawer.

Something rolled to the back, and I reached in and pulled out a vial of liquid. It was the same bottle Ryzen had shown Riddick. My hand trembled as I read the label.

*Alprazolam Clobinax—Benzodiazepines.*

What the fuck was this?

"Nova?" Valik yelled out.

Oh, fuck, he'd gotten out already. I slammed the desk drawer shut and ran over to the bookshelf, pulling off the first book I could grab just as Valik walked into the office.

He narrowed his eyes at me, Dracula clawing up his suit. "Why did you lock me down there?"

We were silent for a moment, a layer of tension in the air. I scrunched up my face and laughed. "I didn't lock you down there, silly. The door shut on its own. Must have been a draft." I walked over and held the book up. "Just came to get some reading material for later."

He opened his mouth, then shut it, handing me Dracula. "OK, get your book and let's get out of here before Ryzen comes back. He doesn't like it when people are in here."

We fussed around with Dracula over the next hour and made him a little bed right next to mine. My chest felt lighter from having this tiny little companion, like I'd found a new friend, which just made me realize how isolated and lonely it was here. Dracula abandoned his bed to lie on my feet and I grabbed the book I'd taken from Ryzen's office.

*The Complete Guide to Norse and Greek Mythology.* I flipped through the pages, stopping every so often to read a snippet.

Thor, the Norse God of thunder and the sky.

Thor. Thor. I kept saying it over and over, something tickling at the back of my mind.

*C'mon, Nova, remember. Please remember.*

My head throbbed, and I squeezed my eyes shut. Thor. Thor.

It was there. Something was there.

I grunted and threw the book against the wall, scaring poor Dracula. He climbed up, nestling his little head in the crook of my neck, and we fell asleep that way.

\*\*\*\*\*

My dreams were filled with terror, and I woke up gasping, covered in sweat. I had been driving, frantic, screaming and terrified. A giant scorpion chased after me, and a man was yelling in my ear, telling me he was coming to save me. Then darkness. A name popped up like a big billboard on the side of the highway.

Thora.

Was it real? Was that a real person? Or was it just the book playing tricks on me?

There was a knock on the door, and then Valik walked in with a small tray of food, along with my tea and pills. "Hungry?" He grinned at Dracula, who meowed at the smell wafting around the room.

I nibbled on a few bits and pieces of my dinner, letting Dracula eat most of the meat until he was content and plopped back down on my feet. I wanted to ask Valik about the name Thora, but something stopped me from doing so.

"I made him a little box, so he won't be peeing in every corner of the house." Valik chuckled and dragged the box in from the hallway. "Ryzen said to make sure you take your medicine and drink your tea."

He handed the pills to me, and I sighed. "But I don't need them, Valik. I'm getting better."

"I don't make the rules, Nova. He just said to make sure you took them." Valik squinted at the pills, as if he was trying to read something. "That doesn't make any sense," he muttered.

"What?" I narrowed my eyes at him. His lips were set in a flat line, and he looked between me and the pills.

"You've been taking these?" His voice was uncertain, and he raised his eyebrow.

I nodded, nibbling on my bottom lip as he muttered under his breath. Something was bothering him, but he wouldn't spit it out. I'd noticed a few things since we'd been here—hell, I'd noticed a lot of things, but one thing was for sure: He was scared of Ryzen. And I didn't know why.

"How about"—I took the pills out of his hand—"I won't tell if you won't?" Valik watched me walk over to the plant in the corner of the room, and I tucked the two pills into the soil, covering it back up. I threw my hands in the air and walked back to bed. "Problem solved. Right?"

He was quiet for a moment, then nodded. "OK, our secret. But drink your tea, it'll help you sleep."

I rolled my eyes and chugged the tea, handing him the cup back. Yeah, just what I needed. More bad dreams. But they weren't all bad. Sometimes I had visions of a man hugging me, telling me he loved me, or me dancing with Juliet. Those dreams were the ones where I would wake up and feel happy. But the others? I shuddered at the thought. I was sick of the nightmares.

*****

## Day 67

I peered over the banister as Ryzen yelled in his office. He had been like that all morning, and a part of me wanted to laugh at how untethered he sounded. The other part of me wanted to take cover in my room so that I didn't end up the target of his anger like poor Glenda, the housekeeper.

"What do you mean you told him to come here? Have you lost your mind, Riddick?" He must have thrown something, because I heard a loud bang and then what sounded like things falling off a shelf. "Get your ass back to the island right fucking now!"

His office door flew open, and I raced back to my room, shutting the door quietly.

*Please don't come up here.*

I held my breath for what seemed like an eternity, but he never came up. My whole body was shaking, vibrating with a level of anxiety I wasn't familiar with. The fact that my body was reacting this way freaked me out even more to the point where I had to take deep, steady breaths. The subconscious mind was a powerful thing, and if I was having this reaction to hearing Ryzen yell, then I knew I had experienced this before. How many times had we fought? Had he yelled at me like that? He'd said I'd gotten mad at him for pushing back the wedding date, and my drunk ass had decided the best way to handle that was to speed down a dark road going over seventy miles per hour. It didn't make sense. How could I turn into a fuck-up like that? Especially after the snippets of happy memories that were starting to come back to me.

There was only one answer that I was starting to accept. And that was that I wasn't a fuck-up. I was just being tricked into believing that.

Something was very wrong here. Something bad. But I was going to get to the bottom of it. No matter what.

The sound of cars pulling into the driveway had me running to the window. Five sedans pulled up, one after another. I narrowed my eyes as men started climbing out of the cars. There must have been twenty of them all dressed the same in black suits. It looked like an army. One man stepped out from the crowd, a whole lot bigger than the rest. He glanced up at the window I was looking out of and took off his sunglasses. I stepped back slowly, just as Ryzen yelled out a slew of cuss words from downstairs. I didn't know who these men were, but he was definitely not happy about it.

A few minutes passed, and I peeked out the window again. Only a handful of men stayed by the cars, and the rest had walked up and were standing on the porch.

Well, no use being a chickenshit and hiding in my room. If we had company, then I wanted to know who they were. I went downstairs and peeked inside Ryzen's office, but they weren't there. Voices were coming from the main living room, so I went in that direction and ran right into Valik standing in the entryway.

"No, no, no," he whispered and tried to block my view of the living room—or more like he was trying to block whoever was in the living room from seeing me. "Get out of here," he murmured over his shoulder.

"Who have we got here?" a man's voice purred from the living room, and I pushed past Valik. "Ah, Miss La Roux." He walked towards me, his eyes widening as he looked me over. Hell, I looked a lot better now than I had two weeks ago, but I still had cuts and scrapes covering most of my body, and plenty of bruises to boot. At least my black eye had finally started to get better, and now was a nice disgusting yellow color. I was used to seeing my beat-up and bruised body; I hadn't realized that it might be jarring to someone seeing me for the first time since the accident.

"Hi." My smile faltered as he got closer. He was massive, bigger than Ryzen, and covered in tattoos. There was an aura of power around him, and something else. Whatever it was, it made the hairs on my arms stand up and I regretted coming down here and being nosey. "Sorry to interrupt."

"Nova," Ryzen huffed. "Go to your ro—"

The man held his hand up and Ryzen stopped talking abruptly. "Did he do this to you?" His voice was low, his eyes assessing me.

Ryzen huffed and opened his mouth, but the man snapped his fingers and Ryzen stopped whatever he was about to say.

"Oh, no, no," I scoffed. "I guess I did it to myself?" I shrugged my shoulders and he raised his eyebrows.

"I was in a bad car accident. Um, I'm sorry if I don't remember you. I'm having trouble remembering a lot of things actually." I was rambling, and my heart was beating so fast I thought it might pop right out of my chest. "You know me? My name, you said it. We know each other?" I hated how eager I sounded. Being locked up in this house with mostly just Ryzen and Valik—and, well, now Dracula—as my only companions had me desperate for contact with another human being.

Ryzen walked up and gripped my hand. "She's not well at the moment. Valik, please take her." He turned me towards Valik and I wanted to scratch his eyes out for making me leave. I wanted to know what was going on. It wasn't normal to be cooped up in a house like this. Desperation washed over me, and I shook off Valik's hand from my shoulder.

"I'm going to make a snack," I muttered and went down the hall. Valik seemed satisfied with that and didn't follow me, just turned back to face Ryzen and the stranger.

I tiptoed across the kitchen floor to the side hallway that connected to the other side of the living area. Their voices echoed down the hall, and I peeked through the little crack in the door.

"What happened to her?" The man's face was scrunched up with anger. He looked terrifying, if I was being honest with myself.

"She was in a car accident and sustained a head injury. Amnesia—well, temporary. We're seeing a psychiatrist."

I gasped, my hand flying to cover my mouth. *Why, you little damn liar.* We weren't seeing a psychiatrist, and he knew it.

"That's none of your concern though." Ryzen crossed his arms over his chest, keeping a distance from the man.

"Oh, but it is," the man purred and took a step closer to Ryzen. "Cian Blackwood is causing problems. Problems that I don't need."

"I will handle him."

"Like you've been handling Covington? Tell me, Ryzen, what have you accomplished while hiding out on this island the past few weeks like a coward?"

"I'm not hiding," Ryzen scoffed and wiped his forehead. "I'm working on closing the deal. It's all going to plan."

"And my money?" the man demanded and took another step closer. He moved his jacket to the side, reaching into his pocket, and I saw a flash of metal.

A gun.

"I need more time. Two weeks tops."

The man sighed and rubbed his temple. "I'm growing extremely tired of your incompetence. You need to understand that I am not my father. You have one week before I take it all away from you. Understand?" He tapped Ryzen on the cheek. "You should be thanking me for not killing you right where you stand."

Ryzen gulped, visibly sweating through his shirt.

"Well?" The man adjusted his cufflinks and smirked.

"Thank you," Ryzen whispered, closing his eyes for a moment.

My hands trembled as I covered my mouth. Who was this guy? This was worse than I'd realized. I stepped back, knocking into a painting, but grabbed it before it could fall and expose me for spying. They were quiet for a second too long and I hauled ass back to the kitchen and ran out the back door.

*OK, Stepford Wife Nova. What have you gotten yourself into?*

I walked toward the water, needing time to process what I had just heard. Out of the corner of my eye, I saw something run through the trees and realized it was a woman. She hid behind a tree, peeking around it, and then took off again.

I trotted after her. She had to have come with those men, except she was wearing just plain jeans and a t-shirt. The landscape scraped my legs as I moved through it, and I stopped to catch my breath. I bent over, placing my hands on my knees as I heaved. My body wasn't used to moving as quickly, and my heart pounded in my ears. She was standing close to the edge of the cliff, granite scattered around her.

"Hey," I yelled to her, but she didn't turn around. She took another step closer, and I yelled louder this time. "Hey, be careful." Couldn't she tell how slippery it was with all those rocks there? I moved closer. "Excuse me."

She took another step and stumbled slightly, and I gasped. Her head fell back, and she stared at the sky, her arms raised above her head. *Oh, my God. This bitch is crazy.* The realization that she was getting ready to jump off gripped my chest and I raced over, slamming into her from the side. We landed in a pile of tangled limbs, pain shooting up my arm, and I yelled out at the sensation.

"What the hell are you doing?" Rocks were digging into my ass, and I groaned, trying to stand up. "Are you out of your mind? That's instant death." I pointed down the cliff.

"You ruined it," she sobbed and covered her face.

I kneeled down and peeled her hands away. "Hey, it's OK." Instant regret ran through me for yelling at her, and she wrapped her arms around my stomach, clinging to me. "Shh, it's OK."

Her tears drenched my shirt, and after a moment she pulled back and wiped her face. She looked up at me and gasped, a flash of surprise crossing her face. "It's you. Pastry girl."

I tilted my head to the side and chuckled. Well, that was a first. "Do I know you?"

"From the park?" She looked at me, her eyes big, and I noticed she had one blue and one gray eye. I sighed, my shoulders slumping forward. I was getting real sick of explaining that I couldn't remember shit from the last three years. We looked behind us as men started yelling out, presumably looking for her.

This was my only shot. "Do you have a phone?"

She nodded and reached into her jeans, handed me her phone. My fingers trembled as I dialed the number engraved in my brain.

"You live here?" Her face was scrunched up with concern, and I nodded my head.

"That's what they tell me." I placed the phone to my ear and crossed my fingers. *Please pick up, Juliet. Please pick up and tell me that this is all a dream and you're out there waiting for me.* It rang and rang, but no answer. "Fuck!"

The men were close now, no more than thirty yards away. Valik was with them, and so was the other man. The scary one.

Fuck. Fuck. Fuck. I opened the browser and typed in the words I had memorized from days before.

*Alprazolam Clobinax.*

The browser loaded and I shuffled on my knees so that they wouldn't see I had a phone. It was so slow to load that I wanted to scream at the top of my lungs.

*Alprazolam Clobinax: Used to treat panic and anxiety disorder. Not approved in the United States. Side effects include amnesia/memory loss, heart palpitations, including heart attack and stroke, and internal bleeding. Can be taken in capsule or liquid form.*

My blood ran cold as I read it one more time.

Out of the corner of my eye, I saw the men approaching and I dropped the phone. "Don't tell them." I looked at the phone and then her. She nodded and put it back in her pocket.

"Milliani, what the hell was that? Were you trying to jump?" The man gripped her shoulders, shaking her slightly.

"I'm sorry, Kaviathin. I just couldn't take it any more." She sobbed and clung to him. "Please don't be upset."

"Don't be upset? That my sister tried to end her precious life?" His voice was filled with anger and I squeezed my eyes shut. This was private and not something a group of people needed to be watching. A man in a black suit started speaking in another language—Italian, I thought. He pointed at the cliff, and then to me, mimicking how I tackled her to the ground.

I turned away, not wanting to get involved in their personal business. Valik rushed over to me, giving me a once-over. He shook his head at the cut on my arm and my torn shirt. "You all right?" he whispered.

"Yeah." I nodded and let him take me back to the house. Ryzen was waiting for us on the front porch, his eyes narrowing when he saw me scraped up.

"What happened?" He was angry, probably because he'd just had his ass handed to him by this Kaviathin guy.

"Just… It's a long story," I mumbled from the bottom of the stairs, which only seemed to irritate him. He shook his head, watching as the men piled back into their cars, the woman with them.

"Valik, I need you in my office now." Ryzen nodded his head to the front door, and Valik walked up the steps. "Come on, Nova. Get cleaned up before dinner." They both stood at the top of the stairs waiting for me.

Before I took my first step, Kaviathin called my name and motioned for me to come to him. I didn't bother looking at Ryzen, because I knew he'd tell me not to go. I walked over to the car, standing behind the open door where Ryzen and Valik couldn't see.

"You saved my sister."

I couldn't read the look on his face or his tone, so I just nodded.

He reached up and brushed his thumb just under my eye, the one that had been black and brown for weeks. "Your lion is tearing the world apart looking for you."

"My lion?" I whispered, my heart stopping for a moment.

"You really don't know?" He took off his sunglasses, his eyes piercing mine—the same as his sister, one gray, one blue.

Ryzen called my name and yelled for me to come

inside. I turned to leave, but before I did Kaviathin grabbed my arm and I gasped. He pulled out a switchblade knife, pressing a button on the side so the sharp point popped out. My eyes widened as he pressed it again and the blade disappeared. He dragged my arm closer to him and stuffed the knife down the cast around my arm.

"I owe you." He nodded and let my arm go.

I ran back to the house, a million thoughts rushing through my head. Ryzen narrowed his eyes. "What did he say to you?" He gripped my upper arm and Valik's eyes widened. He took a step forward, but I shook my head slightly. I didn't need Ryzen yelling at him again.

"Just said thank you because I helped his sister." I patted his chest. "That's all. Let me get cleaned up for dinner, OK?" I reached up and kissed his cheek and that seemed to relax him. He let me go and I raced upstairs, locking myself in the bathroom.

Well… I'd figured out what the problem was…

He was drugging me.

And probably trying to kill me.

*Stepford Wife Nova, you have a lot of explaining to do.*

# Chapter Eighteen

I gripped my fork until my knuckles turned white and stabbed at the salad Ryzen had prepared for me. He raised his eyebrows, and I forced a smile, digging my nails into my palm under the table. Kaviathin and his entourage had left not too long ago, and I had hidden the knife upstairs under my pillow. Why the hell had he given that to me? He knew something I didn't, and that was fucking terrifying. I was in danger here, that much was clear. Every muscle in my body was tight, my body ready to run.

But where? There was nowhere to go. My shoulders sagged, and I swallowed the lump in my throat. "Ryzen, why were all those men here?"

He'd been mostly quiet while we ate, not offering a single explanation as to why a posse of men who looked like they had just stepped off the set of a mafia movie had shown up at our home. "Business associates. Nothing to worry about." He tapped my nose and I had to stop myself from trying to bite his finger off like a wild animal. "How's your memory? No improvement?" He watched me like a hawk, looking for something in my facial expression.

"No, nothing still." I shook my head and put my fork down. "Maybe we should go see a psychiatrist?

Someone to help me remember." My voice quivered and I gripped his hand.

He tugged his hand out from under mine and tilted his head to the side. "The doctor said it would come back when you were ready, dear."

*More like it will come back when you stop fucking drugging me.*

He wiped his mouth and tossed his napkin onto his plate. "You know I've been feeling terrible about your accident. If I hadn't postponed the wedding date, you would have never left so angry. I would like to make it up to you." He leaned back in his chair, crossing his arms behind his head. "How about I have a priest come this week and marry us? Right on the island. Just us?"

I blinked rapidly and jolted back, trying to process what he was saying. Get married? Why would we get married when I couldn't even remember anything about our relationship? The way he looked at me made me realize that this wasn't a choice. He was telling me, giving me the illusion of free will. It was like a game to him, I realized. All of it was.

I didn't even know how to respond to that. There was no way in hell I was going to marry him, but I knew I couldn't say that to his face. Not at this moment.

"Maybe we should wait? Until I get my memory back?" My heart slammed against my chest at my words.

"Oh, it's fine, Nova. Trust me, this is exactly what you wanted all along." He clapped his hands together and stood. "I'll set it up. Now get ready for bed, you need rest." He kissed my forehead and left me at the table.

Later that night, I was sitting on my bed with Dracula, my mind racing. I wasn't going to lie to myself.

I was terrified. I was trapped on this island with almost no connection to the outside world, except for a fiancé who I had a terrible suspicion might be trying to kill me. My only friend was this tiny ball of fur—and Valik, but I didn't know if I could trust him one hundred percent. He seemed to really care for me, but I didn't know if it was just an act. My gut told me it wasn't, but I couldn't be sure.

What I didn't understand was why. Was I in a relationship with a control freak? Had Ryzen always been this way? I balled my hands into fists, banging them against my thighs.

*Why can't you remember?*

It had been days since I had stopped taking the pills. I would have thought my memory would have come back by now. But it hadn't, and the desperation that ran through my whole body was enough to make tears form and stream down my cheeks.

Valik knocked on the door and came in with a tray, and I wiped my tears away. It was our typical nightly routine of him handing me my tea and pills, then turning his back while I hid them in the plant that I had moved next to my bed. I would have to find a new hiding spot for them soon.

Or get the hell out of here.

I sat on the edge of the bed, letting the teacup warm my hands. Maybe I needed to meditate, be my own psychologist and get my brain churning. Hell, perhaps it was the trauma of crashing in such an awful way that had made me forget. *Maybe* I wasn't ready to remember. I brought the cup up to my lips, blowing on the hot liquid.

And then I froze.

*Alprazolam Clobinax—may be taken in liquid or pill form.*

My hands trembled as I held the teacup away from me, the realization sinking in.

It was the tea. Every single night I had been drinking the tea since I had woken up here on the island. Valik had his back turned to me and I placed the cup on the edge of the nightstand, letting it fall to the ground. He snapped his head over his shoulder and rushed over.

"Damn, don't burn yourself, Nova." He grabbed a towel and wiped up the pool on the floor. "Are you all right? You look pale." He narrowed his eyes at me.

"Uh, yeah. Fine, just a long day." I leaned back onto the bed, and squeezed my eyes shut.

"Let me go get you some more tea." He picked up the cup and placed it on the tray, along with the towel.

"No!" I straightened my back. "I'm OK for tonight." He looked at me like I had lost my mind, and I sighed. "What kind of tea is that anyway?"

He shrugged. "Hell if I know. Ryzen makes it."

A tingling sensation moved from the top of my head, down my neck and shoulders. I'd known it.

That son of a bitch.

\*\*\*\*\*

I saw *the* face in my dream that night, the same man from my other dreams. It wasn't completely clear, but I saw scars running down his face and neck. And tattoos. Lots of tattoos. A giant scorpion covered most of his chest. Most of him was blurry, but his smile… his smile made my heart melt and ache all at the same time. I didn't know who he was, but I knew that I loved him more than anything else in the world.

And I also knew that man was not Ryzen.

**Day 71**

I had to get off this damn island.

It had been days since I had stopped drinking the tea. I wasn't sure if I could trust Valik, so when he brought me it every night, I would make sure his back was turned before dumping it into the plant.

My memory was still not coming back to me though, just random bits and pieces that made no sense. Like images of me lying on the grass with a crystal on my forehead. Or stuffing my face with pastries.

Pastry girl. That was what the woman had called me.

It would come back, I knew it. But I didn't want to be on this island when it did. Because something told me I wasn't going to be happy when I remembered why I had tried to leave Ryzen the night I crashed my car.

I had been doing my best to avoid Ryzen over the past few days. He was intent on having a priest come and marry us any day now. Kaviathin had said he would be back in a week, and that had been four days ago. I had thought maybe I could get him to help me, but realized that wasn't going to be an option. He knew something was wrong, that was why he'd given me the knife, but he hadn't offered to take me with him. No, nobody was coming to save me. I had to save myself.

I peered out the window as Ryzen drove off in his Lamborghini and rolled my eyes. *Good, go blow off some of your psychopathic steam.*

Dracula followed me down the stairs, and I dug through the cabinet of cat food to feed him. He rubbed against my legs, and I sat down on the floor with him while he ate.

"Where did you come from, hm?" I asked. He purred while he ate, my heart warming.

Glenda, the housekeeper, was singing along with the radio as she dusted around the living room. An idea occurred to me then, and I peeked around the corner, watching her for a moment. There was no reason not to trust her. I exhaled sharply and walked over to her.

"Hi, Glenda." I clasped my hands together in front of me. "How was your weekend?"

She turned and smiled at me. "Oh, hi, Nova dear. Very good—we caught lots of lobster, so very good indeed."

I took a step closer, trying to appear as casual as possible. "You live on the island?"

She shook her head no and swiveled her hips to the music. "No, dear. I'm out on the mainland. Just come here twice a week to clean."

"Uh-huh. How far is the mainland again?" I glanced around the room and picked off an invisible piece of dust from the fireplace.

"About fifteen miles, dear, about an hour by ferry. It's not too bad, unless you get seasick like I tend to do." She chuckled.

An hour. That was all? "And, um, what time does the ferry come?"

She stopped cleaning and gave me a curious look. "Seven a.m. and p.m., twice a week. Are you and Mr. Goodacre planning a trip?"

There was nothing sinister in her tone, but I didn't want to give anything away.

"Well, his birthday is coming up and I wanted to maybe go to the mainland to get him a present. Um, unless there is a shop nearby where I could find something for him?" I shrugged my shoulders, biting the inside of my cheek.

She shook her head. "Oh, no, dear. There're a few shops by the ferry drop-off, but oh, gosh, that's all the way on the other side of the island, about twenty miles."

Twenty miles? How the hell was I supposed to get twenty miles without a car? And without being seen? That wasn't going to work. I took a deep breath and cracked my neck. "Just curious, but if someone wanted to get to the mainland without getting on the ferry, how would they?"

She tapped her lips and stared up at the ceiling. "Well, you could take a boat. My nephew does it all the time when he wants the peace and quiet. Takes a good chunk of time though. Four or five hours. Depends on the day and the tide really."

I glanced down at my arm wrapped in the cast, my shoulders slumping forward. How was I supposed to row a boat with only one good arm? I would have to face that hurdle when I got to it. This was good news. Great, actually. If I was able to find a boat, then I would be just a short few hours from freedom. My pulse quickened at the realization.

"Just one more thing, Glenda, then I'll get out of your hair." I walked over so that I was standing in front of her. "Where would someone get a boat around here?"

"Well, Mr. Goodacre has some tied up under the pier, dear, don't you know that?" She scrunched up her nose.

I slapped my palm against my forehead and chuckled. "Duh, I've been a little slow since my accident."

She tilted her head to the side and gave me a look that resembled pity, and I wrapped my arms around her tightly. "Thank you, Glenda." I pulled back, her face registering surprise, but I didn't care. Freedom was close. So damn close.

Valik was out front talking to another guard, which meant it was a perfect time to run down to the pier. I changed my shoes and ran out the back door, only stopping to catch my breath when I got to the tree line. I passed the little shack we had found Dracula in and noticed the door was open. Odd, because Valik had shut it last time. Why would someone be messing around out there? I would have to deal with that later though because I didn't know how long Ryzen was going to be gone.

I raced through the trees and down the slope, slipping through the rocks. The last thing I needed was to break my damn neck going down the hill, so I slowed down and took my time. The pier was in sight, and I laughed when I finally set foot on it. She'd said the boats were tied under it, so I climbed down the ladder and walked under the planks.

There were three little boats tied together, just like she had said. I pumped my fist in the air and inspected them. They weren't quite boats, more like dinghies, but smaller. One had a crack on the side with water pouring through it, but the other two looked in perfect shape. There were even oars tucked under the seat. I looked over the water. It was quiet, peaceful, but that didn't mean rowing a boat across it would be easy. The weather had been nice the past few days, the water calm. Maybe it wouldn't be that hard to do.

I could do this. Get away tomorrow night when everyone was asleep, get help. I could go to the police. I bit down on my bottom lip and shook my head. And tell them what? That I was scared of my fiancé? That I thought he was drugging me? No, they would think I was crazy and probably just call Ryzen. I would have to stay somewhere for a few days while I tried to get my memory back. Try calling Juliet again. She would help me. I knew she would. It wouldn't matter if we had fought; she could keep me safe. I just knew it.

The only problem was rowing with only one good arm. But maybe if I tied the oars together? I was a city girl; never in my life had I rowed a damn boat. A million thoughts raced through my head, but it didn't matter. I had a semblance of a plan now, a plan to get away, and I would make it work no matter what, because nobody was going to help me. I had to help myself.

I climbed back up the ladder and walked down the length of the pier, looking off into the distance. There were lampposts running up and down the pier, so I grabbed a handful of rocks and hurled them. I missed the first few times, but then I smashed the first lightbulb, then the second, and third, until eventually I had gotten them all.

I would leave tomorrow night. Ryzen would think I was asleep, that I was drugged up with all the pills he had given me. He would have no idea that I would be running away. Yes. I could do this.

A sense of peace washed over me as I walked back to the house. Ryzen still wasn't home, and I took the steps two at a time to the front door. Glenda was still cleaning, the radio blasting as she sang along to the song.

*Beautiful moon, so bright and white,*
*Won't you be my lucky date tonight?*

I stopped in the foyer, something tickling at the back of my mind.

*Love me wrong, love me right,*
*You belong to the night.*
*Oh, beautiful moon,*
*So bright and white.*

The hairs on the back of my neck stood up, fear gripping my heart like a vice. I stumbled over to the wall, trying to hold myself up. An image flashed in my mind of Ryzen, his words burned into my brain.

*"You bitch!" he screams and leaps towards me. The knight. Push the knight over, Nova. He's chasing me—oh, God, he's so close. Valik. The knife, use the knife, Nova. It's against his throat; blood is dripping. He's coming. Hurry, drive away. Don't let him catch you. Get the flash drive to Cian. Hurry!*

My vision blurred as I tried to go up the stairs, my heart pounding in my ears.

*He's right behind you. The tree, watch out for the tree!*

I screamed out at the top of my lungs, and then all I saw was darkness.

*****

It came flying back to me in an instant. Not everything, just bits and pieces. I'd been at a party with Ryzen. He'd been hiding something. A flash drive. I'd found it, and he'd found me. But I couldn't remember why I'd needed it. What was so important about that flash drive that I'd fled and he'd chased me down like a dog? The crash, someone resuscitating me. Little chunks of memory came rushing back. And Valik. I'd had a knife to his throat. I was the one who'd cut him. Why hadn't he told me? Oh, God, the fear—the fear was unlike anything I had ever experienced before. I couldn't stop screaming. He'd gotten me, and now I was going to die.

"Nova!" Valik was shaking my shoulders, my head whipping back and forth. There was a sharp sting and I gasped as he lowered his hand. He'd smacked me. He'd fucking smacked me. "Nova, stop screaming!" His chest heaved up and down, his eyes wild. "Calm down, it's OK."

"You hit me?" Tears welled up in my eyes and I covered my cheek with my hand.

"I had to; you wouldn't stop." He wiped his forehead and glanced at Glenda. Her face was pale, and she looked at me with wide eyes. "Glenda, it's fine. She's OK. Have Lindell take you back to the ferry." She stood there for a second longer, her eyes darting from me to him. "Go." He nodded at her.

Valik picked me up in his arms and carried me

upstairs to my room. When we got there, he slammed the door and tugged on the collar of his shirt. "Are you OK? You nearly gave me a heart attack."

I blinked rapidly at him, my heart still beating in an unsafe manner. Images of the two of us driving in a car, laughing and singing, popped into my head. We were friends. He had already said that. And when I had asked him about the cut on his neck, he had said it was a misunderstanding. I certainly hoped it was, because I was about to take a giant leap of faith at that moment, and if I failed, I could end up dead.

I stood at the end of the bed and gripped the post. "Valik," I whispered.

He stopped pacing and looked at me, his face turning serious.

"Valik, why didn't you tell me I was the one who cut your neck?"

His eyes widened; surprise flashed across his face. He took a step closer to me, and my nostrils flared. I held my hand out and shook my head. "Don't."

He sighed and sat down in the chair, clasping his hands together. "Is that what that just was? You remembered?"

"Some things, yeah." I nodded, and he muttered something under his breath.

"Fuck, Nova. I thought I was doing the right thing by not telling you. The doctor said..." He twisted his lips, shaking his head. "He said that if you remembered too quickly, it could be too much for you. That it would cause more harm than good."

I narrowed my eyes at him. "That doesn't make any sense though."

He huffed and leaned back in the chair. "Do I look

like a fucking doctor?" I stepped back at his aggressive tone, and he held up his hands. "I didn't mean to yell at you. It's just that's what he told Ryzen, and what Ryzen told us. I don't know shit about amnesia, Nova."

"But why did I have a knife to your neck?" My voice rose with each word. "Why would I do that to you if we were friends?"

His eyes searched mine, and he opened his mouth to say something, but stopped himself.

"Tell me, Valik." I took another step forward until I was standing in front of him.

He looked over his shoulder at the closed door, and shook his head. "I don't think it's a good idea for us to be talking inside. Someone could be listening."

"Stop trying to avoid the question and just tell me." I balled my hands into fists.

"I don't know why you pulled the knife on me." He threw his hands in the air. "One minute everything was fine, and the next you were holding a knife to my throat and kicking me out of the car. I had no fucking clue what was happening. You drove off before I could even help you, and Ryzen fled after you." He shook his head and huffed. "This has all been a damn mess. What else do you remember?"

"Enough. Enough to know that I was trying to get away from him. And enough to know that Ryzen's been trying to kill me."

Valik narrowed his eyes. "No, he—"

"Yes," I snapped. "He fucking is. I found all the pills in his office, Valik. And a vial of liquid that causes amnesia. He's been drugging me to excess so that I won't remember."

Valik genuinely looked frightened at that

moment, his eyes wide and body completely tensed. Was it fear for me or for him? I didn't know. But what I did know deep in my gut was that he was a good man with a good heart. "He's been putting alprazolam in my tea. It causes amnesia. The woman from the cliff—she gave me her phone for a second, and I saw it with my own two eyes," I choked out. "He doesn't want me to remember, Valik. He wants me dead."

Valik's shoulders slumped forward and he held his head in his hands. It was quiet for a moment, and I reached under the pillow and grabbed the switchblade. If he was about to try to turn me over to Ryzen, I was going to have to stop him.

"You're sure?" he whispered. I nodded, and he let out a deep breath. "Fuck."

'Fuck' was right.

He paced around the bed, shaking his head. "I have to get you out of here."

Oh, thank God. "How?" I pushed the knife back under the pillow and stood to face him.

"I don't know. I need a few days to think. We can take the ferry but would need a car to get there."

"No." I shook my head. "There's no time. Ryzen's bringing a priest here to marry us any day now."

Valik's lips curled in disgust. "What? He can't fucking do that."

"He can try. Look, I might have found another way off the island. Glenda told me about some boats down under the pier."

He raised his eyebrows and blinked slowly. "I'll never underestimate you again, Nova La Roux."

I chuckled, shaking my head. "It's dangerous though. If we could call someone to help us… Where are the phones?"

"I don't know." Valik shook his head and peeked out the curtains. "Ryzen took all our phones. We're all at his mercy, Nova. He has a safe in his office, but I've seen inside it… it's empty except for papers."

"Wait, I had a phone with me when I crashed. And, um…" I squeezed my eyes shut. There was another memory on the verge of coming out. What was it? "I had, um… crap. I don't know. But I definitely had a phone. What happened after I crashed?"

He sat down on the edge of the bed, his jaw clenched. "Ryzen and the other guard, Lindell, took you straight into the maids' quarters and had me and the other security stand guard. They didn't want the guests to be alarmed. The doctor came and shortly thereafter we were at the airstrip and headed this way." He gripped my hand and squeezed. "I swear, Nova, I didn't know how bad a shape you were in until I saw you the next day right here in this room. Ryzen said it was just a little accident." He let out a deep breath. "I should have fucking known. After all this time, I should have put the pieces together."

"I've made the mistake of trusting him too, Valik. I don't blame you." I squeezed him into a hug and was quiet for a moment. "You don't know where he put my stuff? My dress? He wouldn't have just left it there, especially not my phone."

Valik's jaw tensed. "Lindell carried a black bag out the maids' quarters and put it in the back of the SUV when we were leaving. Ryzen had it over his shoulder when we got off the ferry here. So, it's here somewhere." Valik's back tensed, and he snapped his fingers. "Wait. The day we got here, I saw Ryzen walk into the woods with a shovel, and I thought it was odd considering there's nothing out in the direction other than woods and that little shack. Do you think…" His voice trailed off.

"Do I think he buried the phones?" I scrunched up my nose. "That sounds like a crazy thing to do. But considering how this whole thing is one big ball of crazy, yes. I totally think he would do something like that. There's only one way to find out."

A car alarm beeped outside and Valik rushed to the window. "Fuck, Ryzen's back."

Panic gripped me again and I shuddered.

"Get into bed and act like you're asleep. Everyone heard you screaming from outside, so he'll know. We can't hide that."

"What are we going to do?" My breath caught in my throat as the front door slammed shut and moments later footsteps pounded up the stairs.

Valik pushed me back onto the bed and covered me with the blanket. "Shh." Valik rushed to sit in the chair and opened a magazine. I closed my eyes just as Ryzen walked in.

"What happened today?" he hissed.

"She took a nap downstairs and had a nightmare," Valik said. "Just resting now."

"Ah, good. You've been watching her take her pills? And the tea every night, right?"

"Yes, sir." Valik cleared his throat.

I didn't dare open my eyes, just tried to make my breath come out evenly.

"Good. I knew you wouldn't disappoint me. Bring her down for dinner at seven. We'll dine on the patio tonight."

The door shut, but I waited another moment before opening my eyes.

Valik's face was twisted with concern. And something else. Anger. Fear. His fists were balled up like he was ready to attack.

"Just get through dinner like normal and we'll check the shack tomorrow on our walk. OK?" He reached over and placed his hand on my foot over the blanket. "I've been a fuck-up my whole life, Nova. But I promise I won't let anything bad happen to you."

"I know," I whispered.

# Chapter Nineteen

Ryzen had a huge fire going in the firepit outside by the time I went downstairs for dinner. He stood with his hands stuffed in his pants pockets, eyes glistening as he stared at the fire. A part of me was dying to know what he was thinking. The other part wanted to push him into the flames.

I'd been practically hyperventilating when Valik said I had to go downstairs. Now that my memory was coming back, things were completely different. It had been easier to face Ryzen when I didn't know that he was actually trying to kill me. But now? How was I supposed to look at him without trying to murder him?

*He did this. All of this. He's trying to hurt me. Well, I'm not going to fucking let him.*

I sat across from him, my leg bouncing uncontrollably under the table. The knife was tucked inside my cast, and I was prepared to use it if I had to. But that was a last resort. I had to keep calm and not let on that I was getting my memory back. As much as it pained me, I reached across the table and patted his hand.

"You're in a good mood?" I smiled, gritting my teeth together.

"Things are working out wonderfully now." He

grinned and his dimple showed, making me want to gag. "I heard you had a bad dream earlier. You're still not remembering?" He leaned forward, his eyes searching my face.

I shook my head, keeping my face as neutral as possible. "No, nothing," I muttered.

"That's too bad." He leaned across the table and kissed my cheek, but not before I saw a hint of a smile on his face.

*You dirty, rotten scumbag.*

"I have to make a few calls. Why don't you go get ready for bed?" He pushed his chair in and held his hand out to me.

"Do you mind if I sit by the fire for a little longer? It's so warm." I batted my eyelashes, hoping that would have some kind of effect on him.

"Of course. I'll have one of the guards come get you in a bit." He strolled off up the back steps, whistling as he went.

I moved to a cushioned seat closer to the fire and sank down. The sky was completely clear and it would have been a wonderful night if I wasn't trapped on an island with an insane person. One of the guards —Lindell, I thought—sat down on the back steps and lit a cigar. The smoke drifted over to me, and I turned in the other direction, my nose tickling. I had seen Glenda place a stack of magazines on the side table earlier that day, and I reached over, grabbing one.

It was one of those interior design magazines, the front covered in cool furniture with vibrant colors. I rolled my eyes as I flipped through the pages. There was a four-page spread on how to pick the best velvet for your upholstery project.

Crushed velvet. Embossed velvet. Cisele velvet. I stared at the magazine, something screaming in the back of my mind. The flames danced around the fire, growing bigger and stronger, as if the universe was trying to tell me something at that moment. Cigar smoke wafted over to me, and I sneezed, glaring at the guard. Cigar smoke always irritated my nose. My father loved to smoke them, and thought it was funny when I would go into a sneezing fit.

The wind blew the page of the magazine over, and I blinked rapidly at the words. Plain velvet. Patterned velvet. Velvet.

A chill ran through me, making the hair on the back of my neck stand up.

*Operation Black Velvet is a go.*

My whole body froze, the magazine falling from my hands as I stared into the fire. Images flashed through my mind like a picture book. My warehouse burning down; the FBI threatening me; snooping around Ryzen's house. And Cian. My hands flew to my mouth, trying to cover the gasp trying to escape. Oh, God, Cian. My love. My heart. The man who would do anything for me, including putting out his freshly lit cigar because it made me sneeze uncontrollably.

I remembered.

I remembered everything.

## Day 72

I tossed and turned all night, images of Cian

flooding my mind. Everything was rushing back to me —the love, the fear, the anger. And Ryzen. Everything Ryzen had done to me. He must be out of his damn mind to bring me to this island, to drug me and keep me locked away from everyone. I couldn't understand what his endgame was. The only answer I came up with made my stomach turn. Did he think we were going to secretly get married to close the deal with Covington? Then what? He'd keep me locked away forever? No, he wouldn't let it end that way. I had a feeling he had something much more sinister planned. But I wasn't going to stick around to find out what. Because I was getting off this damn island, and if he tried to stop me then I was prepared to do what I needed.

I woke up with a new sense of purpose. Enough with the games. Enough with the bullshit. It was time to take action.

Kaviathin's words flashed through my mind.

*Your lion is tearing the world apart looking for you.*

Cian must be going crazy. My heart ached at the thought of him not knowing what had happened to me, only knowing that Ryzen had me. God, the terror in his voice when I'd told him that Ryzen was chasing after me. His frantic instructions echoed in my ears, making me squeeze my eyes shut.

The only thing keeping me calm was the other memories. Juliet's smiling face; Orin yelling in the kitchen that dinner was ready. Cian's lips all over my body; the way he kissed me and told me he loved me unlike any other; his fierce need to protect me.

*I'm coming, Cian. Just hold on.*

I rushed to get ready and waited for Valik, my hands unable to keep still. He came at his regular time in the afternoon, both of us silent as we walked across the back yard and over to the tree line. I gripped his arm, almost unable to control my excitement to tell him the news. When we got past the first row of trees, I turned to him, my eyes big and my smile stretched from ear to ear.

"Are you OK? You look a little crazy." He chuckled, and I leaned in close. We were outside and nobody had followed us, so there was no need to whisper, but I couldn't help it.

"I remember. Everything." I exhaled sharply, watching his reaction.

His mouth fell open and he picked me up in his arms, swinging me around. "Thatagirl! Yes, fuck yes," he hollered.

"Shh." I slapped his chest. "Someone might hear."

"Oh, damn," he whispered and put me down. "Didn't think that through. You remember it all?"

"Most of it, yeah." I nodded and we continued our walk. "It seems kind of like a movie playing in reverse though. Like things are out of order... but it's there." I tapped the side of my head. "There's more though. Look, I can't go into all the nitty details of everything, but you need to know that Ryzen and I were never really engaged."

Valik stopped walking, his eyes almost popping out of his head. "What? Why? No way."

I nodded and faced him. "There's just too much to tell you, but what I can say is that the engagement, the wedding, was all for show. And because of the people Ryzen's mixed up with, well, I've been working with the FBI." I nibbled on my fingernails, hoping this wasn't going to freak him out. "Not by choice. But the good news is, they are definitely looking for me."

Reassurance washed over me at the thought. I'd known Cian would be looking, but the FBI had to have been searching for me as well. I almost couldn't believe they hadn't found me yet.

"But that night that I pulled the knife on you, I found evidence that Ryzen blew up my warehouse. And other evidence against Kaviathin…" My words trailed off as I realized that Valik had to have known at least a little bit what Ryzen had been up to with Kaviathin. "You knew that though, right? That Ryzen was working with the Mafia?" I put my hands on my hips, tilting my head to look at him.

"Yeah, I knew. Not at first though. I was a nobody when Riddick hired me to be one of their guards. Didn't know what I was getting mixed up in. But I found out pretty quickly. By then, it was too late to look the other way or even walk away. The last few years have been a damn mess." Valik wrung his hands together, his lips in a flat line.

"What aren't you telling me?" He was avoiding my eyes, obviously keeping some type of secret from me. The question was, was it worse than mine?

"I don't want to freak you out, so let me explain everything before you say a word. OK?" He gave me a pointed look and I nodded. "I fucked up a while back. Robbed a few banks, and when I didn't get caught, robbed a few more. I never hurt anyone, OK?" He shook his head and kept walking as I tried to keep up the pace. "Was sentenced to ten years, but got out in six for good behavior. I tried to keep straight when I got out, but it's hard out there when you're a felon, Nova. You get the jobs nobody wants like mopping floors and cleaning dishes. Got mixed up with the wrong crowd again."

"How did you end up working for Ryzen then?"

"Fighting. Used to fight for money at an underground club. Riddick came in all the time, became real friendly, and offered me a job."

OK, well, that wasn't too bad. It wasn't like Valik had ever hurt anyone. That was what he said, and I believed him. There was no reason not to.

"I'm not judging you, Valik." I rubbed my hand up his arm. "We all make mistakes. Was that what you were worried about telling me?"

He shook his head. "The thing is, the agent who arrested me for the robberies… when he found out I was in tight with the Goodacres, he made me a deal I couldn't refuse. Turn informant and give them intel on Ryzen, or they would reverse my parole and send me back to prison. I had no choice. I think one of the other guards might be an informant also, but I'm not sure. Agent Dobbs is a fucking prick, I can tell you that."

My mouth fell to the floor at his words. Dobbs? That slimy sleazebag. God, how many other people had they forced to turn informant or be sent off to jail?

"But I swear"—Valik held up his hands and faced me—"they didn't tell me anything about you working for them… they only said that I needed to watch over Ryzen's fiancée and keep her safe. Keep you safe. Which is what I've been trying to do since we got here."

"Wow, that's…. that sounds exactly like Dobbs to pull some shit like that. But wait." I gripped the sleeve of his jacket. "Shouldn't they know we're here then? You had to have told them something when I crashed." My pulse quickened at the realization. Maybe… they were coming… or… the look on Valik's face made me realize that wasn't the case.

He shook his head and scrunched up his lips. "After you crashed, I was able to send one message saying you were in an accident. But Ryzen was quick to handle everything. We went to the airstrip and he took our phones right away. No contact with anyone. I couldn't even tell if the message even went through."

"Fuck."

He scrunched up his nose. "Yeah, fuck."

We got to the shack, a million thoughts running through my head. One was that Valik didn't deserve any of this. Dobbs was an asshole and needed to get his ass handed to him.

Valik opened the door to the shack and looked around as I peeked over his shoulder to see for myself. It was empty except for a few planter pots. The hair on the back of my neck stood up and I looked back where we had just come from.

*Nobody followed you.*

I tried to shake off the uneasy feeling that was creeping up my spine. There was loose dirt around the edge of the shack where it looked like somebody had recently disturbed the area. I dug my shoe in it, and the soil moved easy enough. "Valik, come check this out."

He kneeled down and moved the dirt around with his hand. "Yeah, it looks fresh. Maybe something is buried here." He took off his jacket, and I handed him the metal spatula I had stolen from the kitchen that morning. He raised his eyebrows, his lips curling at the sides. "What the hell am I going to do with that? Make dirt pancakes?"

I swatted him on the arm and chuckled. "It's to dig with, you big moose. Not like we could just walk past Ryzen with a shovel, now could we?"

Valik's back shook with laughter. "You are so weird, Nova. Go grab me one of those branches."

I grabbed two thick branches, handed them to him. I kneeled down next to him, using my spatula to dig through the ground. The soil was completely loose, so within minutes we had uncovered a hole about one foot deep.

"There's nothing here." He sighed and I bit the inside of my cheek.

"It was worth a shot." I leaned back on my heels and wiped my forehead. Damn, I had really thought my phone would be out here. Why else would Ryzen walk out here with a shovel? Maybe he'd been digging my grave. The thought sent a shudder through me and I rubbed my hands against my thighs. Valik pushed dirt back into the hole, and my head snapped in the direction of the sound of a tree branch cracking.

My hand flew to my heart as a small squirrel ran up a weeping willow and bounced from tree branch to tree branch. That little fucker had scared the crap out of me. Something at the base of the tree gleamed where the sun hit it, and I elbowed Valik.

"Look." I pointed, and we both walked over to the tree a few yards away. At the base of the tree a nail was embedded; it looked intentional. A little red ribbon was wrapped around the nail in a bow. My eyes widened and I turned to Valik. "That's suspicious." The grass just below the nail was dead, and when we looked closer, I realized that the earth had been moved not only there, but in another spot a few feet away.

He nodded and grabbed the spatula from my hand. We both were frantic as we dug in the first spot, my hands trembling the deeper we got. With only one good arm, I was doing very little to help him. It was the thought that counted though, which was what I told him when he tried to make me stop. His cheeks were flushed, and he stopped digging with a gasp.

"What is it? My phone?" I leaned over and peeked inside the hole he had dug, about two feet deep. There was a fluttery, empty feeling in my stomach and my hand flew to my chest at the sight of what was in the ground.

Bones.

"Oh, fuck." He leaned back.

I reached down and pulled out the first bone. "Is it an animal?"

He shook his head and moved the dirt around, pulling out another fragment. "I'm no expert, but this looks like a human jawbone." He held it up, his face twisted in disgust.

"Oh, my God, what the hell is going on?" My body was trembling, nausea rolling through me. "Put it back." I tossed the bone back into the hole. "Just put it all back. He can't know that somebody was snooping here." I rubbed my hands together, trying to get the dirt and God knew what else off of me.

This was a whole lot worse than I had originally thought. We had just dug up someone's bones. A grave. I scrunched up my nose, the air suddenly too thick. Who the hell was in this hole? A terrible feeling rested in the bottom of my stomach. These bones had been here for a long time. There weren't any remnants of clothing or anything to indicate the grave was recent.

"C'mon, Nova. Let's get out of here." Valik helped me stand. He was sweating profusely, but I didn't think it was just from the digging.

"Wait, there's another spot here." I walked over a few feet and dragged my shoe through the dirt. "It's fresh."

He scrunched up his face. "I don't think I want to know what's down there." His voice was low.

"Valik, don't wimp out on me now."

We both kneeled and started digging again, dirt flying everywhere as a new sense of urgency rolled through us. The air was filled with tension, which quickly turned to excitement when we got about two feet down and found a black bag.

"Holy shit," we both mumbled, and he pulled the bag out.

"Open it." I was breathless as he ripped it open.

My pulse quickened as each second passed, and he dumped out the contents of the bag. A dress fell out, and I blinked rapidly.

"That's my dress!" Excitement ran through me as I picked it up. It was covered in blood and practically ripped to shreds. It looked like someone had cut it from my body. My stomach rolled as I saw a flash of Ryzen screaming at me, his eyes murderous. I squeezed my eyes shut and shook my head.

*No, don't freak out. Now is not the time.*

The chain of the onyx necklace was tangled in the chiffon, and I tugged it loose. Most of the stones had been knocked loose, except the big black one. The watch lay on the ground, the band broken, and I picked it up.

"The FBI gave these to me. There's a camera in both of them. I just have to..." I pressed the buttons on the side of the watch, but nothing happened. The same thing happened when I pressed on the necklace.

Absolutely no indication that they were working. My gut told me it was a dead end though. If the tracking device in the watch had been working, the FBI would have shown up already.

"Never mind, I think they are too damaged." I tossed them on the ground and grunted in frustration.

"Here's the phone." He gripped it and held it up, his face lighting up with a smile. The screen was cracked, but otherwise looked OK. He pressed the button on the side, trying to power it on. The screen turned white, and then black.

"Is it broken? Press the button again."

Valik pressed the buttons on the side, then all over the screen. "It looks on, but the screen won't work. We can't make any calls. Fuck." He shook his head and handed it to me. "It's garbage."

I wasn't going to give up that easily. Maybe it just needed to be charged.

"OK, if this is all useless, then it's time for a different plan." I stood, almost stumbling over the hole. I threw the dress, necklace and watch back in the ground and started covering it back up with dirt.

He raised his eyebrows as he helped me. "Which is?"

"Come with me."

We made sure the holes were covered back up and that they looked untouched. The last thing we needed was for Ryzen to come out here for whatever reason and find out that someone had been messing around in his little dirty den of secrets.

We made our way up the hill and down the slope of granite. The sharp edges of the rock dug into the soles of my shoes, making my feet hurt. But it would all be worth it when we were out of here. He followed me down the ladder on the side of the pier and over to the little boats.

He let out a whistle and scrunched up his nose. "These are fucking tiny, Nova." He stood next to one, and I gulped. They were the perfect size for me, but to someone like Valik who was well over six feet and built like a firetruck… no, it might be too dangerous for us both to fit in one. It made more sense to take them both. Especially if something happened to one of the boats out on the open water.

"OK, well, let's go over our options again. We have no cell phone, so we can't call for help. What about the walkie-talkies, can we call someone on the mainland from those?" I placed my hands on my hips, nibbling on my bottom lip.

He shook his head and exhaled sharply. "No. The other guards or Ryzen would hear us. We would be caught right away."

"OK, and the ferry is not an option because it only comes twice a week and it's far. We would never get there without a car. Ryzen would find us right away."

He eyed the little boats, his back tensing as if he'd just realized he was going to have to squeeze his big-ass body into one. The silence between us stretched.

"It's fucking dangerous out there on the open water, Nova. If the tide is too strong or the current works against us, we could get lost or be out there for hours." He was talking more to himself than to me. "I don't know, it might be too dangerous."

I dug my nails into my palms, my lips in a flat line. "I'd rather take my chances out there on the open water than here with Ryzen." There was no way I could stay here another day. If Ryzen was having a priest come out here to marry us, then who the hell knew what he had planned after that? Nothing good. No, I wasn't going to die on this island, especially not at the hands of Ryzen Goodacre. "No, we need to go, and it has to be tonight. I'm out of options."

"OK." Valik looked over the water. "OK, if it stays clear all night, then we got a shot."

I wrapped my arms around him and squeezed. "We can do it, Valik. I know my arm is fucked up, but we can make it there. I know it."

He chuckled and patted the top of my head. "I will never underestimate you again, Nova."

We washed our hands in the water, scrubbing all the dirt and grime from them. We walked back, coming up with a plan.

"We'll leave at midnight. Ryzen will be asleep by then," Valik murmured as we got closer to the house. "I'll try to find a lantern or flashlight. We can't use it in the woods, but it might come in handy out on the water."

Butterflies flew around in my stomach, and I held my hand there and tried to control my breathing. I wasn't going to lie, this was fucking terrifying, but there was no choice. Escape or die trying. End of story.

"And Nova, dress warm. We're going to get wet and the last thing we need is hypothermia."

Great, that definitely didn't make me feel any better.

I snapped my fingers and turned to him. "Can you get a backpack?"

"For what?" He raised his eyebrows. "We shouldn't bring anything extra, Nova."

"For Dracula." I narrowed my eyes at him. "We can't just leave him here."

"Nova, we can't take a damn cat out on the ocean. He'll freak out." Valik chuckled and shook his head. "We'll come back for him."

He was lying, but I didn't want to argue with him. Glenda would take care of Dracula, at least that was what I had to make myself believe. We walked up the steps, and Valik gripped my hand. "Go rest for a few hours. You're going to need it. I'll come by in a bit with your tea and medicine."

"Wait, you have your gun, right?" I looked down the hall to make sure nobody was coming.

He nodded and lifted his jacket to show me. Relief washed through me, and I let out a shaky breath. "Good. I hope we don't need it, but..." I shrugged my shoulders. I didn't have to say anything else. We both knew the implication.

*I hope we don't need it, but we might if something goes wrong.*

I wouldn't put that burden on Valik though. I was the one Ryzen wanted. And he was in for a big surprise if he decided to come for me tonight.

Ryzen was locked away in his office like usual, and I hauled ass up to my bedroom. I kept myself busy for the next few hours, mostly squeezing Dracula and promising that I would be back for him. Agent Dobbs' allergic ass would lose his mind if he could see me right now. I chuckled to myself as Dracula cuddled in my arms. Valik came at his usual time with my tea and pills, and I dumped them into the plant.

"OK, all is normal downstairs." He checked his watch. "I'll be back in three hours and we'll go." His voice wasn't as confident as it had been earlier in the day, and I gripped his hand.

"We can do this, Valik. By this time tomorrow, we will be safe and off of this island."

He smiled softly and gripped my hand back. "I'll make sure of it. Don't turn the light back on. I'll be here right at midnight. Not a minute past, got it?"

I nodded, my pulse quickening.

*I'm getting out of here.*
*Thank fucking God.*

# Chapter Twenty

I paced around the room, checking the clock on the wall for the hundredth time. Eleven fifty-eight. Valik would be here any minute now. Dracula lay sprawled out on my bed, and my shoulders sagged. Was it normal to get this attached to an animal? I hovered over him and kissed his little head, promising to come back for him as soon as I could.

My stomach was in knots, the anticipation of waiting for Valik eating me up inside. I was ready, more prepared than I had been hours ago. I had wrapped my cell phone in a plastic baggie and shoved it in my back pocket. The screen was still alternating between white and black, but I hoped—no, I begged to the universe that it would start working again. Maybe it just needed a charge.

I had to call Cian. He would come for me, for us, and bring the FBI. Earlier I had found a sequined dress in the back of the armoire and ripped it until I had several long strips of fabric. If something happened, God forbid, and Valik and I got separated on the water, it might help us find each other if the light reflected off of it. I stuffed the strips into my pocket and checked the clock again.

Three minutes past midnight.

Where the hell was Valik? He'd promised he would be here right at midnight.

My stomach made an obnoxious growling sound, and I exhaled sharply. *Don't freak out. He's coming, just a little late. No need to panic.*

At seven minutes past midnight, the knot in my stomach turned into the size of a boulder. Had he fallen asleep or gone to the boats without me? Had I misunderstood? I raked my fingers through my hair, pacing in front of the bedroom door. No. That was not what we'd agreed to. He wouldn't be out there, and he definitely wouldn't have fallen asleep.

I checked my cast and made sure my knife was tucked in there nice and snug. Something wasn't right about this, and the hairs on the back of my neck stood up. I peeked out the curtains into the backyard, but there was nothing, no sign of anyone moving, no lights… just darkness.

*Dammit, Valik! Where are you?* I wanted to scream at the top of my lungs but knew I couldn't. I had never been the praying type, but I clasped my hands together and squeezed my eyes shut.

*Please, God, if you're listening, please send Valik to my room so we can get off this fucking island.*

I opened one eye and glanced around the room.

My nostrils flared. The only sound in the room was the tick, tick, tick of the clock. If he wasn't here, that could mean only one of two things. Ryzen had somehow gotten to him and was waiting for me downstairs. Or Valik had gotten scared and bailed on the plan. I didn't like either of those options. I squeezed my eyes shut, clasping my hands in front of me.

*Let's try that again. Please, Lucifer, give me the strength I need to get off this island and take this son of a bitch down.*

Dracula meowed softly, and I nearly jumped out of my skin. My hand flew to my chest, and I chuckled. "Thanks for the support, you little monster."

It was fifteen minutes past midnight. I couldn't wait any longer. The door creaked slightly and I peeked my head around the corner. It was completely dark and dead silent. A part of me had been expecting Valik to be outside my door, about to knock, and dread filled me once again. Reality was settling in my stomach.

*Ryzen, you sleazy fuck. Did you take him?* I balled my hands into fists and stepped back into my room, shutting the door quietly. I couldn't leave that big lovable moose here. If Ryzen had figured out somehow what we were planning, then Valik could be hurt. He was my friend, and had been protecting me this whole time. And now I was just about to run away? I couldn't do that to him.

No, I was sick of hiding, sick of being scared of one stupid man who thought he could control every person in the world because he was rich. He wasn't going to get away with any of this. And if I had to be the person to stop him, then I was going to be.

Even if it ended badly for me. Even if it meant death.

Ryzen Goodacre needed to pay.

I glanced around the room and snapped my fingers when I glanced at the wall sconces. I pulled out the switchblade and unscrewed two of them from the wall. They were sharp with lots of pointy edges and could definitely cause some damage if used the right way. I tugged my pillow out of the pillowcase and put the scones at the bottom, twisting and tying a knot.

If Ryzen was waiting for me downstairs, then he was about to get a sack of sconces to the head.

I let out a deep breath, on the verge of hyperventilating as my hands trembled.

*Get it together. You're a badass. Cian is waiting for you. Prove to the world you're not a victim. You are the queen of orgasm-makers. A sex goddess extraordinaire. Not a doormat. Not some simple-minded idiot who's too weak and afraid to stand up for herself.*

Here went nothing.

I opened the door slowly, peeking around the corner, my makeshift weapon over my shoulder ready to be swung. It was eerily quiet and more ominous than it had been moments ago. All the bedroom doors were shut, not a guard or Ryzen in sight. I tiptoed over to the staircase and peered over the banister.

Silence.

I pressed my back against the wall and moved slowly down the stairs. There was light coming from just under the basement door, and my heart nearly stopped. I had seen enough horror movies to know what might be waiting for me downstairs.

*You are not a victim.*

I went down the stairs as quietly as I could and peered around the corner. There was a lantern hanging in the center of the room. Had Valik been down here trying to find us a light for the boat trip?

"Valik?" I hissed and took a step closer.

No answer.

I ducked behind a metal shelf filled with old boxes and odds and ends. There was nothing there that could be used as a weapon. I didn't know why that had surprised me—the lengths Ryzen had gone to protect himself against little old me. "Valik, are you down here?"

A faint noise was coming from around the corner. It sounded like a groan, and my hands tightened around the pillowcase. It happened again, almost a wheezing sound, and I rounded the corner.

My entire body tensed, and I gasped when my gaze landed on a dark liquid.

Blood.

Lots and lots of blood.

I squeezed my eyes shut and inhaled deeply, trying to force my heart to stop beating so erratically. If that was blood, then it had to be Valik's.

Fuck. The braveness I'd been feeling minutes ago slowly began to disappear as the realization sank in. Somebody was hurt down here. And it was probably not Ryzen. He was the one causing the hurting. I shook my head, scrunching up my nose. *No. Not anymore, asshole.*

I followed the trail of blood, my pulse quickening when it ended at a closed door to what looked like a utility closet. My whole body was shaking, and the air in the room was so thick, it was suffocating. I wiped my palms against my jeans and turned the knob, opening the door slowly.

Valik lay in the closet, his face covered in cuts and scrapes. It looked like he had lost a fight with a bear. His face was as pale as a ghost's, and I couldn't control the gasp that escaped my lips.

"Valik," I choked out and leaned down. His hand was pressed to the side of his stomach, and I moved it, my mouth going dry. There was a giant gash there, and

I ripped off my jacket and pressed it against the open wound. I reached up and checked for a pulse, and his eyes flashed open, a gasp coming out of his mouth.

"Nova, run," he wheezed.

"Where's your gun?" I hissed and lifted his jacket, feeling his pockets. "Valik, where is it?" My pulse quickened when he gripped my wrist, his eyes widening as he looked over my shoulder.

"Run," he wheezed.

The hair on my arms stood up, and I didn't need to turn around to know that someone was behind me. I glanced down at the knotted pillowcase next to me, and in one swift movement I grabbed it and hurled it around my shoulders like a helicopter blade with as much force as I could muster.

It smashed into Ryzen's head, and he yelled out, stumbling backwards. "You bitch." He lunged for me, and I swung again, but the ceiling was too low, the pillowcase too bulky. The air swooshed out of my lungs as we landed on the floor, him on top of me.

I was frantic, kicking, clawing, hitting him with all my might, but he had the advantage of being on top of me and blocked most of my blows. His fist made contact with my jaw, and the pain alone was enough to have me screaming at the top of my lungs.

"Shut the fuck up," he roared.

I wailed on him as hard as I could, but he grabbed a fistful of my hair and slammed my head against the ground. The pain was excruciating as it radiated up my neck and the back of my head.

"Thought you were so clever?" He leaned closer, his nostrils flaring. "Not as clever as me."

He was so close, I could smell the alcohol on his

breath. Blood filled my mouth from his punch, and I gathered as much of it as I could and spit it all over his face. He grunted, his mouth twisting as he wiped his face.

"You're going to regret that." He stood up and stepped on my arm, the one with the cast, and I screamed out, tears running down my face. The pain was too much to handle, my own sobs echoing in my ears. He grabbed me by my legs and dragged me. The cold concrete dug into my back, my flesh getting cut as he took me towards the stairs. I tried to grab onto the metal shelf, but he just yanked me harder. He moved up the stairs like I weighed nothing, whistling as he went. My head was hitting each step with such force that I started to lose consciousness.

*No, Nova. Be strong. Stronger than this.*

But at that moment, I couldn't do it any more, and my eyelids drifted shut, a sea of darkness in front of them.

*****

*I think I'm in heaven. Cian is there laughing at something Thora said, while Orin is in the kitchen yelling at Eros for burning the biscuits. Juliet sits next to me on the couch, showing me doodles of her latest and greatest dildo design.*

*Cian wraps me in a bear hug, kissing me deep until I'm almost out of breath. I push back, gasping for air, and his face twists and turns into Ryzen's.*

*I'm screaming at the top of my lungs, then my eyes*

*fly open.*

Ryzen narrowed his eyes at me. We were back upstairs in the living room and I was sitting in a chair with my hands tied behind my back.

"There she is." He chuckled and pulled up a chair, sitting down in front of me. He pulled the gun out and laid it on the coffee table next to us. "Tell me, dear fiancée, when did you get your memory back, hm?"

I stared blankly at him for a moment. He looked completely untethered, manic, his eyes drilling into me. His clothes had blood splattered across them, his fingers covered in dirt. But it was his smile that made me nervous. It was a smile of a madman, and I didn't know how the hell I was going to get out of this one.

He reached up and smacked me across my face, tears welling in my eyes at the sting. "How long, Nova?"

"Just a few days," I sputtered.

"Good." He nodded and pulled out my phone. "Won't be needing this either, now will you?" He threw it next to the gun on the table and laughed. "You know, it's a good thing I was starting to get paranoid. Otherwise, I wouldn't have seen that a little sneaky somebody"—he pressed his pointer finger against my forehead and pushed—"was out in the woods digging up my shit."

'Paranoid' was probably an understatement. His eyes looked wild, and I wondered if he was on something.

"You have been nothing but a pain in my ass since we met in that elevator." He shook his head and leaned back in his chair. "If you had just played by my rules, Nova, you wouldn't be here right now—tied up in a chair, death just minutes away. But you're just like the others. A gold-digger. A whore. Good for only one thing, which surprisingly you never gave me."

His eyes roamed over me, and every muscle in my body tensed up.

*Fucking try it, asshole.*

I let the blood dribble down my chin, and he scrunched up his face. Good. I wiggled my wrists, noticing he had tied the rope around my cast, which made it loose. My heart was in my throat at that moment. If I could get my hands free and grab the gun… or my knife… The switchblade handle dug into my skin where my cast was pressed, and a laugh escaped my throat with my excitement.

He glared at me, his face twisted in disgust as I let the blood flow. I just needed to keep him talking until I could get my hands free. Then I stood a shot. I didn't want to die here. Not on this island and not at the hands of Ryzen. I wasn't going to give up. Not yet. I would fight tooth and nail if I had to.

"I'm not a whore. I had real feelings for you at one time. Real feelings, Ryzen."

He threw his head back and laughed. "Oh, really? When? When you were fucking Cian Blackwood?" He shook his head in disgust, muttering to himself. "He'll get what's coming to him too, don't worry about that."

My jaw tensed at his remark. "You know, Hymen, this obsession you have with him is a little unhealthy." My head whipped to the side as he landed another slap across my face. Obviously, he didn't want to be reminded about his given birth name. The one he had been bullied over and changed in high school.

"Hymen?" Ryzen's mouth twisted into a sneer. "That boy has been dead for a long time. He was too weak." He chuckled.

"And you're not, *Ryzen*?"

"Watch your dirty fucking mouth, Nova. Don't provoke me so I'll kill you faster. I wanted to take my time with you." He trailed his thumb across my cheek and gripped my chin. "You're supposed to be dead already, you know that? You were never supposed to leave that wedding alive. I had it perfectly planned out." He paced in front of me, running his hands through his hair. "My men were supposed to kill you and that whore Juliet. And me? Well, I would be the devastated widower and Covington would have buckled then. Signed the hotels over."

I raised my eyebrows, my eyes widening. What a bizarre fucking way to think. It just reaffirmed that he was on a whole new level of crazy, one that I had never seen before in my life.

My wrist burned as the rope dug into it. It was loosening slightly, but not enough. I had to keep him in front of me so that he wouldn't see what I was doing behind my back.

"But you want to know what the best part would have been?" His eyes glistened and he chuckled. "Fucking Kaviathin was supposed to take the fall for the kidnapping. I was going to hand him over to the feds on a silver platter." He pulled out the flash drive and showed it to me, then stuffed it back into his pocket. "You already knew that though, right? Because of all your snooping."

Ryzen shook his head, clenching his fists. "But fucking Blackwood had to come save the day and ruin everything yet again. He just won't fucking disappear, you know?" His voice was calm, too calm if you asked me. My body tensed as his gaze traveled down my body, every muscle screaming at me to break free.

"Iva did amazing, don't you think?" He threw his hands up in the air and laughed like a maniac. "It was her idea to tell you she was sleeping with Cian. I'm just sad I didn't get to see your face when she told you, although we had a good laugh about it after. And when you agreed to marry me… that was the real prize."

Rage coursed through my body, and I twisted my wrists a little bit quicker now, the rope getting looser.

"You just couldn't let him go, could you? He has this pull over women that I'll never understand. Gretchen was the same." Ryzen clucked his tongue on the roof of his mouth and rolled his eyes.

An image of the black box with her hair and necklace popped in my head, and I sat frozen for a moment. "Is that why you killed her? I assume that's her grave out back."

His face twisted in disgust, and he towered over me. "She was nothing but a whore, just like you. If she had just listened to me and done as I asked… but she didn't want to leave Blackwood." He made a tisking noise. The rope was loosening. I just needed to keep him talking.

"So what, you killed her and kept her hair in a box in your office? That's low-level psychotic. You know that, right? Why would you even keep that? Ugh, I hope you didn't touch yourself and play with her hair, Ryzen, that seems unsanitary," I said all in one breath as the rope finally slipped down my wrist and I grabbed it before it fell.

He slapped me again and again, and I grunted at each blow, tears flying freely around me.

"I do thoroughly enjoy hurting women, Nova. Mostly mentally though. The physical hurting, well, that just tends to happen from time to time. It's the only fucking reason I got involved with Voledetti. They helped me cover up the first one—a mistake, obviously." He chuckled.

Nausea rolled through me at his confession. He'd actually killed someone. And not just one person, but at least two. This fucker deserved to die, and I was more than happy to be the one to put him in his grave.

He let out a deep breath and laughed. "God, that felt good to get off my chest. I've been wanting to tell someone that for a long time. Only Riddick and Voledetti knew."

I dug into my cast, making sure I didn't move my arms too much, otherwise he would see, and pulled the knife out.

He sat down in the chair in front of me and dragged it closer so that our knees were touching. "I'm sorry it has to end like this, Nova." He pushed my hair behind my ears and then pulled out a handkerchief from his pocket. I sat completely still as he wiped away my tears and the blood from my chin. "I had high hopes for us." He leaned closer and pressed his lips to mine, and I gagged, trying to recoil away from him. He gripped the back of my neck and held me in place, his lips crushing into mine. I bit down on his lip as hard as I could, and he pushed back, holding his mouth. "You fucking bitch. That's it. I was going to just give you more benzos, but now, I think you'll take a trip over the fucking cliff."

His voice rose with every word, and when his hand whipped back ready to land another blow, I pulled out the knife and plunged it into his thigh. His eyes widened and he yelled out as I yanked the knife out. I lunged for him and pushed him, and he fell backwards onto the glass table. The glass cracked as he landed, and he bellowed as the little pieces cut into his arm. "You whore," he screamed, but I was halfway down the hall by then.

I flung the front door open and ran as fast as I could. I didn't know what direction I was going in, but when I heard him yelling not too far behind me, I pumped my legs faster. It wasn't fast enough though, and even with a gash in his thigh, he caught up to me and tackled me from behind.

He flipped me over, his hands going around my throat and squeezing. I clawed at him, reaching for his face and pressing my thumbs into his eyes, but that just made him angrier. He cursed and shook his head, picking me up slightly and slamming me back down. The air whooshed out of my lungs, and panic started to set in. I was kicking and scratching, but he was relentless.

I didn't notice the headlights of the cars that started to pull up, the flashing of blue and red lights surrounding me. Men were yelling and then someone tackled Ryzen off of me and I rolled over onto my side, gasping for air.

"I'm going to fucking kill you!"

*Cian.*

Cian was here.

I raised my head and looked over at him. He was on top of Ryzen, landing blow after blow to his face. Ryzen stopped moving, but Cian didn't stop. He kept wailing on him until Delove ran up and pushed him off.

"Cian, enough!" Delove yelled.

Cian ran over to me, his chest heaving, and pulled me into his arms. "Nova, are you OK? Nova? Please, tell me you are OK," he choked out, his eyes glistening.

I squeezed him tight against me, sobbing against his chest. "You found me," I whispered, my body trembling as his fingers dug into me. "You actually found me."

He leaned back and gripped my face in his hands. "I've been searching for you every hour of every fucking day. I never gave up, Nova. I told you I would burn the whole fucking world down for you, and I just about did. I love you so fucking much."

He crushed his lips to mine and I could taste the fear and desperation in his kiss. "I love you too," I sobbed out.

Delove rushed over, his gun drawn. "Is there anyone else inside?"

Valik. "Valik is downstairs in the basement." I choked out. "He's hurt badly."

Delove, Dobbs and a few police officers ran inside, their guns drawn. Cian held me against him, practically suffocating me to the point that I couldn't breathe. But I didn't mind. I wasn't going to let him go. Never again.

Men were yelling from inside the house. The loudest one of all was Dobbs.

"Is there a fucking cat in here?"

# Chapter Twenty-One
## Day 73

Agent Dobbs sat across from me, dried blood splattered across his wrinkled blazer. Whose blood, I couldn't be sure of. Was it mine? I looked down at my hands, grime and something else I couldn't identify embedded under my nails. I could barely move my right arm, the cast almost completely broken off. A ringing noise flooded my ears, and I hunched my shoulders forward, crossing my arms against my chest.

"Nova." Cian's voice was hoarse. "Nova, look at me, little star. It's OK now."

I couldn't. Not now. Not after everything. The handcuffs around his wrists clashed against the metal desk as he strained to move closer to me. I couldn't bear to see him in handcuffs like that. My heart ached and I opened my mouth to speak, but Dobbs cut me off.

"Cut it out, Blackwood. Or I'll put a gag in your mouth." Dobbs huffed and wiped the sheen of sweat from his forehead.

"I'd like to see you fucking try," Cian growled and jerked his arms in an attempt to loosen the cuffs.

"Both of you shut up already." Agent Delove scowled and placed a tape recorder on the table in between us.

They'd patched me up a little bit on the island in an ambulance, and then a helicopter had flown us to a small town right on the mainland. Cian had insisted they take me to the hospital, but Dobbs had wanted my statement right away. I didn't mind going to the police station first. Maybe it was the shock, or the adrenaline, but I just wanted to get it over with. But Cian had not been happy with that and had gotten into a shoving match with Dobbs, which was how he'd ended up in a set of handcuffs right after rescuing me. Now we were in a small police station that only had two interview rooms. We were in one and Ryzen was in the other. I could hear him through the walls yelling like a maniac and I exhaled sharply.

Dobbs snickered and pulled out a flask. He poured a dark liquid into the two cups of coffee and slid one across to me. "Drink. It'll help calm your nerves, honey."

"Take off his cuffs, Dobbs." I gave him a pointed look.

He stood and muttered under his breath. "If you fucking touch me, I'm going to lock you up, Blackwood."

Cian smirked and rubbed his wrists when the cuffs were taken off. He rushed over and I squeezed him as hard as I could.

"You're OK," Cian said. "Just tell them what happened, and we'll get the hell out of here."

My hand trembled as I held the cup and took a swig. The liquid burned down my throat, and I welcomed the sensation. It didn't matter. Nothing did. Numbness swept through my whole body. I looked around the room, the walls painted a terrible brown color that reminded me of Dobbs' blazer. My stomach turned and I took another sip of my drink. The dim light above our heads flickered for the hundredth time, and the urge to stand on the desk and rip it out of the ceiling was overpowering.

"Nova, are you listening?" Dobbs cleared his throat, and I snapped my attention back to him. "Why don't you start at the beginning."

I threw back the rest of my drink and slid the cup back to him, nodding when he held the flask up. The beginning. How stupid I had been. How naïve and foolish I was. I scoffed, my nostrils flaring as I recalled those first few weeks after being snatched away from my wedding.

"I... guess it started..." My voice trailed off as a commotion in the hallway drew all our attention to the door. People were shouting, one voice louder than all the others—a voice burned into my memory forever.

The door flew open, and my chair screeched against the linoleum as I stood up and faced the man who had haunted my nightmares.

Everything was a blur as the men around me scrambled, their chairs spilling backwards, coffee flying across the table.

"Gun, he has a gun!" someone shouted, but I couldn't tell you who. The only thing I knew for sure was he indeed did have a gun.

And it was pointed right at me.

Ryzen stood in the doorway, his face twisted in anger. "You! You ruined everything!"

He pulled the trigger just as strong arms wrapped around me and pushed me to the side. I landed on the floor with a thump just as Cian lunged for him. Another shot went off as they rolled on the floor. Cian pinned him down, grabbing his arm and bashing it on the ground until Ryzen let go of the gun.

Delove rushed over and flipped Ryzen onto his stomach, his knee in his back. He pulled out a walkie-talkie and yelled, "Get a medic in here, now."

My eyes widened as Cian toppled onto the floor, holding his stomach, blood running down his shirt.

"No!" I screamed and crawled over to him. My heart was on the verge of exploding out of my chest as I put pressure over the wound. "No, Cian. Please. Somebody help!" I couldn't recognize my own voice as people rushed around me, a medic running over. Dobbs put his hands under my armpits and dragged me backwards so the medic could get better access to Cian.

"He's losing too much blood." The medic was calm, controlled, and I squeezed my eyes shut.

*Please, God, don't let it end like this.*

# Chapter Twenty-Two
## Day 74

**Cian**

The hospital monitor beeped in a slow and steady rhythm that started to agitate me. My eyes flew open, and I instinctively reached down to where Goodacre had shot me, a bandage covering the area.

Thank fucking God. If I was going to die, it wasn't going to be at the hands of that son of a bitch.

Anger coursed through my veins, my nostrils flaring. The beeping noise coming from the machine grew faster and louder, and a hand gripped mine.

Nova.

My beautiful little star. Her dark hair cascaded down her shoulders, her cheeks flushed and damp. She was a site for sore eyes. I knew the second I had seen her in my club dressed as Lara Croft, that I was done for. Her beautiful blue eyes and plump ruby lips had haunted me since that day. I had wanted to be a part of her world so badly, that I had been willing to destroy mine over it.

"Cian, you're awake." Her eyes glistened with tears, and she leaned down, pressing little kisses all over my face. "I was so scared," she sobbed, squeezing my cheeks between her hands.

God, she smelled good, like sunshine and peace.

My heartbeat immediately slowed back down.

"What happened?" I groaned as I tried to sit up, my stomach still tender to the touch.

The last thing I remembered was Goodacre busting in the room and pointing a gun directly at Nova. I hadn't even hesitated before pushing her out of the way and charging towards him, but not before he got off the first shot.

I scanned her body, my eyes frantic, looking for any type of gunshot wound.

"I'm OK," she whispered and held up her arm. "The bullet grazed my cast. I think the universe was looking out for me." Her eyes welled up with tears again and she pressed her forehead to mine. "Ryzen overpowered one of the cops, knocked him out cold and got his gun and came looking for me." She shook her head, and I noticed her hands were trembling. Never again though. I would never let her out of my sight for the rest of my life. I wrapped my arm around her waist and tugged.

"Get up here."

She bit on her bottom lip and looked down at my wound, hesitating for a moment.

"It's OK, my beautiful star." I moved my legs, hissing at the pain. She climbed up, resting her head on my chest. Her whole body was shaking, which only made me angrier. Angry at myself, angry at Delove and dickhead Dobbs. They should be fired for a slew of fucking reasons.

"They rushed you to surgery. Said that the bullet missed your liver by less than half an inch." She looked up at me with those big, beautiful eyes, and I clenched my jaw. How anyone could ever hurt this woman, I'd never know.

"Cian, how did you find me?" She leaned up and placed her hand on my chest. "Delove said you were the one who told them I was on the island, but he didn't know how you knew. Was it the phone?"

I exhaled sharply and shook my head, thinking back over the last hellish few weeks. God, how frantic I had been when I had heard her screaming that night at the party. My brothers and I had rushed to the party with the FBI in tow, but Goodacre and Nova were already gone. He had taken her away from me, and I vowed a vengeance so fierce, so terrible that I almost couldn't take it.

I had searched everywhere, every major airport and private airstrip, paying off pilots and flight attendants. Nobody had seen them. Not one damn person. I went to all of Goodacre's known hangouts, showing anyone and everyone a picture of him and Nova. I questioned everyone from the maître d' at his favorite restaurant to the hotel staff. There were no fucking leads, and when paying off people didn't work, I resorted to violence. I craved it. I needed it in order to stay sane. Nobody was safe. Not the dirty cops I had tracked down with the help of one of Goodacre's old guards, or even the delivery drivers Kaviathin had on his roster.

And I had had absolutely no regrets about it. Goodacre had taken the most important person in my world away from me, and everyone was going to suffer because of it.

"Did my phone track me? I thought it wasn't working." She scrunched up her nose, and my heart softened. I'd thought I was never going to see her beautiful face again, and I'd been ready to go to the grave and take as many people down with me as I needed to.

"Kaviathin," I muttered.

"He told you where I was?" Her voice quivered and she rubbed the cast on her arm, almost as if she was trying to pull something out of it.

"Not willingly." My voice was low, cold, and I clenched my fists. "There are some things better left unsaid, Nova." I exhaled sharply and brought her back down to my chest, wrapping my arms around her.

She didn't need to know that I had turned into a monster with the snap of Goodacre's fingers. As the days had gone by, and I wasn't getting the answers I needed, I'd started trailing Kaviathin. But I'd soon realized that he had too many guards around him. Everywhere he went, at least ten men would follow him. So we'd switched tactics.

The Mafia only cared about two things: family and money. And if you were prepared to take those away from them, then you'd better be ready for the consequences.

Juliet had cozied up to a low-level guard in one of Kaviathin's bars while Eros made sure the brothers stayed away. She'd enticed him back to her place, and when they got there, my brothers and I had been waiting. He had been hesitant at first to tell us what we wanted, and I'd taken out all my anger and frustration on him until my hands were covered in blood. I didn't care. There were no regrets. I would do it all over again if it meant finding Nova.

After two days, he'd finally given us what we needed. Althazair was trying to offload an arsenal of guns and was meeting with some buyers that night in the parking garage adjacent to a storage facility.

Eros, Orin and I waited until they were all there and we masked up and loaded our weapons. They never saw us coming. There were eight of them, and only three of us, but it didn't matter. We got the jump on them before they even had time to blink. We jumped out of the van, pointing our guns at them. My eyes landed on Althazair, and I hit him on the side of the head with my gun, knocking him down to his knees. I pressed my gun against his temple and pointed my other gun at the three men behind him. "Move, and he's dead."

The other group of men, the buyers, all dressed in gray suits, tried to rush behind their car, but Eros shot a spray of bullets at the car, making them all stop in their tracks. "Put your fucking hands up, all of you!" Orin roared, and when one of the buyers reached like he was going for a gun, Eros jammed the butt of his rifle into his stomach and knocked him down to the ground.

"Are you all prepared to fucking die? One more person moves, and I'll put a bullet in your fucking head!" I commanded, and they all froze.

Thora and Juliet jumped out from the back of our van and loaded it up with the duffel bags of money and weapons.

Althazair had sneered, spitting on the ground near my shoe. "You just dug your own grave, friend."

"Tell Kaviathin I'll be in touch." I aimed my gun and shot him in the back of the leg. He keeled over, screaming in agony, but no one else moved. Not a fucking inch.

It was only hours later that I was able to find out where Nova was. We took a picture of the money and the guns in front of an incinerator and sent it to

Kaviathin. He called less than a minute later.

"You took my money and shot my brother. You've got quite the set of balls on you." His voice was calm and controlled, but I knew. I knew the rage that was just underneath his cool exterior.

"I know you know where Ryzen is. Tell me, or I'll fucking burn it all."

He was quiet for a moment and exhaled sharply.

"Ten seconds, Kaviathin."

"Lilly Island, off the coast of Maine."

I hung up before he could say another word.

Eros and Orin had looked at me, their bodies just as tense as mine. "She's in Maine." My heart roared in my chest. "Burn it all."

There was no honor among thieves. Kaviathin should have known that.

I had no choice but to call Delove and tell him. Who knew how many people Goodacre had on that island with him. And although I was fueled by rage and revenge, I wasn't stupid enough to show on my own. I met the FBI at the airstrip and we flew a chopper to Maine and were on the island soon after.

"He gave me a knife to protect myself," Nova said. "I don't know why he did it."

My jaw clenched and I gripped her to me. I knew why he had given her the knife. The past was trying to rear its ugly head. But I wouldn't let it. I had been down this road with him before, and it wasn't going to end well. There was only one true thing I knew for sure. Kaviathin was no fucking saint, and if he came for me again, I would be more than ready this time.

# Chapter Twenty-Three
## Day 145

**Nova**

I bobbed my head to the music, sipping on my drink as Juliet danced with Eros just feet away from me. Cian had business to take care of tonight at the Hellfire Club, one of the two clubs he owned downtown. The old gothic building was huge with over three floors filled with multiple bars, performers, and people dancing. A group of performers were on a stage to my right dancing with fire hoops, and I stared at them in awe. Cian had insisted that I come with him. He was so possessive now, always watching over me and making sure I was safe, that he knew where I was at all times.

When I had to repeat my story over and over again to the FBI those months ago, Cian had become so enraged, his whole body had shaken when I told them about all the pills Ryzen had forced me to take, and the benzodiazepines that contributed to my amnesia. Ugh, I hated thinking about that. I was better now, my memory completely restored, although I would love nothing more than to forget about Ryzen Goodacre.

So I could understand why Cian was so hesitant

to leave me alone. I had tried to explain that everything was OK now, that I didn't need him constantly worrying about me. He wouldn't listen to reason, just shook his head and kissed me until I was gasping for air. Which of course made me shut up.

Every single damn time.

My heart fluttered in my chest, and I looked up at him standing at the top of the stairs in the VIP section. He was watching me, like always, and I blew him a kiss. We were inseparable, spending every waking minute of every day with each other—when we weren't working, that was. And I loved every second of it.

Valik sat down next to me and signaled the bartender for a drink. He was almost as bad as Cian, taking his new job as my personal security guard very seriously. He was completely healed now, although it had been touch and go for a while. When Ryzen had found out that we had found his hiding spot, he'd waited until he could get Valik alone. Valik was a big guy, and strong, but he was no match for a bat to the head. And when Ryzen had stabbed him, there was no way he could defend himself. But he was a fighter, both physically and mentally, and I had to admit, I loved the big moose in the way you loved your annoying older brother who only wanted to protect you.

The hairs on the back of my neck stood up and I swiveled around in my bar stool, looking through the crowd. I had to stop being so paranoid. The doctors said I needed to keep my post-traumatic stress in check, or it would take over my whole life. My therapist had agreed. You didn't just get kidnapped, drugged and almost murdered and not try to get professional help right after. It had taken some time, but the nightmares had finally stopped, and the need to always look over my shoulder was slowly diminishing.

No, I wasn't going to let Ryzen win. I scoffed and shook my head. He was rotting away in jail waiting for his trial to begin. The FBI had raided his homes and Goodacre Corporation, and every single business that Ryzen had dipped his fingers in they'd searched and seized. It was one of the biggest operations they had done in over a decade. They had more than enough evidence to put him away for kidnapping and attempted murder because of me and my testimony, but the DA had tacked on all the charges she could, including money and real estate laundering, tax fraud, stock manipulation, bid rigging, and murder.

That was right. The grave Valik and I had found had contained the remains of Gretchen Mastillo. But not only her. They had found a gravesite containing the remains of another woman not too far from where Gretchen's had been buried. She still remained unidentified though, and Ryzen was not cooperating with the FBI. Their whole plan to get him to flip on Voledetti was a total shit show, and the worst part was, they couldn't find the flash drive. I'd told them in the ambulance that he had it in his pocket, but after searching Ryzen, they couldn't find it anywhere.

I didn't tell them that Kaviathin had come to the island and had given me the knife. I didn't know why I hadn't. Cian wasn't happy about that part, but I told him I thought it was best to let that go. I wanted nothing more to do with Kaviathin or any of his family.

Luckily, something funny happened a few days after we got home from the hospital. I got an email with a summary of my monthly activity from the meditation app Thora had downloaded on my phone, and it included three audio recordings. The first one was of me and Cian having sex, and when I played it for Cian, it quickly led to us seeing if we could outdo ourselves on the scream meter.

The second was a clip of Ryzen having a phone conversation with someone right after I had crashed, which I later found out had been Iva. And the third, and most shocking, was a snippet of his confession to me the night he'd tried to kill me. It was all there—confessing to killing Gretchen, plus the other unknown woman... his tie to Voledetti. I had forwarded it to Delove, who was ecstatic, saying it was just what they had needed. Ryzen was a sick fuck and deserved to be locked away for the rest of his life. And I was willing to do everything in my power to make sure that happened.

Let them all burn for the parts they had played. Iva was currently in jail awaiting trial for accessory and conspiracy. But unlike Ryzen, who wasn't cooperating, she was spilling the beans on anyone and everything she could to save herself. Covington had hired a team of lawyers, and they were doing their best to get her a deal. But I swore I wasn't going to let that happen. No, she needed to pay, just like Ryzen. Covington had reached out to me several times, and although he was trying to separate himself completely from Ryzen, he couldn't do that to his granddaughter. He had even resorted to calling and begging me to make the charges against Iva go away, at which I'd promptly hung up on him.

My own family had been anything but supportive, except for Grams. She was doing so much better than a few months ago after her heart attack scare. I didn't want to tell her everything and make her worried, but I assured her every week when Cian and I visited that I was OK. That Cian was taking care of me, and that I hadn't been seriously injured.

"That's my tough cookie." She squeezed me tight, just as strong as ever. "Us La Rouxes are fighters. It's in our blood." She gave Cian an assessing stare and clucked her tongue. "You take care of her, young man, or you'll have me to deal with." She chuckled and opened her arms to him.

Unlike Grams though, my mother and Grace tried to put the blame on me when I went to visit them. No, I must have done something to Ryzen to make him crazy. It was my fault this had all happened. Look at what I had done to their reputation. It was completely ruined. And my father, he wouldn't even come out of his office to see me. My spirit had been completely broken when I had left their house, but not for long. They had never really supported me in anything in my life, and this had been the icing on the cake. I vowed that day to never return. There was no point.

Juliet came over to the bar and wiped her forehead. "You coming?" She chuckled and grabbed my hands. She was such a breath of fresh air after everything. And although Cian had told her to keep it hush-hush, she'd let it slip about her little detective work and the smash-and-grab she had participated in to get to Kaviathin. I would say I was surprised, but somehow, I wasn't. Juliet was my ride-or-die best friend, and if the roles had been reversed, I would have done anything in my power to find her also.

With the help of Cian and the payout from the insurance company, we had just broken ground on construction of our new warehouse just outside of downtown Chicago. Cian had offered to have a building built for us, but I had refused, not because I didn't want him involved, but because I didn't want to take a handout. So we'd compromised and he had become a silent partner and investor in the Shiver Box. He was always going to find a way to help me somehow, so this killed two birds with one stone.

I joined Juliet and Eros on the dance floor, letting the music flow through me. My body was sticky with sweat after a few songs, and a young guy came up behind me and started dancing. I glanced over my shoulder and chuckled. He couldn't have been older than twenty-one, his eyes wide and eager as he eyed my body up and down. I didn't even have time to say one word to the poor guy before Cian was standing next to me, his eyes burning into the man.

"Get the fuck out of here." He pushed the guy back, and the guy's eyes widened at the size of Cian. He scurried away, tripping over his own two feet as he ran.

"It's OK." I patted Cian's chest and reached up, kissing his lips.

Cian's gaze traveled down my body, his eyes narrowing where my dress clung to my skin. Before I could say anything else, he grabbed me and tossed me over his shoulder. I let myself hang there and giggled as he marched up the steps to his office. My man, the epitome of a caveman.

He set me down on the edge of the bar, his eyes dark as he pressed between my legs. "What's so funny, little star?" He weaved his hand through my hair, exposing my neck.

"Nothing," I gasped as his teeth dragged up the curve of my neck, his tongue licking along the way. "It's just he was just a kid… didn't mean any harm." I chuckled.

"I don't fucking care. Nobody touches what's mine." Cian tugged my head back, and I bit my bottom lip. "You're mine, Nova. And the whole world needs to fucking know that."

"Yes," I whispered. "All yours." I reached down, unbuckling his belt and lowering his zipper. God, he was an animal, already so hard for me. I moaned as I stroked the length of him, ready for him to fuck me for the third time today.

I needed him, craved him in a way that was probably unhealthy, but I didn't give a crap. His lips met mine, our tongues tangling together in a little dance that I fucking loved. I moaned against him, his hands gripping my thighs roughly and spreading them apart.

"This is mine." He dipped his finger inside of me and stroked in and out. "Say it."

"I'm yours," I gasped, and spread my legs even further. I was so wet for him, always so ready. My body had a mind of her own and knew exactly how to react when he was around. His lips were greedy as he kissed down my body, between my breasts. I arched my back, my chest heaving as he gripped my panties with his teeth and dragged them down my legs. My whole body was on fire, burning for him, and I never wanted that feeling to go away. My breathing was coming in tiny pants by the time he stood and centered his cock at my entrance.

"I love you, Cian." My head fell back as he entered me in one quick thrust. "So fucking much." I gasped as he filled me up.

"I love you, my beautiful bright star. For fucking ever and ever." He emphasized each word with a hard thrust of his hips, pounding into me as a delicious feeling spread throughout my whole body.

I reached up and wrapped my arms around his neck, moaning against his lips as he thrust into me. I didn't know what I'd done to deserve a man like Cian Blackwood, but whatever it was, I was glad it had happened. I would go to hell and back for this man.

He dragged me off the bar top and I clung to him as he held me in place and fucked me with such a relentless passion, I was screaming out his name within minutes. My whole body trembled in his arms as my orgasm shot through me, and he roared out a second later, filling me up with his release.

"I'll never let you go, Nova. No matter what." His eyes burned into mine, my heart bursting.

"I'm not going anywhere, Cian," I murmured and claimed his lips once more.

I had almost lost this man too many times to count. I had been beaten and broken down until I thought I couldn't take anymore. But he had always been the light at the end of the tunnel. And I was never, ever letting him go again.

*****

**Day 146**

The sun streamed through the blinds, birds chirping just outside our window. I lay in bed on my stomach, Cian's arm wrapped around me tightly.

Dracula stretched and meowed as if to say good morning and jumped down from the bed. It was a beautiful morning where the possibilities were endless, and I was going to make the most of it.

I flipped over and straddled him. A devilish grin spread across his face. "Good morning, my love." He reached up and trailed his thumb over my cheek and across my lips.

"Good morning to you, my love." I leaned down, pressing my lips softly to his, grinding my hips against him.

He chuckled and flipped me over on my back, and I screamed out in laughter. His lips trailed kisses down my jaw, my body already responding to him. His phone rang from the side of the bed, and I groaned.

"Fuck that, it'll go to voicemail." He claimed my mouth again. No more than a second later, my phone rang and I reached over, knocking it down on the floor. Whatever it was, it could wait.

"So greedy for me, Nova," he purred against my lips.

"Always," I breathed and gasped as his cock pressed into me.

His phone rang again, and then mine, and we both raised our eyebrows.

"Who the hell could be calling this early?" he grumbled and rolled over. "It's Dobbs," he muttered and hit the accept button. "This better be important, Agent," Cian growled.

I chuckled and grabbed my robe from the floor, wrapping myself in it. When I turned back around, the blood had drained from Cian's face, and my heart slammed against my chest at the look in his eyes.

Something wasn't right.

No. Something was terribly, terribly wrong.

Cian threw his phone across the room, and I jumped, my hand flying to my chest.

"Fuck!" he roared.

## Chapter Twenty-Four
**Day 146**

**Delove**

I sat in darkness in the back of the bar, sipping my gin and tonic. I pushed my sunglasses up and lowered my hat, waving away the server when she tried to offer me another drink. My eyes never left the door as the bouncer searched every person who came into the lounge area. The air was filled with cigar smoke and the desperation of men as they placed their gambling chips down and squeezed their eyes shut. You could see it all over their faces—the fear, the hope that this would be the hand that was going to save them. But it wasn't. It never was.

I gripped my glass as Kaviathin and Althazair walked in and headed straight downstairs. That was where the real gambling was taking place. Unlike up top where people were betting in the thousands, downstairs they were selling their souls.

I chugged the rest of my drink and stayed in the shadows as I made my way downstairs. There was a guard at the bottom, and I let him search me, his hand gliding over my gun and letting me pass through.

Kaviathin sat at a table in the back, a trail of women fawning over him as he took a drag of his cigarette. I walked right up to the table, and his eyes registered shock. He snapped his fingers and the women scattered.

"This is a surprise," he purred and took a sip of his drink.

I raised my eyebrows and chuckled. "What, that I'm on time?"

He stood and came around the table, gripping me tightly in a hug. "In all the years I've known you, you have never been on time, *cugino*."

My cousin wasn't wrong there. Ever since we were kids, I'd always been the one running behind—late for school, work, you name it.

Althazair came over with a tray of drinks and smirked. "Ha, you owe me a hundred dollars. I told you Angelo would be on time today." He laid the tray down and squeezed me tightly.

"How's your leg, Althazair?" I murmured as he walked to his seat, a slight limp in his step. Althazair was the unsteady one, the one to anger easiest. I had always worried about him.

His face twisted in disgust, and he threw a shot back. "Mostly healed. But it will be a lot better when I get my hands on Cian Blackwood."

"No." I shook my head, my voice stern. "You will not touch him, do you understand?"

His mouth fell open, and he looked between me and Kaviathin. "But he fucking shot me." Althazair slammed his hand on the table, the glasses shaking.

"And Kaviathin shot *him* weeks ago. It's done. Even." I gave him a pointed look.

"Listen to the man, Althazair. If Angelo says no, then no." Kaviathin sat down and pulled out the chair next to him, indicating for me to sit. "You have something for me?" He leaned back and crossed his ankle over his knee.

I pulled out a white envelope and slid it across the table. It contained the flash drive Ryzen had been foolish enough to keep and try to use against my family.

"And the recording?" Kaviathin took a drag of his cigarette.

"I've taken care of it."

"Good." He nodded.

"You should have told me, Kaviathin, that Goodacre had her on that island. You should have come to me."

He sighed and shook his head. "I am no saint, Angelo, you know that. I had faith in her. And I was right. Look how it turned out." He chuckled.

There was no point arguing. I knew Kaviathin thought he had done the right thing by giving her a knife instead of calling me for help, and I'd been shocked when Nova hadn't uttered one single word about him. Just another mess I didn't have to clean up, which I was thankful for. If he would have just listened to me when I had told him to stop pursuing the hotel deal with Ryzen, this could have all been avoided.

My phone beeped and I saw five missed calls from Dobbs. This fucking guy needed to retire already, and he had better soon, otherwise he could become a real problem and not the annoying gnat he currently was. I dialed his number and pressed the phone to my ear.

"Delove, where the fuck have you been, man? We have a problem. Goodacre's gone. He was meeting with his lawyers and somehow got free. We can't find him or his brother anywhere."

My head fell back, and I sighed.

Great, just fucking perfect. I did not need to deal with this bullshit anymore.

I would find him though. Or Kaviathin would. Either way, it wasn't going to end well for Ryzen Goodacre.

Not now.

Not ever.

\*\*\*\*\*\*\*\*

Sign up for my Newsletter to be notified when I have a new release, for freebies, and other extra goodies: https://bit.ly/xoxodaniantoinette

## Thank You

I hope you loved reading Venom and Velvet as much as I loved writing it. What a wild ride this series has been. Book three will be released in fall of 2023. Please consider leaving a review, I would really appreciate it! Sign up for my newsletter to be notified when I have a new release and for other extras and fun goodies. Keep reading for a special sneak peek at Wild Talk, book one in the Wild Series.

A special thank you to Chelsi PA for helping me set up my ARC group and keeping me organized. You are the kindest, most lovable person and I appreciate all your hard work. To my critique partner Samantha M Thomas, thank you for all the great feedback while writing. Melissa, who gave me all the great details about her island home – you are amazing! Lys, thank you for all the support. I can't wait to read your book when it comes out. And of course, a major thank you to my ARC group, Dani's ARC Sharks on Facebook and Instagram. This book wouldn't be here if it wasn't for you all and your support. Thank you for always putting a smile on my face.

Xoxo, Dani

**NEWSLETTER**
https://bit.ly/xoxodaniantoinette

**WEBSITE**
www.daniantoinette.com

## GOODREADS
https://www.goodreads.com/daniantoinette

## SOCIAL MEDIA
TikTok: https://www.tiktok.com/@authordaniantoinette
Instagram: https://www.instagram.com/authordaniantoinette/
Facebook: https://www.facebook.com/DaniAntoinetteAuthor/

## About the Author

A total bookworm and a hopeless romantic, Dani Antoinette likes to write the kind of stories she loves to read—stories about hot alpha males who embrace the thin line between right and wrong, and the strong, fearless women who are able to handle them. When Dani isn't devouring books by her favorite authors at her local café in downtown Chicago, she spends her time interviewing prospective characters out loud in public places, all while planning her takeover of the romance world.

# Wild Talk Sneak Peek

"I'm not going to hurt you."

He grabbed my arm, examining where Miles had gripped me, and stroked his finger over the bruise that was already forming. My body heated up at how close he was. His calloused finger felt rough against my soft skin. I looked over at Garret as he lifted Miles off the floor and threw him over his shoulder like a rag doll.

"I'll take care of it, Mason." Garret kicked the door open and walked out.

"Mason?" I questioned. He looked down at me, his face unreadable as he let my arm fall back to my side.

"You should be more careful," he said, his voice like a sweet caress against my whole body. He leaned down and began to pick up the contents of my purse.

I felt a sting of irritation. I should be more careful? He didn't even know what had happened. I kneeled down and picked up my wallet, keys and lip gloss.

"I told you, I can take care of myself," I huffed as I moved my hands around, searching for anything else that might have fallen out.

He chuckled and stood up, my eyes now directly aligned with his crotch. I licked my lips and slowly raised my eyes up his chest to meet his eyes. His lips curled in a small smile as he held his hand out to me.

*Good grief, what is happening to me?*

I grabbed his hand and he lifted me up. "You should carry mace, a weapon," he said.

"I am a weapon," I retorted as I stood with my hands on my hips.

He tilted his head back and let out a thunderous laugh. I stood there with my eyes wide in disbelief.

*Who does he think he is? He doesn't know what I'm capable of.*

I wasn't sure if it was him laughing or the leftover adrenaline that had me grabbing his arm. I tugged him toward me and moved my right leg around his, pushing his chest. His eyes registered surprise as he started to fall back.

I was not prepared for him to grab me. I let out a shriek and we landed on the floor, our legs tangled together. He grunted as my chest slammed on top of him. I put my hands on his chest and pushed myself up. His chest was warm, solid, and he smelled like crisp bedsheets. He grabbed my wrists and tugged to the side, making me fall back on top of him. I felt his heart beating through his chest. Or maybe it was mine. My lips parted and I raised my eyes up, an amused look on his face.

"Careful, girl." His breath felt warm against my lips. The same tingling feeling started to radiate from my toes to my head. He released my wrists and slid his hands down my back, resting them just above my ass. "You poke a bull and there will be consequences."

I pushed myself up from his chest, very aware of the fact that I was now straddling a complete stranger in a dark hallway. I stood and smirked at him.

"Just proving my point." My eyes never left him as he stood and brushed his slacks down.

"What makes you think I didn't let you do that?" he retorted, crossing his arms over his chest. "Maybe I wanted to be on the floor with a beautiful woman in front of the ladies' room. Maybe that's why I came here in the first place." He raised his eyebrow at me.

"OK, pervert." The heat rushed to my head. I turned and squinted my eyes as two women opened the side door and came down the hall. They stopped in their tracks, glancing between me and the big pound of flesh in front of me.

"Well, thanks for"—I waved my hand around the hallway—"all of this, but I will be going now." I turned down the hall and headed out the door.

*Don't look. Don't you turn around and look at him.*

I stopped and turned my head. He stood there watching me, a smile spreading across his face. *He thinks he's won.*

*Jerk.*

"See you around," he said with a nod.

*I don't think so.*

I made my way to the front and grabbed the attention of our waiter with a wave of my wallet. He said our bill had been taken care of and I let out an exasperated breath as I glanced back at the door that led to the bathroom.

I hailed a cab and called Olive, crossing my fingers that she wouldn't be angry. She was, but not with me. I was exhausted by the time I reached our apartment and just wanted to lie down. I dug through my purse for my keys, my heart falling to the pit of my stomach when I realized something was missing.

My planner was gone. No wonder my purse felt ten pounds lighter. I pushed my forehead against the door and groaned. That planner had everything in it from my bank account information to all my passwords. Contacts and all of Henley's wedding to-do items.

Just gone like that.

I pulled out my cell phone and paced down the hallway to my apartment. I called the restaurant, but nobody had turned it in.

I waited on the couch for Olive to come home. When she arrived, she squeezed me tightly and apologized profusely for her boss. She'd had no idea his nephew was a creep, otherwise she wouldn't have agreed to set me up. I told her everything that had happened, from Miles grabbing me to this Mason guy showing up out of nowhere.

I lay down on the love seat, exhausted from the whole ordeal.

I didn't hear my phone go off until well after midnight. There was a voice message from Miles. I was apprehensive as I pressed play and put the phone to my ear. He was babbling like a baby, apologizing every few seconds. Begging me not to sic my goons on him again.

*My goons?*

I pressed end on the voicemail and saw a flashing red sign in my message folder. It was a picture message from an unknown sender.

My planner.

*I found your day planner. Please retrieve at nine a.m. tomorrow morning—M.*

I sent a quick text back agreeing and jotted down the address. I was relieved that it had been found, but wondered if the "M" stood for Mason or if it was just a coincidence.

Something told me it wasn't.

Find it on Amazon (https://bit.ly/WildTalkDaniAntoinetteAmz), iBooks, B&N and many others. Add to Goodreads: http://bit.ly/GRsWildTalk

Printed in Great Britain
by Amazon